A KISS IN THE MORNING MIST

Marie Patrick

Crimson Romance
New York London Toronto Sydney New Delhi

CRIMSON
ROMANCE
Crimson Romance
An Imprint of Simon & Schuster, Inc.
1230 Avenue of the Americas
New York, NY 10020

First Crimson Romance ebook edition APRIL 2017.

CRIMSON ROMANCE and colophon are trademarks of Simon and Schuster.

For information about special discounts for bulk purchases, please contact Simon & Schuster Special Sales at 1-866-506-1949 or business@simonandschuster.com.

The Simon & Schuster Speakers Bureau can bring authors to your live event. For more information or to book an event contact the Simon & Schuster Speakers Bureau at 1-866-248-3049 or visit our website at www.simonspeakers.com.

Cover design by © Period Images.

Manufactured in the United States of America

10 9 8 7 6 5 4 3 2 1

Library of Congress Cataloging-in-Publication Data has been applied for.

ISBN 978-1-5072-0620-1
ISBN 978-1-5072-0444-3 (ebook)

Praise for Marie Patrick

"Plenty of intrigue, romance, and an unforeseen plot twist will captivate the audience of this spirited tale; enthusiastically recommended." *--Library Journal* (starred review)

"This western with a hint of mystery is … a real rootin', tootin', captivatin' read!" *—RT Reviews*

Dedication

Chapter 1

Colorado, April 1886

For the first time in a very long time, Eamon MacDermott could breathe easier. He filled his lungs with sweet, fresh air. The knot in his stomach unraveled a little, just enough to be noticeable, and guilt, his constant companion, eased.

A bit.

He never thought he would come back to Colorado. There were too many ghosts here, too many memories of the day the Logan Gang changed his life, but he didn't seem to have a choice. Something had drawn him back here. Perhaps it was the thought of his brothers, Teague and Brock, and his need to see them, though he wasn't quite ready for that yet.

His stomach growled, reminding him of his hunger and his meager provisions. The piece of jerky he'd eaten earlier had only served to make him hungrier. The coins in his pocket could buy him a decent meal, but only one, perhaps two if he was careful. He needed to find a job. Or a meal. Or both.

He followed the road to Pearce, the rumbling in his stomach a companion to Traveler's steady clip-clop, until he came to a wide path cut between two blue spruces. A big, white sign with black letters stood at the entrance to the path. It read "Morning Mist Farms, est. 1876." Painted in the upper right hand corner was a horse in full gallop.

Eamon eyed the sign from beneath the brim of his hat, then gave a slight tug on Traveler's reins and nudged him up the path.

He had nothing to lose and everything to gain. Even if there was no work to be found on Morning Mist Farms, at the very least, perhaps he could get a hot meal before going on his way.

The house came into view around a bend in the path and made him sigh. A nice place. Made of wood and rock most likely mined from the river he passed a while back, the structure rose three stories with one-story wings branching out to the north and south. Windows, framed by black painted shutters, were open, and lace draperies fluttered in the breeze. Rose bushes, beginning to bloom, were lined up neatly all along the front of the house, as well as the path that curved around the structure toward the back.

A porch ran the length of the three-storied section, sheltering two distinct sitting areas complete with wicker chairs and small round tables. A swing, suspended from the porch's ceiling, rocked gently.

Eamon dismounted and studied the house. A curious sensation settled in his bones. This house was more than just wood and stone—this house was a *home*. He could almost imagine the people who lived here, hear the laughter echoing within the walls.

He tied Traveler's reins to the railing, then took the steps leading up to the porch, his boot heels clicking on the wooden risers, and knocked on the door. While he waited for someone to answer, he studied his surroundings and noticed a rag doll on one of the chairs to his left. Missing a button eye, its black yarn hair in tangles, stuffing leaking from just about everywhere, the doll appeared to be very loved. Perhaps a bit too much, judging by her condition.

There were children here. A little girl, at the very least.

He knocked again, a little louder this time, then shoved his hand in his pockets. When no one answered, he bounded down the steps and followed a flagstone walk around to the back of the house, his gaze taking in and memorizing everything he saw as it came into view—barn, henhouse, icehouse, smokehouse, and huge stable—all well-kept and tidy—and a tall, sparse old woman wearing a big, straw hat. She wandered around a huge garden, talking to the various plants greening up the tilled earth, pulling weeds with gnarled, twisted fingers to fill the wicker basket hanging from her arm while pristine white sheets snapped in the breeze closer to the house.

He removed his hat from his head and approached her. "Excuse me, ma'am."

She didn't jump or stop pulling weeds from between rows of sprouting greenery. In fact, she didn't seem to be alarmed by his sudden appearance at all. Instead, she peered at him from beneath the wide brim of her hat. Her sharp brown eyes boldly assessed him as her scrutiny went from the top of his hatless head to the boots on his feet and back. She smiled, the wrinkles on her face deepening, as she nodded. "Well, now, you certainly took your time gettin' here, son, but you'll do."

Somewhat taken aback by the comment, Eamon peered at the woman and frowned. She spoke as if she'd expected him, but how could she have known? He hadn't known until a short time ago he'd be here.

She continued her frank appraisal, then stuck out her hand. "Lavinia Stark, but you can call me Granny. Everyone does."

Despite her misshapen hands, her grip was strong and solid.

"A plea—"

He never had a chance to finish his sentence or introduce himself. He heard the back door open, then the distinct double click of a shotgun being cocked.

Eamon released the woman's hand and dropped his hat to the ground. Without another thought, he reached for the pistols slung low around his hips but found ... nothing. No holster, no guns. He'd forgotten he no longer wore them—they weren't part of him anymore and hadn't been for a long time. He took a deep breath, turned slowly to face the direction of the noise, and blinked several times. A woman stood before him, the shotgun steady in her hands. Dressed in a white blouse, a split skirt made of fine, soft suede, and tooled leather boots, she stunned him with her perfection. A hank of whiskey-colored hair slipped from the ponytail at the back of her head and fell forward. She swung it out of her face with a practiced jerk of her head.

She spoke, her voice low and gravelly, but exuding confidence. "Mister, I don't know who you are, but if I were you, I'd get off my land. I've never killed anyone, but there's always a first time." She didn't raise the shotgun and point it at him, but she didn't have to. The threat couldn't have been more clear. She would if he forced her hand.

She stood not ten feet away and looked ... angry and unapologetic. Determined to make him leave. Green eyes, as green as spring grass, sparkled with indignation, and the firm set of her mouth left no doubt ... she wanted nothing more than to have him gone, and he didn't think she would hesitate to pull the trigger.

"And you can tell Mr. Pearce I haven't changed my mind." Her voice dropped an octave, becoming more hoarse, sounding like she gargled three times a day with rocks, but still strong and commanding and oddly, very pleasant. "I'm not selling. I'll never sell. I don't care how many men he sends to bully me. He's messing with the wrong woman."

"I don't mean no harm, ma'am." Eamon took a step back ... a slow careful step, and just as carefully, picked up his hat. "I don't know any Mr. Pearce. I'm just lookin' for work. Or maybe a hot meal."

She didn't seem convinced as she stepped closer, her eyes narrowing as she studied his face.

"Theo Danforth! Put down that shotgun!" The woman beside him finally spoke and moved with a swiftness that belied her age, advancing on the woman named Theo.

A heated, whispered conversation, which Eamon couldn't hear, ensued while he watched both women warily, his hat still in his hands, his feet planted firmly to the ground. Their conversation became more animated, though he still couldn't hear their words. The fact Theo still held the weapon tightly in her hands was enough to let him know he wasn't welcome.

"Look, lady, I'll just leave. No harm done." He shifted his weight from one leg to the other, his discomfort growing by the second. No one liked being on the wrong side of a gun, no matter which side of the law one stood on, even if the bore of the shotgun was pointed at the ground. Accidents could happen. "I ain't that hungry."

Despite his words, his empty stomach chose that moment to gurgle loudly. Much to his embarrassment, the noise carried to where to the two women argued. The younger one snapped her mouth shut in midsentence, while the older one, Granny, grinned with smug satisfaction.

Theo relaxed her grip on the gun, but she still didn't smile. "The least I can do is feed you," she said, though her expression made it clear she wasn't happy about it. She turned and marched through the back porch into the house, slamming the door behind her.

Granny held out her hand. "It'll be all right, son. Trust me."

Though doubtful he should trust either one of them, Eamon allowed her to lead him toward the back porch and a long wooden trestle table before she went back to her garden. As he took his seat on one of the benches and placed his hat next to him, he noticed several things at once. Again, he saw toys—a wooden train, a barn that resembled the one standing across the yard, and another rag doll as equally loved as the one on the front porch, except this one had yellow yarn hair and a calico apron. Beside the door, a big bell had been screwed into the doorframe, and rain slickers, in various sizes, hung from hooks along the wall. Beneath the coats were boots, again in various sizes. Dried herbs hung from the ceiling of the porch and lent their aroma to the smells coming from the kitchen.

He jumped to his feet as the woman named Theo came out onto the porch. She had replaced the shotgun with a tray, which she slid onto the table. On a flower-patterned plate, thick slices of ham and cheese were wedged between two pieces of bread. Steam rose from a bowl to the left of the sandwich, the aroma making his stomach grumble once more. She moved everything from the tray to the table, including a huge glass of milk, a napkin, and a spoon. There was also a cup of coffee, but she didn't set that before him.

"Sit," she said as she moved the tray to the side and slid onto the bench across from him. A ray of sunlight settled on her, illuminating her entire being, making it appear as if she had a halo around her head. "Eat." She nodded toward his food, then picked up her coffee cup and took a sip.

Eamon took his seat and changed his opinion of her in that moment. Despite the fact she'd held him at gunpoint just a few short minutes ago, she looked like an angel, and he couldn't stop himself from staring at her. She was older than he originally thought; fine lines radiated from the corners of her eyes. Deeper creases defined her mouth, telling him this woman smiled and laughed. Perhaps not right now, but quite often.

She cocked an eyebrow and pointed to the food on the table once more before her gaze shifted to Granny in the garden.

Embarrassed he'd been caught staring, blood heated his face as Eamon dug into his meal. The sandwich was delicious, the bread, as he suspected, soft and chewy, the ham succulent with the sweet taste of honey, and he couldn't remember the last time he'd had a bowl of chicken soup this delicious, nor dumplings so light and fluffy.

Eamon felt the warmth of her gaze as her attention returned to him. She sipped her coffee while she studied him, but didn't say a word until he took the last bite of his sandwich. "My name is

Theodosia Danforth. And you are?" she asked, her brilliant green gaze never leaving his face.

"Eamon MacDermott, ma'am."

"Mr. MacDermott," she repeated and gave a slight nod, a thick curl of whiskey-colored hair falling next to her cheek. She tucked it behind her ear. "About earlier. I don't normally greet people—"

"No need to apologize, ma'am."

She stiffened and a becoming flush stained her features. "I wasn't about to apologize, Mr. MacDermott. I have every right to defend my family and my property, by whatever means necessary."

Eamon almost grinned but forced it away. She was a thorny little thing, full of bluster and bristle. He liked that. "Yes, ma'am, you do." He rose from his seat and grabbed his hat. "Thank you for—"

She grabbed his arm, her long slim fingers imparting warmth to the flesh beneath the material of his shirt, a slight burst of heat that traveled along his veins, filling him with sensations he couldn't describe. Unnerved, he wanted to take a step back but forced himself to remain exactly where he was ... at least until the unfamiliar feeling passed.

And whatever that sensation was, she must have felt it too. She released her grip on him quickly, as if burned. The flush staining her cheeks grew brighter, and her eyes, those glimmering shards of green, gleamed. "You still need that job?"

"Yes, ma'am, I do, but ... why did you change your mind?"

Her gaze stayed on him, unblinking, and then she shrugged. "Let's just say I'm willing to take a chance on you. Besides, a fancy back east lawyer wouldn't be dressed the way you are nor would he wolf down a meal like he hadn't eaten in three days."

He wished she would smile, but she didn't as she gestured toward the bench. Eamon took his seat once more and laid his hat beside him.

"Tell me about yourself."

"Not much to tell. You already know I'm looking for work."

"Have you worked on a horse farm before, Mr. MacDermott?"

"No, ma'am, but I have moved cattle and milked a few cows. I also washed dishes and waited tables in a hotel in Tombstone, Arizona." He didn't tell her he'd been a U.S. Marshal, a job he loved before he put his guns away. She didn't need to know he blamed himself for the deaths of his brother, Kieran, his wife, Mary, and their son, Matthew, and the near death of his brother, Brock, at the hands of the Logans. If he could forget, he'd be much happier. "Poured whiskey in a little saloon in Cheyenne, too, and once, on a dare, I even sang in that saloon."

His attempt at humor failed. She still didn't smile. Instead, she absorbed the information with the tiniest frown on her face, the corners of her mouth turned down.

"Can you repair fences and the like?"

"Yes, ma'am."

There was another question in her eyes, but she didn't ask. Instead, she took a deep breath, her chest expanding against the stark white of her shirt, distrust evident on her face, and he couldn't help wondering who or what had made her so. She didn't seem like a woman who would normally be full of suspicion, but then, he didn't know her. He only knew what he saw and felt—years of experience taught him to trust his gut. This woman was afraid, though she tried to hide it. Did it have something to do with the name Pearce she had mentioned? Who was he? And why did he want her to sell her farm?

He shook himself out of his musings and listened.

"Regardless, Granny insisted I offer you a job, and truthfully, we do need you. Breeding season is fast coming upon us, and I recently lost a worker," she said, her gaze intent, "but I have rules, Mr. MacDermott. This is a working farm. We work. Hard. Every day. If you're not willing to make that commitment, then I don't want you."

Again, her hair fell in her face, but instead of tucking the thick tress behind her ear, she removed the strip of leather holding the mass together and let it hang loose to curl around her shoulders. Eamon could only stare. Her hair wasn't just the color of whiskey. It was so much more. Rich golds, burnished reds, and deep chestnut shimmered in the sunlight, fascinating him. He resisted the urge to touch the softness and forced himself to listen to her words instead.

"There are children here, none of whom have had an easy time of it. I will tolerate nothing less than kindness toward them." She spoke around the strip of leather clenched between her teeth as she smoothed her hair back one more time. "I will tolerate no abuse to the animals either. None. Some of them have already been abused and are healing. I'll let nothing stop that process."

She finished finger-combing those shining tresses back into a ponytail, wrapped the leather strip around the mass, and tied it off before she stood and smoothed the wrinkles from her split skirt, then stuck out her hand. "Can you abide by my rules? Think carefully before you answer. Many have said my rules are too harsh, and they quickly left."

Without hesitation, Eamon clasped her hand in his and shook. Again that odd sensation filled him, but he chose to ignore it. If she felt it again, nothing gave her away. "Yes, ma'am."

"The job comes with a place to stay, Mr. MacDermott, if you don't already have one. I pay a dollar a day, and you'll earn every cent. You'll take your meals with us in the main house. There's always a pot of coffee on the stove, and you're more than welcome to it. Sundays and Wednesday afternoons are yours to do with as you wish. There's a lake through the woods just to the north if you like to fish."

Gratitude flowed through him. How could he have been so lucky? Not only would he have a place to stay but good food to fill his belly as well. Trusting the instincts that made him turn up the drive to this farm had paid off tenfold. "Yes, ma'am."

A shapely brow rose, and a smile, one he'd been wishing he'd see, hovered at the corner of her mouth. She inclined her head slightly. "I'll show you to your room."

"Thank you, ma'am."

She walked quickly, taking two steps to every one of his, but never stopped speaking as she led him toward a small room built onto the side of the barn. She opened the door and stepped aside. "It isn't much, but it's warm in winter and cool in summer and it'll keep the rain and snow off your head."

"Yes, ma'am." Dust motes danced in a beam of sunlight coming in through the window and swirled as he stepped inside. "Thank you, ma'am."

"Please call me Theo. We'll never get along if you insist on calling me ma'am."

"Yes, ma—I mean Theo. My horse is out front. Would you mind if I took care of him before I begin working? We've had a long journey, Traveler and I."

"Of course. Everything you need is in the barn. Come out to the paddock when you're ready. It's behind the stable." She closed the door behind her.

Eamon listened to the sound of her retreating footsteps as he glanced around the room. The word *comfort* came to mind as he took in the furnishings. Nothing had been spared. Aside from a small bed, he had a bureau with a mirror, a bedside table, an armoire, a commode, and a small Ben Franklin stove to heat the place in winter. There was even a well-padded leather chair in the corner beside a table and a rag rug on the floor. Above the table, a shelf held several books. Plenty of light streamed in through the open windows, allowing him to briefly peruse the titles. A slight smile lifted the corners of his mouth. The woman had good taste in literature.

He stepped outside, closing the portal behind him, and popped his head into the barn through the open doors. Sunshine streamed in through several windows along the sides as well as the open matching doors at the opposite end of the barn. The structure was clean, well designed ... and empty except for a few kittens stalking each other in the hay.

He met no one else as he made his way to the front of the house to retrieve Traveler. When Theo said she needed him, she wasn't lying. Where were the children she had mentioned? And the other workers? He hadn't seen anyone other than her and Granny, and this farm was too big to be run by an old woman and her feisty granddaughter.

Doesn't matter, MacDermott. It's not your business. You won't stay long enough to find out. The thoughts popped in his head as he untied Traveler's reins and walked him back to the barn, his hooves kicking up dust on the wide dirt road curving around the house. He never stayed long for fear someone would recognize him and see his guilt.

He led his horse into the barn, chose a stall, and then removed the saddle, placing it as well as the blanket that had been beneath it on the railing. He slung his saddlebags over the railing, too, then strode down the aisle in search of a currycomb or brush and some oats. He found everything in a small room tucked into a corner at the back of the barn. The smell of leather from saddles, old and new, as well as reins, halters, and harnesses overpowered the smell of hay.

Eamon inhaled the familiar scent and found himself smiling, something he didn't do very often anymore, before he grabbed what he needed and strode down the center aisle. He poured some oats into the trough attached to one of the rails, then clicked his tongue against the roof of his mouth. The horse chuffed and moved toward the trough, sniffed at the oats, and began to eat. "Eat up, boy. You deserve it." He smoothed his hands along Traveler's shoulder, speaking to the horse as if he understood every word, then picked up the currycomb and began to brush him down.

It didn't take Eamon long to get Traveler settled, nor to grab his saddlebags, go back to his temporary quarters, and unpack his belongings. He didn't own much, and everything he did own fit into his saddlebags. Living as he had for the past two and a half years, moving from town to town, trying to outrun his past, he didn't accumulate many possessions. Except for memories and regrets, and he already had plenty of both.

A sigh escaped him as he dug the last item out of his saddlebag. He sat on the edge of the chair and pulled the strings of the bow holding the burlap-wrapped bundle closed. His hand shook, and his heart beat a rapid tattoo in his chest.

The tools of his job—the one he'd given up when he promised himself he'd never wear the holster around his hips or shoot the pistols again. He rubbed his hands over the pearl handles now, feeling the smoothness beneath his fingertips. Memories assailed him, making his heart hurt all over again. It would be so much easier if he'd never see these guns again, but for reasons he didn't understand, he couldn't give them up, couldn't sell them for much needed revenue. He'd tried. Too many times to count.

Deep in his soul, the guns were a part of him, part of his life. And his past.

With a heavy sigh, he wrapped them once more in burlap and found a safe place to hide them.

A short time later, Eamon left his quarters, strode around to the back of the stable, and stopped in midstride, not quite prepared for the beauty of the landscape before him. Pasture spread into the near distance, toward a deeply wooded copse. Separated into various enclosures by white fence, the grass was as green as Theo's eyes, a fact he noticed too quickly. Milk cows grazed to his left. He saw sheep as well. Closer to the back of the barn were chickens and pigs. And in the distance, he saw horses, all shapes and sizes, their colors ranging from blackest black to startling white.

He skirted the side of the stable and saw her. Theo. She stood in the middle of an enclosure, speaking softly to a horse, her voice a low, soothing hum. She didn't move very much, and when she did, she did it slowly so as not to frighten the animal.

Lined up next to the paddock fence, their focus on her, Eamon saw a dog, a duck, and two cats. Not unusual to see on a farm, except these animals were different. The dog's front leg was shriveled and misshapen, one cat had no tail, and the other cat had no ear and part of its face seemed ... odd. The duck had a bandage wrapped around his body, keeping both wings close so he couldn't stretch them out ... and perhaps fly away?

As he approached, Theo's words became clear. "It's all right, Maizie. I'm going to put this ointment on your sores, like I did yesterday and the day before." She stood motionless and he realized she was giving Maizie time. "You felt better after that, didn't you, girl?" The beautiful roan eyed her, then tossed her head, ears pinned back, tail swishing as she backed away. Sunlight struck the slash marks on her dark coat. They were new, but beneath them, he could plainly see older scars. Someone had purposely hurt this animal, and his heart went out to her. Theo had said she didn't tolerate abuse. Well, neither did he.

He turned his attention from the horse to the woman. She should have been named Patience because she stood in the paddock as still as a painting, her voice melodic and soft, almost hypnotizing, as she sang a lullaby. After a while, Maizie finally came toward her and nuzzled her shoulder.

Unable to help himself, Eamon let out his breath, surprised he'd been holding it. "That was amazing."

Chapter 2

Theo didn't jump when he spoke, but did turn to look at him. She'd noticed him the moment he stepped behind the stable. How could she not? The man possessed an assured, confident presence and moved with a natural, easy grace. Easily topping six feet, he possessed broad shoulders and long legs, which filled out his trousers quite nicely. And his mouth ... good gracious, his mouth looked so kissable, even if he didn't smile.

And why am I thinking about his mouth? Or how nicely he fills out his trousers?

With effort, she pulled her gaze away from him and concentrated on dabbing soothing salve on the mare's open sores. "Are the accommodations to your liking, Mr. MacDermott?"

"Eamon, please."

From the corner of her eye, she saw him lean against the paddock fence and rest his forearms on the top rail. A boot-clad foot rested on one of the bottom rails. His hat shaded part of his face, but couldn't hide his utterly kissable mouth.

And she still shouldn't be thinking about that, but she couldn't seem to stop.

I may be a widow, but I can still appreciate a fine-looking man. Nothing wrong with that.

Theo tore her gaze away once again.

"They're quite comfortable. Thank you." He said nothing more, but she could feel his steady gaze as she liberally applied more salve. After a while, he tilted his hat back on his head and asked, "What happened to her?"

"Her former owner thought by whipping her, she'd go faster, have more strength and stamina, but Maizie here is an old girl. She just wants to rest. Her days of pulling the ice wagon are over." She glanced at him and noticed how gray his eyes were, like smoke rising from a fire, and how intently they watched her. "She's mine now. Once she heals, I'll let her out in one of the pastures so she can run with the younger horses." She put the lid on the small container of salve and slipped it into her pocket, then slowly worked the remainder of the cream into her hands, delighting in the subtle smell of roses. Giving one final pat to Maizie's shoulder, she approached the fence where Eamon waited.

And was shaken by a moment of utter doubt. Should she have hired this man? She didn't know if she could trust her judgment anymore, considering what had happened with her last hired hand. Burl Stanton hid his true nature behind a charming smile, but showed it when he took a whip to Circe. Granny said Eamon was different. He needed Morning Mist Farms and the healing to be found here. She said he'd come a long way to find this place, even if he didn't realize it, and if anyone would know that, it would be Granny. Theo never questioned the woman's ability to simply *know* things.

Besides, Theodosia Danforth never turned away a person—or an animal—in need. And she wouldn't now but ...

She watched him warily, studied him actually, looking for a sign that she'd made the right decision and could trust this stranger she'd just met. If he felt uncomfortable with her scrutiny, he didn't show it. Instead, he studied her just as carefully, and in the depths of his smoky gray eyes, she saw pain ... and loneliness. Feelings she knew well. Her heart went out to him, and all doubt fled from her mind. He did need healing, as Granny said. From what, she didn't know, but she would. Eventually.

And he needed kindness. As much as she could give.

A flush heated her face. He needed compassion, and she'd threatened him with her shotgun. The fact that it hadn't been loaded didn't make her feel any better.

It hadn't been kind. Not in the least.

"I apologize about the shotgun. It wasn't loaded. I just … though I would never harm another human being, Eamon, I do think I should be able to protect myself, my family, and my property." She slipped through the space between the rails and came up beside him.

He asked for no further explanation as he gave a slight nod. Theo didn't know if that meant he accepted her apology or not. Maybe he decided it wasn't his business. Taking a deep breath, she asked, "Are you ready to see the horses?"

Again, he didn't speak, just gave another nod.

"Good. If you'll follow me."

She grabbed her hat from one of the posts, plopped it on her head, and led the way. The dog, cats, and duck followed behind her in a single line.

"I should introduce you," she said as she led them down a grassy walkway between fences.

"To whom?"

"Why, the menagerie, of course." She turned around and walked backward so she could see his face and gesture to the animals following her. "The dog is Happy although he answers to Hoppy as well." The dog, hearing his names, leapt forward with a soft *woof* and butted her hand with his head, looking for affection. Theo rubbed her fingers through the dog's silky fur as she spoke. "I'm sure you've noticed he's only got three legs that work. Doesn't slow him down any. The cat missing his ear is Vincent. The other one is Mama." She grinned as she faced forward. "The duck is Mallory, who, I'm sure, cannot wait to leave us once his wing is healed. He's not fond of humans at the moment."

"Why not?" His voice, a little closer now, sent a tiny shiver down her spine. Deep and rich, it had the most pleasing quality to it. She turned her head, intending to look behind her, only to see him right beside her.

"He was shot by some rowdy boys who had no business being on my property. I don't condone killing for killing's sake. It's one thing to hunt for food. It's another thing entirely to kill because one is bored and has nothing better to do." Even now, she had a problem keeping the anger from her voice and glanced at him to judge his reaction to both her words and her attitude. "Living creatures should not be used as target practice."

"I agree." His gaze met hers. Direct. Disturbing—as if he could see inside her heart and knew all her secrets.

She stumbled a bit beneath his intent stare. He grabbed her upper arm, his fingers strong yet gentle, and steadied her. The flicker of *something* when she'd touched him earlier returned, startling her. It made her feel breathless and giddy, like she'd run too far too fast.

"Thank you," she managed, though how, she didn't know.

Goodness gracious, Theo! Quit behaving like a ninny!

Admonishing herself didn't help—she still felt it ... whatever *it* was. She couldn't give this particular feeling a name no matter how hard she tried, though the giddiness remained, persistent and strange.

She took a deep breath and looked up at his face—his utterly handsome face. If he felt anything, his features did not reveal his thoughts, but his hand remained on her arm for much longer than necessary.

He gave a slight nod and released her from his grasp. With effort, Theo resumed walking along the grassy pathway, forcing herself from her momentary lapse into wherever she had gone.

"What happened to the boys?"

"What? Oh ... I spoke to their fathers, and each of them worked on my farm for a week, from sunup to sundown."

"I'll bet you gave them the most unpleasant of tasks."

"Of course. I wanted them to learn a lesson." She chuckled, remembering the looks on their faces when she'd handed them their shovels and given them their chores. Mucking out the stable wasn't a task anyone *wanted* to perform, but it was a necessity of life on the farm. "My barn and stable never looked so clean. Neither did the henhouse."

Theo led him along the grassy path and stopped at the first enclosure. Four horses, three due to foal soon, stood in the shade of a tree beside the small stream that cut through the pasture. Theo gave a short, sharp whistle. Almost as one, they raised their heads and raced to the fence, each one vying for her attention.

"These are my babies." She touched them one by one. "Athena is nine. Electra is eight. Circe and Galatea are both six and about to become mothers for the first time. This will be Electra's second foal."

"Named after Greek mythology. Was that your idea?"

"No, it was my husband, Henry's, idea. He loved Greek mythology and read quite a bit on the subject." She rubbed Electra's nose as she spoke. "A very important part of your job here at Morning Mist will be keeping careful records for each horse: dates of birth, sire and dam when we have a new birth, illnesses, and injuries. Their temperament and the like." It didn't occur to her to ask if he could read and write. She assumed he could since he knew the horses were named after Greek mythology.

"You'll also be recording time." She pulled a stopwatch from her pocket and clicked it open, then closed it with a snap and handed it to him. "It's important for those who are purchasing my horses to know how fast they run on a set course."

Eamon slipped the watch in his pocket. "Who rides when you're recording their time?"

"I don't record the time. Usually, I can get one of the children to do that. I ride."

If he was surprised by her answer, he didn't show that either. In fact, he didn't seem to show any emotion, his features set, though he seemed friendly enough. She studied him once again, her eyes drifting over his face. There was something inherently gentle in his features despite his stoic demeanor, but for reasons she couldn't explain, she got the distinct feeling he hadn't been happy—or laughed—in a very long time.

Theo blinked, tore her gaze away from him, and got back to the subject at hand. "And lastly, I keep track of who comes here to have their mares breed with my stallion and who purchases my horses outright. It's important for me to know that my horses go to good homes. I won't sell to just anyone. A buyer or a breeder must be recommended." She rubbed her arm where his strong fingers had grasped her.

What is wrong with me? It's like I've never seen a handsome man before. Quit staring at him and get on with it!

Once again, though it took effort on her part, she got her mind back on business, and firmly pushed away any thoughts that didn't have to do with the horses or the farm. "I'll show you where the records are later."

"Yes, ma'am."

She didn't correct him for calling her "ma'am" again. Instead, she led him farther down the fence and stopped at another enclosure. The dog, cats, and duck stopped as well. She didn't need to whistle this time. The young horses were already lined up. Theo grinned and touched each one as she named them. "Echo, Ares, and Hestia are three years old. Castor and Pollux are twins out of Athena. They're four. Daphne is five, and I think this year, I'll breed her." Her hand lingered on the side of Daphne's long muzzle before she gave the horse one final pat.

"This way." She stepped away from the fence and strolled across the wide grassy expanse between enclosures. A grouping of trees cast long shadows on the ground, shading several tables and chairs as well as a small wooden bridge spanning the stream that twisted and turned throughout the pasture. Theo stepped across the bridge, her boot heels loud on the wooden planks, and strode toward another fenced area directly across from where her three-, four-, and five-year-olds frolicked in the pasture. Again, the horses were lined up at the fence. "These are my youngest. Phoebe is two and proving to be a fast runner. Her times are incredible. Persephone and Hermes are one and will be as fast as her." She paused as she rubbed Phoebe's nose. "Phoebe will be leaving us soon."

"Leaving? Has she been sold?"

"No, not sold. She isn't mine."

"I don't understand. I thought you owned all these horses."

Theo shook her head. "Not all. The majority, yes. Phoebe's owner will be arriving shortly and taking her home. Hart Jameson brought his stallion, Hart's Pride, a few years ago and bred him with Athena. Phoebe is the result, and Hart couldn't be happier. He left her with me so I could train her, but now he's anxious to take her on the racing circuit."

She moved on, glancing only once to see if she still had his attention, but it seemed like he was absorbing every word she said, his attention fully captured between her and the horses. She stopped at the last enclosure, and joy filled her heart. "And this is Henry's All or Nothing. Or Pumpkin, as I've always called him."

"Strange name for a horse," he said as he leaned against the fence. "Why isn't he named after Greek gods like the others?"

"He was our first and not so strange when you know why he's named as he is." Theo opened the paddock gate and sauntered through. Pumpkin trotted up beside her and nuzzled her pockets. She stroked his long nose, then gave him the sugar cube she'd taken from the kitchen. "Henry and I were there when Pumpkin was born. The birth had been difficult, and we almost lost his mother. We didn't think either one of them would survive." The horse finished the bit of sweet, then nuzzled her pocket again, looking for another. Theo obliged. "Last one, my boy," she whispered as she held out her hand. The horse took the sugar cube with his lips and proceeded to crunch the cube to nothing. Theo pulled a handkerchief from her other pocket and wiped her hand, then turned her attention back to Eamon.

"Henry's father didn't want anything to do with him. To look at him now, you'd never know Pumpkin was a scrawny little thing, so much smaller than the other foals born that year—smaller, in fact, than any other horse born on Turning Leaf Farms in Kentucky. It took him all afternoon to stand and begin nursing. But Henry saw something in him, something special. He bet every last penny we had—every last hope of winning races—on this horse, so truly, he was and is All or Nothing." She continued to stroke the horse's nose and couldn't help the smile that lifted the corners of her mouth as memories came flooding back. There had been some bad days, but luck had shined on her and Henry more often than not, and the good far outweighed the bad.

"For three years, he won every race we entered him in. Sometimes, the purse wasn't even worth the entry price, but for us, it was more than the money. It was pride. Pumpkin was building a reputation as were we." She glanced at him. Again, his foot hooked onto the bottom slat of the fence, and one arm rested on the top. He'd tilted his hat back, and his full attention was on her, though his hand gently brushed against Happy's silky black-and-white coat as the dog leaned against him. She wondered if he was aware he was doing it.

"Eventually, we took the winnings, moved here, and built what you see. Morning Mist Farms." She gave the horse a final pat and stepped through the gate, making sure it was locked behind her. Pumpkin would never run away, but why take the chance? "We are primarily a stud farm. People come from far and wide to have their mares bred with Pumpkin, hoping they'll have another winner. Or they bring their stallions to mate with one of Pumpkin's progeny. They also come to buy Pumpkin's offspring with the same hope. He's proven himself more than once."

"You have yourself a nice place, Miz Danforth."

She peered up at him. "I thought we agreed you were going to call me Theo?"

A flush stained his features as he lowered the brim of his hat, as if he had allowed her to see too much and was now trying to hide it. "Yes, ma'am. I mean Theo."

"That's better. Now, do you have any more questions?"

"Just one. Why Morning Mist?"

"Another one of Henry's ideas." Warmth filled her when she mentioned Henry's name once again. She thought of him every day, but now, two and a half years after his passing, the pain of losing him wasn't as devastating. More and more, his memories brought her happiness and not tears. "In the morning, when the sun is first coming up, there is a fine, soft mist hovering over the pastures. Henry thought it was the most beautiful thing he ever saw, hence the name."

As she began to lead him back toward the stable, Happy gave a short, whiny yip, then nearly toppled her over as he ran toward to the house in his peculiar three-legged gait. The cats followed, and the duck brought up the rear, quacking for all he was worth. "Ah, it's time."

"Time? Time for what?"

"The children are home from school." She led the way down the grassy path toward the house, following behind Mallory, who waddled quickly but not fast enough to keep up with the dog and cats. "I'll show you around the stable after you've met everyone. I'm very proud of what we built. Henry and I designed it while we were still traveling to Colorado. We hadn't even found the land yet, let alone purchased it, but we had faith."

She glanced in his direction as they came out from between the barn and stable to the commotion in the yard. She expected to see Quincy driving the buckboard, Marianne beside him, but they were nowhere in sight. Neither was the buckboard. Instead, the children—her pride and joy, although they weren't her own—stood in the dust of the drive as Happy danced and barked, running from one to another, sticking his nose in places it didn't belong, giving soft *woofs* of happiness as hands stroked his fur. The duck quacked and waddled after the dog while the cats meowed and rubbed themselves against five pairs of legs, one right after another, welcoming the children home.

Beside her, Eamon stopped and stood with his hands on his hips. Theo studied him, noting the expression on his face. Some people found it intolerable to have their peace broken by a cacophony of noises such as her barnyard had become. Others accepted it for what it was. And others still, like her, loved it. Eamon seemed to like it, although she couldn't be quite sure. Humor danced in his eyes, and the corners of his mouth twitched. "Is it like this every day?"

She shook her head. "Not every day. Only when the children attend school. Usually, there are two more—Quincy and Marianne Burke. They live here as well. Quincy is my farm manager and Marianne cooks for us, but you'll have to meet them later."

She so loved this part of the day, when the children came home from school and her family became complete once more.

The only one missing was Henry.

He would have loved seeing how Thomas and Charlotte had grown. He would have marveled and been as proud as a father could be by how Lou and Wynn had matured into fine young men. He would have adored Gabby, as precious as she was.

Henry Danforth had loved children and wanted a house full, but they had never been blessed.

Mentally, Theo gave herself a little shake, pushing the thought from her mind, then gave a quick nod to Granny, who opened the back door and waited on the step as she and Eamon approached the children. Theo clapped her hands, gaining their attention from greeting the animals, which were barking, meowing, and quacking. In seconds, the three youngest of the group swarmed her, wrapping their arms around her so she could give them a little squeeze. Theo loved this part of welcoming them home the best and reveled in the love they gave her. It was more than reciprocated.

She glanced upward to find Eamon's intent stare on her. She thought she saw an unmistakable yearning flash in his eyes, but it was gone too quickly to be certain. She cleared her throat. "Everyone, I want you to meet Mr. MacDermott. He'll be working with us." Theo drew his attention from herself to a boy she motioned forward. "This is Lou Burke, Quincy and Marianne's son." He had a smattering of faded freckles across his nose, lively blue eyes full of mischief, and a thick sheaf of dark hair over his forehead. He gave a slight nod, but an impish smile graced his lips as he put down the large crate he held and stuck out his hand.

Theo watched carefully as Eamon shook the young man's hand and exchanged pleasantries. She could tell a lot about a person in the way he or she responded to others. So far, Eamon MacDermott seemed to genuinely like people.

After the two greeted each other, Lou turned toward her and shoved the hair out of his eyes. "Pop and Mama heard Mr. Osuch fell from his roof and broke his arm so they went over to see if the Osuches needed any help." Again, hair was pushed out of his face as he picked up the crate. "Nice to meet you, Mr. MacDermott."

Why does his name seem familiar? She'd thought so before when he first introduced himself, but couldn't place it. She knew for a fact she'd never met him, so why did his name jiggle something in her memory?

She ignored the question as well as the dull pinprick of disquiet. Her nephew stepped forward, a stack of books held together with a leather strap in his hands. Solemn brown eyes measured the man before him. After a moment, he introduced himself. "Wynn. Wynn Danforth. Theo is my aunt," he said in a tone that was a warning and a welcome at the same time, though the warning was quite clear. He would protect his aunt.

Theo grinned, very proud of the young man she and Henry had taken in over six years ago when Henry's brother passed. Then she forced the smile from her face, schooling her features into a mask of solemnity equal to his own.

Eamon offered his hand. "Nice to meet you."

"And these angels are my wards." Theo released the three children from her protective embrace. "I'd like you to meet Thomas and Charlotte White and Gabrielle Bainbridge. Say hello to Mr. MacDermott."

Theo's heart swelled as Thomas stepped forward first and held out his hand. "P-p-pleased to make your acquaintance, M-m-mr. MacDermott." Pride grew as he shook the man's hand, then stepped aside and gestured to his younger sister. "M-m-may I present my s-sister, Charlotte?"

"How do you do?" The young girl extended her hand as well and dipped a little curtsy, her face flushed, her voice barely above a whisper. She pulled her hand away quickly and hid behind her brother.

"You can't forget me. I'm Gabby."

Theo took a deep breath and let it out between her lips in an effort to keep her emotions at bay as Gabby tugged on Eamon's sleeve. He knelt on one knee to be eye to eye with her. Gabby hardly ever touched anyone. She very rarely allowed herself to be touched either and quickly squirmed free, but that was getting better. She let herself be hugged a little more often now, but that progress had taken over two years. The only exception was on those nights when the nightmares came and she relived, once more, the tragic loss of her family in a fire. She'd been so young, only four, when it happened, but the memories lived on, not only in her mind but in the faint scars marring the soft skin of her hands, her back, and the backs of her legs. She was still self-conscious about her hair, which had been singed off in the fire, but was now long enough to pull into pigtails.

Theo glanced at Granny and saw the woman struggle with the same emotions, although Granny hadn't managed to keep the fine sheen of tears from her eyes.

"How do you do, Miss Gabby?" Eamon asked, the tone of his voice gentle. If he noticed the faded marks the fire had left on her hands, he didn't show it.

"I do jes' fine." Her smile was engaging, her soft baby-blue eyes glimmering with a hint of understanding as she shook his hand, and then she did the most surprising thing of all. She wrapped her little arms around Eamon's neck and hugged him. The small display of affection was Theo's undoing, and she turned away, swallowing hard against the lump in her throat. She had tried for so long to get Gabby to open her soul of the sorrow that dwelled there, longed for the day when the six-year-old child would allow herself to be held without pulling away, and here, she'd taken the first step herself.

Perhaps she felt a kindred spirit in Eamon MacDermott or recognized the same sorrow dwelling in his soul, as Theo herself had done.

She studied Eamon with a new appreciation.

No matter why the child did as she did, it was a good beginning.

The best beginning.

Chapter 3

Eamon watched Granny shepherd the young people inside for milk and cake, except for Lou, who sauntered over to the hen-house, the crate in his hands, the dog, cats, and duck tailing behind him in a single line.

The yard quieted once more.

For a man who spent so much time alone except for his horse, the noise had been jarring. Now, the hush was deafening and reminded him how much his life had changed over the past two and a half years. All of it was his own doing. He didn't deserve more. If he had pursued and captured the Logan Gang when they had crossed his path, he could have prevented Zeb Logan from killing Kieran, Mary, and Matthew, then shooting his brother, Brock, leaving him for dead. He might even have avoided being shot himself by Tell Logan. His head told him he couldn't have gone after the Logans—he was transporting prisoners to Canon City at the time—but his heart wouldn't listen. Seeing how Theo's family acted with one another, despite all of them not sharing the same blood, made him miss his brothers and his nephew and niece more than he usually did. Though he'd been a U.S. Marshal, traveling from place to place, he'd always been able to see his family on a regular basis, often having dinner at Kieran's ranch.

All that changed in the blink of an eye with a bullet from a gun.

He shook himself from his thoughts and turned toward the back porch, catching sight of Gabby as she darted toward a chair in the corner and grabbed the much loved rag doll from her perch.

She squeezed the doll tight, then disappeared into the house once more. The corners of his mouth pulled down in a frown as another unbidden memory—or perhaps it was his heart's desire—flashed through his mind. Desi Lyn, Kieran's daughter, would be a year or so younger than Gabby now, but he hadn't seen his niece since he recovered from Tell's bullet. The loss of Kieran, his wife and son, and the near loss of Brock had left a gaping hole in his heart that made him wonder how and why he should still be alive.

He heard laughter coming from inside the house through the open windows, adults' as well as children's, and longing stirred. He'd always been fond of children, had wanted a family of his own at one time.

The children were Theo's wards and not hers, but the fact they were not borne of her didn't seem to matter at all. Theo's love for them was obvious. He didn't doubt they were the children of her heart. All three of them seemed happy and carefree, as children should, but he couldn't help notice a touch of sadness in them as well. Nor could he deny something had happened when Gabby wrapped her little arms around him and hugged him. Tears had sprung to his eyes, and he'd had to blink them away.

That had never happened to him before, but it wasn't the only odd thing he'd experienced since coming to this farm a few hours ago. There was something here ... something he couldn't define.

Theo's warm fingers upon his arm brought him back to the present. "Are you ready to see the stables?"

"Yes, of course."

She gave a slight nod, then headed across the yard, the hem of her split skirt swirling around the tops of her boots with her purposeful stride. Despite her quick pace, Eamon had no problem keeping up with her. For all her bristle and mere *presence*, Theodosia Danforth was a tiny thing. Her head only came up to his shoulder, and if she weighed much more than one hundred pounds, he'd be surprised, although every one of those pounds seemed to be all in the right places. His gaze drifted to the gentle sway of her hips and nipped-in waist before he made himself focus on the stable ahead of him. He shouldn't be admiring his brand-new employer like that—she was a married woman.

He forced himself to listen to her words. Once again, he found that he'd missed some.

"—the house after that. By then, the children should be done with their snack." She stopped at the entrance to the building, her slender hand on the doorframe, and looked at him for a long time. Her eyes were wide and so very green ... and filled with gratitude. "Thank you."

Startled, he stopped as well and couldn't help asking, "For what?"

"For not laughing at Thomas's stutter or Charlotte's shyness. For letting Gabby hug you and not staring at her scars. They haven't ..." She cleared her throat, then stopped speaking as she moved through the stable's open door and down one of the two main aisles.

"Tell me about the children. You mentioned they are your wards. How did they come to be here with you?"

Theo shrugged, but when she faced him once more, he saw the glow of love on her pretty face. "They had nowhere else to go, Eamon. No family left to love or care for them." She turned away, but not before he saw the sheen of tears that made her eyes luminous. "Thomas and Charlotte's mother, Angela, was my very dear friend. She contracted diphtheria when there was an epidemic in town. Being so far away out here on the farm, we were spared that tragedy so I brought the children here to stay with Granny and Marianne while I cared for Angela and her husband. She begged me to take her children, to give them a home after she was gone. She wanted them to be loved and cherished. I gave my word. Thomas was only five. Charlotte four. They've been with me ever since ... it's been four years now."

"And Gabby? Did her family die of diphtheria as well?"

She shook her head, but didn't speak for a long time. Her body stiffened, and she clasped her hands in front of her. He shouldn't have asked her or delved into things that were not his concern. He wanted to know, but at the same time, he didn't. He didn't plan on staying long, and the last thing he needed was to get involved with this family, such as it was. "I'm sorry. I shouldn't have asked."

Theo swiped at her eyes and shook her head slightly, dismissing his apology. She swallowed, her throat moving as she did so, drawing his eye to her smooth, sun-kissed skin. His gaze followed her jawline; then shifted to her high cheekbones, pert nose, and almond shaped eyes framed in thick, dark lashes; and once again, he had to remind himself to pay attention.

As a former lawman, he'd always had to be aware of his surroundings, but this woman, in the course of a few hours, distracted him like no one else ever had, married or not.

And it wasn't only her. It was this place.

His gaze moved to her mouth, and finally, her softly spoken words penetrated his mind.

"Gabby's parents and older sister perished when their house in town caught fire. Doc Foster, Gabby's neighbor, heard her screaming and pounding on the window in her bedroom, trying to get out. Her clothes were starting to smolder, and her hair ... He broke the window and saved her before the flames could ... She wouldn't have survived if he hadn't. She ..." Her voice tight, she stopped speaking. She turned away and her gaze focused on a spot in one of the stalls, but he could still see the way her throat moved as she swallowed. When she continued, her voice seemed much more hoarse.

"You noticed the faint scars on her hands, but there's more ... on her legs and back. Doc Foster—he's a good friend—brought her to me while he searched for her relatives. He never found any so she stayed with me instead of going to an orphanage."

She gave an elegant shrug of her shoulders, as if taking in and raising someone else's child was an ordinary occurrence. Perhaps for Theo, it was. "She was a scared little thing when she came to me, hurting in so many ways. I didn't think I could help her. It took time and patience and a lot of Granny's special salve, but eventually, most of the scarring faded. At least on the outside. She is the darling little girl you see, but she doesn't touch people very much. She accepts very brief hugs but never gives them like she gave you, so thank you."

Eamon didn't quite know how to respond. His throat constricted, not only because of what had happened to that sweet little girl—to all of them—but because no one had thanked him for anything in a very long time. He was warmed by the show of gratitude … and afraid of it as well. He'd been kind. Nothing more.

She cleared her throat, then continued down one of the two aisles between stalls, pointing out things he'd need to know, as if they'd never had their conversation, dismissing her brief emotional moment.

He followed her lead, pretending she hadn't been upset. Still, his heart ached for all of them. She'd given him a peek inside her heart and was obviously embarrassed that she had. He would respect that. The children's stories touched him more than he wanted them to.

He pushed such thoughts aside and focused on what she showed him.

He liked the stable. He'd seen bigger in his travels, but not many. None nearly so clean or well ventilated and bright. Windows at the end of each stall along the walls, as well as both big doors, had been opened to catch the spring breezes and sunlight. There were thirty-two stalls in all, eight along each wall and sixteen in the middle with a narrow space between them big enough for a man to pass. Fresh hay carpeted the dirt floor in each. He looked up toward the roof at the loft filled with bales of straw and noticed birds' nests in the rafters. There were no lanterns near any of the stalls, but there were several attached to the wall at the front and back, near the doors.

The corners of Eamon's mouth twitched as his gaze went from the birds' nests over his head to the floor below ... and Theo's menagerie at his feet. The last he'd seen of them, they'd been following Lou. Happy waited patiently, big brown eyes silently begging for attention. He couldn't resist and scratched the dog under his chin. He'd always loved dogs, although he'd never had one growing up, nor did he have one while he was a U.S. Marshal. His life, such as it was, wouldn't have been fair to the animal. The cats rubbed their bodies against his legs, the sound of their purring a low rumble. And the duck? Mallory just stared at him, probably still deciding if he was a worthy human. He wasn't.

He turned his attention to Theo, who had been speaking, though he'd missed some of what she'd said. Again.

"... have simple chores, such as helping to wash the supper dishes, making their beds, and keeping their rooms clean. They also help in the stables, but only under supervision. Either Wynn or I do that, sometimes Quincy. In a pinch, Granny will supervise, too. Gabby, Charlotte, and I collect the eggs every morning. Thomas is learning to milk the cows but isn't quite comfortable with it yet. Lou and Wynn do it now. I think it's good for children to learn responsibility early, but I try to match their chores to their strengths, something they do best. A talent, if you will."

She shrugged her slim shoulders as she led the way outside, the small parade of animals once again following her into the bright sunlight. At the end of the paddock where Maizie grazed from a feedbox in the shadows, several chickens joined the procession as they turned and headed back toward the barn and the house. Theo gestured to the garden to her left, either unaware of the growing number of followers behind her or so used to it, she didn't notice anymore.

Either way, Eamon found it amusing as he followed the strange procession.

"Granny grows things—flowers, vegetables, herbs. She also makes her special salve, guaranteed to cure just about anything. As I mentioned before, Marianne cooks and bakes. That's her special talent. It's what she enjoys doing, and she does it well. She's teaching Charlotte, who seems to have a knack for it, too. Wynn has a gift for the horses. They run like the wind for him. Lou can build or repair anything. Give him some wood planks, a hammer, and nails and he's happy. And Quincy ... well, he manages everything."

She laughed then, a musical lilt that filled the air and made him suddenly feel *freer* than he had in a long time.

"It's his strength. He organizes nearly everything here, and there's a rhythm to the days that's pleasing. The only thing he doesn't do is manage the breeding business." She glanced at him and flashed a smile in his direction, a beautiful smile that captured his attention and actually scared him. For in that moment, she once again looked like an angel.

As if an angel or this place could help him. The sarcastic bite of his thoughts shot through his mind, and his muscles tensed. Is that what he wanted? Did he want to settle someplace and stop running away from his dreams as well as his nightmares? If he were honest with himself ...

He nearly scoffed aloud. He had quit being honest with himself some time ago. "—to find your special talent, Eamon."

He tried to concentrate on everything she'd told him. For a man who often didn't hear another human voice for days on end, it was a lot of information to take in, especially in one fell swoop, all of it spoken in her hoarse, much too pleasant voice. He did notice that not once since he'd been shown the horses had she mentioned Henry, and suddenly, he had to know why. "And Henry?"

She smiled, though it was a sad smile. "Henry?" She shrugged. "Henry dreamed. Big dreams about what we could accomplish. Coming to Colorado and starting this farm was his idea."

"Does he help with the horses?"

She shook her head, and the sadness of her smile reached her eyes before she averted her gaze. "Henry's not with us anymore."

Not with us anymore? What did that mean? Had he left, abandoning her and the dreams they'd had? Had he passed away? He would have asked, but the pensive look on her face stopped him and he didn't press for an answer. "What about you, Theo? What's your special talent?"

"Mine?" She stopped and faced him. "I'm not sure I have one, Eamon, although Granny insists I have a gift, but I wouldn't call it that. What I have is common sense and patience, enough to help an animal heal itself. Like Maizie." Her eyes were wide and such a beautiful shade of light green, almost peridot, it almost hurt to look, but he couldn't turn away nor did he want to. He saw hints of gold and sparks of blue in their depths ... and love.

Eamon found himself being drawn into the love he saw shining there but somehow managed to resist the magnetic pull. He didn't deserve the kind of comfort he saw there. He closed his eyes and counted to ten, hoping to break whatever spell Theo Danforth had cast over him.

"You saw the barn when you settled Traveler so let me show you some of the other outbuildings." She led the way to the chicken coop, a large square building where chickens pecked at the grain scattered on the ground. There must have been at least a hundred of them, all clucking and chirping and scratching at the dirt, both inside the fenced-in area and outside, as the gate was wide open. A rooster, perched on top of the henhouse, flapped his wings and crowed, but the hens simply ignored him.

"Ninety-two at last count, not counting the chicks," she answered his unspoken question, as if she could read his mind. Was that her special talent? "And all of them great layers."

As he suspected, the inside of the building was clean, despite being home to so many chickens. He even spotted an egg, one that had been missed earlier in the morning, or perhaps the egg had been laid after collection. Why, though, would anyone need ninety-two hens? That was a lot of eggs, even for a family of her size, although Wynn and Lou were in that age between child and adult when they grew quickly, like weeds left untended. If he remembered correctly, when he and his brothers were that age, they ate everything that wasn't nailed down.

"Quincy sells eggs, milk, butter, and cream to the hotel in town. It's part of our agreement, and we all help." Again, she answered his unasked question and drew his attention as she stepped away from the henhouse. "Only a few more things to show you out here."

Eamon tried to take it all in, but Morning Mist Farms was big. Too big by far for a man who spent so much of his time alone. His gaze took in the ice house she pointed out as well as several other buildings, though he already knew what they were, having seen them when he first walked into the yard. It was good to know he hadn't lost his powers of observation though. What he hadn't noticed before was one curious-looking thing that reminded him of a gypsy wagon, minus its wheels. Instead, it perched on a platform, never to be moved again. Wooden steps led up to a bright red door. Painted flowers adorned the surface. He was about to ask about it, but never had the chance.

She touched his arm again, her fingers infusing him with warmth and that curious feeling he was beginning to like and dread at the same time. "Come into the house," she invited. "Henry and I designed it on our journey here, though neither one of us could be considered an artist. I can't draw a straight line, even if I use a ruler, but I knew what I wanted, and as long as we were dreaming, I dreamed big. A big house with lots of room, but not just a house. I wanted a home. A place where people could be comfortable and feel welcome. A place that didn't move."

A place that didn't move? It was a strange thing to say about a home, but he didn't ask for clarification. Again, it wasn't his business.

She led the way through the porch and opened the back door into the kitchen. "It took someone with real talent to turn our scribbling into what you see now."

Eamon stopped as soon as he entered the house. He understood there were a lot of people living and working here, himself included now, but the kitchen reminded him of the one in the hotel in Wyoming, where he'd spent a month washing dishes and waiting tables for very little pay and even less respect. It still amazed him what he was willing to do to fill an empty belly and emptier wallet—anything except sell his pistols or strap on his gun belt once more.

He nodded at Granny, who turned to glance at him, a warm, welcoming smile on her face, though she never stopped peeling vegetables. She stood at the counter beside the sink, working the knife over a potato while the children sat at a long table, doing their homework. He became the center of attention in moments as the children turned their eyes in his direction. Pencils stopped scratching on paper and a primer lay spread open on the table, forgotten, while curiosity brightened their faces.

He tried not to notice—surely, there had been other farm hands before him—and continued his survey of the room. A huge stove, one of the biggest he'd seen, and an icebox, smaller than the one in the Cheyenne hotel, but not by much, graced one wall amid ample counter space and glass-fronted cabinets. Several windows, covered with lacy curtains, were wide open to catch the breezes and filled the room with bright light. He inhaled and smelled rosemary. Though he'd eaten a short time ago, his stomach still growled and he wondered what mouthwatering entrée would meet his tongue for supper. If it tasted anything like it smelled, he would be in heaven.

"Eamon?"

He glanced away from the oven and its tempting aroma to see Theo standing in a short hallway between the kitchen and dining room, glass-fronted cabinets on both sides of her, a long polished table covered in fine lace behind her. "The dining room is this way."

He gave a quick nod to Granny, then started to join her in the passageway but stopped when he heard the rumble of wagon wheels over hard-packed dirt, followed quickly by a chorus of barking and meowing with a few quacks thrown in. The rumbling ceased, replaced by a man's booming voice as he greeted the animals and followed by the sound of horses' hooves moving toward the barn.

"They're home." Theo touched his arm, startling him. He glanced at her fingers on the sleeve of his shirt, then at her face, and came to the conclusion that she liked to touch as she moved passed him toward the door and held it open.

A few moments later, a woman with dark auburn hair twisted into a coronet atop her head walked through the open door, a wicker basket filled with paper-wrapped packages and letters hanging from her arm. A generous smile lit her face and excitement made her amber eyes twinkle as she pulled the letters from the basket and dropped them into Theo's hand. "They're all coming, Theo! Two more than last—" She stopped midsentence as her gaze fell upon him. "Oh, I'm sorry. I didn't realize we had a guest." She rushed forward, her hand extended in greeting, her mouth still spread in a generous grin. "Hello, I'm Marianne Burke."

Eamon took the hand offered. "Eamon MacDermott. A pleasure to meet you."

"Marianne, Eamon will be working with us." Theo offered an explanation to his presence.

The woman bobbed her head. "Welcome." She slid her warm hand from his grasp and moved toward the sink beside Granny, where she started removing the packages from the basket and laying them on the counter.

A moment later, an older man with a touch of gray at his temples and a square jaw that seemed chiseled from granite stopped in the doorway of the kitchen. Again, Theo performed introductions. Curiosity gleamed from the man's lively blue eyes as the two men shook hands. "Welcome to Morning Mist Farms. Are you ready to start working? We've got a lot to do."

"Of course." Eamon put his hat on his head, nodded to everyone staring at him, and followed the big man outside.

•••

An hour or so later, face and hands clean after helping Quincy move the silver galvanized canisters from the back of the buckboard into the springhouse, Eamon answered the timid knock on the door to his room to find Charlotte standing on his tiny front porch, her long brown hair done up in braids, honey brown eyes wide and filled with anxiety.

She shifted from one foot to the other and opened her mouth several times, but no words came out. Her fingers twisted the hem of her shirt, the one she'd changed into when she'd come home from school. A smudge of dirt could be seen on the garment of brown calico with tiny yellow flowers. Again, her mouth opened and a bright blush stained her cheeks as she shoved her hands into the pockets of the trousers she wore.

Her shyness was painful to see, and the kindness Theo insisted he extend to everyone came to the fore, though he hadn't needed her reminder. He tried to be kind always as one never knew the journeys of others or what hardships they faced, just like no one would ever know that he himself wasn't worthy of the same compassion.

"Hello, Charlotte," he said, careful to keep his voice calm and friendly, the same gentle tone he'd use on a frightened animal.

"Mama Theo says come for supper, Mr. MacDermott," she blurted in a rush, bobbed a quick curtsy, and fled back to the main house. Eamon watched her for a moment, then left his little room, carefully closing the door behind him.

The aroma hit him as soon as he entered the back porch. His mouth watered as the scent of rosemary, garlic, and fresh baked bread joined together to tickle his nose. He made his way to the doorway and stopped, unable to take another step despite the delicious aromas tempting his appetite. The kitchen bustled with activity, a chorus of children's voices mingled with adults'. There was nothing formal here ... just people who truly loved each other, and it showed. A family, as his own had been before tragedy drove them apart. It was all too familiar.

He didn't belong here, not in the midst of all this ... *love*. He certainly didn't deserve to be breaking bread with these good people. Seeing the joy in which Theo's family interacted with one another made him long for things he wasn't worthy of having. He backed up a step, intending to head back to his room and the solitude to be found there, even though his stomach growled in hunger again.

Before he could make his escape, Theo caught him, those lovely eyes of hers beckoning him closer, the smile on her face welcoming. "Eamon, please come in."

Still, he hesitated, but her smile widened. The decision was taken from him as Gabby grabbed his hand and pulled him inside the homey kitchen, for despite its size, the room was indeed homey. "We saved a place for ya," she told him as she led him toward his seat, then lowered her voice into a stage whisper. "Don't be 'fraid."

Eamon took his seat, aware that every eye was on him, and the urge to escape from this room was so strong, he nearly bolted. He took a deep breath and forced himself to look around the table. The expressions on the faces he saw were welcoming and friendly. Not one of them looked at him with censure or blamed him for his brother's death. Of course, they didn't know about Kieran. Or his failure to keep him and his family safe.

"Thank you, Marianne. Everything looks wonderful," Theo said as she took her seat.

The woman blushed as she set a basket of bread on the table, then slipped into her chair. A warm glow colored her face as she smiled. "Whose turn it is to say grace?"

"I do believe it's Gabby's turn tonight," Quincy replied, his lips twitching at the corners, "but I should check my list, just in case."

"It's my turn." The little girl nodded with enthusiasm, her grin infectious. "Yesterday, Tommy said prayers, and the day before, Charlotte did." She folded her hands, closed her eyes, and recited a blessing Eamon remembered his own mother saying almost every night.

Eamon didn't pray, not in the usual sense. Rather, he spoke with God, talking to Him more than he spoke to anyone aside from Traveler, but he listened now, showing the proper respect, even folding his hands and bowing his head as the familiar words flowed over him. "And thank you for makin' Mr. MacDermott come to our farm."

Gratitude shook him, rocked him deep in his soul. In the past two and a half years, no one had reason to be thankful for his presence, and now, in the space of an afternoon, one person had thanked him and the other was pleased he was here. He wasn't quite sure how to react to that, and along with the gratitude filling him, he experienced panic as well.

He jumped, startled, when Charlotte called his name and passed him a bowl of mashed potatoes, the bowl so much bigger than her hands and yet she managed. He focused, took a big spoonful of the potatoes, and passed the bowl to Gabby—the chatterbox—on his left just moments before another bowl came his way, this one filled with green beans topped with slivers of almonds.

Theo's family talked, all of them, often at the same time as they passed plates and bowls from one hand to the other, and this, too, reminded him very much of his younger days. His mother had always set a nice table, no matter where they were, and there was always enough to eat. She'd often say if you left the table still hungry, it was your own fault.

He did not contribute to the conversation and instead concentrated on the food on his plate. He took a bite of his dinner and sighed. He'd had leg of lamb before, but not like this. The lamb melted in his mouth, the rosemary and garlic the perfect complement. Marianne Burke was a genius.

"Who wants to start?" The question came from Granny, who held court at the head of the table.

Lou leaned toward him and drew his attention. "Every day, we all tell one good thing that happened. It can be something simple." He grinned, his lively blue eyes twinkling. "Or it may be something truly momentous."

"M-me!" Thomas nearly jumped from his seat with excitement. "I g-got an A on m-my spelling test t-today."

And so it began.

Earlier in the day, when Eamon had breathed in the fresh Colorado air, he'd known a moment of peace so rare, it had taken his breath away. Now, sitting around this table, listening to the children talk about their day, something shifted in his heart. Despite the tragedies they had suffered, the children still had the capacity to look for the things that made living worthwhile.

His entire body stiffened with the thought, and he shook his head just in time to notice that the entire room had gone silent. All eyes were on him. Again.

He focused and his gaze traveled from one to another, finally settling on Theo. Again, he saw no disgust or revulsion on her face. In fact, he saw the opposite. Kindness. It was there in the warmth of her startling green eyes.

"It's your turn, Eamon. Tell us one good thing that happened for you today," she encouraged him, her smile soft and sweet.

He swallowed his mouthful of green beans, stifling the urge to admit he'd found a bit of paradise when he stumbled on to Morning Mist Farms. Instead, his gaze shot to Marianne. "This is the best dinner I've ever had."

Chapter 4

Eamon tugged on the reins and stopped Traveler on a rise overlooking Whispering Pines Ranch. He pulled his hat lower to block the sun from his eyes.

Something was wrong. He felt it deep in his bones.

The ranch seemed deserted. The big two-story house set in the middle of a vast green lawn looked forlorn and empty. Brock and Kieran must have headed out, but if that were so, then why was the wagon still in the crushed stone drive near the front door?

He squinted, focusing on the house. Nothing moved except the horses tethered to the wagon, nervously pawing at the ground, moving the buckboard to and fro. A chill skittered up his spine, and his muscles tensed.

Where were his brothers? And Mary? Had stopping to remove the rock from Traveler's shoe made him too late to help? Had the Logans already come as Jefferson Logan had threatened?

His gaze roamed past the wagon to the front door. The feeling that something wasn't right persisted. He clenched the reins in his hands, then nudged Traveler's sides to move forward. The horse walked down the slope as silently instructed. Eamon didn't take his eyes from the house, fully expecting to see one of the MacDermotts—his brothers or Kieran's beautiful wife, Mary—open the door but it remained closed.

The horses and wagon rolled back and forth as he approached. The wind moaned and sighed, bringing with it the faint echo of cows lowing in the field and the whinny of horses in the pasture beyond the barn and stable. A window shutter slammed against the wall somewhere in the back of the house. Or perhaps it was the back door that hadn't been closed properly. The unexpected bang made him jump a little every time.

Eamon tugged on the reins, bringing Traveler to a stop beside the buckboard. He peered over the wooden slats and saw several cloth-sided valises filling the interior. A small smile lifted the corner of his mouth. He wasn't late after all. He was just in time. They hadn't left yet.

He slid from the saddle, letting the reins dangle to the ground and strolled around the buckboard toward the porch. He mounted the steps and strode across the porch, then slowed his pace. The front door was already open, but the scent wafting through the door wasn't Mary's well-known apple pie. It was the coppery smell of blood and the acrid burn of gunfire.

"You must be that other MacDermott, the U.S. Marshal. Too bad that badge ain't gonna help you."

The voice came from his left as a man stepped around the corner of the porch. Eamon turned, and his heart constricted. He knew this man, though he'd never met him face to face. Tell Logan. Thief. Rustler. Murderer. His Wanted posters, along with the rest of his family's, graced the walls of every sheriff's office from here to Albuquerque and a hundred places in between. He—and his brothers—were the reason he was here.

Eamon reached for his weapon, but he wasn't fast enough. He had just cleared leather when Tell Logan grinned, blinked twice, and fired.

Eamon awoke with a start, a harsh sob stuck in his throat, the sound of the shot Tell Logan fired ringing in his ears. He swallowed the cry and concentrated on breathing deeply until the visions in his head vanished. Reaching up, he smoothed his fingers over the ugly scar on his chest between his collar bone and his heart. The action brought pain—not physical, but emotional, the ache never disappearing completely though his flesh had healed. Half an inch lower, and he wouldn't have survived the bullet at all. Kieran hadn't. Neither had Mary. Or Matthew, their young son.

Only he, Brock, and Desi Lyn, Kieran's daughter, had managed to stay alive after the ambush.

He sat up slowly, momentarily disoriented by the soft mattress beneath him and the roof over his head. He had expected to see stars, but instead, saw the heavy beams of the rafters above him. Moving the thin blanket aside, he sat up, planting his bare feet firmly on the rag rug on the floor, then scrubbed his hands over his face, removing the last vestiges of sleep. The hazy light of the morning sky before dawn brightened the room.

He sat still, letting his body calm after reliving the devastating events that had sent him on this journey of isolation—punishment for failing to protect Brock and Kieran and his family, a penalty for being late on that fateful day, penance for not going after the Logans prior to them descending on Paradise Falls and Whispering Pines, Kieran's ranch. If he had been five minutes earlier, he wouldn't have been taken by surprise. Tell Logan wouldn't have shot him and left him to die. Ten minutes earlier and he might have stopped Zeb, Tell's brother, from killing Kieran, Mary, and little Matthew. He could have stopped the outlaw from shooting Brock.

He could have prevented it all ... if he hadn't been late, if Traveler hadn't gotten a rock in his shoe. Such a small thing to dig a rock out of a shoe, but the precious minutes it had taken caused devastating consequences.

Eamon swiped at his face again, then rose from the bed, slid into a pair of trousers, grabbed his shirt, and headed for the door. There was a rocking chair on the little front porch, the perfect place to watch the sun rise and see the mist for which this farm had been named while his heartbeat returned to normal and the last of the nightmare disappeared. He slipped into his shirt, but didn't button it, and grabbed the doorknob.

He opened the door and nearly collided with Theo, her hand poised to knock. If she hadn't been paying attention, she would have rapped on his chest. As it was, she appeared startled and a little flustered as her eyes widened and slowly drifted from his chest up to his face.

"Oh! You're up," she stated the obvious, her voice, usually hoarse, sounding a little breathless as a blush colored her cheeks, making the new-grass green of her eyes more brilliant. If she noticed his scar, she was too well-mannered to mention it, but he did observe her gaze dart back to the patch of smooth, discolored skin as she handed him a cup of coffee and stepped off the porch. "Lou and Wynn are waiting in the barn for you. They'll show you what to do."

Eamon watched her as she beat a hasty retreat and started walking toward the henhouse. Marching, actually—the hem of her dark brown split skirt swirling around the tops of her tooled leather boots as she quickly crossed the yard, muttering to herself.

He lifted the corner of his mouth a little ... until she stopped and faced him once more, her gaze seeming to burn him as it traveled from his bare feet to the top of his head, and his halfhearted smile disappeared as quickly as it had come. "Breakfast will be ready by the time you're done with the milking." She tilted her head and gave him a tremulous smile, one that made his heart beat faster, though why he couldn't begin to understand. He'd just met her *yesterday*, for pity's sake. Not even twenty-four hours ago. And she might or might not be married!

Maybe he was just as startled by her as she had been by him.

"If you need anything laundered, just leave it on the chair."

She gave him another beautiful smile, then disappeared behind one of the buildings, the dog, cats, and duck following behind her. He remained in the doorway, coffee cup in hand, just staring. Bringing the cup to his mouth, he took a sip and promptly burned his lip and tongue.

That's what you get for ogling the boss lady!

He brought the cup to his mouth once more, but this time, blew on the hot brew before he sipped.

Tonguing the slightly burned place on his lip, Eamon stepped back inside his room to get ready for the day. A few minutes later, he dropped his dirty laundry on the chair on his little front porch as instructed, then pushed open the barn door and stepped through, greeted by the warm smell of animals and hay. Pale sunlight streamed in through the windows, but a few lanterns had been lit to create a glow that reflected on four tall, galvanized canisters in the walkway between stalls. Like the stable, the barn was huge. It would have to be. There were a lot of animals—draft horses, sheep, and pigs, as well as the cows. The buckboard he'd seen the day before, as well as a buggy and a sleigh, was housed here, too.

He greeted Traveler in one of the stalls near the door, rubbing the horse's nose, promising to let him run in the field after breakfast before he turned his attention to the sixteen cows lined up in the middle of the barn, waiting to be milked. The calves were already outside in one of the pastures, waiting for their mamas. He could hear them bawling beyond the barn as he walked closer to the cows and spotted Lou squatted on a stool, his hands in constant motion, milk squirting into the pail beneath the cow's udder.

"You milk cows before?" the young man asked as he turned his head and noticed him. He twisted his hand a little and spurted milk at one of the kittens waiting patiently beside a bucket.

"I have." He didn't lie, but it had been a long time ago ... in another life—when he had been young and innocent, before guilt became his constant companion. He watched the boy. Lou had a nice, steady rhythm, which he didn't break as he nodded toward Wynn, who was just putting his stool and two pails on the ground beside one of the other cows.

"Wynn, would you show him where the stuff is and what to do?"

"Sure. Come on back, Mr. MacDermott."

"Eamon, please."

The boy gave a nod and walked back the way he'd come in his loose-hipped gait, a gangly youth, all elbows and knees and long legs. Eamon would bet the boy hadn't stopped growing either. Neither had Lou, for that matter.

Eamon followed the young man to a small room at the back of the barn, opposite the one he'd been in yesterday. Instead of harnesses and halters and the other accoutrements for the draft horses, this room contained several three-legged stools, piles of small fluffy towels and washcloths in glass-fronted cabinets, and galvanized pails, like the one Lou filled. A large sink nestled beside a potbellied stove above a floor made of brick. Water simmered on top of the stove, steam rising toward the ceiling.

"Grab a stool," Wynn said, and handed him two pails, then walked over to the cabinet against the wall.

Eamon looked at the pails. "Why two?"

"One is for the milk. The other is for the warm water. We wash the cow's udder with Granny's special soap and dry it with one of these towels." The boy took a towel, a washcloth, and a small square of soap from the glass-fronted cabinet and tossed everything at him one at a time. "Quincy's rule. Not only is it healthier for the cow, but he says it calms them and they give more milk. I'm not sure if that's true or not, because I've never milked cows anywhere else, but I can tell you we get a lot of milk." He grinned then, his lips spreading wide to stretch the beginnings of a mustache on his upper lip. The youth grabbed the ladle out of the vat of water on top of the potbellied stove. "You'll have to mix this with some from the pump. You don't want it too hot. And you don't need much in your bucket. We get fresh water for each cow. Clean towels and washcloths, too. No sense spreading anything."

Eamon shook his head as the boy slipped out of the room and walked to his waiting cow. He didn't remember doing anything like this when he milked cows before, but then, it had been years. Many years. And certainly not on a farm like this.

He placed the towel, washcloth, and soap on a small table near the sink; prepared his water, making sure it wasn't too hot; then grabbed everything including his stool; and sauntered down the aisle toward the waiting cows. He dropped the stool and maneuvered it into place with his foot, then sat with his pails beside him. The towel, washcloth, and soap went in his lap as he studied the udder before him, not quite sure where to begin. Or how. It had been longer than he thought. He turned slightly and studied Wynn's actions, then mimicked them, washing the cow's udder, then drying it with the towel. He dropped the used washcloth into the pail, then grabbed the other and moved it into place. Once again, he sat back and studied the cow in front of him.

"It helps if you talk to them," Lou offered, his voice disembodied by the big animal hiding him.

"Talk to them?"

"You talk to your horse, don't ya?" Wynn asked, then nodded toward the bovine. "Same thing. That one there is Nessie."

Well, of course he talked to his horse. Didn't everyone talk to their horses? He and Traveler held long discourses on any subject under the sun. Traveler may not participate in the conversation with words, but he whinnied or snorted in the appropriate places. He was a smart horse. Nessie, however, was a cow. He'd never spoken to a cow before. "What should I say to her?"

"The same kinda things you say to your horse. It's not the words, but the tone. You can call her the biggest pain in the a— rump, as long as you say it in a nice voice. Oh, and don't forget to breathe. If you're nervous, they'll feel it." The boy shrugged, then grinned. "Got no scientific proof of that. It's my own theory and experience."

Eamon took a deep breath and let it out slowly. He made himself more comfortable and said, "Good morning, Nessie," in the same tone he used when speaking to Traveler, then grabbed hold of a teat and squeezed like Lou and Wynn were doing. Nothing happened. No milk spurted into the pail.

Nessie shuffled her hooves a little, then turned her head and looked at him. He could have sworn she was laughing at him and his feeble attempts to milk her.

Eamon flushed, the heat rising up to his face, then smirked at the cow. "Wouldn't it be easier for both of us if I placed the pail where it needs to be and you just … gave me the milk?"

Nessie continued to stare at him. She didn't respond, though he knew she wouldn't, nor did she just spontaneously drop milk into the bucket. Eamon inhaled deeply and tried again … and again, all under Nessie's curious, mocking brown eyes. She was patient with him though and didn't kick, although she could have.

It took more than a few tries, but eventually, the rhythm of milking came back to him. A feeling of accomplishment accompanied the tentative squirts of liquid into the pail. One of the trio of kittens that had been watching—and waiting—next to Lou waddled over to him and sat, big yellow eyes on the milk making its way into the pail.

Eamon glanced at the kitten. "Sorry, pal. None for you today. I'm lucky I'm getting it where it's supposed to be." The kitten mewed and watched for a long time, eyes focused on the pail. He licked at the milk already on the fur around his mouth, but Eamon concentrated on getting the milk in the bucket, ignoring the feline and his occasional *meows* until the kitten wandered toward Wynn across the aisle, willing to take his chances on another human.

By the time Eamon moved on to his third cow, he had his own rhythm. True, he was slower than either Lou or Wynn, but in his own defense, it had been a long time. "What's this one's name?" he asked Lou as the boy emptied a pail of milk into the galvanized canister in the center aisle.

Lou glanced at the cow and grinned. "Silly Boy."

"Silly Boy?"

"It used to be Sally, but Gabby renamed her. She doesn't seem to mind." The young man shrugged and shuffled back to the little room to clean his buckets, get fresh water and towels, and begin again with another cow.

They worked in companionable silence, the only sounds in the barn that of the cows' hooves shuffling against the straw on the floor, the rhythmic spurts of milk into buckets, the soft murmur of words spoken to the animals. Peaceful. Soothing. Like the rest of Morning Mist Farms, as he'd discovered yesterday. Despite the number of people and the sometimes boisterous conversations, there was tranquility here he couldn't deny. This place was different from anywhere he'd ever been. It wasn't just the geography, although the farm was nestled in a natural Eden—bright sunshine and blue sky, meandering streams, lush green grass, towering trees, and mountains in the near distance—it was the people. Theo and her *family*. No wonder everything thrived here.

Eamon took a deep breath and let it out slowly, his hands in constant motion.

The barn door slid open, allowing more light to spill into the interior of the building. Quincy tugged off his gloves as he stepped inside. "How we doing, boys?"

"Almost done, Pop. Got more milk today than yesterday."

"Excellent." He rubbed his hands as he came farther into the barn. "I'll take the cows to the back pasture today. Give them a change of scenery. Plus the grass is getting a little high back there." He came even farther into the big room and stopped short. "Oh, Eamon, didn't see you there."

Eamon gave him a nod, but his hands never stopped moving. He had found a comfortable rhythm and didn't want to lose it. "Morning, boss."

The big man grinned, then moved a little closer, inspecting the contents of Eamon's pail. "Good, good."

One of the kittens chose that moment to pounce on Quincy's boot. "And good morning to you, little one." He stooped and picked up the silver-and-gray-striped kitten, holding it close to his chest. He shook his finger, and the kitten immediately swiped at it with his paw. "Have you had enough milk today?" The kitten purred, then rubbed his milk-wet chin on Quincy's finger.

Eamon watched the man interact with the kitten and couldn't help noticing the expression on his face.

That's what happy looks like. The thought rumbled through his head as he turned away. Long forgotten memories sprung free from the place in his heart where he kept them locked away, reminding him that he, too, had once been happy and as close to carefree as one could be and still be in the job he'd had. He glanced back at Quincy. The joy on his face hadn't changed. If anything, his smile grew as the kitten snuggled closer. For reasons Eamon couldn't explain, seeing Quincy's expression made him a little jealous. It had been a long time since he had worn a similar look or felt that way.

And whose fault is that? the little voice in his head, the one that sounded suspiciously like his brother, Kieran, demanded. *You're the one who walks away when things are going well. You're the one not allowing yourself to be happy. I forgave you a long time ago. So did Mary. Teague and Brock, too. Isn't it time you forgave yourself?*

With effort, Eamon forced his brother's voice to shut up, then turned away and finished milking the cow. He rose from his stool, then poured the milk into the canister.

"All right, little one. Get along." Quincy placed the kitten on his own four paws and grinned when he scampered toward the closest pail, his already full belly making him waddle.

When the milking was done and the last pail of creamy liquid had been poured into one of the four big canisters and two smaller jugs, Quincy placed the tops on them, then gave instruction to Lou and Wynn. "Roll those canisters into the spring house, boys, and start separating the cream from the milk in the canisters from yesterday. After that, you can wash up for breakfast." The boys moved quickly—the sooner they completed the tasks, the sooner they could eat. He turned and tilted his head slightly, his eyes gleaming. "Help me clean up in here, would you?"

"Of course." Eamon reached for the stool he'd recently vacated, as well as the pails, towel, and washcloth, then followed Quincy, who did the same with the items the boys had left. After putting everything away—the towels and washcloths in a basket to be washed, pails left to soak in the vat of simmering water on top of the potbellied stove—the farm manager offered another invitation.

"Walk with me, Eamon. You haven't seen Morning Mist when it's the prettiest. I love the mornings here. Nothing better than sitting on the back porch with a cup of coffee and my pipe and watching the world come alive." He grinned. "Not that I get to do that often, but every once in a while ..."

"Sure." Eamon hooked his thumbs in his trouser pockets and trailed him from the little room.

Quincy stood in the doorway and gave a short, sharp whistle followed by a longer one. Almost as one, the cows gave him their full attention. "Move it out, girls. We're going to the back pasture today. Number eight to those of you who can count."

Eamon burst out in a chuckle at the thought cows could count, but as if they understood every word Quincy said, the cows moved out of the barn and strolled in a semiorderly fashion toward the farthest pasture without being led by either person or dog, then disappeared into the fine mist hovering over the landscape. He and Quincy walked behind the last cow, which just happened to be Nessie. She gave Eamon one final look, bovine humor still gleaming in her eyes, and sauntered through the gate. Quincy closed it behind her and folded his arms on the top rail.

"Breathe in that fresh morning air, Eamon." Following his own advice, Quincy pulled air into his lungs, the grin on his face widening. "Ever smell anything so wonderful or see anything so beautiful?"

"No, sir, not in a very long time."

Quincy turned toward him, his brows raised but his grin still firmly in place. Curiosity danced in his eyes, and his mouth opened as if a question waited on the tip of tongue, trying to force its way over his lips, but he was too polite to ask. Then again, maybe he was as straightforward as Theo, blunt and direct. "Tell me about yourself, Eamon."

Eamon stiffened, just a little. He hated that invitation to blurt out his life's story. "Not much to tell. I've been around. Done a few things."

A subtle change in the man's complexion and the nearly imperceptible flicker of an eye, not enough to be noticeable to everyone, but for a man who spent most of his adulthood risking his safety, even his life, on reading a man's expression, Eamon noticed and his muscles tightened. Quincy didn't believe his noncommittal answer for a minute.

"You aren't a farmer," he stated rather baldly.

"How could you tell?"

"Oh, you milked the cows just fine." Quincy gave a little chuckle. "A little rusty, like you hadn't done it in a long time, but there's something else." His eyes shifted over him, before he focused on the cows in the pasture, and the fine mist hovering over the field once more. "You're not a drifter, either. You may have been traveling, but—"

Though he tried to remain casual and relaxed, the simple fact was that Quincy Burke guessed too much for Eamon's comfort. He covered up his unease with another question. "What makes you say that?"

The man shrugged. "Just a feeling," he admitted, confirming for Eamon that he had no proof to back up his statements, just a hunch that probably settled low in his belly, the same sensation

Eamon experienced quite often when something just wasn't quite right. "You watch everything, constantly alert, like you're waiting for trouble, like—"

Quincy stopped speaking, just cut himself off and once more turned to study him. Eamon's mouth dried. For a moment, he thought Quincy would see his guilt and blurt out his shame. Instead, the farm manager gave him a slight nod. "Morning Mist Farms is a wonderful place, Eamon. It can help you if you let it." He adjusted his hat, pulling the brim a little lower. "Come on, let's eat."

Relief surged through him that Quincy hadn't prodded deeper. He wasn't ashamed of his life as a U.S. Marshal. He'd been a good one, a fair one. No, that part of his life he could share, if and when the moment presented itself, but why bring it up if he didn't have to? The inevitable question as to why he quit would open a Pandora's box of misery, and he just didn't want to relive that particular time in his life.

Eamon followed the man down the path between enclosures, passing the sheep already munching on sweet grass, the fine mist hovering over the fields beginning to dissipate, giving way to the vibrant green that extended all the way to the tree line in the distance. Neither man spoke as they sauntered across the barnyard to the back porch. If Quincy had questions, he kept them to himself, but his last comment about letting the farm help him wormed into Eamon's brain. Was such a thing possible? Could a place help him? Help him with what?

He pushed the questions away. Firmly. Things in life didn't happen like that. A place could never take away his guilt nor could it bring forgiveness or happiness.

"You comin'?" Quincy's voice intruded into his thoughts, and Eamon realized the man was waiting for him, holding the kitchen door open in invitation.

His feet moved forward of their own accord, bringing him across the porch to join the farm manager. "Thanks."

His mouth began to water as soon as he stepped past Quincy and into the kitchen, the aromas rising into the air tantalizing his nose. His belly growled, though he'd eaten his fill last night and left the table groaning. Marianne and Granny were busy putting out the last of the food. There were flapjacks and eggs and crispy bacon. Fluffy, flaky biscuits. Triangles of toasted bread with four different types of toppings aside from butter—blackberry and strawberry jam, peach marmalade and apple butter, each jar labeled in neat handwriting Eamon assumed was Marianne's. Granny's twisted, gnarled fingers didn't leave much confidence she could hold a pen in the way required to form the fancy loops and twisting curls of the letters. Of course, the handwriting could have been Theo's.

"Is there anything I can do?" he asked as he stood beside the chair he'd occupied last night at dinner. Without a word, Marianne handed him a pitcher of milk and pointed to the glasses beside the children's plates. Eamon poured, then took his seat as everyone took their places at the table, except for Theo. He hadn't seen her since she'd handed him his coffee earlier. Where was she? In the stable with the horses? Did she not join the family for breakfast?

Thomas said grace, and as soon as everyone repeated "Amen," plates and bowls were passed around, much the same way as the night before.

"Since it's Saturday and none of you have school, what's on the agenda for today?" Quincy asked as he spread strawberry jam on a triangle of toast and slipped it onto Gabby's plate.

"We've been invited to a picnic," Lou announced and grinned, showing white teeth with a small gap between the two front ones, then nudged Wynn with his elbow. "Lanie Tuttle invited Wynn personally. I think she's sweet on him."

Wynn turned a deep red, the color staining not only his cheeks but his neck as well. "She is not!" He returned Lou's nudge with a little more enthusiasm. Milk sloshed from the glasses. Indeed, the entire table moved a bit as the younger children started chanting "Wynn loves Lanie!"

"I do not!" Wynn declared and elbowed Lou once more. More milk soaked the tablecloth as the table moved a little more. A coffee cup, thankfully empty, tipped over, and once again, Eamon was struck by how familiar the scene was and how much he missed his brothers. He'd been on the receiving end of that chanting and elbowing more than once before his father put a stop to it.

"Besides, you're sweet on Evangeline Davis. I saw you carrying her books!"

In an instant, the chanting changed from Wynn and Lanie to Lou and Evangeline, accompanied by the thwack of spoons hitting the table.

"All right," Quincy cut into the antics with a stern, no-nonsense voice. "That'll be enough now. Boys, behave. There is no jostling at the table." He turned his attention on the younger children and raised one eyebrow. The chanting died immediately. He picked up the platter of flapjacks and began passing it around the table as Theo rushed into the kitchen and grabbed the coffeepot from the stove. "Sorry, I'm late. I was reading yesterday's mail."

She turned to face Eamon and smiled. His world tilted, his breath stuck in his lungs. Maybe he was suffering from mountain sickness. He'd heard some people had headaches and dizziness, queasiness, and difficulty breathing from being too high up in the mountains. Perhaps he had a touch of that and his problems would disappear once he became accustomed to being in the Rockies again.

"Mr. MacDermott," Gabby whispered and tugged on his sleeve to gain his attention.

"What?" He looked at the platter in his hand. "Oh, I'm sorry," he said and quickly plopped two flapjacks on her plate, then passed the platter to Charlotte, but that didn't stop him from glancing up and studying Theo as she went around the table to fill the coffee cups for the adults. He stiffened when she came closer and leaned between him and Gabby while she poured the steaming brew. Eamon inhaled, catching the scent of roses that seemed to waft around her.

He closed his eyes for a moment in an effort to get his world back on its axis and tried to concentrate on the conversation around him. The task was easier said than done.

"Before you can go on your picnic, I promised Mr. Osuch we'd fix his roof." Quincy addressed both his son and Wynn as he nodded his thanks to Theo when she filled his cup. "We can do that after we get back from our morning run into town."

"But Pop!" Lou stopped in the middle of dishing eggs onto his plate, his features a study in disappointment. That, too, was familiar as Eamon had given his father the same expression on more than one occasion.

"We'll be done long before your picnic." The older man drizzled syrup on his flapjacks, then passed the small glass pitcher to his left into Charlotte's hands. "It's a small repair. Mr. Osuch has been a good neighbor to us. We are returning the favor."

Assured he wouldn't miss any of the picnic, the boy finished piling fluffy scrambled eggs onto his plate and passed the platter along.

"You and Wynn can take the buggy, as long as you promise to bring it back in one piece. No racing. And no seeing how many people you can fit inside at one time, either. Took me forever to fix that spring after the last time." He waited until his son nodded in agreement before he asked, "What else have we got?"

There were other plans, but none as exciting as the picnic the older boys would attend.

Theo seated herself in her customary chair, which just happened to be directly across from him, and once again, Eamon found himself drawn to her, his attention captured by her luminous grass-green eyes and generous smile. His flapjacks turned to sawdust in his throat, despite the thick, sweet syrup he'd poured over the stack.

Quincy cleared his throat. "Eamon, would you like to come into town with us this morning? I could drop you off back here before the boys and I head over to the Osuch place."

Eamon stilled, a strip of crispy bacon halfway to his mouth. He hadn't been to Pearce in quite some time, and it would be nice if he had more tobacco for his father's old pipe, but would the magic—though he hesitated to believe such a thing existed—of this place disappear as soon as he stepped off the property? He'd never been a superstitious man, never believed that a black cat crossing one's path could bring bad luck or that walking under a ladder would do the same. He carried no good luck charm and never had, but the thought of leaving this farm—even for an hour or two—made him think twice. He'd only been here one day, not even a full twenty-four hours. How would he feel a couple weeks down the road when he had some money in his pocket and struck out on his own again? "I would love to ... but I think Theo has plans for me and the horses." He glanced in Theo's direction to confirm his suspicions.

She smeared peach marmalade over a triangle of toasted bread, then raised her gaze to his and took a dainty bite. After she chewed and swallowed, she said, "That I do. Are you ready?"

"Yes, ma'am."

"All rested?"

"Yes, ma'am."

"Good because you have a long day ahead of you."

She grinned then, and Eamon wondered if she was teasing him. He felt the corners of his mouth starting to lift in response to her—in response to all of them around the table as he caught tidbits of several different conversations. He couldn't seem to help himself. It was this place and these people. "I'm ready anytime you are."

Fifteen minutes later, belly full, the taste of strawberries lingering on his tongue from the jam he'd liberally spread over his toast, Eamon drained the last of the coffee from his cup and wiped his mouth.

He and Theo were the only two still sitting at the table. Granny had grabbed her big floppy hat and headed outside to the barn to begin the process of washing clothes. Lou, Wynn, and Quincy had already left to prepare the buckboard for their morning run to town. Marianne scraped the plates the younger children brought her into a bucket to be given to the pigs, then slid the dishes into the sink to soak for a few minutes—everything organized and efficient, like the rest of the farm.

His attention focused on Theo. She leaned forward in her chair, elbows on the table though it wasn't proper, her chin resting atop her folded hands as she focused her attention on Thomas. Though he cleared the dishes along with Gabby and Charlotte, he told a story at the same time, his speech pattern alternating between rushed and halting, the words tripping over his lips in his excitement only to become stuck on his tongue where he struggled to get them out. And it didn't matter. Not to Theo, who patiently encouraged the boy, such love showing on her face, Eamon could feel the intensity of her emotions all the way across the table.

Even though there was work to be done, he didn't want to interrupt. It wasn't his place. And Theo didn't seem like she was in any kind of hurry. Taking his cue from her, Eamon sat back in his chair and listened until the story ended and the boy wandered over to the sink, his turn to wash the dishes while Gabby and Charlotte dried.

A moment later, Theo put down her coffee cup and cleared her throat as she rose from the table. Her gaze settled on him, and her lips spread into a grin. "Shall we?"

"Of course." He pushed his chair away from the table and quickly followed.

She led the way outside, grabbing her hat from the hook next to the door and plopping it on her head. "We'll move the horses into the pastures, then we'll muck out the stable." She grinned at him. "You ready for that?"

It was on the tip of his tongue to say no. Mucking out the stalls had never been a favorite thing to do, but it was part of his job here. He gave a quick nod. "Yes."

Theo laughed, a bright bubbling sound that filled the air. "You can admit it, Eamon. No one likes mucking out the stalls."

He didn't deny or agree with her statement, but a flush warmed his features as they reached the stable. Eamon stepped in front of her and pulled the heavy door open. His heart jumped a little when Theo gave him a beaming smile and stepped through. "Good morning, my lovelies!"

Her greeting was answered with a few neighs, some nickers, and a whinny or two as she strolled down the aisle, the dog, appearing from wherever he'd been, on her heels. The cats and duck brought up the rear. Stroking a nose here, patting a neck there, speaking softly, Theo opened the gates as she moved forward. Eamon followed her example and did the same on the other side of the aisle.

Eamon watched her, as amazed as he'd been yesterday by the way the big animals responded to her. They left their stalls at a leisurely pace and followed her, behind the dog, cats, and duck already in line.

She turned to him as she came up on Pumpkin's stall and opened his gate, but instead of letting him roam free as she did the others, she laid her hand on his neck, said a few words close to his ear, then led him toward the big door at the back of the stable. He stayed right beside her, needing nothing more than her touch to guide him. "Do you remember in which enclosures the horses were yesterday?"

"Yes, ma'am."

"Theo," she insisted and grinned again. "Let's do the same, except I want Daphne with Pumpkin here."

He gave a quick nod, though he didn't remember exactly which horse was Daphne. It didn't matter. He'd find out soon enough.

Theo clicked her tongue as she slid the door open, and the horses strolled through, heading up the grassy path between enclosures. Eamon opened gates and led them into their respective fields.

Theo closed the gate to Pumpkin's paddock closest to the stable, the faint murmur of her voice reaching Eamon, though he couldn't decipher her words. He did admire the subtle sway of her hips and the way the hem of her dark brown suede split skirt rippled around the tops of her boots. It took a moment or two before he could force his attention back to the task at hand.

Standing in the middle of the grassy path between enclosures, he studied the horses behind the fences. "All right, which one of you is Daphne?"

A soft nicker met his ears as one of the horses moved toward the gate, her ears pricked in his direction, her soft brown eyes alert and on him. "Are you Daphne?"

The horse let out another nicker, this time a little louder. Eamon took that as confirmation, though he glanced at Theo. She gave a slight nod, letting him know he had chosen correctly. "Well, that was easy enough." Eamon approached the horse, grabbed her halter, and gently led her to the paddock where Pumpkin waited.

The rest of the morning passed in a blur of heat and dust as they groomed the horses, one at a time for each of them, then cleaned the stable together, all while keeping an eye on Daphne and Pumpkin in the paddock, the mare seeming to be receptive to Pumpkin's pursuit, though she led him on a merry chase over the gently rolling hills. And though he tried not to, Eamon couldn't help stealing glances in Theo's direction before forcing himself to turn away.

Who was this woman?

She worked as hard as he, perhaps even harder. Perspiration glistened on her face. She'd taken off her hat earlier, and a hank of whiskey-colored hair slipped from the ponytail at the back of her head to curl near her cheek. He resisted the urge to tuck it behind her ear at the same time he squelched the desire to just stand back and watch her. Theo fascinated him. Perhaps it was the way she moved, graceful ... even with a pitchfork. Perhaps it was the way she talked with the children and the animals. Perhaps it was ...

Eamon dumped a shovelful of manure into the wheelbarrow, determined to keep his mind on his task instead of the boss lady and failed miserably, as once again, almost beyond his control, his eyes flicked toward her. She stood in the aisle, pitchfork in her hand, tines up, as she surveyed her completed task. Sunlight streamed through the door behind her, making her entire being glow, as she tucked that errant lock of hair behind her ear and smiled in his direction.

Eamon didn't dare move as a thought occurred to him: *Do angels exist?* And if they do, had he found one? Or maybe she was a sorceress. It was the only explanation he could come up with ... she'd cast some kind of spell over him. And not the first spell. Why else would he feel this way? He'd known her for less than a day, and yet he was fascinated with her, unable to stop stealing glances in her direction. Reminding himself she might be married didn't help either.

On the heels of that thought came another, one more likely to be closer to the truth than thinking Theo Danforth was an angel or a witch. Perhaps he'd been so lonely for so long, he saw and felt things that weren't true.

With a strength he hadn't known he possessed, Eamon gripped the handle of the shovel harder and forced himself to turn away from the vision that tempted him, determined, more so than ever, to keep his distance.

Chapter 5

Aldrich Pearce moved his chair closer to the crackling flames in the fireplace, kicked the footstool into place, and extended his slipper-clad feet toward the fire. He took a sip of the aged brandy filling the snifter in his hand and felt the trail of heat the liquor left as he swallowed, warming him from the inside out. Despite the fire burning brightly, he was still chilled—was always cold. He supposed that had to do with growing up so poor, there was never enough money for firewood. His hands. His feet. Even the tip of his nose never seemed to be warm.

There were those who said his cold hands and feet matched his icy heart, and to those, Aldrich would tip his hat and agree. One didn't get where he was with a warm heart. To get what one wanted in life, one needed to be cold. Calculating. Manipulative. Or so he learned early on from the man who sired him, then left him and his mother to face the world on their own while he went to seek his fortune elsewhere.

He smiled as he swirled the amber liquid around the bowl of the snifter, took another sip, and slid the glass onto the table beside him. His gaze wandered to the map of Colorado above the fireplace. The map had recently been altered—new, darker lines denoted the growth of his personal holdings with the acquisition of the Flying Cloud Ranch and Barclay's Stock and Feed. The Pearce empire, centered on the town bearing his name, was growing, and that gave him some satisfaction, however short-lived it might be. The pleasure and the feeling of accomplishment never lasted. Nor did it erase the memory of growing up poor and watching his mother struggle without the protection of his father. It didn't erase the memory of being hungry or ridiculed either.

He rubbed his hands together to generate warmth in his frigid fingers and studied the map. His focus shifted to Morning Mist Farms, five miles south of Pearce and one prime piece of land, not to mention horseflesh ... and the Widow Danforth.

He wanted it. All of it. The land. The horses. And the enticing, green-eyed widow.

He hadn't been able to devote much time to pursuing that goal, leaving the details up to his son, AJ, and the handful of lawyers he kept on retainer. Things had changed though. The Flying Cloud was his, as was Barclay's, thanks to Tell Logan, the outlaw he'd hired to do a little less than friendly coercion on his behalf. He had time now.

He heard the front door open and close. A moment later, his son greeted the butler, despite the lateness of the hour, before his rapid footsteps crossed the marble tiled hall, heading for the broad staircase, the second floor of the Pearce mansion, and the comfort of his suite. "AJ, come in here."

The footsteps stopped, followed by silence. Aldrich pursed his mouth and waited, silently counting the passing moments until those footsteps fell against the marble tile again, bringing his son to the study. AJ leaned against the doorframe and folded his arms across his chest as if he hadn't a care in the world, an action Aldrich had seen many times, and a lie if ever there was one.

"You wanted to see me, Father?"

Aldrich reached for the brandy beside him and finished the liquor in one swallow, then rose to his feet. Moving away from the warmth of the fire, he settled himself behind his massive desk, not because it was more comfortable—he'd be cold again in no time at all—but because it afforded him the perfect vantage point to study his son as he sauntered across the room toward the wet bar in the corner. Once again, he heard the vindictive, poisonous words AJ's mother had whispered just before she died fifteen years ago. "He's not yours."

There were times, like now, when he believed those words, when the hatred Millicent Grant Pearce harbored toward him felt more like the persistent jabs of a knife than mere words. As a child, AJ had looked nothing like him. As a thirty-year-old man, even less so. Whereas Aldrich had pale blue eyes and blond hair, nearly white now, AJ was dark. Very much like his mother and the man he suspected of being his father.

Even his stature did not resemble Aldrich. Not in the least. Tall and lanky, with not an ounce of extra weight, AJ was the complete opposite of himself, which again, made him think of the man he assumed had truly sired his son. Aldrich, even on his best day, could never be considered tall or lanky, but Carter Preston, his late partner, could.

His son didn't act like him, either. There was none of the drive or ambition that had made Aldrich one of the richest men in Colorado, not that he could see anyway. The only thing that AJ did have, which Aldrich credited himself for, was a devious mind.

Aldrich mentally shook himself as, bourbon in hand, AJ sauntered toward the desk and slumped into the chair, his dark eyes a little red-rimmed, as if he hadn't had enough sleep. And in this case, it was true. The grandfather clock in the corner kept perfect time as the minute hand swept toward twelve, the hour hand firmly positioned on two. He had never needed a lot of sleep and actually did some of his best thinking in the small hours of the morning, when the world was quiet. The same could not be said for AJ, which was another difference between them.

His nose detected cigar smoke, cheap toilet water, and cheaper booze, not the good liquor that filled his wet bar or the expensive perfume worn by his last mistress. "I've been thinking about our little problem."

"And which little problem is that, Father? There are so many."

"Sarcasm, AJ?"

"My apologies, Father. It's late and I'm tired." He swallowed some of the liquor in his glass. As he did so, Aldrich noticed how his hands shook, the tremor slight but noticeable. Too much booze could do that to a man. So could fear. "Please go on. To which problem were you referring?"

Aldrich forced his attention from AJ's shaking hands to his slightly flushed face. "Theo Danforth."

It gave him some pleasure to see his son sit up straight, one hand clutching the glass, knuckles white, the other curled into a fist as if he might strike him. That would never happen. The day AJ raised a hand to him, son or not, would be the day he died. He understood the reaction to the woman's name, though, and it suited his purposes well. AJ had a soft spot for the spirited widow. That soft spot began the day she drove her gypsy wagon into town, despite the fact her husband sat beside her. AJ had been smitten upon first glance. If the truth were told, Aldrich had liked what he'd seen, too. "Ah, you thought I'd forgotten about Morning Mist Farms."

AJ shook his head as he reached into the humidor on the desk and selected a cigar. He took his time clipping off the end, then swiped the head of a match against the striker. The match sparked into flame. He stared at that little bit of fire before holding it to the end of the cigar and puffing it alight. Smoke circled his head before dissipating toward the ceiling. "Not forgot. Just thought you decided to let her be."

Aldrich scoffed. "And why would I do that?"

"Because you don't need another farm. Or ranch. Or business. You don't need those horses."

"Who said anything about need, AJ?" He gestured toward the expensive, one-of-a-kind paintings adorning the walls and the rare objets d'art created especially for him, each piece worth so much more now that the artist was dead. "I don't *need* anything. *Want* is a whole different story." He paused, his eyes focusing on the map once more. "I'm thinking of letting Logan help us persuade our lovely widow that selling Morning Mist Farms and her horses to me is her best decision."

Movement caught his attention and his focus shifted.

AJ rose from his seat and sauntered across the room to the bar filled with fine liquor. He poured himself another glass of aged Kentucky bourbon, then tossed it back like it was water. "I thought you were going to let me court the widow Danforth, marry her, and gain control of all that fine horseflesh."

Aldrich grunted as he rifled through the papers on his desk. "You're taking too long. You should have wedded and bedded her already." He looked up from his papers and grinned. "Or bedded and wedded her."

"She isn't ready." AJ filled the glass one more time, then resumed his seat.

"She's a woman, isn't she? Change her mind."

AJ shook his head. "She's still in love with her late husband."

Aldrich smirked. "She might say she is, but I know the truth. How can she still love a man who left her with a mountain of debts when he died? Who'd give money to every poor slob who asked for it rather than save it for their future? She'd be a very rich woman if Henry Danforth had kept his money in his wallet." He pulled a cigar out of the ornate box on his desk, bit off the tip, and stuck it in his mouth. "Take my word for it, son, she's ready." He struck a match, but instead of lighting the cigar, he waved it in the air as he spoke. "Convince her. Show her she needs someone to help her run that farm. I'm sure she's tired of shouldering the responsibility on her own." He grinned and finally puffed the cigar alight. Blue-gray smoke wreathed his head as he leaned back in the chair and held out his empty snifter. "I'd do it myself—I'm still young enough. I haven't lost my looks or my powers of persuasion, but for some reason, Theodosia Danforth doesn't like me."

AJ grabbed the glass, rose from his seat, and, once again, strode toward the bar. "I wonder why, Father? Do you think it has anything to do with the nasty, reprehensible things you said about Henry when she paid off the debt he owed you?" He poured a healthy portion of brandy, more than the usual amount, the amber liquid filling the snifter halfway. "And she isn't alone, either. She has Quincy Burke and the rest of her family."

Aldrich took the glass before AJ slumped into his chair. "Ha! He's another one. I will admit he's a good farmer. His cows produce more milk than average, but he's got no head for business. He has himself a sweet deal at Morning Mist, but he's not Theo's husband or her protector." He lifted the snifter to his lips and swallowed, feeling the warmth of the liquor slide down his throat.

"You could always buy out her mortgage, then call the loan in."

"And why would I want to do that?" He tapped ashes into the crystal bowl on the desk, then stuck the cigar in his mouth and inhaled deeply.

AJ shrugged, then adjusted the sharp crease in his trouser leg. "It's worked for you before."

He exhaled the smoke in one perfect smoke ring after another and watched them distort and become shapeless wisps of vapor. "True, true, but those were dire circumstances. That gambit failed for me, too, and I lost money on the deal. No, I won't go that route again unless it becomes absolutely necessary." He leaned back in his chair and brought the cigar to his lips once more while his focus went from AJ to the map and back. After a moment, he sighed. Now that Flying Cloud and Barclay's were his, he felt a little generous, not something that happened very often. "I have decided, dear boy, to let you continue with your plan to seduce the widow Danforth, but there is a time limit. You have two months before I have Logan ... *persuade* her to see my point of view. No, make that six weeks to court her, so you'd best hurry. She's already got Ben Foster and Jim Kennedy sniffing up her skirts and that new hired hand, too."

"What new hired hand? What happened to Stanton?"

Aldrich barked laughter and almost spit his cigar from his mouth. "Stanton? She sacked him, as I suspected she would. Damned fool thought he could hit me up for money when she did. Sent him packing before you even learned of it. And you're more of a fool. You should have known better than to have him try to work on her farm. Theo isn't stupid, nor is she tolerant of abuse."

"No, she isn't stupid. Every man I've sent there to work for her and spy for me hasn't worked out."

"I told you that idea was worthless." Aldrich's chest puffed out with satisfaction as redness crept into AJ's face and sweat beaded on his forehead.

"No more worthless than you sending your fancy lawyers to bully her. She ran off the last three with a shotgun."

That satisfaction died quickly.

"Theo requires a more subtle touch."

"Then do what needs to be done, AJ. You have six weeks to woo her and get her in front of a preacher. You can start by asking her to that dance up at the church. She'd like that, I'm sure." He leaned forward and folded his hands on the desktop. "And while you're asking her, find out who that new man is."

"Yes, sir." AJ finished the bourbon in his glass, rose to his feet, and left the room, his footsteps loud on the marble staircase rising up to the second floor. Aldrich watched him go. Had his late wife lied all those years ago? Had she been telling the truth and AJ truly wasn't his son? Was he Carter Preston's?

Aldrich sighed. He'd never know. Dead women didn't talk. Neither did dead men.

Chapter 6

"Mama Theo, why is Mr. MacDermott so sad?"

Theo stopped in the midst of braiding Gabby's hair, the question taking her by surprise, though it shouldn't have—Gabby was a sensitive child. Theo mentally shook herself, then grabbed a ribbon and tied it around the end of the braid, the bright blue silk making Gabby's eyes brighter. "I don't know, buttercup. Perhaps something terribly sad happened to him."

"Like me? And Charlotte? And Tommy?"

She gave a slow nod. "That could be. Perhaps you should ask him. Be kind though. Always kind." She inspected her handiwork, then caught the child's gaze in the vanity's mirror. "And maybe you can help him. Show him how to be happy. Some people just don't know how. Or they forgot."

Gabby turned around on the stool, but she didn't look up. Instead, she studied her feet, dangling above the floor. "But I'm just little."

"Ah, buttercup, that's all right." Theo reached out and gently clasped Gabby's chin between her thumb and forefinger, raising her ward's face upward so she could see into her baby-blue eyes. "You just haven't grown tall yet, that's all. It's there. One of these days, you'll sprout up like Granny's plants, but that isn't the important thing. You may be little on the outside right now, but your heart is as big as all Colorado." She released the child's chin, then stooped to wrap her arms around the girl, hoping this time Gabby wouldn't hold back.

The girl hugged her, a quick squeeze that was over much too quickly, before she scrambled off the dressing table's matching stool. "It's your turn, Charlotte," she said as she skipped from the room.

"Where are you going?" Theo grinned and had a moment of sympathy for Eamon at the same time. She knew exactly where Gabby was heading. *Poor man doesn't know what's about to hit him.*

Her prediction proved correct as the girl responded, her cheerful little voice trailing down the stairs. "To help Mr. MacDermott be happy."

"I know it's Saturday and you have no school, but we still need to collect eggs." Theo moved into the hallway and yelled down the stairs. "I'll meet you at the henhouse in a few minutes."

"Okay, Mama Theo!"

Theo shook her head as she walked back into her room. Gabby Bainbridge was a force to be reckoned with. She did not touch people often and she carried scars from her past, but there was no escaping her persistence or her charm. "I'm so sorry, Eamon."

"Why are you sorry, Mama Theo?" Charlotte asked as she sat in the vacated seat, her honey-brown eyes intent upon the mirror.

"Because Mr. MacDermott is about to get blown over by Hurricane Gabby. You know what a chatterbox she can be. And you know how determined she is."

The little girl sighed and nodded in agreement. "I know." She sighed again as her fingers plucked at the hem of the shirt she wore over her trousers. "Not sure how it happened, but she ended up with all my peppermint sticks."

"She did?" Theo picked up the brush and drew the bristles through Charlotte's light brown hair, making the thick strands curl and gleam in the light coming in through the window. "Braid or pig tails?"

"Pig tails." Her fingers continued to pick at her shirt, pulling at a loose thread. "Mr. MacDermott *is* very quiet."

Theo nodded as she chose several ribbons—two each of red, green, and yellow—from the little ceramic box on the dressing table and held them up. "No, he doesn't say very much, does he?"

Charlotte shook her head, and a blush rose to her cheeks as she chose the green ribbons. "But he's not like me. He's not ... shy."

"No, he's not shy, rosebud. He's just ... sad for whatever reason." She rested her hand on Charlotte's shoulder and gave a light squeeze. "But you can help him, too."

The little girl's face brightened, although doubt flickered in her eyes. "Me?"

"Of course. Why not you? You're a sweet girl, and you have a big heart, too. Be kind to him and he'll be kind back, and maybe, between all of us, he won't be sad anymore." She drew the brush through Charlotte's hair, then parted it down the middle, and separated the sides. A few more quick strokes and she tied the green ribbons, creating two perfect pigtails, the ends curling like a true pig's tail.

The ribbons would be lost or stuffed into a pocket and her hair would be tangled and knotted after a day of hard play, but it didn't matter. Not in the least. This time Theo spent with the girls was not so much about doing their hair, but more about talking and listening and loving. Over time, it had become a ritual, one that she enjoyed. "You're done."

Charlotte slipped off the stool and threw her arms around Theo, hugging her tight. "Thank you, Mama Theo."

"My pleasure, rosebud. Now scoot with you. I'll be down in a minute, and we'll collect those eggs."

As Gabby had done, Charlotte skipped from the room, then ran down the stairs, her sock-clad feet light on the risers.

Theo listened, a smile on her face, then pulled the brush through her own hair, tying the heavy mass into a ponytail at the back of her head. Her thoughts flew to Eamon, and her smile grew. The man didn't stand a chance at remaining sad, not with two very persistent little girls showing him how to be happy. She smirked at her reflection in the mirror, then sat on the stool the girls had utilized earlier, and pulled on her thick wool socks and boots. A moment later, she left her room and went downstairs to find the kitchen empty.

No Marianne, no Granny, no children. She glanced out to the porch, but only saw Charlotte pulling on her boots. Closer to the barn, she saw Gabby, one of the rag dolls she loved dangling from her fingertips with its stuffed feet dragging through the dirt and the small cigar box where she kept what she called "medico supplies" tucked under her arm.

Again, a smile crossed her lips. The little girl was going to see Eamon right now and begin her battle to make him happy, starting with "fixing" her doll.

"Was I right?"

The voice came from behind her, and though Theo recognized it, she still jumped, startled, her hand flying to her chest as she sucked in her breath. She turned to see Granny shuffle into the kitchen from the butler's pantry, folded napkins in her hand, still dressed in her nightclothes, her robe tied securely around her waist.

"Granny! You frightened ten years off my life!"

"Sorry, Theo, didn't mean to startle you." She moved around the table in a slow, halting gait, placing the napkins beside their plates, then adding fork, spoon, and knife with her twisted fingers.

"Why are you setting the table? Isn't it Thomas's turn this morning?"

"I sent the boy out to the barn to help with the milking." The older woman shrugged as she finished the process and each place setting had a full complement of silver, napkin, plate, and glass or cup.

"Where is Marianne?"

"Sent her out to the springhouse for more butter." The woman inhaled deeply and released the air from her lungs through her pursed lips, an action Theo had seen more than once and generally meant Granny was in pain, her joints stiffer than usual. It also meant there would be rain before the day was over. Her arthritic hands and knees never lied.

"She was looking at me like you're looking at me," Granny grumbled. "Stop it right now."

"You shouldn't be doing this. It's the children's chore." Theo was careful not to mention the real reason for her concern.

"And don't you be tellin' this old woman what to do." Even as she said the words, Granny winced, the pain pinching the woman's mouth until her wrinkles deepened, nearly swallowing her eyes in the creases. "I need to be moving around this morning."

Sympathy rushed through Theo, but it would be useless to argue with the woman. She knew from experience when it came to stubbornness, Granny held all the cards. Despite her discomfort, there would be no resting, no coddling herself. Granny's attitude didn't promote pampering.

"Don't worry about me. I'll be as right as rain soon as these old bones get the idea I ain't ready to lie down just yet." She drew in her breath and rested her hands on the back of a chair. Gnarled with arthritis, they seemed more swollen today. "And we're not talking about me. Answer my question."

"What question?"

The look Granny gave her was pure Lavinia Stark—fierce, yet loving.

"Was I right about him?" she asked again.

"Oh." Theo placed her hands on her hips and returned her unflinching stare. "I'll answer your question if you'll sit down and let me make you a cup of your special tea."

"I told you not to bother with me. I'll be fine. And you have eggs to collect."

Theo crossed her arms over her chest and shook her head. "The eggs can wait. So can everything else. Sit. Don't argue." She moved to the stove and grabbed the tea kettle, filled it with water from the pump at the sink, then placed it back on the stove as Granny eased herself into her chair. "I'll be back in a minute."

Breakfast would be late, but that didn't matter. Granny was much more important. She discussed her concerns about Granny with Quincy and Marianne, both of whom she'd found just outside the barn, talking in hushed tones. After consulting with them, she rushed back into the house in time to hear the water in the kettle boiling merrily and see Granny already struggling to get up from the chair where she'd finally rested, her hands flat on the table, though that pained her as well.

"Oh no, you stay right where you are," Theo ordered as she rushed to the woman's side, realizing Granny's discomfort was worse than she'd first thought.

"I told ya I don't want no fussin'."

Theo let out a long sigh as she grasped her elbow in a firm, yet gentle grip with one hand and rested her other hand against her shoulder blade. "Don't argue with me, Granny. For once, let me take care of you. Just sit. Fifteen minutes. Long enough to drink your tea. That's all I ask. Will you do that for me?"

Finally, with as much dignity as she could muster, Granny acquiesced and allowed Theo to help her into her chair again, though her expression conveyed her unhappiness with the situation ... and her own physical limitations.

Theo sprinkled Granny's combination of tea and healing herbs into a tea ball, closed it securely, and then dropped it into the cup and poured boiling water over it. When it had steeped, she added a dash of cool water so Granny could drink it, then carefully brought the malodorous concoction to the table. She had no idea what plants Granny used to mix into the loose tea or what made it smell so horrible, but it always seemed to help.

Granny pulled the cup closer to her and wrapped her twisted fingers around the fine china, her body visibly relaxing just a bit as the warmth settled into her swollen hands. She raised the cup to her lips, blew on the liquid, and then took a careful sip. Her intent gaze never left Theo, though. As she placed the cup in the saucer, she said, "Well, girl. You got your way. I'm sitting. I'm drinking this foul tea—"

Theo ignored the sarcastic bent to Granny's words. Instead, she poured herself a cup of coffee from the pot Marianne made before the sun rose that morning and brought it to the table. She slid into the chair beside Granny. "The tea always helps you, even though you don't like—"

"Hmmm. You're avoiding the question."

"What question?"

"Theodosia Danforth, you're a smart girl." She sipped her tea and made a face. "But I'm just a bit smarter. I know when you're stalling. Was I right?"

Theo didn't have to ask what Granny was talking about. And though she hated to admit it, the woman had been right. She always was. She'd warned Theo not to hire Burl Stanton. Two days after he started, the man had gone after Circe with a whip. The unforgivable sin had Stanton packing and on his way within five minutes of the incident. She'd witnessed no such actions from Eamon nor did he need any reminders to be kind.

"He seems to be a good man from what I can see," Theo admitted with a helpless shrug. "Patient. Tolerant. Doesn't talk very much. But he's been here less than a week. Time will tell."

The older woman raised an eyebrow as she drank more of the foul concoction. She said nothing, but the twinkle in her eye was something Theo recognized. And almost feared. Granny was not above playing matchmaker. After Henry passed away and a respectable mourning period had come and gone, Granny had *arranged* for Theo to meet several eligible men, sons and nephews and so forth of her many acquaintances in town—she had even recruited Dr. Foster—but none of them had interested her.

Oh, they had been nice enough, not to mention attractive, but perhaps Theo hadn't been ready to be courted—though she liked the men Granny introduced her to, there'd been no spark. No sudden rush of longing. No desire like she'd experienced with Henry, right from the very beginning. She still didn't feel anything romantic in nature for those men, although all four remained treasured friends. She hadn't been sure she'd ever feel passion and yearning again, but then Eamon MacDermott had walked onto Morning Mist. And everything seemed to have changed.

Did mature, respectable thirty-three-year-old widows feel the same things as a fifteen-year-old girl? Most definitely not. And she didn't expect to. She had changed. Grown up. Experienced life, the good and the bad, but when all was said and done, she couldn't deny there was definitely ... *something* there with Eamon. More than something, if she could admit the truth, and so much different from what she'd experienced with Henry.

A subtle flicker of warmth if Eamon should touch her as they worked with the horses, however unintentionally, or a delicate tingle that rushed through her and set her heart to beating more quickly when he looked at her a certain way. And there were many occasions when he did just that ... looked at her with an expression she couldn't define, his eyes darkening from the light gray of smoke to the dark slate gray of a storm cloud on the horizon. *That* look always gave her a breathless feeling, like she'd run too far too fast.

She'd been able to ignore these new and confusing feelings—mostly—but since she was being honest, he did cut a fine figure of a man. Long and lean, with a backside so firm she wanted to glide her hand over it—repeatedly. He possessed a handsome face, too, and a smile—when he smiled—that could jolt her world, especially when it reached his eyes and made the skin at the corners crinkle. She often wondered what his lips would taste like, feel like, beneath her own, and if his mustache would tickle.

Startled by the turn her thoughts had taken, her face warming with embarrassment that matched the heat settling low in her belly, Theo studied the woman in front of her with a critical eye. Granny returned her direct stare with an expression of innocence. Theo didn't believe that look for an instant. "Old woman, I am not interested in you playing matchmaker, nor am I interested in getting married again. I'm still ... I still love Henry."

Granny placed her nearly empty teacup in its matching saucer, rested her hands, one on top of the other, on the tabletop, and studied Theo before she asked, "Who said anything about marriage? And even if I was, he's a damned sight better than AJ Pearce. Coming 'round here, talkin' all pretty, lookin' and smellin' like he's never done a day's work. *Hmph!* As if we all don't know what he's really after."

Theo chose to ignore the reference to AJ. She, too, knew what he—and his father— wanted. Morning Mist Farms. Although AJ seemed to want her just as much if his attempts to kiss her were any indication. "If not marriage, then what?"

The woman said nothing for a long time, then finally shrugged, her dark eyes gleaming with mischief. "He's a handsome, powerfully built young man. You're a healthy young woman."

Theo inhaled, surprised, though she shouldn't have been. "Are you suggesting what I think you are? That I should ..."

Granny shook her head, then finished the tea in her cup, and dabbed at her mouth with a napkin before she rose from her seat, her movements a little less stiff as she shuffled to the sink and placed her teacup into the basin. "I'm not suggesting a thing," she said over her shoulder as she left the room, but Theo swore she heard laughter in the woman's voice.

She stared at the doorway where Granny had disappeared without really seeing it. Idly, she raised the mug to her lips and sipped at the dark brew, but her thoughts were far away from the coffee.

Take a lover? Me? But I couldn't. I wouldn't dare.

A small smile found its way to her mouth. In the two and half years Henry had been gone, she had thought she would get married again if she could find the right man, but never, not once, had she ever considered taking a lover. Now that Granny suggested it without really saying the words, she supposed it could be a possibility.

Since I'm telling myself the truth, I can admit that I've missed the closeness and intimacy Henry and I shared. I may not get that again, but it doesn't mean I should shut myself off and not even be open to the idea. What have I got to lose? Not only is he handsome, kind, and well read, Eamon MacDermott is a good man. I know it deep in my bones, just as I know he's hiding something.

She shook her head as she took another sip of coffee, the thoughts in her mind whirling faster, becoming more appealing as a flush heated her from the inside out and the warmth in her belly grew.

Why not? I'm young. I'm fairly attractive.

She laughed. She couldn't help herself. *I'm being ridiculous. Am I convincing myself to do it? Or trying to talk myself out of it? What about Eamon? Would he consider …*

He'd given her no reason to think he wanted to be involved with her—romantically or in any other capacity than he already was—except for that look in his eyes. That look said more than words ever could. That look conveyed …

Darn you, Granny, for making me think of this, for making me realize the possibilities and the pitfalls. What if … I asked him to consider an "arrangement"? What if he said no? She drew in her breath, and her heart thumped in her chest.

But what if he said yes?

"Theo?" A decidedly masculine voice came from the doorway, and it wasn't Quincy or Lou or Wynn. It was *his* voice, the man she'd been thinking about in the most inappropriate yet enjoyable way.

Theo jumped, startled, and turned in her seat, her gaze locking with Eamon's eyes. Humor danced in those eyes as he sent her *that* look. Her heart beat faster and heat flooded her, rising up from where it had settled in her belly to burn her chest, neck, and cheeks. He couldn't know what she'd been thinking, but how much had he heard of her conversation with Granny? How long had he been standing there?

"Gabby, Charlotte, and I collected the eggs after I performed minor surgery on Gabby's doll." He stepped into the kitchen, a basket filled with eggs slung over his arm, but she wasn't looking at the basket or the eggs.

Instead, she was looking at ... his smoky-gray eyes beneath the dark slash of his brows before her attention was drawn to the lushness of his thick mustache and the stubble on his chin and cheeks. She drew in her breath. She had never kissed a man with a mustache, but she certainly wanted to right this moment. Her gaze moved lower and stopped on the strands of dark hair at the base of his throat, exposed by the open collar of his red shirt. The urge to unbutton his shirt and lightly rake her fingers through that hair on his chest raced through her.

The seed had been planted, the idea more than appealing, and in that realization, subtlety fled to the far corners of the earth. Indeed, the compulsion to touch him surged through her blood like a racehorse coming off the starting line, leaving too much heat in its wake.

He touched two fingers to the brim of his hat and strode toward the icebox without another word.

Goodness gracious, look at that behind! And how long his legs are!

"Th-thank you," she stammered, trying desperately to find her composure. Again, he flashed that smile as he opened the icebox door and glanced in her direction. Her hard-won poise simply vanished. "I'll ... I'll meet you at the stable." She fled outside, her face burning as she grabbed her hat from the hook beside the door and attempted to escape the emotions that suddenly overwhelmed her.

The dog, cats, and duck followed as Theo let herself into the stable and closed the door behind her.

"Good morning, my lovelies," she greeted the horses as she always did and received the same greeting from them in return as she walked among them, hoping their calming effect would slow the quick beat of her heart and the riot of thoughts going through her head, but it didn't help. She stopped at Pumpkin's stall, grabbed the halter hanging from the post, and raised the latch holding the gate closed. The horse chuffed and moved forward, ears perked, as she slipped inside. "What do you think, Pumpkin? Should I? Could I?" She guided the halter into place, then smoothed her hand down the side of his face.

Pumpkin nuzzled her pockets, looking for a bit of sugar or an apple, but she hadn't thought to bring either with her.

She led the horse outside and placed him in one of the smaller paddocks, Happy, Mallory, and the cats close on her tail. After closing the gate, she stepped onto the bottom rung of the fence and leaned over the top rung. Pumpkin sidled close to the fence, then nudged the hat from her head. "Oh, Pumpkin, I wish you could talk. You knew Henry as well as I did. Would he approve of Eamon and me?"

Pumpkin didn't offer any advice. He nuzzled her hand once more, nickered softly, and then strolled toward a small grouping of shade trees beside the stream. She turned and studied the menagerie that had followed her down the grassy path and now waited patiently for her attention. "What do you think?" None of them held the answer she sought.

She turned, intending to head back into the stable, but stopped as a sharp whistle rent the air. The other horses were coming through the open stable door, their hooves kicking up clods of dirt and grass as they ran up the wide path between paddocks, Eamon behind them. He waved his hat, then pointed to the enclosures. Theo understood his intention and rushed to open the gates on either side of the path.

The horses thundered into their usual fenced areas, neighing to her and to one another, racing against each other, full of energy and the taste of freedom.

After locking the last gate, Theo breathed a sigh and turned, expecting Eamon to be close by, but he was nowhere in sight. Neither was Electra and her heart skipped a beat. The mare was close to foaling. Had her time come? Had Eamon noticed something before he led the other horses through the stable door and deliberately kept her behind?

She rushed toward the stable but slowed her pace as she neared the open door, captivated by the most pure tenor voice coming from inside the building. She peeked inside. Electra was there, her belly still bulging with the foal yet to be born, her eyes full of adoration for Eamon as he approached her with a currycomb in hand. His rich voice vibrated against the walls and ceiling, vibrated within her. She hadn't known he could sing. How could she? There were days when he hardly spoke. She never expected such a beautiful voice to come from this man, nor did she expect how it made her feel.

Her heart thudded in her chest, not from the exertion of putting the horses in their paddocks, but from desire, liquid and hot, as the melody and his wonderful voice floated over her like the gentle mist that covered the farm in the mornings. She may not have thought herself ready to fall into any kind of romantic entanglement, but her body remembered the pleasure of making love and had a mind of its own. It had been too long since she'd been touched by a man.

She slipped into the stable, but remained near the door, unable to take another step. Despite the earliness of the morning, it was warm inside the building. Too warm. Or perhaps it was the rush of heat to her belly and lower. Eamon stood before her, his bold red shirt conforming to his broad back, his black trousers hugging his behind—the one she wanted to caress. Theo looked her fill. She could see the muscles in his back ripple as he used the comb to loosen the dirt from Electra's creamy, champagne-colored coat. She licked her lips. He was so gentle with Electra, so patient, she couldn't help wondering if that was how he made love ... slowly, taking the time to leisurely touch every inch of her skin, building the flames of desire until he ...

The bell beside the back door rang, signaling that the morning meal was finally ready, breaking whatever spell she'd been under. Theo jumped, startled, and raced from the stable before Eamon saw her, certain that her face was the color of his shirt. She needed a moment or two or ten to find her control and banish the erotic thoughts that had crept into her head.

Chapter 7

Keeping his distance from Theo proved to be an impossible task. How could he? They worked together every day, side by side, with the horses. And her unending kindness demanded that he respond in ways he never thought he could again.

It wasn't just Theo, either. It was himself, too. He could easily walk away … find a new town, a new job, like he always did, but now? Eamon couldn't ignore the fact he'd grown comfortable here on the farm. There was a peaceful flow to the days that appealed to him. No one hurried, but all the work got done. And there was a lot of work, hard work that helped him sleep at night. The nightmares had only plagued him twice, which was an improvement, and the dark circles shadowing his eyes, like bruises from a fistfight, had disappeared.

It hadn't taken long to settle into a routine. After the morning milking with Lou and Wynn, Eamon led the cows out to the pasture where he and Quincy would stand at the gate and watch the mist dissipate before heading into the house for breakfast with the family.

He liked Quincy Burke. And therein lay another problem. He found Quincy easy to talk to. Too easy, like his own father, Shamus, had been. Both men had a certain way about them that invited confidences, but Quincy was not the exception on Morning Mist—he was the norm, along with Theo, Granny, and Marianne. The care and concern they had for each other had been extended toward him without question or hesitation, though, in his opinion, they should have had reservations about taking him into their fold. For their own protection.

He wasn't quite sure how to handle all the caring, feeling deep in his heart that he didn't deserve it—not after what happened. He wanted it, though. Like the misty morning air he drew into his lungs, he grasped at the kindness they offered. Especially from Theodosia Danforth.

A little more than a week had passed since he stumbled upon this little piece of heaven, and he'd yet to meet Theo's husband, although she talked about him all the time. Her statement when he'd first met her—that Henry wasn't with them—still sparked his curiosity, but he just couldn't bring himself to ask her. "Where is Henry?" he blurted out, his interest getting the better of him as he helped Quincy ready the wagon for town.

Quincy glanced at him but didn't answer as he backed one of the draft horses toward the buckboard and proceeded to connect the harness traces to the singletree. He patted the horse's shoulder, then repeated the process with one of the other draft horses.

Eamon waited for a response, his eyes following Quincy's every move as he checked the ropes holding the canisters of milk against the side of the wagon. He suspected the man was biding his time, perhaps trying to figure out the best way to answer, which meant the answer wasn't an easy one. Had Henry Danforth built his wife this beautiful place, then abandoned her? He couldn't see that happening. From what he'd been told and by the way Theo spoke of him, Henry was a fine man. He wouldn't have done that. Something else had happened, and it wasn't good. A trickle of unease rippled up his back.

"I keep forgetting you've only been here a short time." The big man took a deep breath and glanced at him as he adjusted a harness strap. The horses shifted, moving the buckboard slightly. "Easy, boys," Quincy murmured, calming them with his soft voice and soothing touch. He turned his attention back to Eamon. "Henry ... passed away."

"I'm sorry. Was it the diphtheria epidemic that took Tom and Charlotte's folks?"

Quincy shook his head as he led the horses and wagon from the barn into the barnyard. "Henry was killed."

"Killed?" The word shocked him, like a sucker punch to the gut—unexpected and painful. He'd learned over the past few days that Henry was loved by everyone, so who would kill him? Why?

"Got caught in the crossfire with an outlaw gang. He never had a chance." Quincy brought the horses to a halt, then sauntered to the back of the wagon, checking the ropes around the canisters one last time while he waited for the children. He didn't stop speaking, though his voice had grown hoarse. "They were coming out of the hotel when the first shots rang out. Henry stepped in front of Theo to protect her while trying to push her back into the building. He ended up catching a bullet in the heart."

He turned, and Eamon caught the sadness in the man's eyes. It was obvious Quincy had held the man in high esteem and his passing still hurt. Along with the mental and physical ache, there was anger, too. Eamon sensed it in the way the farm manager stood, his body tense, one hand clenching a leather strap, knuckles white.

"He died in her arms." He watched the door for the children, and Eamon got the distinct feeling the young ones didn't know the details of Henry's death, nor should they. "Henry was a good man, the kind that never met a stranger. He'd give you the last penny in his pocket if he thought it could help. I'm not embarrassed to admit that I loved him like a brother." Quincy drew air into his lungs, then blinked several times in quick succession, as if that could keep the telltale shine of tears in his eyes from showing. "He and Theo hadn't been married for very long when Marianne and I first met them, but I saw right away how much they loved each other. They'd already done so much for being so young—raced Pumpkin on every track that offered a purse and some that didn't from Georgia to New York, then traveled across country and built this farm from nothing, but they did it together. They were devoted to each other."

He turned away but not before Eamon saw his Adam's apple bob as he swallowed, then cleared his throat. "I didn't think Theo would ever recover from his death, and there are times even now, when I look at her, that I know she's thinking about him. I'm sure she would tell you the same about me. I think of Henry often. I miss him. It took me a long time to accept the fact he's gone. My biggest regret is that I should have been there that day. I could ..." He stopped speaking, perhaps realizing there was nothing he could have done or because the memories were too painful, then he plodded back into the cool shadows of the barn, his steps slow and heavy.

Eamon's own heart was heavy as sympathy washed through him. Who better than he to know the pain of loss? The grief and guilt that could cripple a man? He should say something to Quincy. And to Theo. Offer his condolences for Henry's loss. Something.

They would be just words though, and no matter how heartfelt they might be, they wouldn't be enough. In the end, he said nothing. He waited a moment or two for Quincy to return, but when the man didn't reappear, Eamon headed toward the stable to begin his chores with the horses, remorse for opening old wounds filling him. He shouldn't have asked, should have left well enough alone.

The big heavy door to the stable was already opened wide and he stepped inside, only to stop short and drag in his breath. Though he assumed Theo was already there, waiting for him, he wasn't prepared to see her. The horses were still in their stalls, the gates closed. The dog, the cats, and the duck waited in silence, their attention on Theo, who stood with her forehead pressed to Daphne's nose, as if the two shared a secret.

She pulled away from the horse and turned to look at him, those eyes of hers, as bright as new blades of grass sprouting up from the earth, crinkled at the corners with her smile. "Ah, there you are."

Eamon blinked and shook himself, as if suddenly aware he stood in the middle of the aisle, gawking at her like an idiot ... or like Nessie's besotted calf, who now followed him around whenever she could. "I was helping Quincy." He jerked his thumb in the direction of the barn.

"I know. I saw you when I passed by." She gave Daphne a final scratch behind the ears. "You seemed to be in deep conversation, and I didn't want to interrupt." She tilted her head as she walked up the aisle toward him. "What were you talking about?"

If there was ever a time to offer his condolences, it was now, but he couldn't. Saying the words out loud would take the smile from her face, and he didn't want to be responsible for that. How she managed to remain kind and loving after how Henry died, he didn't know, but his admiration for her grew. He hadn't done so well with his own grief. Perhaps she could teach him, show him how to let the past rest and look toward the future.

An image popped into his head as she traversed the aisle between the stalls. He was used to thinking of her as an angel, but now? With the mist at her back, that strange cool glow all around her, she looked like a bride. The only thing missing was a veil and flowers.

His heart hammered in his chest and he blinked several times, but the vision remained. Could it be possible he'd fallen in love with this woman? In such a short time? Even though, up to this moment, he had thought she might be married.

He couldn't breathe, the air stuck in his lungs with wanting ... wanting something he couldn't have. Yes, it was possible ... and terrifying.

In fact, he'd have to be made of stone to *not* fall in love with her. Anyone with eyes—and a brain—in his head would fall in love with her. She was everything good in the world, everything right.

And he was wrong. He wasn't good enough for her, would never be worthy of her love. He took a step back, hands shoved deep in his pockets. "Tobacco."

Theo snorted with surprised laughter, a most unladylike sound he'd heard on occasion, and whatever spell he'd been under, broke. He could breathe again. Thankfully. Once more, she was Theo Danforth, dressed not in bridal lace, but in her usual uniform of a split skirt, this time a dark brown suede, and white blouse, the long sleeves already rolled up to her elbows.

"Tobacco?"

He nodded, his gaze on her face. "I asked Quincy if he'd get me a tin of pipe tobacco after he drops off the milk and eggs at the hotel."

She didn't believe him. That much was evident by the expression she wore, but she didn't press it. He had told the truth—somewhat. He *had* asked Quincy to purchase him a tin of tobacco for his pipe, but he'd done so last night, giving the man the last of his money as they settled the cows in the barn just after sunset. He turned away and started opening the stall doors, letting the horses roam toward the big door at the back of the stable.

It didn't take long to lead them out to their respective paddocks then muck out the stable. They'd developed a pattern—another routine Eamon found comfort in. When the stalls were all cleaned to her specifications and fresh straw padded the dirt floor, Theo turned toward him and grinned. "I thought we'd do something different today."

"Something different? Like what?" Usually, at this point, they exercised the older horses in a small ring, then after a quick break for lunch, exercised the younger ones.

"You'll see." Her grin widened as she moved toward the back of the stable and tossed him some leather halters and several lead ropes, then picked up the saddle that had been laid over a sawhorse, one that wasn't as big or as heavy as the saddles he was used to. She hoisted it over her shoulder before he could help her, grabbed another halter hanging from a hook, and exited the stable. Her quick strides ate up the distance on the grassy path, affording him the uplifting opportunity to admire the sway of her backside as he quickly caught up to her. She turned toward him, the smile on her face warm and enticing.

In that moment, he wanted to kiss her, to touch his lips to hers and see if they were as sweet and supple as they looked. He wanted to pull the tie holding her hair in a ponytail and let the whiskey-colored tresses tumble down her back so he could run his fingers through the curls. And unbutton the blouse she wore, the collar already open, revealing the long, slim column of her throat and the soft skin that seemed to beg to be touched. Her pulse beat steadily there; he could see it sometimes.

He stopped short, stunned by the turn his thoughts had taken, equally stunned by how quickly his body reacted. He had no business wanting that. Wanting her. She was a respectable widow who was still in love with her late husband and he ... well, she deserved so much better than him. And as soon as he had his pay filling his pocket, he'd be gone, although that plan didn't hold the same appeal as it once did. How could he think about leaving this place? These people?

"You're scowling." She stopped at the gate to the paddock where Echo and Ares frolicked with Hestia. The horses, seeing her come closer, raced to the fence, nickering and blowing in greeting, as if they knew what was in store for them.

"Am I?" He made an effort to remove the scowl, but he couldn't force himself to smile.

Theo raised an eyebrow as she tilted her head and studied his face. "Hmmm, you were. Did I say or do something to upset you?"

she asked as she settled the saddle on the fence railing, swung the gate open, and strolled through.

He shook his head. It hadn't been her at all, unless he could place the blame on how lovely a woman she was, not only on the outside, but on the inside, where it really counted. "No, ma'am."

"Ah, we're back to calling me 'ma'am,'" she commented quietly, almost as an aside, but he still heard the disappointment and hurt in the simple statement as she slipped the halter over Echo's head. A flush crept up his face. He should apologize ... but he couldn't, afraid of the words that might slip from his mouth, words and the desire behind them that he had no business saying, much less thinking. She watched him, her gaze sliding over his face, before she drew in a deep breath and hefted the saddle onto Echo's back. After tightening the cinches, she led the horse out of the gate. "Would you bring Ares and Hestia?"

Eamon quickly maneuvered the halters into place for each horse, then attached their lead ropes, and followed behind as Theo led them farther up the grassy path toward the woods. "There's a dirt straightaway before you get to the tree line with a grass track right beside it. I've measured them out at four hundred yards each. Do you have the stopwatch I gave you?"

Eamon always carried it, though she hadn't asked about it since she'd given it to him. He switched both lead ropes to one hand, then pulled the watch out of his pocket and handed it to her. Theo pressed the button and watched the second hand sweep over the numbers printed on the face, then handed it back to him. "Oh, I forgot my journal. And the starter pistol. Would you mind terribly going into my office and grabbing them? The journal should be on my desk, and the pistol should be in a small box on the top shelf of the bookcase."

"Of course." He handed her Ares's and Hestia's ropes.

"I'll meet you at the straightaway."

Eamon gave a nod, then headed toward the house, excitement whispering through him. Today would be the first time he'd actually get to see the horses put through their paces. He'd spent enough time watching them race each other in the paddocks to know they were fast, but more importantly, he would get to see Theo ride. She'd told him that she did, but he hadn't actually seen her do so. Did she ride as gracefully as she did everything else?

He entered the kitchen and stopped in the doorway. He'd never been farther than this room and had no idea where to go, although he could see part of the dining room and parlor depending on which way he turned. Marianne stood at the table, canisters of sugar and flour beside her, and crimped the edges of soft, pliable dough around the rim of a pie pan.

"Sorry to bother you, but Theo asked me to get her journal and starter pistol from her office."

The woman smiled, her face lighting up as she grabbed the loose material of her apron to wipe her hands. "And you don't know where to go. Come, I'll show you."

He forced himself to pay attention as Marianne led him through a small, but well appointed butler's pantry into a formal dining room. The long table, covered in yards of lace, easily sat twenty guests. Splashes of color adorned the walls—paintings in oil, pastels, and watercolor, all horses in various settings from exciting racetrack to serene pasture. His feet went from carpeted floor to bare wood polished to a high gloss as Marianne led him out into a long hallway. A flight of stairs led to the second and third floors, but she didn't lead him up. Instead, she stopped before a set of closed pocket doors near the entrance of the house and slid them open. "Here you are."

"Thank you."

Marianne gave a slight nod and headed back to the kitchen. Eamon poked his head into the room and blinked before he stepped inside. He wasn't sure what he'd expected—perhaps an extension of Theo herself—dainty, feminine, neat, and orderly. What he saw in her office was the opposite—a completely masculine room filled with heavy, sturdy furniture and paintings of horses on the walls. He recognized Henry's All or Nothing, the beautiful horse forever memorialized in oil.

A big desk in dark mahogany dominated the room; stacks of newspaper clippings, letters, receipts, and magazines—some piled high and in danger of becoming small avalanches, some just spread out over the entire surface—hid the desktop from view. Behind the desk, two floor-to-ceiling bookcases on either side of the window held books and more stacks of paper. On the top shelf, as promised, he saw a small box with carved cutouts in a pattern he couldn't quite discern.

From the corner of his eye, he spotted another rag doll, this one with bright red yarn hair and denim overalls, perched on one of the leather chairs in front of the desk. She sported a bandage around her head and seemed a little newer than the other two dolls he'd seen, but no less loved.

His gaze slid over another pair of pocket doors and a long, leather sofa, angled in front of the fireplace, a colorful afghan folded and spread across its back. The crocheted afghan was the only thing neat in this room.

Eamon moved toward the bookshelves and grabbed the box. Flipping it open, he found a small pistol and several cartridges he recognized as blanks—all sound but no bullet. There was a difference between this pistol and the ones he'd used in his former life ... this one wouldn't kill anyone. And yet, that didn't matter. It was still a gun.

He stared at the revolver. The scar on his chest seemed to throb in rhythm with his heart, the puckered skin drawing tighter as images flashed through his mind. He recalled the wide grin on Tell Logan's face as the outlaw aimed, blinked twice, and pulled the trigger, relived the pain of that bullet finding its mark ...

Eamon shook his head to clear it of the memories, as if that action could help, and forced himself to breathe. He could do this. He could hold the gun in his hand and pull the trigger. He could.

Closing the box, he tucked it under his arm and moved around to the front of the desk. There were eight journals on the desktop, lined up side by side between two bookends carved as horses. He bent over a bit and scanned the red leather-bound books, but there were no dates imprinted on the covers and no way to know, without looking, which one was the most current. He picked up the first one, the binding soft, yet sturdy in his hand, and flipped it open to the first page, looking for a date. Neat, meticulous writing—not the elaborate swirls and loops that labeled the jars in Marianne's pantry—filled the page. Noting the dates written there, he realized he'd started with the wrong journal.

Placing it back in the same position he'd found it, Eamon put the carved box on the desk, then picked up the journal at the other end of the row. As he did so, a photograph fluttered to the floor and landed face up. His gaze focused on Theo as he put the record book on the desk and stooped to retrieve the keepsake. Her smile, even in black and white, lit up her entire face. Though he knew having one's photograph taken was a sometimes tedious procedure, one would never know that by looking at her. She stood next to a dapper gentleman dressed in a fine light-colored suit, his hat in his hand. Light hair, slicked back against his head, emphasized his striking features. Theo had her hand tucked into the crook of his elbow, her head turned in a way that she could look at him but still see the camera. Such love showed on her face, there was no doubt in Eamon's mind the man beside her was Henry.

Emotion whipped through him. Not jealousy, though that demon was certainly in the jumbled mix of feelings. No, this was deeper, more intense. Almost painful.

It was longing. And hopelessness. And fear, too. All wrapped up in one bubbling mass that sped through his veins. No one had ever looked at him the way Theo looked at Henry. Nor had anyone loved him the way she loved her late husband. He wanted the kind of love and passion he sensed within her. Or perhaps he was just losing his mind, seeing things that weren't real, wishing for what he couldn't have.

"Did you find what you were looking for?"

Startled, Eamon jumped, and the photograph once more floated to the carpeted floor as he turned toward Marianne in the doorway, embarrassment warming his face.

She wiped her hands on her apron as she came farther into the room, then bent down and retrieved the photograph from the floor. A smile crossed her lips. "Ah, I remember this." Fondness crept into her voice, though Eamon quite clearly heard sadness too. "This was taken just a few months before Henry passed." She handed the souvenir from happier times back to him. "We'd gone to the county fair when it passed through town a few years ago. A nice man had set up a photography booth, and Henry thought it would be fun to have our photographs taken so we did. And it was fun. You can't see it here, but we were laughing and carrying on and having such a wonderful time. Theo wanted that day to last forever so she asked the photographer to take a picture of all of us together." She nodded toward the heavy oak mantle above the fireplace and another photograph in a frame made of silver. Eamon placed the photograph on the desk, stepped closer to the mantle, and studied the picture ... everyone was accounted for: Henry and Theo, Marianne and Quincy. Granny. The children.

He leaned closer to the photograph and noticed that not all the children were present. A particular pigtailed moppet was missing. "Where's Gabby?"

"She wasn't with us then. She came to us later. After Henry ... passed. He would have adored her though." She joined him at the mantle, her eyes glowing as she glanced at the photograph, then at him. "He was a good man, and he loved our Theo more than life itself. I still miss him."

Eamon didn't doubt it. If he had known Henry Danforth, he probably would have felt the same. He took one last look at the photograph, then turned away and headed for the door. Marianne's humor-filled voice stopped him before he passed over the threshold.

"Eamon, didn't you come in here for these?"

He turned and caught the twinkle of mischief in her eyes, as well as the journal and box with the starter pistol in her hand. The flush that had warmed his face now heated the rest of him as he took the items from her and quickly exited the room, though not quick enough that he didn't hear her chuckle.

He practically bounded up the grassy path, then slowed his pace as he drew closer to where Theo waited on the track beside several tree stumps. Once again, she seemed to be in quiet conversation with a horse. Echo lowered her head to allow Theo to press her face to her forehead while her fingers gently stroked the horse's nose. Her ears were positioned forward, a sign of relaxation, and her tail swished the air in a slow, regular back-and-forth motion. One would have assumed Echo would be anxious for a chance to stretch her legs over the four-hundred-yard course or be pulling at the reins Theo held loosely in her hand, but she did none of those things. Perhaps that was why Theo spoke to her as she did.

The other horses, Ares and Hestia, were off to the side in a long, narrow fenced-in area that paralleled the track for about twenty yards. Shaded by several trees, cooled by the mist that had never dissipated this morning, they galloped beside the fence, racing each other back and forth. In the short time he'd been gone, Happy, Mallory, and the cats had decided to join the activities as well and sat in front of the fence, their attention on Theo.

She turned to face him as he approached, the smile stretching her mouth contagious and he found himself smiling in return. She loved this—loved every part of breeding and raising these horses, training them to be the fastest on the track. The truth was there in the happiness shining from her eyes.

Stepping away from Echo, but still holding the reins in her hand, she started to step up on a tree stump.

"Here. Let me help you."

"Eamon, I don't need any help. I've done this a thousand times."

Ignoring her statement, he put the journal and starter pistol down on the other stump, then took her hand in his and helped her up. After so recently convincing himself that he wasn't nearly good enough for her, holding her dainty yet strong hand just seemed to intensify his longing ... and his regret. His entire body stiffened. If she noticed the sudden tension, she chose to pay no heed to it as she slipped her hand from his and fitted her foot into the stirrup.

She swung her leg over, then seated herself comfortably in the saddle. She held the reins loosely in her hands, her back straight but not tense. She said a few words to the horse, and the big bay moved forward several paces, stopping at a line in the grass Eamon hadn't even noticed.

"Are you ready?" He pulled the stopwatch from his pocket, then took the pistol from the box. His muscles tightened just holding the revolver, even though he reminded himself there were no bullets, just blanks. Once again, the scar on his chest began to throb, and pain, whether real or imagined, seemed to center on the spot where his skin puckered. He knew it wasn't possible. He had healed long ago. Yet the ache remained.

"Eamon?" Her voice reached him and he blinked. "Are you all right?"

He wasn't aiming the revolver at a criminal, nor was an outlaw aiming at him. He forced himself to relax and grip the handle just a bit harder. The pain lessened, and his scar stopped its throbbing. He tightened his grip a little more and marveled at how familiar and comfortable, albeit frightening, the wood handle felt in his hand, like the feel of his father's pipe cradled in his palm as he filled it with tobacco.

"I'm ready whenever you are." She grinned, her hands loose on the reins, then gestured toward the end of the track with a nod of her head. Beneath her, Echo pawed at the ground, anxious to be running, but otherwise didn't move. "Why don't you move farther down the track toward the finish line? You'll get a more accurate time. At least, that's the way we've always done it."

Eamon walked to the other end of the track, the cats, dog, and duck following behind him, which was unusual. Normally, they stayed where Theo stayed ... at least until the children came home. A tree stump at the end of the track acted as a table. He put the journal on the stump, then turned and waved. The mist for which the farm was named seemed to have grown thicker here, casting a haze around everything ... the line of trees at the forest's edge, the grassy track, Ares and Hestia racing each other to the right of him ... and Theo. She waved in return, then settled into position. He aimed toward the sky and pulled the trigger. The blank cartridge did exactly as it was supposed to, the loud bang echoing in the trees. He pressed down on the timer with his other hand even as he brought the pistol down to his side.

Echo responded to the shot of the pistol as if suddenly free from earthly chains, and her hooves pounded the grass track, throwing clods of dirt into the air. Theo crouched low over her neck as she raced toward him out of the mist like a wraith from another world. The wind whipped the hat off her head to leave her long ponytail rippling behind her.

Eamon sucked in his breath, his heart pounding in his chest. He'd seen people ride before. He himself was more comfortable in the saddle than on his own two legs, but he never saw anything like Theo and Echo.

She raced past where he stood, her laughter filling the air. He didn't look at the stopwatch in his hand—he couldn't—the sight before him was too alluring for him to turn away, though he stopped the instrument from recording time. Even without looking, he knew the horse had made great time. Indeed, Echo had flown as if she had wings like Pegasus.

With her cheeks pink, her eyes twinkling, and her mouth parted into a delectable grin he wanted to taste, Theo looked like a woman who'd just come from bed after a delicious romp between the sheets, and he couldn't resist. He helped her from Echo's back, lowering her to the ground so she stood in front of him. Despite learning she was a widow, despite his own rules and the knowledge he'd never be good enough for her, before he could stop himself, he dipped his head and captured her mouth with his own.

She didn't stiffen in his arms, nor did she push him away. Instead, she made a small sound in the back of her throat before she wrapped her arms around his neck, Echo's reins, still in her hand, brushing against his skin. Her lips were softer than he imagined as she returned his kiss with as much enthusiasm and ardor as she'd ridden Echo across the finish line. Eamon pulled her closer, moving his hands from her waist to around her back, crushing her breasts against his chest as his lips slid over hers.

He couldn't stop. Didn't want to. The taste of her was ambrosia for the gods her horses were named after, and he was a man starving for that heady concoction. He wanted more. So much more. Now that he had tasted her, it wasn't nearly enough. He pulled her closer and teased her lips open, his heart drumming in his chest so hard and loud, he thought she could hear it.

Echo nudged them, her long nose coming between them to force them apart and break the kiss. Theo stared at him, the warm blush on her cheeks spreading to her entire face. Her eyes sparkled, but seemed darker, more like emeralds than the bright green of grass sprouting from the ground. She drew in a shaky breath through lips slightly swollen and took a step back.

"We ... we shouldn't."

"I know." He lowered his head and stared at the ground for a moment before looking her straight in the eye. "But I'm not sorry."

"Neither am I."

Eamon gave a slight nod, touched the brim of his hat with his fingers, and walked away as quickly as he could while maintaining his dignity, forgetting all about recording Echo's time, but keeping in mind he could never, for his own sanity, kiss her like that again. His original goal to keep far away from her wasn't possible. He hadn't been able to before, but now?

Perhaps it was time to leave Morning Mist Farms.

Chapter 8

Eamon didn't leave, even though he knew he should. He couldn't force himself to pack his belongings and walk away from the warmth and acceptance he'd found here. He couldn't stay away from Theo either. He tried to keep himself busy so he'd fall into bed at night too exhausted to think about holding her in his arms, too worn out to remember that kiss in the morning mist, as if fatigue could make him forget the sweetness of her response.

And so he worked. As much and as hard as he could, but none of the physical exertion helped, as it left his mind free to wander. Wanting Theo became a tangible thing, and his body reacted to the visions flashing through his mind at all hours of the day, but most especially at night.

Eamon shook his head to clear the images once more—a futile effort if there ever was one—and dumped the last shovelful of manure into the wheelbarrow. He pushed up his hat with the back of his hand, wiping his brow at the same time, then turned to find Quincy at the barn's entrance, pitchfork in hand. He seemed intent on whatever was happening outside.

Curious, hoping to catch a glimpse of Theo, Eamon sidled up beside him and glanced outside. A man he'd never seen before had Theo's full attention as they walked across the yard toward a small top-of-the-line buggy parked near the garden. Not a cowboy. Or a farmer. What Eamon would call a "dude." A fancy lawyer from back east, perhaps. He might be a buyer, here to purchase one of her horses, or a breeder. She'd said they were coming soon. Dark hair slicked back with a healthy dose of pomade, mustache and goatee carefully trimmed, the man was dressed in a suit that cost more than a year's salary. "Is that one of Theo's horse breeders?"

"Hardly." Quincy scoffed. "That's AJ Pearce, son of the legendary—at least in his own mind—Aldrich Pearce. AJ rides, but prefers not to. I can't blame him there. It's a wonder he knows the back end of a horse from the front end. He acts like the back end more often than not."

"I've heard his name before ..."

"Of course you have." He pointed toward AJ and scoffed again. "The town is named after that buffoon's father. Richest man in Colorado I'm told. Nastiest, too. For a town benefactor, he leaves a lot to be desired."

Eamon straightened, his muscles tightening. He'd never heard Quincy say a mean-spirited thing about anyone, let alone two people in the same breath. He hadn't thought the big man was capable of harboring an unkind thought or deed, so his obvious dislike of AJ Pearce and his father meant something.

"What's he want?"

Quincy shrugged but didn't take his gaze away from the couple in the barnyard, his hands gripping the side of the door so tightly, his knuckles were white. It was a wonder the wood didn't splinter and crack beneath the pressure. "Probably bringing another offer from his father."

"An offer? For what?"

"Aldrich Pearce has been trying to get Theo to sell this farm for the better part of six months now. To him. Sent a couple lawyers out here to try to convince Theo the farm is too much for a woman without a husband. When the lawyers failed, Pearce started sending AJ out here." Quincy chuckled as Theo gave another shake of her head. "As you can see, AJ's not having any better luck than the lawyers. Our Theo can be a bit stubborn." He chuckled again, though there wasn't any humor in the sound. "At least she's not running him off with a shotgun, though I'm thinkin' maybe she should."

A memory clicked for Eamon. The first time they'd met, Theo had held a shotgun on him. He remembered everything about that moment, her words as well as her stance. "*And you can tell Mr. Pearce I haven't changed my mind.*" Her voice had dropped an octave, becoming throatier and oddly alluring, but it was her words that came back to him now. "*I'm not selling. I'll never sell. I don't care how many men he sends to bully me. He's messing with the wrong woman.*"

He shook the memory away, though it took a little effort. "Why does Aldrich want this farm so bad?"

"Can't rightly say, but I can tell you that he always wants what he can't have, and the more he can't have it, the more he wants it. Doesn't necessarily matter what it is—could be a hotel or a farm like Morning Mist. Or someone else's woman. If he wants it, Aldrich pursues it with a single-minded persistence that can be impressive. And downright scary at the same time because no one really knows how far he'll go to get what he wants." He took a deep breath and forced his hands from the door, flexing his fingers to get the circulation back.

"Should we do something?"

Quincy shook his head and let out a deep breath as his gaze focused on Theo and AJ in the barnyard. "Theo can handle him. This isn't the first time AJ has come around. I'd bet my last dollar it won't be the last. The elder Pearce might be interested in the farm, but young AJ there seems to be sweet on our Theo. He is persistent, I'll say that much, but I'd best keep my distance." Quincy moved away from the door toward the coolness of the barn's interior. "Last time he came by, I almost punched him in the mouth."

"You really don't like him, do you?" Eamon asked the man's back.

Quincy stopped and turned around to face him. He took a moment, probably to get his emotions under control, then shrugged. "What's to like? Sure, he can be charming, like right now, but deep down in his soul, he's a nasty piece of work. I've seen a few things, heard a few more, but at least he isn't cruel like his father. Now there's a snake in the grass with his tail rattling, just warning everyone of how mean he can be, and just like a rattlesnake, you don't want to rile him. I've heard how he treated his wife—AJ's mother—and the women who came after her. It isn't pretty."

Eamon didn't follow Quincy. Instead, he stood in the doorway and continued to watch Theo and her visitor. As Quincy suspected, AJ *was* sweet on Theo. It was obvious in the way the man stood—shoulders thrown back, smile wide and confident, head tilted as he spoke with her. He reached for her hands and grasped them within his own, his expression one of a man trying to convince someone his intentions were good.

Jealousy, unbidden and surprising, tightened Eamon's belly, and his hands, like Quincy's had done, gripped the door frame.

How dare he touch her!

He forced himself to breathe. It wasn't his business, but telling himself that and making himself believe it were two different things.

He pulled air into his lungs just as Theo shook her head and pulled free of AJ's grasp, her body tensing. A flush colored the man's cheeks as he took a step back, his arms folded across his chest, obviously unhappy. He nodded several times as Theo spoke. Though her words did not carry to where he stood, Eamon had the feeling, just by watching them both, that she was dashing AJ's hopes, but something just didn't feel right.

He had always drawn his own conclusions regarding a man's character, trusting his gut more often than not. Expressions said a lot about a person. So did the way a person stood and gestured. Someone smiling at you did not necessarily mean that person was happy to see you. Tell Logan had grinned to beat the band before he pulled the trigger and left him for dead.

And perhaps Quincy had tainted his judgment, but it looked like AJ Pearce would not take no for an answer. His eyes narrowed as he took a step closer to Theo. She took a step back, like they were in some kind of dance, avoiding the hand that reached for hers, clearly uncomfortable by AJ's persistence. Eamon's jaw clenched as his belly tightened even more. Not with jealousy this time, but with something else entirely.

He'd always had a soft spot for damsels in distress, and Theo seemed to fit the description at this moment, though he doubted the dog at her side would allow anything untoward to happen. The cats were there, too, winding around AJ's ankles while Mallory pulled at the laces of AJ's shoes.

If he hadn't been jealous or afraid for her, Eamon would have laughed. Theo's menagerie would protect her, but still ...

He left the shelter of the barn and sauntered across the barnyard, tugging the brim of his hat lower on his face to shield his eyes from the sun. He studied Pearce as he approached and his opinion matched Quincy's, though he really had no reason, except his gut, to dislike the man. It didn't matter. The urge to get Pearce away from Theo and escort him off the farm couldn't be denied. Would Theo appreciate his efforts? Would she think he was interfering where he didn't belong? He reminded himself he was just her hired hand, nothing more.

He slowed his pace as that thought slid into his brain and removed the gloves from his hands, pushing them into the back pocket of his trousers as he decided exactly how he would handle this situation. Brute force wasn't the answer. Theo was all about kindness—she wouldn't like him physically removing Pearce from the property simply because the man had the audacity to touch her. No, this required some finesse, some subterfuge.

"Forgive the interruption," he said as he nodded toward Theo's guest, then turned his attention to Theo, "but could you take a look at Circe? She's acting strange. I think she's about to foal."

"Of course. Thank you for telling me." Was that relief flashing in her eyes as she stepped farther away from AJ and closer to him? "Eamon, I'd like you to meet Aldrich Pearce Junior. AJ, this is Eamon MacDermott."

They shook, AJ's palm so damp within his grasp, Eamon had to squelch the desire to pull away and wipe his hand on his pants.

"Thank you again for the offer, AJ, but I'm afraid I couldn't possibly. I have three horses ready to foal ... Circe might be ready right now. If you'll excuse me?" She flashed him a smile that didn't quite reach her eyes, then scurried away, followed, as always, by the dog, the cats, and the duck.

It didn't surprise Eamon that both of them watched her hurry past the stable toward the corral where the pregnant horses had been brought earlier, the hem of her split skirt flirting with the tops of her boots with each step she took. When she disappeared behind the building, he turned toward their unwelcome guest, then held out his hand once more, though he hated to touch the man again. "Nice to meet you, AJ."

Without a word, AJ shook his hand, then turned and walked to his waiting buggy ... or perhaps slogged would be a better description, as if each foot weighed a ton and became heavier with every step. If he noticed that one of his shoes was untied, he gave no clue. He turned once, his gaze searching the last place he'd seen Theo, the look in his eyes enough to make Eamon feel almost dirty, as if that single glance summed up the way the man truly felt. Brazen. Lustful. His intentions impure.

Quincy had been wrong ... at least the senior Pearce had a rattle to warn of his true nature. The junior Pearce had no such thing.

AJ climbed into his buggy. Eamon squelched the desire to smile as the man grabbed the hat on the seat beside him with quick, jerky movements and jammed it on his head before he reached for the reins. Wrapping the leather straps around his wrists, he flicked them with a well-practiced twist and drove out of the yard. Eamon grinned. That man was angry enough to bend an iron poker with his bare hands. He stayed right where he was, standing sentinel as it were, and waited until he could no longer hear the buggy's wheels before he walked around the stable to the paddock behind the building. Galatea and Electra stood in the shade provided by several trees, their sides bulging with life, but no Circe.

Theo must have taken her inside. He entered the stable through the back door. It took a moment for his eyes to adjust to the cool shadows of the interior and spot Theo. She was inside Circe's stall, brushing the horse's smooth sorrel coat, the menagerie calmly watching her every move from the aisle.

By now, she knew he had lied and the mare was not quite about to foal. His heart picked up an extra beat as he strode down the aisle toward her, hoping she wouldn't be angry.

"Theo?"

She glanced in his direction for a split second before she went back to her task, but in that brief glance, he saw all he needed to see. Her cheeks were pale except for two bright spots of red high on her cheekbones and her cheerful smile was nowhere in sight. She didn't seem angry at him for lying to her. She seemed sad and lost, and it took every ounce of his willpower not to simply enfold her in his arms, although that's exactly what he wanted to do. "You all right?"

She didn't answer, but her body stiffened.

"Theo?" He moved around the dog, cats, and duck sitting guard, passed through the open gate to Circe's stall, and then closed it to lean against the smooth wood.

"Yes. I'm all right." Her voice was more hoarse than usual. Tight, as if she suppressed the urge to cry.

"Did he upset you?"

This time, a quick shake of her head instead of words, and though she responded in the negative, he knew she lied by the way she grasped the brush in her hand, her knuckles white. And the fact she wouldn't look at him, her gaze focused on the horse.

"I think he did." He pushed away from the gate and reached for her, grasping her upper arms gently, physically forcing her to stop brushing Circe, and pulled her against him.

She trembled, but didn't move away, and they stood in silence, his hands still grasping her upper arms, her back against his hard chest, her delectable behind pressed against places it shouldn't. He could wrap his arms around her, instead of just holding her as he was, and pull her closer. He could kiss the side of her neck where it met the curve of her collarbone or nibble at her earlobe.

He didn't do any of those things, though he wanted to. Instead, he inhaled deeply and let the delicate, intoxicating fragrance of roses linger in his brain before he turned her around to face him.

A hank of whiskey-colored hair escaped the ponytail at the back of her head and he finally gave in to the desire he'd had for a long time. He tucked that errant tress behind her ear, his fingers smoothing over the soft strands. Her eyes were wide and filled with worry, but that wasn't the only emotion they reflected. There was wonder—and doubt, too.

"Talk to me."

If possible, her eyes widened even more. Disbelief was added to the other emotions displayed so clearly.

"He really didn't upset me, Eamon. He just made me remember too many things I'd rather forget. And I can't help wondering if he's right. Maybe this farm is too much for me to handle."

He led her to a bale of hay, then took the brush from her hand. Theo settled herself, bringing one knee up to rest her chin on. Eamon didn't sit beside her. Instead, he started brushing Circe. Sometimes, it was easier to share when people didn't look at each other. Side by side, during a task, was often the best, as he'd witnessed since coming here. The children all seemed to be able to whisper confidences while standing at the sink and washing dishes.

But perhaps that only worked with children. As the silence stretched, the only sound in the stable was the brush against Circe's side and her occasional chuffs.

"I ... with Henry by my side, I always felt I could do anything, and when he died, I ... realized I couldn't. I tried though. I still try. Every day, but things changed, especially when I learned ... how far in debt we really were. He was a good man. Please don't think he wasn't. He didn't drink. He didn't ... he was faithful to me. He did gamble a bit. Racing Pumpkin had been a gamble. Coming out here to breed horses when we could have stayed in Kentucky was an even bigger one, but it wasn't gambling that got us in trouble."

She rose from the bale of hay. Eamon didn't see her do so, but he felt her presence come closer and heard her boots shuffling the straw that covered the stall floor. He wasn't surprised when she grabbed another currycomb and started working on Circe's other side. She didn't stop speaking though.

"What got us in trouble was Henry's generosity. He was much too giving by far. He never loaned money. He gave it freely with the understanding he'd probably never get it back. And he was right. He never did get it back. It was the one thing—the only thing really—we ever argued about. He'd give you the last penny in his pocket if you needed it, whether *we* needed it or not."

So Henry Danforth wasn't perfect. The knowledge made him feel a little lighter. Hell, if he wasn't anchored to the ground by gravity, he'd be floating on air with the realization that Henry had not been a paragon among men ... he'd been human, like the rest of the mortals who inhabited this earth. Like himself.

"He let it get out of hand, Eamon. I've never told anyone this. Not even Granny knows, but he gave away so much money, there wasn't enough for us, and before I knew it, he ended up borrowing. Small amounts from people we knew. Friends and so forth. Bigger loans from less savory persons." She took a deep breath. Eamon glanced over the top of Circe's back and caught a glimpse of her brushing her fingers beneath her eyes to wipe away the wetness there.

"Not only were we in debt, but that first year after Henry passed, I sold only one horse and I think Hart bought Thalia out of pity. He'd been Henry's friend since they were born. None of the other breeders came. I thought I was going to lose the farm. Oh, we make money on the sale of milk, eggs, and butter, but it's not enough." She smiled a little. "Sometimes, it's not even enough to keep the children in shoes and clothing, they grow so fast."

She grew silent and again, Eamon's gaze sought her out over Circe's back. She stopped brushing the mare and moved to the open window at the end of the stall, where she just stared at the horses in the pasture outside, her face in profile.

"Last year was a little better. I was able to sell three of Pumpkin's progeny, and several breeders came. I think Hart bullied them into it. I managed to pay off every single debt we had but there is still a mortgage on the farm. Not a very big one. I make my payments in person every month to Mr. Schilling at the bank and I'm never late—never—even though some months are a little harder than others, but if the bank called in my note at this moment, I'd have to sell all the colts and fillies, all the broodmares ... *if* I could find buyers. I couldn't sell to just anyone." She folded her arms across her chest and leaned against the window frame, her focus going back and forth between him and the horses outside. "I don't think Mr. Schilling would allow such a thing, but it doesn't mean that someone couldn't buy my mortgage and demand full payment. It's been known to happen. Especially if a certain someone wants it to happen."

"What does that mean?"

She didn't turn around and face him, nor did she move away from the window. Keeping him at a distance? "I've heard of a few mortgages being bought and called in because Aldrich Pearce wanted a particular business. Giselle at the White Palace nearly lost her hotel because he suddenly wanted it. Fortunately, she was able to come up with everything she owed." She took a deep breath and let it out slowly. "I could take Aldrich up on his offer and sell to him before he decides to buy out my mortgage." She shook her head vehemently. "No. I don't think I could do that—just sign everything over to him because I ... I ..." She blinked several times, but her gaze remained on the corrals beyond the window. "No, Henry and I worked too hard for me to give up without a fight. I won't lose the dream we had. I can't."

"Did AJ threaten you?"

She shook her head. "No, not in so many words, and this isn't the first time AJ made an offer on his father's behalf. I'm just surprised Pearce is being so patient. He's asking. Not taking, which is normally what he does. Actually, I'm amazed he hasn't come out himself. So far he's only sent his lawyers or his son to remind me how difficult it can be for a widow to manage a farm like this."

"What else?" The lawman in him came to the fore, and the urge to protect this woman and the farm she loved nearly overwhelmed him. Perhaps a visit to Aldrich Pearce was in order. They could speak man to man—although Pearce was more of a snake—but he'd make it clear Morning Mist was not for sale nor would it ever be. He could speak to AJ as well and warn him away from trying to court Theo.

All that could wait. Right now, he wanted to comfort her, but she didn't seem to want reassurance.

She still hadn't moved away from the window or glanced his way. Instead, she stood perfectly still, her face in profile, jaw clenched so hard he thought her teeth might shatter, her eyes focused on the horses in the fields. She blinked several times as if she'd been about to cry but through sheer force of will, stopped herself, then took several deep breaths. Finally, she asked, "What do you mean 'what else'?"

"Is that what he was talking to you about today? Holding your hand to ease the devastating news that Pearce is thinking about buying and calling in your mortgage?"

"Actually, no. He invited me to a dance being held by our church."

A dance? An opportunity for AJ to hold her in his arms? Jealousy, that new and completely irrational emotion, surged once again. "You're not going, are you?"

There must have been something in his voice or the way he asked the question because she bristled, her body stiffening as she moved away from the window. Had he gone too far and stuck his nose into affairs that weren't any of his business? Had she actually considered going with AJ?

"That's really none of your concern. I'm a grown woman. I can see whom I please when I please, and I don't need permission from you or Granny or anyone else." She laid the currycomb on the railing between stalls and unlatched the gate. She hesitated for a moment, her hand resting on the wooden railing, before she pushed the gate open and grabbed her hat from the post where she had placed it earlier. She was about to say something more. Her mouth opened and closed several times as she studied the ground, that stubborn hank of whiskey-colored hair once more in her face. After a moment, she glanced up at him, her eyes filled with sadness. "I'm sorry. You didn't deserve that. I ... I just ..." She didn't finish her thought. She didn't ask him to accept her apology, either. In fact, she didn't say anything more about it. "Please don't mention the mortgage to the children. They don't need to know, and it would only upset them."

He nodded, letting her know he would keep silent, but he couldn't help wondering why she had snapped at him. Was it because she thought he was trying to tell her what to do with her life? How many others had done the same? She was a widow, trying to make a success of the horse farm she and her late husband had built. He could just imagine how many said she would fail. And how many said she shouldn't even try. Or that she needed a husband to help her. They didn't know about the streak of stubbornness that ran through Theo.

He watched her as she headed toward the door, then stop before she passed through. There was more on her mind—he could tell—but she didn't say anything. Instead, she placed her hat on her head and strode into the bright sunshine, leaving him in the stable with Circe, his face much, much too warm.

He was a fool. What had he been thinking? "Well, Circe, that didn't quite work out how I planned."

The horse snorted as if to agree with him.

• • •

It was cozy in the kitchen, the air still redolent with the aroma of the freshly baked bread they'd had with dinner, the residual warmth of the oven just right to take the chill off the evening. Several lamps spread their golden glow throughout the room as Theo spread a thick towel over Thomas's shoulders and pinned the ends together just beneath his chin. The boy sat in one of the kitchen chairs she had pulled to the middle of the room, several pillows beneath him so he'd be high enough. "Now don't move, Tommy."

"I won't," he replied even as his foot swung back and forth and he tried to see what was happening in the other room where everyone else had gathered. He was the last one to have his hair cut, having pulled the highest number from the hat.

Theo wielded the comb and scissors she pulled from her apron pocket, but her mind wasn't on trimming the boy's hair nor was it on the chatter coming from the parlor. It was on *him*.

How could she not?

He had kissed her.

The moment his lips touched hers, the well-ordered and safe world she had created and clung to ceased to exist. Excitement filled her, raced through her veins, leaving her hot and cold at the same time—not just when his mouth had taken possession of hers, but even now. Her stomach quivered with anticipation day and night but nighttime was the worst. When she should have been sleeping, she thought of him. Perhaps that was why she had snapped at him in the stable. It wasn't so much his question about accompanying AJ Pearce to the dance, which had been innocent enough, it was because confusion filled her. She doubted not only her sanity but her loyalty. She *had* considered going to the dance, except not with AJ. She had wanted Eamon to accompany her, but the thought had made her feel as if she was betraying Henry's memory. How could she want someone else when she still loved him?

Of course, Henry wouldn't want her to live without someone special in her life. He would want her to be happy, to be loved, of that she had no doubt.

So, why not? Why shouldn't she take a lover? Widows sometimes did. Giselle at the White Palace Hotel had not only taken one lover, she'd taken three, though not at the same time. And she was still with Sebastian Milner, the wealthy rancher she'd taken to her bed more than five years ago.

They were happy. Why couldn't she have that same happiness?

Watching Eamon work with the horses had become not only a guilty pleasure but a mild form of torture. The horses loved him, following him as they followed her, watching him with adoration in their big, brown eyes. They sensed his innate gentleness, and the goodness he carried inside. His touch was always calming, and every time he laid his hand on one of them, she wished it was she he caressed.

Startled by the path her thoughts had taken—again—Theo made herself pay attention to what she was doing. She smiled down at the crown of Thomas's head as she drew the comb through his dark blond hair. The boy didn't speak as she snipped at the curls his hair had a tendency to take when too much time passed between haircuts. He hated the curls, claiming they made him look like a girl.

Theo smiled as she snipped another curl, the strands falling to the towel around Thomas's neck. That was another thing. Since Eamon had stepped onto Morning Mist, her usual routines had gone by the wayside. Haircuts were late, laundry took longer, and sometimes, she left the clothes on the clothesline overnight, which was highly unusual. She'd rather listen to the sound of his voice, which was deep and rich, with a slight Irish accent that sometimes snuck into his speech when he spoke to the horses, rather than fold those clothes.

He sang, too. She'd heard him several times, and his voice sent ripples of desire—yes, desire, something she didn't think she'd ever feel again—rumbling through her. Different from what she'd experienced with Henry but definitely blossoming, growing in strength seemingly day by day. The intensity made her drag in her breath, made her blood zing along her veins, but still, she couldn't bring herself to act upon any of her feelings or the longing that seemed to have taken up permanent residence within her. She wasn't nearly as bold as she used to be. Actually, she wasn't bold at all. She ... was a coward.

Just because she felt like this didn't mean he did.

Except that he had kissed her—just that one time, but oh, what a kiss. Her toes curled just thinking about it. And yesterday, he'd shown a streak of jealousy, which she had seen quite clearly despite his using Circe as a ruse to get her away from AJ, though she was grateful he'd done so. If he could be jealous, then perhaps he cared. He'd certainly seemed interested when she blurted out her confession about Henry and the debts he'd owed when he passed, which was another thing she'd never thought she'd do—tell that secret. No one had known except the parties involved until yesterday.

Eamon MacDermott was turning her world inside out and upside down. And she liked it. And him. And it was all fine and good that he could become jealous and that he cared enough to listen to her, but none of that knowledge told her how she should go about making *it* happen. Should she just go to him, wrap her arms around his neck, and kiss him until neither one of them could breathe and let nature take its course? Or make it a business deal with rules and obligations? In writing?

Was that how taking a lover was done?

The scissors in her hand stilled as visions of Eamon's broad back, muscular arms, and perfect backside invaded her mind. How she longed to glide her hands over those muscles and squeeze that sweet behind as his slim hips settled between her thighs.

"Are you d-d-done, Mama Theo? Can I go?"

Startled by the young voice invading her daydream, Theo shook herself free of the images and realized both comb and scissors hovered in midair above Thomas's head. "What? Oh, no, almost though."

She took a deep breath and forced herself to finish the task she'd started, and she made a bit of progress ... until her heart, already beating much too quickly because she thought of him, picked up its erratic pace even more. There was no sound to alert her, but she knew without looking *he* stood in the doorway between the kitchen and back porch. His presence seemed to fill the entire room, even though he hadn't entered it yet. A surge of excitement rippled through her as a flush rose up to warm her face and she turned her head slightly to the side to see him.

"You're just in time, Eamon." She slipped the comb and scissors into her pocket, then removed the towel from around Thomas's neck. Grabbing a small whisk brush from the table, she swept the clippings from his shoulders. "And you, young man, are done."

The boy ran his hands over his new haircut, then scooted from the chair, taking the pillows with him. Whether he thanked her or not, she couldn't say—the hum in her ears seemed to drown out every other sound.

Eamon hadn't moved, just stood in the doorway, his fingers worrying the brim of his hat. His gaze darted from her face to the chair, then back to her face. "In time?"

"For a haircut, of course." She hoped he couldn't see the frantic beat of her heart through the blouse she wore.

Eamon shook his head and gestured to the coffeepot on the stove. "I just came in for a cup of coffee."

She grinned at him then. She couldn't help it. If he only knew the thoughts going through her mind, he might run. Like Pollux, the four-year-old colt out of Athena, he was a bit skittish—anytime someone got a little too close, he excused himself rather quickly and flew off as if he had wings like Icarus. He could ask questions of others, but he never talked much about himself—just the tiniest pieces of information in response to a question—so his past was his own, but one couldn't help wondering. And she did. Perhaps a bit too much.

"It'll only take a minute. I'm already set up." She pulled comb and scissors from her pocket and gestured to the chair Thomas had just vacated.

Her smile remained in place as she watched him shift his weight from one foot to the other. If reluctance had a name, it would be Eamon MacDermott. Finally, he gave a slight nod as he hung his hat on one of the hooks outside the back door, then entered the kitchen, his movements slow and unsure, so different from his normal confident stride. A sheepish grin lifted the corners of his mouth as he hooked his thumbs into the sides of his pockets. Theo watched him come closer, his eyes conveying a rare vulnerability.

A thought she'd had earlier made another foray through her mind, and the urge to kiss him and keep kissing him until his confidence came back took root and refused to let go.

She took a step back, instead of moving forward into his arms like she wanted, and gestured to the chair once more. It creaked a little as he settled himself into it and folded his hands in his lap. To hide his nervousness? What about her own nervousness as she draped the towel around his shoulders, then pinned it closed beneath his chin? Her gaze went from the lump of his Adam's apple to his kissable mouth beneath his thick black mustache and finally to his eyes, which were the most amazing shade of gray, like smoke rising from a fire.

She could kiss him right now, but didn't. Couldn't. Oh, but she wanted to as she moved to stand behind him.

Why oh why had she started this? Her fantasies had been hard enough to deal with when he wasn't in the room, but now? It was a wonder she could stand with knees suddenly turned to pudding. *This* had never happened to her before, this overwhelming desire to live for the moment and forget everything else, to throw herself into his arms and take from him what she wanted.

No, not take. Never take. Share. Their bodies. Their warmth. Yes, even their loneliness, for she had no doubt he was as lonely as she. It was there in his eyes, though he did try to hide it.

Theo took a deep breath and tried to concentrate on the task at hand, but that seemed just a bit beyond impossible. His hair, thick and luxurious, curled over the collar of his blue-and-white-checked shirt and was slightly damp, like he had washed it a very short time ago. She noticed hints of burnished red reflecting the lamplight as she first ran her fingers through the soft strands, then used the comb to follow the furrows she'd made.

He didn't speak, which was probably just as well—her tongue was tied anyway, and she probably couldn't utter an intelligent word if she tried.

After a few strokes of the comb, the tension left his shoulders and his head moved forward just a bit. He still didn't speak, but at least he seemed somewhat relaxed.

Too bad she couldn't say the same for herself. She bit her lip as she wielded the scissors, tension strumming through her, making her insides quiver. Standing behind him as she was, she could easily caress his broad shoulders or kiss the back of his neck. She could wrap her arms around him and just hold him.

This is ridiculous! You're a coward. Just kiss him already!

All too soon, his haircut was over, though how she managed, she'd never know. Theo removed the towel protecting his shoulders, then, unable to resist a moment longer, she smoothed her fingers across the back of his neck to brush away the clippings.

Eamon jumped up from his seat at the touch of her fingers and backed himself away from her, the rosy color adorning his cheeks bringing out the bluish specks in his gray eyes. He swallowed several times, his Adam's apple bobbing, then licked his lips as if his mouth had gone dry. "Th-thank you. That was m-most kind." He ran his hand through his hair, then dipped his head. "Good night."

Kind? Kindness had nothing to do with it. She had wanted to touch him—and wanted him to touch her—so why couldn't she just say that? Theo opened her mouth, the words flooding her throat and watched her opportunity walk out the door before she could summon up the courage to stop him. He'd even forgotten the coffee he'd come in for.

Theo sighed, tossed the towel on the table, and grabbed the broom leaning against the counter.

Coward! I'm no silly young girl. If I want him, I should tell him.

She swept the kitchen floor, cleaning up the remains of seven haircuts.

I do want him. The thought raced through her mind as she settled the children into bed for the night, then changed into her own nightgown and brushed out her hair.

I will tell him. She slipped beneath the light blanket and snuggled into the mattress. *Or ask him. In the morning.*

She yawned and listened to the familiar creaks and groans of the house settling, which normally soothed her, but tonight, those comforting sounds brought no rest. Knowing that the children were happy and healthy should have put her at ease as well, but instead of sleeping, Theo found herself staring at the moonbeams coming in through her bedroom window. Even with her decision made, she had no respite. Visions of Eamon, and what she'd like to do with him, rushed through her head, making sleep impossible.

Her body thrummed with need, a wanting so strong, tomorrow wouldn't be soon enough. It had to be right now, when she was brave, when she wanted him so much she could barely breathe.

She rose from her bed and slipped into her robe, tying the sash tightly. Moonlight guided her way as she stepped from her room and tread the stairs, avoiding the third riser from the bottom because it squeaked.

A single candle within the protective glass of its holder on the table cast a steady glow throughout the kitchen. Theo quietly opened the back door and stepped out onto the porch. The dog, cats, and duck didn't move from their beds, exhausted, she was certain, from a long day of following her and chasing the children.

The golden glow of a lantern cast its light through the window of his room beside the barn. What was he doing? Sleeping? Reading?

His door opened and more light spilled through as he stepped onto the small porch.

Theo tucked herself into the shadows, suddenly unsure of her decision, and just ... admired the sight before her. Though she wasn't close enough to see details, she could see that he wore no shirt and his feet were bare, the rest of him covered in a pair of tight trousers. In the space of a breath, her heartbeat picked up and the tension within her tripled.

He lit his pipe, then leaned against one of the posts, his head lifting to look at the night sky before lowering to look at the windows on the second floor of the house. Her window or so it seemed, but it was impossible to know for certain with the only light, besides moonlight, behind him.

What is he thinking right now? What would he say if I just walked across the barnyard, threw myself into his arms, and begged him to make love to me? Would he say no?

She took a step forward, then stopped as he tapped the ashes from his pipe into the glass dish sitting on the small table beside the door and went inside. If she was going to do this, she had to do it now, before she lost her nerve, before common sense made her stop. Determination spurring her on, she took another step. She wanted this, wanted his hands on her. Needed to feel his body filling her.

Behind her, the back door swung open. Startled, Theo jumped, and spun around to see Charlotte stumble across the threshold, her long white nightdress ghostly in the pale glow of moonlight. The meager light reflected on the tears on her face, and her breath came in huffs and gasps, as it always did when she cried.

"Charlotte, honey, what's wrong?"

The little girl walked toward her, wrapped her arms around her hips, and rested her head against Theo's stomach. "I had a bad dream, Mama Theo." Hiccup. "And then ... and then I couldn't find you." Hiccup.

In an instant, the plans she had been trying to set into motion disappeared as Charlotte hiccupped into her stomach. She patted the girl's back. "It's all right, rosebud. Do you want to tell me about your dream?"

The girl shook her head and let out a long sigh as her arms tightened around Theo's hips.

"You don't have to tell me if you don't want to. Let's get you back to bed."

Charlotte raised fearful eyes toward her. "Will you stay with me?"

"Of course, sweetheart." She brushed the bangs out of the girl's eyes, marveling at the poor job she'd done of trimming them earlier tonight. Not only were they still too long, but they were crooked as well. She wondered if everyone else's haircut was equally bad, the results of thinking about Eamon when she should have been paying attention to what she'd been doing.

She led Charlotte inside and settled the girl back in her bed. She drew the light blanket up to her chin, then lay down beside her atop the covers as she only intended on staying just long enough for Charlotte to fall back to sleep.

Within minutes, Charlotte's breath whispered between her lips in a steady rhythm. Theo started to slip off the bed, but as soon as she moved, the girl whimpered and reached out for her. All thoughts of seducing Eamon fled at Charlotte's touch. Without hesitation, she moved beneath the covers and held the little girl she loved so much.

Chapter 9

Aldrich's slippers made a scuffing noise across the marble tiles of the foyer as he headed toward his study, a plate with the last slice of apple pie in one hand, a glass of milk in the other. His mouth was already watering. His cook made the best apple pie in the county, and he looked forward to having the last piece.

The sound of the doorknob turning and the front door creaking open stopped him before he could gain his sanctuary. He turned to see AJ sneak into the house, shoes in hand, the smell of alcohol and cheap perfume suddenly overpowering in the hall. He took in his son's appearance and frowned. His clothes were askew and a little dusty, as if he'd fallen in the street or perhaps had a tryst in a dark alley, and his hair, normally plastered to his head with pomade, stood straight up in spiky furrows. "Drunk again, AJ?"

Startled, AJ dropped his shoes, but stood up straight and faced him. There appeared to be no remorse for his condition. Indeed, he seemed a little proud of his semi-inebriated state. "Not nearly as much as I should be."

Aldrich raised an eyebrow. He didn't judge a man badly for having a drink or two, but he didn't condone a man drinking to excess. At least AJ hadn't slurred his words, which meant he wasn't *that* drunk. "I gather the evening didn't go as you planned. Wasn't tonight the church dance? I thought you asked Theo Danforth to go with you."

AJ said nothing, but the expression on his face revealed everything, making Aldrich chuckle. "Ah, let me guess. You asked and she said no. In fact, I'd go so far as to say the little filly wants nothing to do with you."

"You don't have to sound so ... happy about it." AJ stiffened and his lip stuck out, pouting like he'd done when he was a little boy and hadn't gotten his own way.

He shrugged, unconcerned about his son's feelings. "Not happy, son, just glad to be proved right. Again. I knew wooing Theo would be a waste of your time."

The look AJ gave him would have put a lesser man in his grave. It only made Aldrich chuckle harder.

AJ scowled, then bent down to retrieve his shoes. "If all you're going to do is laugh at me and gloat, then I'll just head up to bed."

"Now, don't go off in a huff." He gestured toward the study. "Come on in and share some pie with me. It's the last piece."

"I'm not in the mood for pie, but I will have another drink." He followed Aldrich into the comfortable room and headed straight for the bar. He dropped his shoes on the floor, poured himself a large portion of aged Kentucky bourbon, and then slumped into a chair and pinned his father with a glare. "And I don't want to talk about her."

Aldrich waved away his concerns as he took his seat behind the desk, nearly spilling his milk. "I wasn't going to ask about her. What I want to know is if you found out the name of her hired hand."

AJ sulked—mouth pulled down in either a scowl or a frown, Aldrich couldn't tell which. "I don't want to talk about him either."

He said nothing, but watched his son take another swallow of his bourbon. If he stayed quiet, if he didn't ask or bombard AJ with questions, he just might find out what he wanted to know. Sometimes, patience could be a friend. The silence stretched as he dug his fork into the flaky crust and soft chunks of apple, then brought the sweet, gooey concoction to his mouth.

"She's not interested in me, but she's sure as hell interested in him," AJ admitted after a while, and Aldrich smothered a grin.

His son was so predictable. "You shoulda seen the way she looked at him, like she was ready to peel off her clothes—and his—right there in the barnyard. And he was lookin' at her the same way. It was disgusting."

"I see," he said and took another bite of pie, waiting for AJ's inevitable malign of both Theo and her hired hand. He wasn't disappointed.

"I bet she's taken him to her bed." He buried his fingers in his hair, leaving more furrows in the pomaded locks. He slumped farther into his chair, the soft leather almost cradling him. "I bet they're in bed right now. If I had known Theo was a slut, I'd have gotten between her legs a long time ago. Instead, I wasted all that time trying to court her."

Aldrich smirked. He didn't even try to hide it. "You should have known she was like that, AJ. What kind of woman takes a hired hand—what did you say his name was—to her bed?"

"MacDermott."

"Did you say MacDermott?" He sat up, instantly alert, the name completely erasing the vision in his head of Theo naked and ... writhing on the bed beneath him. He'd heard the name recently but who had mentioned it? Someone ...

AJ nodded as he swirled the bourbon around the bottom of the glass, then finished the last of it in one swallow, oblivious to how easily he'd been tricked into revealing what he knew.

"Does he have a first name?"

"Aiden. Arden. Something like that." He sighed, then stuck his finger in the glass and wiped out the last of the bourbon before he stuck his finger in his mouth. He sat utterly still as he sucked the liquor off his finger, his eyes glazed and distant. "Eamon," he said after taking his finger out of his mouth and wiping at the glass once more.

"Eamon MacDermott," Aldrich repeated as he laid the fork on the dish, the last bite of apple pie forgotten. He leaned back in his chair, steepled his hands over his robe-clad stomach, and stared at the ceiling. "Eamon MacDermott. Hell, I know that name, but who said it?" He repeated the words, then jumped from his seat, the leather chair rolling backward and crashing into the wall. "Logan," he breathed as he recalled the outlaw bragging about all the men he'd killed. He wasn't surprised his son hadn't made the connection with the hired hand's name. AJ hadn't been with Logan when he spoke of it.

He had to be sure though. Needed to know the facts. "Go wake up Ed Dancy."

AJ jumped from his chair as well, a startled, wary expression on his face before confusion registered. "Now? It's after midnight."

"I'm well aware of the time, AJ. Just go wake him up and tell him to open up his newspaper office."

"Why?"

"Don't question me, boy. Just do it." He grabbed a half-smoked cigar from the brass tray and stuck it in his mouth, though he didn't light it. "I'll meet you there in fifteen minutes. Now, go!"

AJ didn't run to do his bidding. Instead, he stood there, swaying a bit on his feet, befuddled.

"Why are you still here?" Without waiting for an answer to his question, Aldrich came around to the front of the desk, grabbed AJ by the arms, and shook him. There was no time to get him sober. Truthfully, he didn't need him sober. Just obedient. "I said to wake up Dancy." He started walking toward the door, at first nearly dragging AJ but then propelling him through the study, across the marble tiles in the foyer, and out the front door before any further protest could be voiced. "Go. Now. Fifteen minutes and he better be waiting for me."

He slammed the door on his shoeless son, then turned and shouted for the butler. "Wilson!"

Despite the fact the older man had gone to bed over an hour ago, a moment later, he tied the sash of his robe as he shuffled from his room just off the kitchen. "Yes, Mr. Pearce?"

"Saddle my horse. I'm going out."

If the butler thought anything odd about the order and the lateness of the hour, he said nothing except, "Yes, sir," and turned back the way he'd come.

Feeling much younger than he had in years, Aldrich practically jogged up the stairs and got dressed.

Twenty minutes later, he tugged on the reins and brought his horse to a stop in front of the *Pearce Intelligencer*'s office. Lights blazed through the plate glass window, creating a warm glow on the street as he dismounted and tied Jezebel's reins to the post.

"Coffee, Dancy," he ordered when he let himself into the office and came face to face with the sleepy newspaperman standing next to AJ. "And keep it coming. We might be here awhile."

"Of course, Mr. Pearce." The man tried to make himself presentable and tuck his shirt into his trousers, but gave up when the garment seemed to defy the laws of order. "May I ask what you're looking for?"

Aldrich didn't answer the question but asked one of his own. "Does the name Eamon MacDermott mean anything to you?"

Dancy scratched his head, causing his hair to stand up on end, like AJ's, and did almost exactly as Aldrich had done earlier: kept repeating the name. "It's familiar, I will say that. I seem to recall ... wait!" He turned quickly and headed toward several file cabinets along one wall of the room, his shirttails flapping behind him. He pulled glasses from his shirt pocket, fitted the earpieces around his ears, and started reading the dates clearly labeled on the drawers of the cabinets. He mumbled beneath his breath, loud enough to be annoying but soft enough so the words were not recognizable, then he grinned as he tugged open a drawer and pulled out a thick sheaf of past issues of the *Pearce Intelligencer*. He handed the stack to Aldrich. "You can start with these. I'll get that coffee."

Aldrich made himself comfortable in one of the room's two leather chairs and wheeled himself closer to the desk. He handed several newspapers to AJ. "Here, you read these. There was a shooting a few years ago, and if I remember correctly, MacDermott was involved. I want to know everything."

AJ said nothing, but he pulled up the room's other chair and began leafing through the stack.

Several hours later, the coffee in his cup stone cold, Aldrich Pearce folded the newspaper in his hand and smiled. He looked around at the other newspapers scattered all over the floor, the drawers of the file cabinets in the back of the room standing open and empty. He'd read them all, finding pleasure and perversion in every account of the day the Logan Gang shot up Paradise Falls. He learned about the deaths of Kieran, Mary, and Matthew MacDermott, and Henry Danforth, who'd been visiting the town with Theo, as well as the many townsfolk caught in the crossfire. Mention was made of the near fatal injuries suffered by Brock and Eamon MacDermott, but not very much. For the most part, their recoveries had been ignored while the reporters paid rapt attention to the subsequent trial and sentencing of Jefferson Logan.

Most importantly, he learned of three members of the Logan Gang who survived the shootout. One of those men—Zeb Logan—was now dead, killed by Brock MacDermott just a few months ago. Jefferson Logan, the young man the rest of the Logans had tried to break out of jail, which had precipitated the shootout, remained in prison, but the last brother, the one that interested him the most, Tell Logan, seemed to have disappeared, according to the newspaper articles ...

Except Aldrich knew exactly where he was. The man was the reason the Flying Cloud Ranch was now his. He had helped to *convince* the owner to sell it for a paltry sum. As a gun for hire, Logan had no qualms about using whatever means were necessary, no matter how low-down and questionable they were.

The smile on his face widened as he glanced at Dancy and AJ, who both slept. He leaned over and shook his son. "Wake up, AJ."

The young man opened bloodshot eyes, then lifted his head from the desk, his cheek stained with ink.

"I need you to ride out to the Flying Cloud Ranch and bring Tell Logan back with you."

At the mention of Logan's name, Aldrich watched the blood drain from AJ's face. Fear clouded his son's eyes, and his mouth dropped open before he snapped it shut. "Logan," he whispered, his voice filled with awe as well as horror.

AJ's reaction was exactly what he was looking for.

• • •

Hours later, the expression on AJ's face still played over and over again in Aldrich's mind. Excitement continued to speed through his body, making it difficult to sit still ... so he didn't even try. Instead, he paced the floor of his study, stopping at the window occasionally to peruse the drive outside and what lay beyond. Living on top of the hill had its advantages. He could see everything, and it made him feel like a king on his throne to look down from this height on the town that bore his name.

People scurried here and there, busy with the daily chores of life. He caught sight of AJ climbing the back stairs to Mimi's place for the second time today, this time to drown his sorrows with a bottle of rotgut whiskey and the comfort of one of Mimi's girls. The boy—man actually, though Aldrich didn't like to admit it— had done well in finding Tell Logan. He hadn't been at Flying Cloud Ranch nor any of Aldrich's other holdings, but AJ had finally tracked him down at Mimi's. And Logan wasn't happy being interrupted in the middle of the woman he was about to do, according to AJ who informed him that Logan would be with him whenever he damned well pleased.

And so Aldrich Pearce, a man who wanted satisfaction immediately in some cases, but was willing to wait in others, waited. His gaze was drawn to the map over the now cold fireplace. Yes, he could be patient when the circumstances dictated. He turned away from the map and headed toward his desk.

The door to his sanctuary burst open and crashed against the wall. Aldrich flinched, but otherwise didn't move as Tell Logan stood in the doorway, his hands hanging loosely at his sides, but looks were deceiving. Aldrich knew, despite Logan's relatively relaxed stance, he could draw the pistols from his holster and pull the trigger so fast, you'd be dead before the smoke cleared the barrel.

A snarl curled Logan's lips beneath the bushy handlebar mustache, and his eyes were squinted beneath the brim of his hat as he scanned the room, which made the scar running down his cheek appear more sinister. He looked like the devil himself, come to earth to wreak havoc and mayhem, leaving nothing but heartache in his wake.

Aldrich studied the man and waited for thunder to rumble and lightning to strike, as he thought it should whenever Satan—or his henchman—took center stage. He'd seen that in a play once and the image had never gone away, but it didn't happen today as Logan crossed to the bar in his slow, rambling walk, his spurs jingling with every step he took. "I'm a busy man, Pearce." He didn't pour himself a drink. Instead, he pulled the cork from a bottle of whiskey and drank directly from it. He wiped his mouth on his sleeve when he was done. "I don't have time for you to send your sniveling son up to fetch me every time you got a bee in your bonnet."

All of it—his attitude, his looks, his slow movements—were meant to intimidate. And for the most part, it worked. AJ was terrified of the man. Most people were, but not Aldrich. He could intimidate people as well as—or better than—a two-bit desperado like Tell Logan. "You're on my payroll. You'll come when I tell you to come."

The fingers on Logan's right hand twitched as they inched toward the gun handle gleaming dully in the light spilling through the window. For a split second, Aldrich thought he might have gone too far, but instead of drawing and shooting, Logan simply patted the gleaming ivory handle and grinned. "Had ya goin' there for a minute, didn't I?"

Aldrich did not respond. He simply glared at the gunslinger and hoped the relief he felt to still be alive did not show. A lesser man would have fallen into his chair, his knees suddenly unable to support his weight. Not him. He stood straight, shoulders back, lips pressed together, not willing to show any sign of weakness to the bully in front of him. And that's what Logan was—a bully.

After a moment, Logan shrugged and slumped into the chair opposite him. He took off his hat and laid it on the seat of the chair next to him, revealing dark hair that looked like it hadn't been washed—or combed for that matter—in weeks. He took another swig from the bottle. A little whiskey dribbled down the side of chin and dripped onto his filthy shirt. Aldrich didn't know what stained the shirt other than dirt, but from his viewpoint, it could have been egg. Or maybe gravy. Difficult to tell as Logan was never one to be concerned about appearance. As long as he did the job, Aldrich didn't care what he looked like.

"What the hell was so damned important?"

"I have two words for you." Aldrich placed his hands on his desk and leaned forward, pinning the outlaw with his stare. "Eamon MacDermott."

Logan paused with the bottle halfway to his mouth. A curious look came into his nearly black eyes. Aldrich recognized it for what it was—panic. "What did you say?"

"Eamon MacDermott. Or should I say Marshal MacDermott?"

In all the time he'd known him, Aldrich had never seen the hired gun sweat. He did now and it wasn't pretty. Perspiration beaded on his forehead and cheeks. It even beaded at the base of his Adam's apple, something Aldrich had never seen before. He himself never perspired. He was never warm enough or scared enough to sweat.

Logan tried to cover his sudden agitation and took another quick swig from the bottle. "What about him?"

"Did you know that he's here? In Pearce?"

The scar on Logan's cheek stood out in stark relief as the man lost all color in his face and more sweat beaded on his forehead. A pink tongue licked pale lips. "He ain't dead?" The question was asked in a tone that spoke of disbelief until Logan sat up straight. "Shit! I shot that son of a bitch in the chest. How can he not be dead?"

Aldrich shrugged, enjoying this little game immensely. It was one thing to not show fear to Tell Logan, but it was another to turn the tables on the killer in front of him and watch him squirm. The outlaw seemed truly surprised MacDermott wasn't dead ... and he was afraid, which suited Aldrich's purposes perfectly. "You missed."

Logan jumped from his seat. The whiskey bottle dropped to the floor as he drew his pistol in one smooth motion, and pointed the bore at Aldrich's chest, the barrel shiny in the late morning sun. "Missed hell! I was this close, Pearce. I saw him go down, an' he wasn't breathin' when me an' Zeb hightailed it outa there."

Again, Aldrich shrugged and slowly lowered himself into his chair, even though the gun was still pointed at his chest. "I wasn't there, Logan. I don't know what happened. All I know is that Marshal Eamon MacDermott is alive and well and working on Morning Mist Farms."

Logan uncocked the revolver and sat as well, the pistol resting on his lap where he could caress the ivory handle. He continued to sweat. Several beads of perspiration rolled down his face and were absorbed in his thick handlebar mustache. "Farmin'?"

"Does it matter what he's doing? He's breathing and that's all you need to know." He pinned Logan with another glare when what he really wanted to do was laugh in the outlaw's face. Tell could be intimidating, frightening everyone from little girls to grown men, that was true, but he could be manipulated too, by someone who knew how. And Aldrich Custer Pearce knew how.

"He should be dead. I shot him." A belligerent note crept into Logan's voice, but beneath his tanned skin, his face was pale with the slightest hint of green. Sweat left wet rings on his black shirt and the odor emanating from that sweat became unbearable in the room, despite the windows being open to catch every little breeze. "Don't you want to know why?"

"Why what?"

"Why he needs to be dead."

"Logan, I don't give a damn why you shot him or why you want him dead. I just want to know what you're going to do now."

"Kill him, o' course." He picked up the pistol and stroked the barrel before taking aim at a painting on the wall. He didn't pull the trigger, but imitated doing so.

"Good. Good. You do just that." If Logan wasn't sitting across from him, Aldrich would be rubbing his hands together in anticipation of Theo Danforth coming to him for help. The more he thought about it, the more he liked it. Truly, it would be the best possible scenario for him. She'd been strong enough when Henry died to carry on and keep their dream alive. Would she have the heart to continue the struggle when everything she worked for went to hell, or would she decide to give it all up? He loved nothing more than seeing a strong woman finally break, and with MacDermott out of the way, he could get what he wanted— her, the farm, the horses. Everything. The hell with how much AJ thought he was in love with her.

But first, he wanted to see her beg. Needed her to realize that Aldrich Pearce always got what he wanted. She should never have turned him down all those months ago. He'd come to her as an honorable man, asking for her hand in marriage. She had been kind, had said all the right things, but in the end, she had declined his offer. Still, he didn't want anyone to hurt her. That would be his job once she was begging him. "Go ahead and kill MacDermott, but don't hurt the woman. She's mine. I want her strong enough to crawl to me on her knees."

"Woman?"

"Theodosia Danforth. Theo. She owns Morning Mist Farms. I want that farm and all that glorious horseflesh. And I want the woman."

"I see." A grin settled on Logan's lips, but it wasn't a nice one.

Aldrich chose to ignore it as he rose from his seat. "No, you don't." He gave a slight nod to the outlaw. "We're done here. You can let yourself out."

Chapter 10

Eamon took a deep breath, grabbed his shovel and rake, and laid them over the wheelbarrow, then pushed the wheelbarrow beyond the stable door, grateful for the cool breeze that dried the sweat on his face and back. Mucking out the stalls was hard, hot work—a task that seemed to never end. For the moment, he was finished, and the results would fertilize Granny's garden.

He had done it alone today. No Theo beside him, which didn't make keeping his mind on his chores any easier. Beside him or not, she remained a distraction. The kiss they'd shared, even though it had been days ago, lingered in his mind. As did the haircut she'd given him; her fingers running through his hair, then across the back of his neck had been one of the most enjoyable, but agonizing, experiences he'd ever had, affecting him not only mentally but physically—even a second dip in the ice-cold water of the swimming hole where he usually washed up hadn't diminished his ardor.

If they'd been alone, if her family hadn't been in the parlor, he might have brought her down on his lap and kissed her again ... and again, but he hadn't dared to touch her. He might not be able to let go this time. He might forget he was an honorable man and she was a respected widow.

Ever since that haircut, though, she'd been busy getting ready for the horse breeders and buyers who were expected to be here within the next couple days.

He stopped the wheelbarrow beside Granny, who, on her hands and knees, pulled the weeds from between rows of beans and peas and potatoes. "Where do you want it?"

The woman peered up at him from beneath the wide brim of her hat, her smile wide. There was dirt on her face as well as her hands, which were without gloves. She never wore them, claiming she wanted to feel the earth between her fingers. She aimed her little spade at the far corner of the garden where corn would soon grow tall. "Over there would be fine. Thank you, Eamon."

"Yes, ma'am."

As he spread the manure where Granny wanted, his mind wandered back to his favorite subject: Theodosia Danforth. Theo didn't have just one gift. She had two. Whereas Quincy organized, Marianne cooked, and Granny grew things, Theo Danforth *loved*. Hard. With every ounce of her being. She opened her heart and accepted people for who and what they were—with passion and a completeness that stunned him and, sometimes, unnerved him, too. That's not to say she did not get angry or outraged. She did. Especially over cruelty or injustice, but if one were lucky enough to be in her circle, one felt the depths of her love and was better for it.

And she healed. Took something broken or hurt and nursed it back to health. He saw it with his own two eyes and still didn't know if she had a magic touch or if she, by sheer force of will and patience, demanded it be so. Maizie, the former ice-wagon horse, had done a complete turnaround. Her wounds had mended, leaving very faint scars that marred her reddish-brown coat, but it was more than physical healing. Her spirit rebounded, her joy contagious as she raced the younger horses in the field, tail flying behind her.

Mallory the duck, too, had healed and the bandage had been removed. He tested his wing, extending it, flapping it about in preparation for flight, but he did not leave the farm and, instead, waddled after Theo wherever she went, usually behind the dog and cats.

If Eamon wasn't careful, she'd probably try to mend him, but what he suffered from couldn't be fixed with Granny's special salve spread liberally over a wound or warm, soapy water and a soft touch. How many times could he hear "You will open up to me, Eamon MacDermott. Eventually, everyone does" before he did just that and revealed all his secrets?

I should leave. The thought rambled through his head, as it did from time to time, but less frequently than when he'd first come here, and the truth was, every time he thought about leaving ... well, he just couldn't bring himself to do so. He liked it here. Perhaps too much.

Finished spreading the manure, Eamon took his tools back to the stable, walked down the aisle toward the back door, and stepped outside. He meandered along the grassy path between paddocks and stopped at one of the gates. Arms resting on the top slat, he watched the younger horses chase each other up and down the fence line. He pushed his hat back, his gaze stopping briefly on each horse, even those Theo wouldn't try to sell or breed. His own horse, Traveler, roamed one of the fields with some of the draft horses. He seemed happy. That was important. Traveler had served him well and deserved to be content, but Eamon wondered if his trusted mount missed the danger and excitement of his former profession. He shook his head. No one, not man or beast, enjoyed being shot at.

His gaze flickered toward another paddock, and he spotted Daphne, his favorite out of all the horses Theo owned. The color of roasted chestnuts, she had a white star on her head and was, in his opinion, the most beautiful. Her sweet temperament and gentle brown eyes had Eamon enthralled. She had a sense of humor, too, and stole his hat a few times, running off so he'd have to chase her. She also liked to roll in the water rushing through the stream crisscrossing the pasture, then find a patch of dirt or mud to dry off with—and required more care than the other horses.

And she was doing it now! Just looked at him, that expression on her face, and rolled in the mud. "Daphne! Stop that!"

She stopped rolling and stood, her gentle brown eyes guileless and guilt-free, as if to say she'd do it again as soon as he wasn't looking. He let himself into the paddock, making sure to close the gate behind him, and approached the mare. "Didn't I tell you to stay clean? Theo's going to think I can't do my job."

Daphne nickered at him, then moved closer and dipped her head so he could scratch her in the middle of her white star. He smiled as he did so, then reached for her halter. "Come on, let's get you cleaned up ... again." He led her toward the small corral right behind the stable and grabbed one of the currycombs hanging just inside the door. "Don't you know the breeders and buyers will be here soon? You have to look your best."

He shook his head and grinned. He'd become the joke of the ragtag group of people Theo called her family because he spoke to Daphne more than he spoke to anyone else. What amazed him was that he didn't mind the teasing. It was good natured, and because they all did it—spoke to the animals—getting teased made him feel like he was part of the family, something he had missed since the Logans had turned his world upside down.

Brock, Teague, and Kieran were never far from his mind, and though he missed his brothers, missed the camaraderie and the trust, he didn't miss the painful memories. Theo's family made him feel welcome. And wanted.

"Oh, who am I kidding, Daphne? I think I've found a little bit of paradise here, but don't tell anyone." The mare looked at him, her serene brown eyes shining with unequivocal love, assuring him she'd keep his secret.

"Mr. MacDermott?"

Eamon continued brushing Daphne, but looked over the horse's back. Gabby stood on the other side of the fence and peered at him through the slats. He forced himself not to smile, but failed miserably when he noticed a doll in one of her little hands and the fancy cigar box filled with bandages, small wooden splints, and other supplies tucked under her arm. It wasn't the first time Gabby had brought him one of her *patients*. She'd told him the first time she'd asked him for help that she was going to become a doctor like Dr. Foster. He walked over to the gate and laid the currycomb on the railing of the corral, then studied the little girl. "Yes, Gabby. What seems to be the problem?"

"Mandy has a broken leg. We need to fix her."

"All right." Eamon left the corral, closing the gate behind him, and went down on one knee as she offered the doll like it was the greatest gift one person could give to another. He inspected the doll, gently turning it this way and that, making note of the stuffing escaping Mandy's leg, his expression as serious as he could make it. He had no experience with little girls, never having had children of his own. His only knowledge came from Desi Lyn, Kieran's daughter, but she'd only been a little over two years old the last time he'd seen her. She wasn't a precocious six-year-old like the girl looking to him right now. "Yes, I can see her leg is broken. What do you have in mind, Doctor Gabby? Should we operate?"

The girl shook her head. "No, she doesn't need a operation. It's a small break." She maintained her serious expression as she sank to the ground, her legs in the shape of a *W*, which looked extremely painful to him, although she seemed quite comfortable. She took the cigar box from beneath her arm and laid it on the ground. Flipping open the lid, she rummaged about, choosing several colorful ribbons before deciding on a plain white length of cotton. She clicked her tongue, shook her head, and mumbled something about Mandy being clumsier than a six-legged horse wearing shoes. Where on earth had she heard an expression like that?

"Hold her still, Mr. MacDermott. This is very serious."

Eamon grit his teeth to keep himself from laughing. He held Mandy in his hands as Gabby wrapped and tied the white cotton strip around the doll's leg.

"Okay, she's as good as new," Gabby proclaimed as she packed up her cigar box and tucked it once more beneath her arm. She grabbed for the doll by her freshly bandaged leg and stood up. "You have to come to tea now."

"Tea?" He shook his head. "I have work to do, Gabby. I can't just ..."

The little girl stared at him, baby-blue eyes wide, her usually smooth forehead crinkled, her gaze so ... hurt, he couldn't stop himself. "Of course I'll join you for tea."

She gave him her brightest smile, then grabbed his hand and led him toward the gypsy wagon. A canvas had been stretched from the side where it met the roof and extended outward to two slim poles stuck in the ground to shade a small table. He spotted Thomas slouched in one of the chairs as he drew closer, looking like a thundercloud had settled over his head. How long he'd been sitting there, waiting, Eamon hadn't a clue, but he certainly didn't look happy.

The table had been set with a miniature tea set made of white porcelain and decorated with tiny green ivy leaves. The girl had spared no expense on her guests as there were plates with Marianne's blueberry muffins as well as some of the almond cake left over from dessert last night. Despite himself, Eamon's mouth watered. He was a bit hungry ... plus, he'd developed a fondness for Marianne's almond cake—*kuchen*, as she called it—a traditional German cake she'd learned how to make from one of their neighbors. It was almost as good as her strawberry rhubarb pie.

"Glad to see you here, Thomas," he greeted the boy as he approached, but Thomas merely rolled his eyes, the epitome of little boy boredom, and continued to twiddle his thumbs. He made no comment, though his expression spoke of long suffering. Apparently, this wasn't his first tea party. Nor would it likely be his last.

Eamon thought of offering the young boy some advice, but decided against it. Truly, what could he say? At almost ten years old, Thomas didn't understand being more or less forced to participate in a children's tea party but he'd learn as he grew older that there were many things a man did in the name of love and kindness. Eamon kept his mouth closed and gingerly sat in one of the too small chairs, his knees coming up to nearly hit him in the chin.

"You can hold Mandy," Gabby informed him as she handed him her doll, indicating that he should hold her in his lap. Then she pointed at his hat. "And you have to take that off. It's proper."

Eamon did as he was told. He propped the doll against his stomach as best he could in his current awkward position, then removed his hat. Finding no other place to put it, he fitted his knee into the hole where his head should have been. Thomas grinned at him with an expression that seemed to say "I told you so" before his gaze darted past Eamon.

Eamon turned in his uncomfortable seat in time to see Charlotte, a fancy, too big hat with flowing feathers on her head, lead both Wynn and Lou toward the gypsy wagon. He heard a snippet of conversation and grinned as well. He couldn't help himself. Apparently, neither Lou nor Wynn thought they had the time for this impromptu tea party, but neither boy could say no. The last to arrive was Quincy. He took a seat next to Eamon—he, too, with his knees nearly to his chin as Gabby poured *tea* and Charlotte passed around the plate with the muffins.

"Sorry I'm late, Princess Gabby, Princess Charlotte, but the queen needed my assistance," Quincy said, falling easily into make-believe, which made it clear the tea party was just one of many and all the males in the family participated, whether they had time or not.

Charlotte, with a regal air of indifference, and for once, not the least bit shy, gave a slight nod. "You are forgiven, Sir Knight."

Quincy took off his hat and made himself comfortable. Eamon grinned at him. "Sir Knight?"

The man shrugged. "It makes them happy and doesn't hurt me any. Doesn't hurt any of us." His eyes flickered to the doll in Eamon's lap, and an eyebrow rose before his lips parted into a huge smile. "It's a nice break in the day." He placed a blueberry muffin on his plate and passed the platter along. "Plus, it gives me a chance to have another one of Marianne's muffins." He took a bite and a look of pure pleasure crossed his face. After chewing for a moment, he swallowed, then said, "Take a minute and enjoy this, Eamon. It'll be the last moment of relaxation for a bit. The horse breeders will be here either tomorrow or the next day, and then you'll be wishing for a tea party."

•••

"I thought you could use a cool drink and a short break."

Theo jumped and whirled around, a dust rag in her hand, as Marianne entered one of the bedroom suites on the third floor.

"You didn't come down for lunch, and dinner won't be for another two hours or so." She carried a small tray with a sandwich, a piece of almond kuchen, and a glass of something cold—Theo distinctly heard ice tinkling. She rested the tray on the bureau, then picked up the glass and moved across the room. "And there's something you have to see."

Theo took the lemonade Marianne handed her and swallowed half of it without coming up for air. She hadn't realized how thirsty she was. Or how warm. Perspiration beaded on her forehead and trickled between her breasts to soak her corset and chemise. She'd been on the third floor, cleaning the bedroom suites since right after breakfast and had worked through lunch. She should have hired some help for the task, but she didn't want the extra expense. Money was still a little tight. Although she had managed to pay off all Henry's debts, her budget did not include employing anyone else to help with the breeding season. This year was better than the last though. She had definite confirmation from five of the breeders, one maybe, and a few requests from people who simply wanted to take a look at her stock.

A little hard work never killed anyone, and besides, she was almost finished. She just needed to shake the dust from the rag rug and sweep the floor, and this last room would be done. She could take a well-deserved break then and perhaps sit down for a minute or two. She finished the lemonade in another two gulps. "What did you want to show me?"

Marianne beckoned her toward the open window, pushed aside the lacy curtains, and pointed toward the gypsy wagon just to the left of the barn. Theo peeked outside and her heart fluttered as her gaze came to rest on Eamon. She could see him quite clearly as he sat at the small table beneath the canvas awning. She could also see Quincy, but not the boys, though she was certain they were there as well. Charlotte and Gabby flitted into her line of vision, pouring tea and passing out muffins, then moved away to serve the others, affording her an unobstructed view of Eamon.

She couldn't help smiling. In his lap, he had one of Gabby's dolls, and in his hand, he held the handle of a tiny teacup between thumb and forefinger—pinky out as Charlotte or Gabby had probably instructed—and laughed. The sound carried. She had never heard him laugh before, and her heart melted. Such a carefree, happy sound, that laughter.

"They've been out there for quite some time." The corners of Marianne's mouth tilted upward as she grinned. "I think they're going to be there for a while longer. Charlotte just came in for more tea."

There was something special about the male species willing to spend some time at a little girl's tea party.

As if he felt her watching him, Eamon turned. Theo held her breath as his gaze scanned the house and finally came to rest on her like a gentle caress. A whirlwind of sensations rippled through her from that simple look. Desire burst into a full-blown conflagration so quickly she thought she could incinerate on the spot. Need made her heart thump harder, made her knees weak. She wanted him. Right now. Right this minute.

"Theo!"

Theo shook herself and forced her gaze away from him, difficult though it was, and turned her attention to Marianne. "What?"

"My goodness, Theo. One would think you'd never seen a handsome man before."

The warmth of a blush infused her face. Indeed, her entire body felt flushed. "What are you talking about?"

The woman shrugged, her warm amber eyes twinkling with ... what? Happiness? Mischief? Had she and Granny been talking? "Just that I had to call your name four times before you finally answered me." She glanced out the window and shrugged again. "I will admit he's attractive, but not nearly as much as my Quincy." She chuckled as she turned her attention away from the tableau outside and pinned Theo with her stare. "You should ... no, never mind."

"I should what?"

She tilted her head slightly and grinned, her eyes still sparkling with a sentiment Theo couldn't name. She grabbed Theo's hand and squeezed gently. "Follow your heart, wherever that may lead." There was more she wanted to say—her mouth opened and closed several times before she shrugged one last time, released Theo's hand, and moved away from the window. She pointed to the tray on the bureau. "Don't forget to eat." She grinned again as she left the room.

Theo watched her, then turned her attention back to the window. Eamon still studied her, the corners of his mouth turned up into a silly grin.

A new thought exploded in her head and she struggled for air, her hand flying up to her chest to rest over her heart. Had

Marianne just given her permission to take Eamon MacDermott as her lover? Or was it permission for something more? She just didn't know, and it was so unlike her to be this unsure. She hadn't been this uncertain with Henry. She'd known exactly what she wanted, though she hadn't acted right away. It had still taken a long time for her to show him what she'd been feeling.

And look at all the time I wasted. Not this time. I don't have to wait.

Tonight? Could she sneak out of the house and bravely knock upon his door? She had come close to doing that once before, hesitated, and lost her chance.

Not this time. Theo stepped away from the window, pulled the rag rug from the floor and shoved it into the hallway, and then picked up the broom and swept, the sandwich and *kuchen* forgotten in her rush to get things done. She grabbed the rug, slung it over her shoulder, and went downstairs.

"Did you eat?" Marianne asked as Theo cut through the kitchen.

"Not yet."

By the time she got outside and hung the rug over the clothesline, the tea party had broken up—the only evidence there had been a tea party at all was Mandy the doll sitting, forlorn and forgotten, in a chair, her bandaged leg stretched out. The small table had been cleared and the adults had gone back to their chores, but she could hear the children laughing on the other side of the barn. Granny, bless her heart, had finally stopped digging in the dirt ... for now. She wasn't finished for the day because her little garden spade and straw basket were still in the rows between the melons and the beans.

Theo shook her head as she straightened the edges of the rug, then picked up the rattan rug beater. Before she could take the first swing, the distinct sound of carriage wheels rolling over her hard-packed-dirt drive drew her attention. She stepped away from her chore to see Hart Jameson, the first of the horse breeders and a very dear friend, drive around the corner of the house into the barnyard. Two stocky, well-built men followed in a buckboard with his trunks and other baggage. Theo recognized the Collier brothers and gave a nod in their direction. They would be engaged to bring the rest of the breeders when they arrived as they'd done for several years. A pretty white mare with a nearly black mane and tail walked sedately behind the wagon, looking none the worse for wear after her long journey from Kentucky, where Hart lived.

As happy as Theo was to see him, she realized two things immediately. She was a dirty, sweaty, smelly mess—she had been cleaning most of the morning and afternoon and hadn't had a moment to bathe—and her plans to seduce Eamon just flew out the proverbial window. Finding a moment alone with him while the horsemen were here would be next to impossible.

With a sigh of defeat, she laid the rug beater on the small table beside the clothesline and went to greet her guest.

"Theo, my love, it's been a long time!" As handsome as ever in a tan suit that brought out the honey brown of his eyes, Hart jumped from the carriage and grabbed her in one smooth motion. Theo squealed as he swung her around.

"Hart! Put me down! I'm dirty, and I'm getting you dirty, too!"

"And I don't care! Even with dirt on your face, you're still the prettiest girl I've ever known!" He gave her another squeeze, then let her down, although she could tell it was with great reluctance. He didn't release his hold on her even though she stood on her own two feet, but he did loosen his grip a bit, his hands loosely clasped behind her back while she rested her hands on his shoulders.

"You're early. I wasn't expecting you until tomorrow."

"I couldn't wait to see you, sugar. Give your old friend Hart a kiss hello." Still holding her, he presented the smooth-shaven side of his face to her. Theo obliged, drawing a huge smile from him, his eyes shimmering with a touch of naughtiness. "When are you going to marry me and make me a happy man? I've been waiting for you a long time, my sweet."

Theo took the proposal for what it was—a greeting between old friends. Hart wasn't serious. He never was. At least, she didn't think his proposal was genuine as he asked her the same question whenever they met and had been doing so since before she married Henry ... and even after. He'd probably never marry, and as much as she loved him as a friend, she had never had any romantic thoughts toward him. She shrugged and shook her head. "You'll just have to pine away for me."

"Oh, so that's the way of it." He grinned, reminding her of what a jokester he'd always been, a man who lived by his charm with never a serious thought to mar his play, but then his smile disappeared and the mischievous spark in his eyes faded as his expression became most sober. He took a step back and held her at arm's length, the intensity of his scrutiny making her a bit nervous. "How are you really, Theo?"

Touched by the rare show of true tenderness, Theo swallowed the lump that suddenly sprang into her throat. It took her a moment to find her voice, but when she finally did speak, there was strength and truth in her words. "I'm good, Hart."

"You're sure now? You're not telling me a fib because you think it's what I want to hear?"

"Yes, I'm sure." She still missed Henry and would probably always miss him, but the pain of his loss wasn't nearly as devastating now. Over time, she'd become accustomed to the idea he wasn't ever coming back and though that was true, *she* was still here, still alive, and needed to live her life. That realization had taken a long time to come, even longer to accept. And yes, there were times when she was overcome with guilt ... especially when she harbored brazen, fanciful thoughts for Eamon.

Hart continued studying her, his gaze roaming over her face until, finally, his smile returned and he released her. He gave a slight nod as the impish glow came back into his eyes. "I believe you. There are roses in your cheeks, and your smile isn't nearly as sad as it used to be. In fact, you look happy and, for that, I am grateful, but if there should ever come a time when you need me, all you have to do is ask. I promised Henry that I'd always be there for you and I fully intend to keep that promise."

Again, the truth in his words touched her. "Thank you, Hart." She slipped her hand into the crook of his arm and walked with him the few paces toward the buckboard. "Let's get you settled."

She greeted the Colliers, then directed the burly men to bring the trunks up to the Rose Room on the third floor, so named because of the huge painting of Granny's roses on the wall, and the best suite in the house.

"This is Gloriana," Hart said as he untied the horse's reins and brought the mare forward. "She's as fast as the wind and as sweet as can be. Won every race I've entered her in, just like Henry's All or Nothing did. I have great hopes for their offspring."

Theo examined the mare, her hands running up and down the horse's legs to look for straightness, then running along her body, feeling her strength. Muscles quivered beneath her fingertips and she sensed this horse's speed without ever seeing her run. She continued her assessment, slowly walking around the horse before stopping in front of her. Intelligence gleamed from Gloriana's eyes as Theo pet her nose. "She's beautiful, Hart. Have you had her bred before?"

"She's five now and ran her last race a couple weeks ago. I didn't want to try before." A blush colored his smooth-shaved cheeks as he shrugged. "I wanted Pumpkin to be her first. Henry would have been pleased, I think."

She laid her hand on his arm as gratitude warmed her. He did not have to wait to have Gloriana bred nor did he have to travel as far as he did. There were many successful stud farms in Kentucky, including Turning Leaf Farms, owned and managed by

Liam Danforth, Henry's brother, after the death of their father. And if Hart didn't want to make use of one of those farms, he could have simply stayed home. The Jamesons owned Clover Hill, one of the biggest and most successful stud farms in Kentucky, and had for generations. "Yes, he would have." She took a deep breath and smiled. "We should probably get Gloriana into one of the stalls so she can rest. She's had a long trip." She glanced at him and grinned. "I'm sure you've had a long journey as well."

Theo took Gloriana's reins from him and waited while he intercepted the Collier brothers as they left and tipped them for their service. "I have a better idea," he said as they started leading the horse toward the stable, "Let's put her in with Pumpkin right now and see how things go. At least then we'll know if she's ready."

"I can't do that, Hart. That would be unfair to the others. You'll have to put your name in the hat and take your chances on being first like everyone else."

"No one would have to know." He lowered his voice to a conspiratorial whisper, and the grin that spread his lips had her fighting not to smile in return.

"I would know."

"Ah, you're an honorable woman, Theo." He gave her a quick kiss on the cheek. "No hard feelings for making me wait."

She felt it then. The heat of *his* smoldering smoky glare. The one that made her heart beat pick up its pace and caused her knees to go weak.

Eamon stood in the doorway of the stable, his gaze going from her to Hart and back, his expression unreadable.

"Hart, I'd like you to meet Eamon MacDermott. Eamon has been with me for a few weeks now. He's helping with the horses."

The two men shook as Theo continued her introduction. "Eamon, this is Hart Jameson. I've known him for as long as I knew Henry. They've been friends since they were old enough to walk. Went to school together—"

"Chased the girls together. Got into trouble together." Hart picked up the threads of her comment as he pulled her in closer for a sideways squeeze. "Our farms shared a common border and our folks were close friends so it was only natural that Henry and I became good friends as well. In fact, we were inseparable ... until this little minx stole his heart. She stole mine, too."

Theo saw his eyes flick from her to Eamon, then back to her, and she wondered at the expression on his face—on both their faces. Hart was his usual charming self, but there was an underlying tone in his voice she didn't quite understand and he didn't seem to want to let go of her. His hand was either on the small of her back or around her back so he could hold her upper arm and pull her closer. The behavior was a little unusual, even for Hart. Had he guessed that she was wildly attracted to Eamon? Was he letting Eamon know by some unspoken manly code that she was his?

But that was foolish. His proposals were never serious. Furthermore, she didn't love him ... at least, not in a passionate way.

Hart moved his hand from her arm to her waist and, once more, pulled her closer so they were side to side as he continued. "You only had eyes for Henry though. Do you remember that summer we met as fondly as I do? The three of us—you, me, and Henry—going on picnics down at the swimming hole ..."

He didn't finish his comment, but Theo blushed anyway.

Why was he telling Eamon all of this? To embarrass her? To make sure Eamon knew of the history she shared with Hart? Of course she remembered. How could she forget sneaking away from her chores to meet them in the little secluded spot where two streams met and deepened, armed with a folded napkin filled with Granny's stolen poppy seed or lemon cakes? How could she forget swimming in just her chemise and pantalets, unaware of how the cotton clothing had stuck to her skin and became nearly transparent, revealing more than it hid? Nor how upset Granny had been on those occasions, threatening to tan her hide for being so naïve? She wasn't the only one to be reprimanded though. Granny made sure Henry and Hart received their punishment, too.

Theo mentally shook herself free of the memories and gained her composure. This wasn't the time to be thinking about that, especially in front of Eamon, who studied her with such intensity, she shivered despite the heat coursing through her. Instead of being smoky gray like usual, his eyes had lightened to an almost silver color, which drew her in. She shook her head, then cleared her throat, forcing her attention away from his eyes. It didn't help that by doing so, her gaze landed on his utterly kissable mouth. His mustache twitched as his lips spread into one of the most charming grins she'd ever seen him wear.

Startled by his generous smile, his second that day, she blurted, "And this is Gloriana." She handed him the reins. Their fingers touched. Such a simple thing but combined with the look on his face and the undeniable heat sizzling through her, it was enough to make her giddy. Theo struggled to gain her bearings and her voice. "W-would you mind brushing her down and giving her some oats? She's had a long journey. I think stall number ten would suit her."

"Of course." He tipped his hat and led the mare to the stall she recommended. He turned only once as he opened the gate, and again, the intensity of his stare held her spellbound—until Hart squeezed her arm and led her to the back door of the stable.

"Now that Gloriana is settled, why don't you show me Phoebe? I'm anxious to see how fast she is."

"You won't be disappointed, Hart," she said even as she turned her head and caught one last look at Eamon before he disappeared from view.

Chapter 11

Old friend, my foot!

Eamon spread fresh straw in each of the stalls in the stable, his agitation growing with every passing moment. Once again, he worked alone, which was fine, except he just couldn't stop thinking about Hart Jameson or how he behaved with Theo.

He doesn't act like an old friend. Always touching her. Looking at her like he's a starving man and she's his last meal.

He took a deep breath and moved toward the window at the end of the stall, which afforded him the perfect view of the small sitting area Theo had arranged beneath the trees in the middle of the grassy path. Even from this distance, the sappy expression on Hart's face made Eamon want to punch him.

Hart wasn't the only one, though. Simon Taylor, Pete Marlowe, and Oren Hallowell, the other three men sitting at the table occasionally watching Pumpkin in the paddock with one of their mares, wore the same silly, stupid look on their faces—like they could die happy men if she would just smile at them. The only one who didn't grin at Theo and try to win her favor was Sylvia Veith, the lone woman in the group. She had eyes for Mr. Hallowell, and she made no secret of it.

Taylor and Marlowe arrived the day after Hart, bringing with them their horses as well as their hopes that those mares would successfully breed and produce a racing winner. Oren Hallowell and Sylvia Veith had arrived the following day, but only Hallowell stayed at the house and took possession of the last suite on the third floor. Sylvia had relatives in Pearce and stayed with them, but her mare, Delightful Encounter, was here.

Eamon didn't mind the extra work. His labors made him tired enough to sleep, sometimes dreamlessly. What he did mind was those men looking at Theo. None of them as blatant as Hart though. The man may have been joking when he asked Theo to marry him, and she may have thought he wasn't serious with his proposal, but Hart really was in love with her. Just like AJ Pearce. It was evident on their faces, at least from what he could see.

He forced himself to move away from the window and took several deep breaths to clear his thoughts, but it was impossible. Theo's laughter rippled into the stable, carried by the breeze, and drew him to the portal once more ... just in time to see Hart tuck that errant curl of whiskey-colored hair behind Theo's ear.

Eamon tightened his grip on the pitchfork's handle. The urge to punch the man doubled and, with it, the certainty he was jealous.

Yes, that was it. Hart Jameson could take Theo's hand or caress the soft skin of her cheek with his thumb, touching her with ease when *he* couldn't do the same ... though he wanted to. Every moment of every day.

Not only did jealousy tie him in knots, but fear did, too ... fear of making himself that vulnerable or that he'd never be worthy of her. She belonged with a man like Hart, one who could give her what she needed.

He sucked air into his lungs and closed his eyes, determined, once more, to ignore Hart's easy way with Theo, though his grip on the pitchfork didn't lessen.

"What did that pitchfork ever do to you?"

Startled, Eamon whirled around, dropping the tool in the process.

Quincy stood a few feet from him, a jar of milk in one hand, and a napkin wrapped around what he hoped was a sandwich in the other. "Marianne thought you might be hungry. You didn't come in for lunch, and I know you didn't eat with Theo's guests."

Eamon picked up the pitchfork and propped it against the wall, then took a seat on a bale of hay. Quincy sat beside him and held out the sandwich. He unwrapped the napkin and sighed. The sight of thin slices of meatloaf from last night's dinner on Marianne's freshly made bread made his mouth water. He liked her meatloaf as much as he liked her rosemary chicken, almond *kuchen*, and strawberry rhubarb pie. Actually, there wasn't anything she made that he didn't like.

"You should be out there, Eamon, not hiding in the stable."

Eamon shook his head as he took a bite of the sandwich, the flavors melting on his tongue as he chewed. He didn't know what seasonings she put in her meatloaf, but he knew she ground pork in with her beef and mixed them together. He always meant to ask her where she'd learned to cook so well, but never did—he was too busy eating. He swallowed and glanced at the farm manager. "I'm not hiding. I'm working."

Quincy raised an eyebrow. "Working, huh? Looks to me like you were just standing here, staring out the window, trying to strangle the pitchfork. As if I didn't know why."

"I thought I heard something." He took another big bite of the sandwich, the bread soft and chewy, and pretended that the comment didn't make blood rush to his face.

If possible, Quincy's brow rose a little higher. A smile hovered around his mouth but he had the good graces not to let it show. "And that's why you were gripping the handle of the pitchfork like you could break it in half?"

There was no censure in the man's voice, just humor, and if he wasn't mistaken, understanding. Eamon couldn't help himself. Even though his face heated with a blush, he had to chuckle. "You saw that, did you?"

"Yes, sir, I did." Quincy didn't chuckle, but he could no longer hide his grin as he pointed toward the window and the pastures beyond. "You should go out there."

Eamon took a swig of milk, then wiped his mouth with the napkin the sandwich had been wrapped in. "No, I don't belong out there."

"Is it Hart?"

Eamon didn't respond. He didn't quite know what to say. For a man who prided himself on hiding what he felt, he wasn't doing such a good job of hiding anything from Quincy.

"Don't mind Hart. He isn't serious when he asks her to marry him. Not really. Oh, I know he loves Theo and I know he'd do anything for her, including marrying her, but if you watch them, you'll see there's no passion there. At least not from Theo. She loves him like a brother. I don't think that will ever change." The man took his pipe from his pocket and held it in his hand. He didn't fill it with tobacco or even attempt to light it, not here in the stable, but he did gesture with it as he spoke. "You're a good man, Eamon MacDermott. As good or better than those men sitting out there watching the horses. I know—" Quincy didn't finish his thought. Instead, he stuck the stem of the pipe in his mouth, clamped it between his teeth, and stared at his feet.

"What were you about to say?"

The man shook his head and spoke around the stem. "Nothing, Eamon. I ... it's nothing."

Eamon shrugged. "I have all day, Quince ... you have something on your mind, you might as well say it."

After a moment, he removed the pipe and just cradled it in his hands. When he looked up from his feet and pinned Eamon with his stare, he said, "I know who you are."

Eamon inhaled and closed his eyes for a brief second, but in that second, his entire life up to this point flashed before him. The sandwich, which had been wonderful, now tasted like sawdust and felt like a boulder in his stomach ... or perhaps several boulders, all piling one on top of the other. "What did you say?"

"I know who you are, Eamon. Or should I call you 'Marshal'?"

He studied the expression on Quincy's face. Again, there was no reproach, just acceptance and perhaps a little pity.

That the man knew was devastating. He never should have stayed here. Hell, he never should have come here to begin with. "How?" He didn't recognize the low, hoarse voice coming from himself as his own.

Quincy shrugged but never looked away. "Something about your name was familiar, and then it hit me. I remembered reading about you and your brothers." His voice cracked as he continued, "And what happened in Paradise Falls." He took a deep breath as if to control his emotions, then wiped at his eyes with the back of his hand. "Remember I told you we lost Henry in a shootout with an outlaw gang?"

Eamon nodded, already dreading what Quincy was going to say next, knowing, somehow, that the Logans were involved in Henry's death.

"That's where it happened. In that little town on that God-awful day."

Worse than he could have anticipated, Quincy's statement hit him like a mule's kick to the stomach, pushing all the air from his lungs. He tasted metal in his mouth as his stomach roiled. He felt like he might lose the sandwich he hadn't even finished.

Theo had lost her beloved husband the same day he'd lost Kieran, Mary, and Matthew, nearly lost Brock and his own miserable life all because Teague had locked up Jeff Logan for horse rustling and his brothers wanted to free him. If he could cry, he would have, but he'd never been able to shed a tear for what had happened nor had he ever read a word written about the incident that changed his life. In the beginning, he'd been too busy trying to recuperate from the bullet that almost killed him. After that, he'd been too busy trying to outrun the memories.

Beside him, Quincy hadn't moved. He sat tall and straight and held the pipe in his hand, as if it brought him comfort. Or strength. He didn't turn away either. He kept his gaze steady. "The reporters gave vivid accounts of everything, but I know they sometimes exaggerate to sell newspapers so I'm not sure how much was fact and how much was fiction." He paused, as if not quite sure how to say what he needed to say. After a moment, he appeared to get his thoughts in order. "They said you were shot out at your brother's place. You almost died."

Eamon gave a slight nod. "There are times, Quincy, like right now, when I wish I had."

"Son, never say that. There is a reason why you survived ... and Henry didn't. There is a reason why you ended up here, and I think I know why." He rose from the bale of hay and crossed the stall to the window. "It's because of her."

Eamon didn't have to ask who *her* referred to. He swallowed over the lump in his throat. "Does she know?"

He shook his head. "I don't think she does, Eamon. And I haven't told a soul, not even Marianne, and I've never *not* told her anything. I won't, either. At least not yet, but there may come a time when I'll have to. Theo's a smart woman. If I can figure it out, so can she, even though she doesn't read newspapers the way I do." He looked away then, his gaze on the view outside.

"She doesn't remember much of the day Henry died, just that he died in her arms. We've talked a time or two about it and I know she feels guilty she wasn't able to save Henry's life, but in truth, there was nothing she could do. Nothing anyone could do. Took her a long time to accept that. I'm thinking it's taking you a lot longer to accept what you couldn't prevent." When he turned back and faced him, his eyes were shiny. "But I think she deserves to know, don't you? Especially since you're in love with her."

The words, said out loud and so matter-of-factly, were a bit of a shock, and there was nothing Eamon could do except deny them. "I'm not in love with her."

Quincy tucked his pipe in his pocket and let out a long sigh. "You can lie to yourself for as long as you like, Marshal, but those of us with eyes in our heads can see the truth."

"I'm not in love with her," he repeated, as if saying so made it true, and joined Quincy at the window. "But even if I was, there's nothing I can do about it. Look at her. She's all kindness and good, and I'm not nearly worthy enough for her."

Quincy said nothing for the longest time, but his expression had changed and his gaze bored into Eamon with enough intensity to be uncomfortable. The silence dragged on until finally, when he didn't think he could stand it anymore, Quincy shook his head. "You know, Eamon, sometimes you say the stupidest things." He moved away from the window, grabbed the empty jar of milk, the napkin, and the half-finished sandwich ... and left.

The smart thing would be to pack his belongings and move on. Right now. This very minute before she realized he'd left. But he couldn't do that to her. Or to himself.

Her laughter came in through the window, carried on a breeze, and in that moment, his path was made clear. He would stay and give himself a chance ... at life. At love. At happiness. And perhaps even forgiveness. And somehow, he'd have to find the strength— and the words—to tell Theo everything.

• • •

Theo stood behind her chair instead of sitting in it. Truthfully, she couldn't sit—too nervous to relax. She had so much at stake with this breeding season. They were here, some of the finest horse breeders in the country. They could have gone anywhere, but they'd come to Morning Mist Farms. Hart and Oren, old school friends of Henry's, came out of loyalty, she was certain. Simon and Pete came because they knew personally of Pumpkin's reputation, having seen him race—and win—before his retirement. And Sylvia came because she was a woman in a man's world who knew exactly what she wanted, but more importantly, she knew how to get it. She'd taken the small, run-down ranch her late husband left her and turned it into a profitable venture with a reputation for producing winners.

Yesterday evening, after Sylvia arrived, Theo had made a big production of writing down the names of the mares on small squares of paper, folding them up, and tossing them into the crown of the old hat Henry had always worn. She'd recruited Eamon to draw those names, each one of her guests hoping his or her mare would be chosen to be first to share the paddock with Pumpkin. Much to Hart's disappointment—and everyone else who hoped to be first—Scottish Lass's name had been drawn. Simon had beamed from ear to ear then. He was still beaming now as out in one of the smaller paddocks, Pumpkin, the pride and joy of Morning Mist Farms, covered Scottish Lass for the second time. Theo would allow one more time today. Then tomorrow, Pumpkin would be paired with Delightful Encounter. Moonglow would have her turn the following day, then Starburst the day after that. Poor Hart. Gloriana's name had been pulled last.

If all went as she hoped it would, all the mares would be breeding in no time at all. And if she could sell a horse or two in addition to the monies she received for stud fees, she would be in great shape, maybe even able to put some funds away for a university education for the children, including Wynn and Lou, if they wanted it.

Thinking of the children, she held her hand to her forehead, shading her eyes from the midafternoon sun and studied the tree line, expecting to see them coming from the lake where they'd gone fishing. There might be trout for dinner.

"Theo, I'd like to see those two run."

She turned toward Simon, affectionately called Colonel by those in the group, as he gestured to Castor and Pollux racing each other along the fence line in one of the other paddocks. Echo, in the same enclosure, did not join in their rambunctious race, preferring to munch on the sweet grass instead, though she did lift her head to watch the display.

The twins were neck and neck as they splashed through the small stream bisecting the large space, sprinted along the back fence, and then circled back to the gate. They nickered and huffed, perhaps daring each other to race again, before doing just that. One could tell they ran simply for the joy of it. "Against each other or separately?"

The man grinned, revealing white teeth and a dimple. "Separately, I think. Wouldn't want sibling rivalry to up the ante even though being twins, they intrigue me. I love their spirit and their speed." He pushed blond hair away from his forehead with his fingertips, his grin widening as if he could already picture the races they'd win and the prize money filling his bank account. A shrewd businessman, she'd met him when Pumpkin first started racing many years ago. He knew a good thing when he saw it ... and often bet on Pumpkin winning. He never lost.

"Of course."

She took a step or two toward the stable but stopped when she saw Marianne heading toward her, a silver coffee service in her hands. A few moments later, the woman slid the tray onto the table. "Thought you'd all like some fresh coffee."

"Thank you, Marianne. You must have read my mind."

Marianne wiped her hands on her apron, then stood with her hands on her hips, surveying the table. "I have a pitcher of lemonade, too. I'll bring that out as well as some *kuchen*. It's still warm from the oven."

Again, Theo thanked her, grateful Marianne thought of people's stomachs and not just horses like she did. "On your way back to the house, would you stop in the stable and ask Eamon to come out here with the saddle? He'll know which one I'm talking about. And if you wouldn't mind, have Wynn or Lou bring me my starter pistol."

Marianne gave a slight nod and rushed toward the stable in her usual quick, no-nonsense gait as Theo picked up the pot and began to pour for those who wanted coffee.

She didn't know what made her turn and look at that precise moment. Perhaps it was the subtle change in the air, or Sylvia's *hmmm* of appreciation as Eamon stepped out of the stable, the small saddle in his hand. Theo's heart started to race nearly as fast as Castor and Pollux in the paddock. He passed Circe, Electra, and Galatea, each heavy with the foals they waited to drop, in the corrals closest to the stable, then sauntered up the grassy path in his loose-hipped swagger, cowboy hat pulled low to shield his eyes.

"Theo."

Shoulders back, he wore a red shirt that stretched across his massive chest, straining the buttons holding it closed. She inhaled as she imagined those buttons popping, one by one, and his shirt flapping open to reveal what lay beneath.

"Theo!"

She jumped, startled. Peeling her gaze away from Eamon, she glanced at Sylvia, then the cup. Coffee filled the thin china cup nearly to the brim. "Sorry. I was woolgathering."

Sylvia, a woman who fought hard for what she had and was now used to getting what she wanted, raised an eyebrow over one of her dark brown eyes. "Hmmm, and I know exactly what you were gathering wool about." She showed her risqué side when she licked her lips and added, "He's absolutely delicious. I wouldn't mind having a taste of him. Or two. Or three."

She liked Sylvia, she really did, but the woman's actions and comments made Theo want to take the coffee and dump it in her lap. Or dunk her in the swimming hole and let the cold water cool her down.

"Is he taken?"

Without a second to think about it, she answered, "Yes. He's taken."

The woman chuckled, then winked. "That's my girl," she murmured, then lowered her voice a little more. "You gotta grab what you can out of life, and he's certainly worth grabbing."

A quick retort built in her throat, but then the subject of their short conversation approached the table and smiled that grin that made her feel like she'd run too far too fast, and whatever was on the tip of her tongue simply disappeared.

Eamon hefted the saddle as if it weighed nothing, but didn't hand it over to her. "You wanted this?"

Sweet mercy, how she wanted him!

"Y-yes, th-thank you." She hoped he hadn't noticed that she stammered. "Would you bring Castor and Pollux to the track?"

"Yes, ma'am." With a slight nod, he headed for the paddock and gave a few short, concise whistles. Castor and Pollux stopped their rambunctious play and trotted toward the gate while Echo remained in the middle of the field.

Beside her, Sylvia chuckled again. "Oh, dear girl, you have got it bad."

"I don't know what you're talking about," Theo said, a little irritated by Sylvia's apparent amusement at her expense.

"Don't you?"

Heat rose to her face as she became aware of all eyes on her— not only Sylvia's, but the men's as well. Even Hart had stopped talking and looked from her to Eamon, then back to her, questions dancing in his eyes.

Theo didn't say another word. What could she say anyway? Sylvia told the truth. She couldn't deny it. The evidence colored her face as Eamon saddled Castor and tightened the cinches, then led the three-year-old horse to the track, Pollux trotting along behind his brother.

To a person, her guests rose from their seats and traversed the short distance, pulling stopwatches from their pockets as they settled themselves against the fence railing to watch. Theo followed a moment later, her knees already weak, not from the thought of riding, but because Eamon turned and granted her that heavenly smile once more. If they were alone, if no one else was about, she would have, at that moment, fallen into his arms and let nature—and her own desires—take their course.

But they weren't alone. Her guests were there, watching, waiting. As was he, his head tilted just a bit, his smoky-gray gaze roaming over her face.

"Are you ready?"

Theo swallowed the dryness in her throat, but her voice came out much hoarser than she intended. "Yes."

He threaded his fingers together to form a step, ignoring the tree stump she had always previously used. Theo grabbed the pommel with one hand and rested her other hand on his broad shoulder to steady herself as she placed her foot in his hands, and he lifted her into the saddle with an ease that caused her to draw in her breath. Her gaze came to rest upon his eyes, which caught and held her attention. Despite his grin, there was a sadness lurking within their gray depths. Theo waited for him to say something—anything—then the sadness was forgotten as his big hands lingered a moment longer than necessary on her leg after he fitted her boot into the stirrup.

"Here's the starter pistol." Breathless from his run from the house to the track, Lou handed the carved box to Eamon. The cowboy of her dreams tipped his hat, then sauntered to the end of the track, and she watched, unable to tear her eyes away from his perfect backside. He turned to face her, then raised the pistol over his head.

Theo forced herself to focus on the task at hand. Not doing so could endanger the horse, herself, or someone else. She exhaled, then hunkered down, gripped the reins tighter in her hands, and whispered, "Show 'em what you got, Castor."

The shot rang out. Birds flew from the surrounding trees, and Castor exploded from the starting line as she had trained him to do. His hooves pounded the track and sent clods of grass and dirt into the air as he extended his stride to eat up the distance between starting line and finish. The ride was nothing less than exhilarating, made more so by the smile on Eamon's face at the end where he waited.

They crossed the finish line in record time, or so Theo thought. Truly, it felt like Castor's fastest time ever. On the sidelines, her guests compared their stopwatches.

Eamon lifted her from the saddle, his hands around her waist, and a rush of heat zinged through her veins—whether from the race or from his touch, it didn't matter. He released her, and she grabbed for the fence railing to try to regain her balance. She had to settle this, do something about these feelings he stirred within her before she made a complete fool of herself over him.

She'd better do it soon, too. Just watching him remove the saddle from Castor's back left her heart thundering as much as racing the horse had. And why were her knees weak and her palms sweaty? She'd never experienced that before. Never. She wasn't some green girl in the midst of her first love. She was a mature woman who had experienced life, the good and the bad ... but she remembered what it was like to be loved, to be held and caressed—

"If I were you, my girl," Sylvia sidled up beside her and hooked her arm with hers, interrupting her thoughts, but somehow, thinking the same thing, "I'd grab that with both hands ... and not let go."

Theo allowed herself to fall into step with Sylvia as they followed Eamon to the other end of the racetrack, where he saddled Pollux ... and waited for her.

She repeated the whole process with Pollux, although how, she couldn't begin to know. Like his brother, though, the horse needed nothing more than her encouragement in his ear and crossed the finish line in less time than Castor. Once again, Eamon helped her from the saddle, her body almost sliding against his as he lowered her to the ground. If they had been alone, she would have …

What would she have done? Kissed him? Most certainly. Lead him away from the paddocks to a secluded place where sunlight dappled the soft, green grass beneath her feet, then make passionate love to him? Yes, she could do that as well. And she should. Sooner rather than later, because just the thought of feeling his hard body against hers caused a blush to heat not only her face, but her entire body.

She turned slightly, lest she do something she shouldn't in front of her guests, and caught Hart watching them intently as Eamon released her. He took a step forward, his mouth open, then backed off when Simon grasped her hand and pumped it, his grip firm with his enthusiasm. "Draw up the papers, Theo. I'll take them both."

Chapter 12

It was the first quiet moment since the horse breeders descended on Morning Mist. Theo had made arrangements with Giselle at the White Palace Hotel—her guests would have dinner, see a play at the opera house, and then stay the night in town. And the family would have a moment of peace and quiet. Grateful for the reprieve, Theo sank onto a bale of hay with a long sigh and leaned against the railings of the stall where she'd just put Scottish Lass for the night. The horse, brushed and fed—and hopefully, already breeding—stretched her neck over the rail and nuzzled the top of her head as well as her cheek.

"I'm so glad they're all gone for the evening," she said as she took off her soft kid gloves and laid them to the side, then reached up to smooth her fingers along Scottish Lass's face. She'd already sent Wynn, Lou, and Quincy into the house for the night, all of them exhausted, which left just herself and Eamon in the stable. "I do love this, but there are times when it's just too much. I'm tired."

She stretched the kinks from her tense muscles, then bent one leg, and brought her foot up to rest on the hay. Her chin rested on her knee as her gaze drifted to Eamon. He should have been worn out, but he wasn't. At least, he didn't seem to be. He brushed Daphne with the same amount of enthusiasm he always did, the muscles in his back and shoulders bunching and relaxing with his movements, mesmerizing her. His dark hair, visible beneath the brim of his hat, curled at the collar of his shirt.

This wasn't the first time she'd just watched him, nor would it likely be the last. She had to admit, watching him had become a pleasurable pastime, though sometimes, it felt like torture to look, but not touch. Even when she was in the company of the others, she found herself looking for him, searching for his familiar cowboy hat among the other men and always, when she spotted the black crown encircled with a band of hammered silver, her heart would flutter in her chest.

And her plans to seduce him? She could never seem to find the right moment. Or if the moment presented itself, she backed away, afraid and unsure.

But maybe ...

He straightened as if he felt her gaze on him and turned slightly. That smile she looked forward to seeing appeared, stretching the mustache on his upper lip, and butterflies danced in her stomach. She patted the bale of hay. "Come. Sit beside me and rest for a minute."

He didn't move, not until Daphne nudged him forward. Theo suppressed the urge to chuckle. The horse deserved another treat.

He closed the gate and walked across the aisle slowly, as if suddenly realizing they were alone. All alone. The last time they were alone, he had kissed her. Was he remembering that? Did the touch of her lips against his linger in his mind as it did in hers? Did he want to kiss her again? She wouldn't mind. Not one bit. And if she were anything less than a coward when it came to him, she wouldn't wait ... she'd grab him and kiss him until neither of them could breathe.

She patted the bale of hay beside her again. Eamon sat as far away from her as possible, his back rigid, both feet firmly on the ground. He removed his hat and laid it down between them as if it were a barrier neither one of them could break.

"Relax, Eamon. I'm not going to bite you."

He glanced at her. Such naked emotion showed on his face, Theo sucked in her breath. In that brief moment, his expression said that maybe he wished she would bite him ... as well as do other things. If there was ever a time to follow through on her desires, now would be it.

And yet, she couldn't. Still the coward, she forced her mind to think of something else ... anything else. He never talked much about himself. Direct questions usually received a nod or a short answer so that wouldn't do, but she had noticed a change in him over the past few days. He'd become more quiet than usual.

After a few moments of silence where the only sounds were the shuffling of horses' hooves against straw and her own breathing, Theo blurted out, "I didn't have a home that didn't move until Henry built the house for me."

"A home that didn't move? I don't understand."

"The playhouse the children play in? Where you had your tea party?"

A flush colored his face and the sheepish grin curving his lips made her heart thump a little wilder, but he made no comment.

"By the way, thank you for taking the time to play along with the girls. I appreciate that more than you know."

If possible, his face turned a bit redder. "I couldn't resist Gabby's invitation."

Theo laughed, finally feeling a little less conscious of his presence. "She is a force to be reckoned with. Not many people can say no to her."

"No, they can't. Believe me, I tried."

If she were a braver woman, she would, at that moment, just grab him and press her lips to his. Instead, she continued talking, forcing her eyes away from his definitely kissable mouth. "I ... uh ... I was telling you about the gypsy wagon. It wasn't always a playhouse for the children. At one time, it had wheels. I had them removed, but I was born in that. My father traveled from horse farm to horse farm, looking for work, and I went with him."

"Where was your mother?"

"She died giving birth to my brother when I was three. My brother passed with her. I don't remember what she looked like, but I do remember her voice. It was sweet and pure, and she sang me lullabies. Sometimes, if I close my eyes and the world is silent, I can still hear her singing to me."

"I'm sorry."

She continued as if she hadn't heard him, the loss too far in her past now. "We never stayed in one place very long. Papa had … Papa … drank. Oh, he was wonderful with the horses, and I always knew he loved me, but he missed my mother very much." She looked at him. "Eventually, Papa's drinking would get in the way, and he'd have to find a new job." She pulled a piece of straw from the bale and started breaking it into little pieces. "I was fifteen when Papa got a job at Turning Leaf Farms. That's where I met Granny. She was gray-haired even then."

"Where you met Granny?"

Theo laughed at the expression on his face. "You thought she and I were related? That she's my grandmother?"

"Well, yes. You call her Granny."

"We *all* call her Granny, even you, but no, we're not related by blood, just by love. Papa and I had pulled around to the back of the house at the farm, but the horses were a little frisky that day and Papa … well, Papa wasn't exactly paying attention. We almost ran right through the vegetable garden, and we would have if I hadn't grabbed the reins. I brought the wagon under control and looked over to the back door, hoping no one had seen what happened, but things didn't turn out as I wished. The door flew open, and this tall, thin woman with glorious gray hair twisted into a loose topknot rushed out of the kitchen. She was brandishing a wooden spoon, and I thought for certain she was going to take me to task for nearly riding through her garden." She laughed, recalling the look on Granny's face, then sobered. "It was the strangest thing, Eamon. She'd stopped before she reached the wagon and just stared at me ... for the longest time. I was so embarrassed. I knew what I looked like. Short hair that had been cut willy-nilly by my own hand and stood up in all directions no matter how many times I brushed it. Hand-me-down clothes that were too big and never seemed to get clean. She narrowed her eyes at me—you know that look I'm talking about—and lowered the spoon as she came closer. I was still afraid she'd swat me, but she didn't. The expression that came over her face ... it was love, Eamon. And kindness. And acceptance. I felt it ... like a hand caressing my cheek. For a girl like me, that was like ... I can't even tell you." She brought her attention back to him, then reached out and touched his arm. "I'm sorry, I'm boring you."

Eamon shook his head, his eyes glowing with curiosity. "No, please continue."

She studied his face and gave a slight nod. "She was the head housekeeper at Turning Leaf." Theo mimicked Granny's voice and mannerisms. "Lavinia Stark—call me Granny. She took me under her wing and became the mother I didn't have. She taught me ... so many things and ..." She paused and leaned back against the railing. "That's where I met Henry, too. He was the youngest of the Danforth boys, and I ... I fell in love with him the first time he came home from school. Never even had to think about it twice."

"Papa died shortly after we arrived. After all the years he worked with horses, he fell taking a jump he shouldn't have taken and broke his neck. He left me with nothing except my little traveling home, but I was lucky. The Danforths let me stay on and work. Even Ely Danforth could see that I inherited a little of the magic Papa had with horses. He didn't really like me, but he couldn't deny how I could get his racers to run like they had wings instead of hooves. Turning Leaf's horses won nearly every race for the next two years."

"You don't only make them run, you heal them, too," he said slowly as he took her hand, his thumb gently caressing her knuckles. "I've seen what you've done with Maizie. She's happy and healthy now. I can barely see her scars. And look at Happy and the rest of your menagerie ... despite their deformities, despite what was done to them, they're happy and healthy as well, and that's all from you. They know love."

"You give me too much credit." Though she denied his compliment, she was touched nonetheless. He had noticed. Did he notice other things as well? Like the fact that she wanted him more than she wanted water to drink and food to eat?

He shook his head, brought her hand to his mouth, and kissed each knuckle, his mustache tickling her as it touched her flesh. "No, I give credit when credit is due. You've done amazing things, Theo." Despite the hat between them, he leaned toward her and hope sprung in her heart. He was going to kiss her again and make her feel things she hadn't felt in a long time.

A sudden attack of nerves made her blurt out, "I know nothing about you, Eamon MacDermott."

Out of all the things she could have said, she chose the wrong thing because he stiffened and stood quickly, forgetting all about the kiss that might have been. Face pale and unreadable, he stammered, "I ... I ... tomorrow promises to be a busy day so I ... I should get some sleep. Good night, Theo." He grabbed his hat and left the stable at a quick pace.

Theo sat on the bale of hay and watched him disappear into the dark night. He didn't go to his room beside the barn, but cut through one of the paddocks, heading, she was certain, to the swimming hole not too far away. She stood as well, determination no longer whispering through her, but shouting, and smiled. "Good night, indeed, Eamon MacDermott."

• • •

An hour later, Theo stood at the door to Eamon's room beside the barn. Indecision stilled her hand, though she'd come this far.

Earlier, he'd held her hand and listened while she poured out memories. And he'd wanted to kiss her. If only she hadn't opened her stupid mouth! She still wanted him though, wanted him more than ever.

A slight breeze molded her silk and lace negligee against her skin, intensifying her sense of longing as the smooth fabric touched her.

She turned and glanced at the house behind her. No one noticed she'd snuck out, not even the cats or the duck that slept together in the box on the back porch. Happy had only raised his head, gave a muffled woof, and then went back to sleep, his muzzle resting on his paws. No lights glowed from any of the windows, except for the candle on the kitchen table, which she could see clearly. The windows on the third floor were dark as well—her guests would not be home until sometime tomorrow.

She raised her hand, ready to knock on his door, then lowered it again. *What am I doing? I shouldn't be here. I'm a respectable widow.*

But she couldn't turn away. Nor could she deny herself any longer. She wanted this. Wanted him. She closed her eyes and drew in her breath, searching for the courage that had brought her this far.

The door swung open without her knock. Eamon stood on the threshold in just his trousers, his feet bare, pipe in hand as if he were about to step outside for a smoke. Moonlight struck his bare chest, highlighting the light matting of dark hair over the ripple of muscles borne of hard work and the patch of flesh above his heart where no hair grew, the skin puckered around a smooth indentation. Theo sucked in her breath and raised her gaze to his. If he was surprised, he hid it well, although concern wrinkled his brow.

"Is something wrong? Has something happened to one of the children?"

She shook her head. "No, nothing is wrong."

His eyes bored into hers, and she looked away, warmth rising up to her face.

"Why are you here?" he asked, his voice gentle and soothing and almost her undoing.

Her courage faltered. How could she possibly say that she needed to be held and feel his hands caress her skin? Wanted to feel the weight of him on top of her, in her, stroking the fires of desire until she couldn't hold a coherent thought in her head.

"I need ... I want ..." she stammered and tears stung her eyes. Why couldn't she just say the words and tell him she wanted him? "I'm sorry. I shouldn't—"

"Theo," he whispered, and the sound of her name eased some of the doubts. He took her hand and slowly brought her inside his room, closing the door behind them. A lantern glowed on the table, casting soft light upon the book open on the chair, where he'd just left it. His bed hadn't been slept in, but the blanket had been turned down.

He didn't say a word, just put down his pipe and gently drew her into his arms. Her head rested on his chest, the soft, dark hair tickling her cheek as she clung to him, his heartbeat strong in her ear.

"I feel so much, but I don't know what to do."

"We don't have to do anything." His voice rumbled in his chest as his arms tightened around her. "We can just hold each other."

"I'm afraid."

"I know." He gently caressed her hair, his touch light and comforting. "So am I."

"You?"

"Yes. Does that surprise you?"

She pulled back to study his face. He hadn't lied. Anxiety danced in his smoky-gray eyes, but the corner of his mouth quirked upward. Somehow, she felt much better that he shared the same fears. Encouraged by his admission and the truth of it in his eyes, Theo rose up on her toes, entwined her fingers in his soft, thick, still damp hair and pulled his head down toward hers. Trembling with both fear and excitement, she touched her lips to his.

That first taste of him sparked through her veins like the electricity that lit up the lightbulbs in Denver. Restraint flew to the wayside—and propriety with it—as she deepened the kiss, her lips sliding over his. He pulled her closer, pressing her body into his, fitting her softness to his hardness from chest to thigh and everywhere in between. She quivered within his embrace, overwhelmed with the need building inside her.

He threaded his fingers through her hair. Then his hand smoothed along her back, causing a familiar ache to flare between her thighs. Her sex swelled and became wet.

She broke the kiss and took a deep breath, forcing air into lungs that desperately needed it, then gazed into his eyes.

"Theo?" His voice was a little deeper now, and sent a thrill straight to her core.

She didn't speak, afraid that if she did, she'd say something stupid again. Instead, she caressed the side of his face, memorizing every detail—the subtle crinkles extending from the corners of his eyes, the smile lines around his mouth shadowed by the thickness of his mustache. Joy filled her ... his eyes were the darkest she'd ever seen them and glinted with undisguised longing. Did he see the same in hers? Could he feel how much she wanted him?

She didn't need to voice her questions. They were answered in the next moment as he brought his mouth to hers and kissed her so tenderly, tears stung her eyes. Her heart raced. No, not raced. Thundered. So loud, surely he could hear it.

And perhaps he did, if the expression on his face when he broke the kiss was any indication. He dipped his head again and took possession of her mouth, his arms holding her so close she could feel every delicious, muscled inch of him. Her knees turned to the consistency of pudding.

His tongue slipped between her lips to caress her teeth and tongue, and a groan escaped him, as if he'd been waiting to touch her, taste her again. He backed her toward his bed until the backs of her calves touched the thick mattress, and then, as if she would break, he stopped kissing her long enough to lay her down. He stood above her and slowly removed his belt, letting the leather strap fall to the floor as his gaze roamed her satin clad body, touching her here and there, igniting the hunger within her even more. Desire settled in her belly, burning brightly, sending sparks radiating outward. "Make love to me, Eamon."

The mattress dipped beneath his weight as he joined her, the rock hardness of his body half covering her, leaving his hand free to settle on her fabric covered belly, the heat of his palm nearly scorching her. She sucked in her breath. Waiting. Anticipating what he would do next, wanting to take his hand and place it where she needed it most.

"Are you certain, Theo?" His question, whispered in her ear as his hand moved across her ribs and upward to lightly caress her breast through the silk of her negligee, made her shiver. Gooseflesh rose on her skin. Her nipple hardened. His hand didn't linger on her breast but continued upward to caress her throat, then cupped her chin before kissing the corners of her mouth.

"Yes." She was certain. More than she'd ever been. She drew his head closer and kissed him back, her lips parting beneath the insistent pressure of his. Her hunger for him climbed as his tongue swirled into her mouth, caressing hers, and his body pressed against hers so tightly, she felt his steely arousal against her hip.

Yes. This was what she wanted. Who she wanted. And she wanted him now, but he had other intentions as he rose up on his elbow and gazed in her eyes, determined to go slower than she would like. "Do you know how beautiful you are?"

"I am?"

He smoothed his fingertips along her cheek, then followed the curve of her jawline. "Has no one ever told you? Your eyes are the color of the new grass growing in the pasture, and when you look at me like you're doing now, I am lost." He touched his lips to the tip of her nose, then her eyelids and cheeks before consuming her mouth once more in a kiss that stole her breath as well as her thoughts. He gathered a curl of her whiskey-colored hair and rubbed it between his fingers, then flashed a smile. "Soft. So soft. Like silk." He smoothed her hair back into place, then lowered his mouth to hers, but he didn't kiss her. "Shall I tell you about your mouth? And what your smile does to me? And how it makes me see your goodness and your heart? Or should I tell you how much I want you?"

"You want me?"

He chuckled and it pleased her. More than that, it touched her heart that he could laugh with her. "Yes, Theo. I want you." He chuckled again, his breath against her ear sending a cascade of gooseflesh down her arms and legs. He took her hand and pressed it against his heart so she could feel it beating. "Do you have any doubt?"

His heart raced, thundering in his chest like hers. "No."

He lowered his head and took possession of her mouth, making her ache for more. Much more. Whatever doubts she had had, whatever shyness that had stopped her before was completely gone, replaced by a certainty that this was right.

She slid her hand over his behind and squeezed gently, finally getting to touch the perfect backside she'd been admiring for so long. Firmer than she had suspected, she allowed herself a few moments to caress him before she tugged at the waistband of his trousers, surprised by her own wantonness. She pushed him away, breaking the kiss. "These are in the way."

He laughed then, from the belly, the sound reverberating through his chest and against her body. "Greedy little thing, aren't you?"

"Not greedy. I ... just want to feel all of you against me."

"As you wish, but only if I can feel all of you as well." He tugged on the pale pink ribbon below her breasts that held her robe closed. The bow slipped free, and he pushed the edges of silk away to reveal the nightgown beneath, then nuzzled his face against her lace covered breasts. Theo squirmed beneath his ministrations, her eyes closed. The heat of his breath, the wetness of his mouth and tongue as he nibbled and grazed first her right nipple, then the left through the open weave fabric had her clenching the blankets with one hand and his backside with the other. And then he stopped.

Startled, her eyes flew open to see him staring at her, the corner of his mouth quirked upward as he climbed from the bed and stood beside her, his hand extended. Theo took it, and he helped her stand. He slid the robe from her shoulders, letting it fall to the floor in a soft whoosh. The lacy nightgown came next, skimming down her body to land in a pale pink puddle around her ankles. She resisted the urge to cover herself. She hadn't been naked with a man since Henry died, but the admiration glowing in Eamon's eyes told her all she needed to see. He might say she was beautiful—anyone could say the words—but his gaze let her know he truly meant it.

"I've waited a long time to touch you like this." His hands came up just underneath her breasts, his thumbs caressing her already pebbled nipples, before his mouth descended on hers.

"And this," he whispered as he pulled away, and his lips moved lower to replace one of his thumbs and draw her hard nipple into his mouth, his tongue teasing the tight crest.

Theo threw her head back with a moan even as she grabbed his head and pulled him closer, the exquisite combination of his soft mustache and hot mouth on her sending sparks straight to her core. As he licked and scraped his teeth lightly across one straining bud, then the other, her body tensed with anticipation. It had been so long since she'd been touched like this, she'd forgotten the power of such an intimate caress, and her knees buckled. If it hadn't been for his arm around her waist, supporting her, she would have fallen.

And would that be so bad? The bed was behind her. She could fall onto the soft mattress and bring him down with her.

"Your trousers are still on." How she held that coherent thought in her head, she didn't know, but she wanted them off, needed to feel his bare skin beneath her hands. She didn't wait for him to respond or to stop what he was doing—*oh, please, don't stop!*—and reached between them, but she couldn't find the buttons, not with his body pressed so close and her fingers so clumsy.

"Patience." He murmured against her breast, then gave another chuckle that tickled her, and sent a ripple of lusty need through her, straight to her already swollen, wet sex. She couldn't help herself. She moaned and squeezed her thighs together, pressing her body as close to him as possible. He slowly lowered her to the bed, his knee nudging her legs apart, the fabric of his trousers rough on her already sensitized skin.

She felt the loss of his heat as he stood, but desire smoldered in his eyes as he slowly unbuttoned his trousers, then pushed them down his hips and long muscular legs.

Her eyes widened as she looked her fill. *Sweet merciful heavens!* She didn't have time to study him, nor touch him, but in the brief moment before he joined her on the bed, she liked what she saw.

And then she couldn't think anymore as his lips found hers once again and his fingers slid through the curls surrounding her swollen sex and caressed her ever so gently. She reached for him, wrapped her fingers around his hard, hot shaft and squeezed. Just a little. He groaned into her mouth, and the sensation was heady indeed. Her hips rose off the bed of their own accord in a bid to deepen the pressure of his hand, and he complied without a word, his entire palm covering her. Exerting just the right amount of heaviness, he moved his hand in a tight, circular motion, alternating the speed from slow to fast, then back again.

She whimpered with need, the sensations he evoked too incredible not to, then closed her eyes, and gave herself over entirely to just living in that moment: the sound of his breathing, the taste of his kiss, the smell of him, the heat and heaviness of his body so close to hers, familiar yet different. Her body tensed and tightened. She was close, so close to the ecstasy she knew she could attain, but she wanted him inside her, wanted to feel him filling her.

"Now, Eamon! I want you now!"

He moved between her thighs, his hard shaft poised at her entrance. Then slowly, so slowly she thought she would die, he pushed into her, filling her completely, and she gasped, unable to help herself.

Eamon stilled. "Theo? Did I hurt you?"

"No," she whispered as she dug her fingernails into his backside, pulling him in deeper. "I had forgotten how good this feels."

He let out a deep sigh. "So did I." He nuzzled her neck at that sweet spot where her throat met her collarbone, then started to move in her, slowly at first, then faster, all his weight either on his elbows or nestled between her thighs. She wrapped her legs around his hips, holding him close. He shifted then, moving upward, pressing harder, deeper into her.

"Oh!" She shouted as her body convulsed around him, joy shattering her senses. The breathless pleasure rippled through her, wave after cresting wave. "Oh, Eamon! Yes!"

He kept his steady rhythm as her hips met his, stroke for stroke, thrust for thrust. Her body tensed again, preparing for what was to come. She tightened her legs around his hips, pulling him deeper. He changed his pace, going fast, then slowing to almost not moving at all except for his body pressing into hers. The muscles in his arms bulged, and sweat beaded on his head before he stiffened and groaned. Heat exploded from him, filling her completely as she cried out in satisfaction once more.

Breathless, he pulled from her body, leaving her feeling suddenly bereft yet so fulfilled she could barely breathe.

He rolled onto his back and gathered her close. "Are you all right?" His voice rumbled in his chest as he twirled a lock of her hair around his finger.

She nodded, unable to speak for a moment as she laid her head on his shoulder, her hand splayed across his chest so she could run her fingers through the light matting of hair. She listened to his heartbeat return to normal, but doubted her own would for a long time. "Are you?"

"I have never been so all right in my life." There was humor and wonder and awe in his voice and a rush of warmth flowed through her. He sounded ... happy. As if he'd found something he'd been missing for a long time. Was it this? Lying in bed in each other's arms, satisfied from their lovemaking?

She let out a long sigh as a sense of contentment whispered through her and the heat of his body kept her warm. Her eyes closed and her limbs became heavy as her body relaxed, the tension she'd been carrying around for weeks finally gone. Her finger circled the puckered scar on his chest, curious as to how he had acquired it. "What is this? Were you hurt?"

She felt him stiffen, his muscles bunching beneath his skin. "Yes. A very long time ago. In another life," he said as he turned, his mouth lowering to hers once more. She forgot what she had asked as the pleasure of his kiss claimed her.

• • •

Eamon opened his eyes as the soft, misty glow of morning crept in through his window. The sun hadn't risen yet, but would shortly and another day with its accompanying chores would commence, but for right now, he wrapped his arms tighter around Theo, surprised yet grateful that she was still in his bed. She had intended to go back to the main house after they'd made love for the second time, but exhausted and sated, she'd fallen asleep in his arms instead. Some time during the night, they had spooned, her back against his stomach, her soft backside pressed against his shaft, which was beginning to stir. It wouldn't be long before he was fully erect, more than willing to make love again.

A slow smile crossed his lips as he pushed her hair away from her face, then held the silky strands to his nose. He inhaled and smelled roses, the scent that had haunted him for months. Her scent.

He hadn't lied last night when he said he was afraid. It had been a long time since he had allowed someone to get this close to him. She hadn't laughed at him for his fears. Indeed, admitting them had seemed to ease hers as well.

He hated to wake her. She looked so relaxed, her body warm and soft, but she wouldn't want to be caught stepping out his door when the rest of the household rose. He moved a little, one hand splayed across her belly, pressing her backside closer to his hardening shaft. With the other, he turned her face toward him. A long sigh escaped her. "Wake up, sleepyhead," he whispered as he nuzzled her ear.

A slow smile lifted the corners of her mouth as she shook her head. "I don't want to wake up. What if I open my eyes and this turns out to be a dream ... just my imagination playing tricks on me?"

He chuckled and moved his hips a little, so she could feel his hardness. "You're not dreaming, Theo. Feel me." The corner of her mouth rose a little higher, but her eyes remained closed. Eamon grinned, determined to play this game with her and win. His hand swept up from her belly to cup her breast, his thumb gently caressing her nipple, which tightened instantly. She inhaled deeply and arched her back, deepening the pressure but pushing against his groin at the same time. "Open your eyes and look at me."

"No." There was laughter in her voice, though she didn't laugh. He kissed the side of her face, then nuzzled the spot on her neck where he could feel her pulse with his lips. His fingertips brushed her hip and she turned in his arms, opening herself to him. He lowered his head and kissed her as his hand smoothed over her belly, then settled between her thighs. Her skin was hot to the touch, and she was wet, so very wet, as he began to caress her.

A soft moan escaped her, followed by a deep sigh as she opened her legs a little wider, granting him more access. Her hips began to move, keeping up with the rhythm he set. He'd been surprised by the quickness of her response last night, but he shouldn't have been. Theo had a joy for life, a passion he saw every day. Why wouldn't it extend to lovemaking? Why wouldn't that joy be contagious?

He ravished her mouth, slipping his tongue between her lips even as he slipped a finger into her sheath while his palm continued to stroke her, the pressure light and meant to tease.

The first wave of pleasure made her moan deep in her throat as her sheath tightened and relaxed around his finger, but still, she kept her eyes closed. Eamon smiled, enjoying this, loving the way her face reflected her emotions, but what he wanted to see most, she denied him. What would it take for her to look at him? He wanted to see what he'd seen last night in the warm glow of the lantern. For a brief moment, when she gazed into his eyes just after pleasure made her body throb, the color of hers went from the new-grass green he loved to something closer to jade and he saw something within their depths. It lasted only a second ... a brief moment in time ... but he wanted to see it again.

What could he do?

His smile widened and he shifted, pulling his left arm out from beneath her warm body even as he kissed her forehead, her temple, her nose, and finally, her mouth, his hand still between her thighs, but no longer caressing her. Instead, he pushed into the mattress for leverage and slid down the length of her body.

The bed was too short for what he had in mind so he knelt on the floor beside it. He kissed his way down her leg to her foot, marveling at how dainty and small it was—he'd only ever seen her in boots—then placed her leg over his shoulder. She made not a peep although it did seem like she stopped breathing for a moment. She didn't try to cover herself, either, as he nuzzled her thighs and inhaled her musky scent, then blew lightly on the curls surrounding her sex. A soft moan met his ears as he gently parted her swollen folds. Dark pink skin glistened and beckoned, and he responded by tasting her, his mouth covering her, his tongue flattening and lapping at her.

Theo's hips bucked upward, and he laid a hand on her belly, his fingers splayed across her smooth skin. Her fingernails dug into his scalp as she pulled his head closer, her hips moving nearly as fast as his tongue as it swept across the little nub that was the key to her release. Her breaths came in little pants, and her body tensed, as if waiting. Her thighs quivered as he pushed her over the edge.

Before she could catch her breath, he rose from his kneeling position on the floor, and plunged into her, hard and deep. Her eyes flew open as she yelled his name, and in that moment, he saw what he wanted to see. In the depths of her eyes, he saw her goodness and a reflection of himself, unburdened by his sins and his guilt, his damaged heart whole once more. Her legs wrapped around his hips, pulling him deeper as he began to rock into her. The ropes supporting the thick mattress creaked beneath them. Sweat beaded on his forehead. The muscles in his arms bunched on either side of her head as his hips ground between her thighs. She let out a triumphant shout as her body pulsed around him, and he quickened his pace, unable to help himself. She felt so damned good, her body hot and tight, and he spilled his seed into her with his own hoarse cry.

"Good morning." He kissed the tip of her nose as he slowly slipped from her body and stood. There would be no cuddling, no falling asleep in each other's arms like they had done last night.

"Good morning yourself." Theo grinned as she stretched, her face and chest flushed, then took his hand as he helped her from the bed.

Despite their lack of sleep, she moved with quick efficiency, washing up, then dressing once more in the pale peignoir. Eamon leaned against the wall near his comfortable chair, trousers in hand, and simply watched her, amazed and overwhelmed by so many things, but the fact that she'd come to him, as frightened as she was, astounded him more than anything else. How could he have been so lucky?

He moved away from the wall, grabbed her around the waist, and brought her closer, the silk of her nightgown soft and sensuous against his shaft in contrast with the thick trousers sweeping his legs and hers.

"I have to go," she whispered even as her mouth sought his.

His lips left hers to move against the soft column of her throat, then the sensitive spot just below her ear. "I know." Yet, he was reluctant to let her.

"Eamon, I really have to go. The children. Quincy." She inhaled and named the last person she would want catching her sneaking into the house. "Granny."

"Granny," he repeated and finally released her. He had no doubt Granny would take one look at Theo and know instantly what she—they—had done. She wouldn't hesitate to box his ears either or take a switch to him even though he was a full-grown man. He chuckled at the thought as he slipped into his trousers, then gave her one last sweet kiss and opened the door ... to find Theo's menagerie—Happy, the cats, and the duck—lined up at his bottom step, waiting for her. How long they'd been there, he couldn't have guessed, but his heart sank. If anything could give away the fact Theo was trying to slip into the house unseen and unheard after spending the night with him, it would be them. Or rather, it would be Mallory, the boisterous duck whose quack could be heard throughout the farm.

Eamon eyed the duck and prayed, *Don't quack. Don't quack.* The duck eyed him back and shook his tail feathers.

"Good morning," Theo whispered to the audience awaiting her. Tails wagged, ears perked and twitched, except for Mallory. He simply ruffled his feathers again as he switched his focus from Eamon to Theo. "You'll be quiet for me, won't you? And let this be our little secret?" Happy's tail wagged harder, producing a miniature dust cloud as it swept the dirt. Mama cat padded up the step and onto the porch, then rubbed her body against Theo's leg. Vincent, the one-eared cat, remained where he was, but his whiskers twitched. And Mallory? He seemed to consider the request, then waddled back to the porch and the blanket-cushioned box that was his bed. Not a quack was heard.

"Amazing." Eamon breathed a sigh of relief. "How do you do that?"

"Do what?"

"Never mind."

She nodded once, smoothed her hand along his face, then dashed across the yard, her bare feet slipping over the dew-kissed grass as she made her way to the back porch, escorted by the dog and cats.

She gave him a quick look before the back door closed without a sound. Eamon waited for the hue and cry but none came. She hadn't been caught. At least, he didn't think she had. There was no startled shriek of surprise. In fact, there was no sound at all and Granny didn't come racing from the house with a rolling pin or wooden spoon in her hand. Neither did Quincy or Marianne, who were already up and moving about their suite of rooms ... he saw a silhouette move closer to a window before the drapes were opened. He breathed a sigh and turned to go back inside his quarters, then stopped as shadows moving behind the gypsy wagon caught his attention. He stared at the gaily painted playhouse, then took a step in that direction.

A moment later, a big black crow came into view, pecking at the ground ... the early bird catching his worm. Nothing more. Eamon chuckled with relief and went back inside to wash up, brush his teeth, and finish dressing. Maybe, if he was lucky, he'd find another moment alone with Theo, but in the meantime, he had work to do.

Before Theo's house guests arrived, Eamon had started the mornings with milking the cows along with Quincy, Lou, and Wynn, but since there were more horses residing in the stable now, he started his day there. He slid the big door open and stood for a moment, his gaze taking in everything at a glance. Imitating Theo and her way of greeting these beautiful animals, he said, "Good morning, my lovelies!" and received the same response she did. The horses nickered and neighed. Some of them snorted and huffed, but all of Theo's horses returned his greeting. He strode down one of the central aisles, unlatching gates as he did so—except Pumpkin's and the guests' mares—then opened the door at the opposite end of the stable as well. The horses that lived at Morning Mist knew the routine well and followed him outside. After leading them to their respective paddocks, he took a moment, his gaze taking in everything—the mist hovering above the ground, the barn, the stable, the house. Lou and Wynn, followed by Quincy, headed into the barn, ready to begin the milking. He followed their progress before his eyes moved upward to Theo's window. If she was standing there, watching him, he couldn't know. The distance was too great, but he felt her presence as surely as if she stood next to him. A smile spread his lips. He pushed at the brim of his hat and hooked his thumbs in his trouser pockets as he headed back for the rest of the horses. As he strolled along the grassy path, he began to hum.

By the time he reached the stable for the guests' mares and attached lead lines to their halters, he was singing, his voice echoing in the rafters. If the mares found it offensive, none gave evidence. In fact, they seemed to enjoy it and followed him, the lead lines he had attached to their halters slack.

He was still singing on his last trip into the stable to get Pumpkin. The stallion was supposed to be in the same enclosure as Delightful Encounter today, according to the list Theo had created and tucked into the ledger she left on a shelf in the tack room, but he didn't feel comfortable leaving him with her until Theo could watch over them. He put Pumpkin in one of the smaller corrals closer to the stable and the pregnant mares to wait until she could be present.

He turned, ready to begin the loathsome, but necessary, job of mucking the stables, then stopped in midspin.

Where was Electra?

She wasn't with the others mares waiting to foal. His gaze scanned all the horses in their respective enclosures. She wasn't there either. Could it be that she hadn't left the stable with the other horses? That was odd because she was usually one of the first ones sprinting to the door. Was she ill? Had she come up lame?

Heart beating faster than normal, he raced into the stable. "Electra?" The horse responded with a nicker, but remained in the birthing stall, though the gate was open.

Eamon drew closer to her, looking for any indication she might be stressed or unwell, but she appeared in fine fettle. Her brown eyes were soft but alert, her ears perked, as she watched him approach. "Don't you want to come outside?"

She tossed her head and let out another huff, then nudged his hat, almost lifting it off his head. He smoothed his fingers along the side of her face, and she nipped at his wrist with her lips even as she tilted her head and leaned into his hand. She stood still for some time, accepting the attention he bestowed upon her, then shifted to the right and allowed him to enter her stall. His breath whistled between his lips when he saw what she had been hiding behind her.

"And who do we have here?" he asked, his voice gentle and soothing, as he took a step closer to the foal.

Sometime during the night while he was making love to Theo, Electra had given birth, and they had missed it. She appeared no worse for wear though. Indeed, she seemed proud of her accomplishment. The foal, a deep sorrel like its mother, looked healthy as it hid behind her back legs, eyes curious as it took a wobbly step toward him.

Electra huffed and nudged him again, pushing him closer to her baby.

He took a quick peek to check the sex, oddly pleased by the fact she was a little filly. She butted against his hand, then started sucking at his fingers. Eamon laughed. He'd never seen a newborn foal or one with so much spirit. "Theo's going to love you. And I'll bet she has the perfect name picked out for you, too."

The filly lost interest in his fingers and nudged at his trousers. "Ah, there's nothing there for you, little one," he said as he guided her toward Electra and mother's milk.

He watched her nurse for a moment or two, his heart light, then glanced around. What should he do first? Clean the birthing stall? Or head into the house to let Theo know about the new addition? It wouldn't take long to rake out the old straw and put down fresh.

Decision made, Eamon set to work as the filly nursed and Electra kept a watchful eye, skillfully nudging her baby out of the way as he maneuvered around them. He hummed as he raked and shoveled, which both mother and daughter seemed to like. Then the humming became words, and once again, his voice lifted to the rafters with a melody that had always been his favorite.

Finished with the task at hand, he came out into the aisle with the wheelbarrow full of dirty straw to see Gabby and Charlotte standing in the doorway. Both were looking at him like he'd grown an extra head. Embarrassed that he'd been caught singing, heat rose to his face and he clamped his mouth shut midnote.

"Were you singing?" Charlotte stared at him, curiosity dancing in her eyes. One of her pigtails was much higher on her head than the other, as if someone, namely Theo, had not been paying attention when she had brushed the child's hair. That made him want to grin, but he refrained, if only to save Charlotte any embarrassment.

"Well, yes, I was," he admitted, then couldn't resist asking, "Was it that bad? I was always told I sang well. No?"

"It was nice." She tilted her head, evening out the pigtails. Eamon made the conscious effort to remain as serious as she. "We just ... we never heard you sing before."

Gabby took a step toward him, rag doll clutched in her arms—this one had red hair and a bandage wrapped around its arm. She squinted just a bit. "Why are you singing?"

Eamon shrugged. "Electra gave birth to a little filly. She's really sweet." He shrugged again and admitted, "I guess I'm happy." As soon as the words popped out of his mouth, he knew them to be true. It made him pause in awe.

The little girl heaved in a breath, her face awash in delight. "He 'membered!" She took to her heels and raced toward the house, shouting with every footstep, the rag doll forgotten in the dirt. "He 'membered!"

"What was that about?"

Charlotte grinned. "Just something Mama Theo said." She turned and started heading back to the house at a much slower pace, then stopped and faced him. "I forgot to tell you. Breakfast is ready."

"I'll be in shortly." Eamon pushed the wheelbarrow after her and dumped the contents in a pile to be spread in Granny's garden when the rest of the stalls were cleaned. He'd just finished when the back door slammed, and Theo, dressed for the day in her typical uniform of split skirt and white blouse, rushed toward him, her brows drawn together.

"I have a new filly? And Electra is all right?"

He watched her come closer and noticed several things at once—her blouse had been buttoned incorrectly; her hair, which she usually wore tied back in a ponytail, had been left free to curl and wave with wild abandon; and there was a glow about her that could not be missed, although that might be just his imagination. All of these things made him smile, and he wanted nothing more than to sweep her into his arms, but he lost his chance as the back door of the house slammed again and the rest of the family, despite the fact breakfast was ready, trooped outside behind her.

He turned his attention back to her as Theo approached. "Yes. To both questions. At least, I think they're all right. The filly is nursing and doesn't seem to be having any problems doing so. She's a bit wobbly, but I think that's normal, isn't it?" She nodded and he continued, "Electra appears very proud of herself." He grabbed the handles of the wheelbarrow and pushed it back to the stable as Theo fell into step beside him. "Have you chosen a name for her?"

"Not yet. I won't know until I see her." She glanced at him and grinned even as roses bloomed on her cheeks. "Don't forget to record her birth in the ledger."

"I won't." He lowered his voice and moved a bit closer to her. "You realize she was born while you and I were making love."

The blush on her cheeks spread to her entire face, and her step faltered. "Maybe I should name her Aphrodite."

Eamon grinned and followed her into the stable. "Hmmm, very appropriate, I'm thinking."

Chapter 13

Theo accepted one last kiss, then stepped down the porch stairs from Eamon's room, and ran across the barnyard toward the house, her bare feet noiseless on the grass. She turned once to see him still standing there, his shoulder resting against the support post, the top button of his trousers undone, his bare chest almost ghostly in the pale light before dawn. He blew her a kiss, but otherwise didn't move from his spot until she slipped into the house.

Closing the door behind her, Theo leaned against it and closed her eyes, her heart pounding so hard, she though she could break a rib. One of these days, she'd be caught sneaking into the house, but so far, she'd been lucky. She'd come close only once as June melted into July, though she spent nearly every night in Eamon's room beside the barn.

What would be the harm of being caught? And why was she still keeping her time with Eamon a secret? Granny would approve. Heck, Granny had given her permission. Sort of. Marianne and Quincy would approve as well. And the children? It was obvious they all adored him.

There was a certain amount of excitement in the knowledge they could be caught at any time though. And they had taken some chances—moments stolen in the stable, where he had her against the wall, or in the secluded spot where the grass grew so soft and, shielded by a few bushes, he laid her on that soft grass and made love to her, bringing her to breathless ecstasy time after time. Anyone could stumble upon them. Perhaps that was part of the exhilaration and anticipation, though she *was* careful about the children. She always made sure Gabby, Charlotte, and Thomas were busy elsewhere before she slipped off with Eamon.

Just thinking about what he did to her—and how quickly she responded to even his slightest touch!—made her sex swell. A flush warmed her chest and spread upward to encompass her face.

"So that's the way of it."

Theo jumped and squelched the surprised squeak that threatened to wake the entire household as Granny shuffled into the kitchen in her nightgown and light cotton robe, her gait slow and a little unsteady.

"Granny, you just scared ten years off my life!"

The woman *tsked* as she made her way to the stove where the kettle was just beginning to spout steam. "That's what you get for sneaking in here like a thief at this hour."

Was there humor in Granny's voice? She couldn't tell. "A thief? I'm doing no such thing."

Granny said nothing, just *tsked* a few more times and raised an eyebrow as Theo's heartbeat returned to normal. Better to be caught by Granny than one of the children, although why Granny was awake this early was another question, one which was answered much too quickly—she winced as she reached for the jar containing her special tea. The woman was in pain, her knuckles swollen more so than usual. There would be rain before the day was over. Granny's arthritic joints never lied.

Theo stepped away from the door and pulled a chair away from the table. "I'll do that. Come and sit."

For once, Granny didn't argue as she shuffled to the chair and eased herself into it. Twice, she inhaled deeply, as if a certain movement caused her more pain.

Theo poured water into the teacup over the little ball containing Granny's special tea concoction and allowed it to steep for a moment or two. As she did so, and to take Granny's mind off her pain, she asked, "How long have you known?"

The woman shrugged and said in her matter of fact voice, "Since the beginning."

At that, Theo stiffened. Here she thought she'd been so careful only to acknowledge she couldn't hide anything from the woman who'd known her since she was fifteen. She let out her breath and poured a little cold water into the teacup.

"I wasn't quite sure until I saw you and Eamon together. Neither one of you could stop grinning, and you ... you couldn't stop blushing every time he looked at you."

Theo shook her head. She would have made a terrible spy—all her emotions were on her face and so easily read. "Who else knows?"

"Quincy, I'm sure. He seems to know everything. And if Quincy knows, then Marianne knows, too. As for anyone else, I don't know." She shrugged her shoulders.

She brought the teacup to the table and slid it in front of Granny, then took a seat. "What about my guests?"

Granny wrapped her gnarled fingers about the cup and sighed. "Aside from that woman, I don't think anyone has paid any attention to you. They're all more interested in the horses, as well they should be."

"And Hart? Do you think—"

"Does it matter, Theo? In the grand scheme of things?" Granny blew on her tea, took a tentative sip, then another. Her shoulders relaxed a little. She took another sip, this one bigger than the last—the healing power of the herbs wouldn't take long to work, but in the meantime, the simple act of holding the cup and breathing in the vapors did wonders. Some of the color came back into her face. "Did you ever really consider marrying Hart?"

Theo studied her fingernails even as she shook her head. She loved Hart dearly, but she just couldn't imagine engaging him in a passionate kiss, let alone inviting him into her bed. Yes, he was a good friend. He was reliable and patient. He would be able to provide for her, the children, and Granny, but she wanted ... more than steadfast. If she were to ever marry again, she wanted more than a companion. She wanted passion and love. She'd had that once. It wasn't so wrong to want it again.

And why was she even thinking about this? Marriage hadn't entered her thoughts since she made the decision to invite Eamon to her bed. Well, rather, she invited herself to *his* bed, but he didn't exactly turn her away.

"You're not upset with me? Or disappointed?"

Granny laid her hand over hers, her soft flesh hot from holding the teacup. "How could I be?" She smiled, although it took some effort. "You've been alone too long, and I know you didn't make this decision lightly. I'm certain you took everything into consideration."

Granny took a deep breath, her gaze steady and straight forward as usual. "He's a good man. Anyone can see that, but the most important thing is that you're happy. You are happy, aren't you?"

She didn't have to think before answering. "Yes. I am."

"Do you love him?"

The question brought her up short. She hadn't thought about it, just as she hadn't thought about marriage except in the most fleeting way. Not really. Oh, he made her feel things she hadn't felt in a long time and the time they spent together was more than wonderful, but did she love him? Like she had loved Henry?

No, this was different, but was it love? She didn't know as she'd never quite felt this way. She certainly didn't know what he felt. Not at all. They talked, but only spoke of tomorrow—never of next week or next month, or even yesterday. After all this time, she still knew nothing about his past, and sometimes the nights she spent in his arms seemed like only a dream when the sun rose. They never spoke about the first time she went to his bed ... and he never asked. They made no promises to each other, nor did they lie.

"Well, good morning!" Marianne grabbed the apron from the hook beside the door, slipped it over her head, and tied the strings behind her back as she came into the kitchen. "Nice to see everyone up and about on this fine morning! I trust everyone slept well?"

Theo faced the much too cheerful woman and stifled a groan. "You know."

Eyes glimmering with merriment, Marianne's smile widened. "Of course I know." She poked at the coals already in the wood compartment of the stove and added several nice size pieces of oak. After closing the door, she filled the coffeepot with water, poured in the ground coffee, and set it on the range top. Over her shoulder, she said, "I saw the love bite on your neck."

This time, Theo couldn't squelch the groan. "I had a love bite? On my neck?" How could she not have seen that? Worse, how could she not have known?

The woman nodded as she turned to face her. "I don't think anyone else saw it. The collar of your blouse covered it up quite nicely, but there was that one moment when you turned your head in a certain way, and well, there it was."

"And you're not upset that I've been ... with Eamon?"

"Why should I be upset? Why should anyone? It isn't anyone's business but yours. I will say this, though, like Granny, I haven't seen you this happy in a very long time and I think it's wonderful." She stood with her hands on her hips, her head tilted just a bit, her eyes aglow with mischief. "So answer Granny's question. Do you love him?"

Her brain said one thing—this was just an affair—she wasn't looking for anything beyond the physical. But she lied. Theo Danforth was not a woman made for a short-term tumble with a handsome man, as much as she might tell herself she could be. Her heart demanded more.

Despite Eamon's silence and his propensity for changing the subject when she asked one question too many, she'd witnessed his goodness, his kindness, and a gentleness born to him that he couldn't deny as much as he wanted to. It was in the way he spoke to the children … and the animals on the farm … and the way he touched her, revered her almost …

Both Granny and Marianne stared at her, waiting for her answer, and the truth came to her not with thunderbolts and lightning strikes, but rather like the fine mist that hovered over this farm in the mornings—gentle, all encompassing, life-affirming, joyful. She *did* love him and had from the moment he stood in front of her, hat in hand, afraid to move because she held him at rifle point.

"Mama Theo!" The sound of Gabby's voice from the top of the stairs jolted her out of her thoughts. "Come brush my hair!"

Saved from having to answer any more questions, especially *that* one, Theo bolted from her seat just as Quincy came into the kitchen, a big grin on his face as his gaze met hers. She didn't need to see herself in a mirror to know her face flushed—she felt the heat under her skin. She fled upstairs, away from the chuckling of all three but grinned as she stepped onto the landing and saw Gabby in the doorway to her room. The child was dressed for the day in a pair of old trousers that had once been Thomas's and a calico shirt that had a small tear in it. Her feet were bare and her hair was a mess, but she wore the brightest smile as she threw herself into Theo's arms and hugged her tight. "Good mornin', Mama Theo!"

Theo's heart swelled within her chest. Was it possible to be this happy and not burst from it?

• • •

Eamon sat straight up in bed, his breath seized in his lungs, mouth open in a shout that he refused to let out. Pain blossomed in his chest, above his heart. He laid a hand over the taut skin, feeling the scar that reminded him he still lived while others did not, as if he needed such a physical keepsake.

Slowly, the nightmare dissipated and the pain receded, but not completely. Never completely. He climbed out of bed. The moonlight streaming through the window fell upon Theo, still asleep among the twisted bedclothes, evidence of their spirited lovemaking. Strange, he hadn't had this nightmare since Theo first came to his bed and he'd seen the mirror image of himself in her eyes—the reflection of a good man.

Grateful he hadn't woken her, he drew the light blanket up to her chin, then tenderly caressed the soft, smooth skin of her cheek with the back of his fingers.

Her eyes were open, her gaze searching his face.

Startled, he pulled away. "I'm sorry I woke you."

She shook her head, her whiskey-colored hair tangled on his pillow, moving with her actions. "It's all right. I wasn't really sleeping. Tell me."

Eamon stumbled back. "I ... I can't."

"Of course you can. And you should. Whatever it is, Eamon, you can trust me." Theo lifted the covers, inviting him back into the warm cocoon.

Eamon hesitated, but only for a moment, then slipped between the blankets, her heat enveloping him, making him feel as if he could tell her everything, but he still held back. Since the night when she'd come to him and they'd made love the first time, he'd felt things he never thought he would.

Forgiveness.

Acceptance.

Healing.

After all this time, he was learning to forgive himself for arriving at Whispering Pines too late to save Kieran, Mary, and Matthew and for not going after the Logan Gang weeks earlier when he could have. And it was Theo—and the rest of her family—who'd made him see that even though, aside from Quincy, they didn't know about the heartbreaking events of that day long ago.

The family had accepted him as he was, a silent, solitary man, and slowly, through kindness and love, changed him so much, he hardly recognized himself.

And those changes brought about the biggest one—healing. Through the power of goodness, which was Theo herself, his broken heart was finally mending.

The nightmare, after an absence of several months, seemed so much more real and shocking. The guilt of that fateful day lingered, a dull throb that reminded him always of what he'd lost, but not nearly so debilitating that he couldn't participate in a little girl's tea party or appreciate the beauty and simplicity of life on this farm. Or laugh. It felt good to laugh again.

And Theo didn't even know what she had done for him.

The plain, unvarnished truth was he was scared. Out of his mind. What if he did confess everything, told her about his past, about the loss of family and the part he had played? And what if she pushed him away? Looked at him with revulsion instead of happiness? Or worse?

It would kill him, mentally and spiritually, changing him back to the solitary, lonely man he used to be. The newfound lightness in his heart would be gone, and once more, stone would fill that space where his heart should be. He couldn't let that happen. Refused.

So he kissed her. Instead of talking, which she expected, he rolled to his side, drew her into his arms and took possession of her lips, sliding over them gently, tugging a little at her bottom lip until she opened her mouth for him. Her breathing sped up, and her arms slid around his neck. She pulled him closer, her fingers entangling in his hair as her leg moved over his thigh and held him captive.

"Eamon, you really can—" she began when they came up for a breath but never finished her statement as he responded with another kiss, this one gentler than the last.

"This is not going to work, you know. Kissing me—" Again, her words were cut off as his mouth descended once more and his hand smoothed over her bare hip, along her belly to lightly caress her breast. Her nipple puckered and hardened instantly. He loved how quickly she responded to him. Theo drew in her breath, then released it in a sigh. "It's working," she muttered against his mouth as her back arched, pushing her breast into his hand, trying to make him exert more pressure. "Make love to me."

He chuckled, then rubbed his whiskered cheek against the side of her neck, making her giggle. The woman had the softest, most sensitive skin—ticklish in so many places that sometimes the gentlest caress could bring her to fits of laughter. He loved that! And enjoyed discovering those places on her body as well as the ones that simply made her sigh with pleasure—like the inside of her wrist. A stroke of his tongue on that sensitive spot made her melt in seconds.

"That was my intention." He dipped his head and captured a nipple between his lips, laving the stiff peak with his tongue, then drawing the whole areola into his mouth, alternating his suction between hard and soft. Theo let out a hoarse groan, then threaded her fingers into his hair, pulling his mouth closer even as her body arched against his. Her legs opened, releasing the musky scent that was her own, letting him know that she was ready for him.

He slid his body over hers, even though he had no intention of giving her what she wanted so quickly. He wanted to tease her, touch her all over, and bring her to the brink before he sought comfort in her hot sheath. He trailed kisses down her neck and throat, stopping long enough to encircle first one nipple then the other with his lips, grazing his teeth against the sensitive skin.

"Eamon!" She stiffened beneath him, then cradled his head against her breast, forcing him to stop, which she sometimes did when the pleasure became too intense for her. "Do you hear that?"

"Hear what?" Truthfully, he hadn't heard anything except the sound of her breathing and her little moans of pleasure. He cocked his head and listened. The wind blew, not in gusts but steadily as it buffeted against the side of his room. Above the sound of the wind, he heard the horses. They were restless, whinnying and snorting, but sometimes they reacted to the wind that way. "Sounds like the wind has picked up. Maybe it's that storm you told me was coming. It's spooking the horses."

He turned his head the other way and heard quacking. The sound grew louder then softer then louder again, as if the duck ran from one side of the barnyard to the other, passing in front of his door as he did so. "Seems to have riled up Mallory, too." He listened more intently and only heard the duck making a ruckus and the sound of the wind, becoming louder, but no barking from Happy, which wasn't usual. If the duck was squawking like a broken hurdy-gurdy, then the dog should be at least whining.

Something wasn't right.

He sat up and looked toward the open window, the one nearest the door. White cotton and lace curtains fluttered and flapped in the wind. He caught glimpses of moonlight, which illuminated the wisps of smoke curling along the ceiling, the acrid smell distinct. Beyond the cool glow of moonlight, a warmer, brighter light flickered and grew more intense with each passing moment. "Fire!"

Theo wiggled free of his embrace and scrambled from the bed, fear making her voice higher and sharper than normal. "The children!"

Eamon jumped from the bed at the same time, pulled his trousers from the back of the chair, and slipped them on. He rushed to the door and flung it open, his heart in his throat, afraid of what he might see. In an instant, a mix of emotions skittered through him. Relief that the house, full of sleeping children, family, and guests, remained safe—no smoke or fire issued from the structure, but the stable was a different matter. Flames of orange, red, and yellow consumed the bales of straw he had stacked under the awning in front of the building earlier in the day and licked at the walls. The stable door smoldered though it hadn't yet burst into flame. Billows of white and black smoke rose upward as ashes floated on the wind currents created by the blaze. The whinnying and snorting of the horses grew louder as they panicked from the smell and the heat.

He jumped from the porch, ran toward the burning structure, and started pulling and pushing the bales away from the wall as flames licked at his bare hands.

Theo rushed past him, now dressed in her familiar split skirt and blouse, but her feet were bare. "The horses!" She ran to the door and struggled with the heavy beam that fitted into slots to keep the stable door closed, but couldn't budge the stout slab of wood. "Help me!"

His heart in his throat, his hands already burned from moving the bales, Eamon rushed to her side and shoved her out of the way. "Wake the others!" Intense heat stole his breath as the flames licked at the wood, but he managed to lift the smoldering beam, toss it aside, and open the door. Flames shot toward the awning, pushing him back from the heat.

From a distance, over the roar of the blaze, he heard the bell by the back door ring.

Theo sprinted past him again and ran straight into the thick, black smoke billowing from within the stable. "Theo! Stop!"

He was too late. Either she didn't hear him or chose to ignore him as she opened the stall gates in the darkness of the building. If she was as afraid as the horses were, she didn't show it. Her voice remained calm and soothing as she called to them, and they rushed past her to the back of the stable where no fire threatened. He followed her as well, his eyes adjusting to the gloomy interior and the glow of firelight coming in from the front door, opening the gates for her guests' mares and grabbing their halters to lead them toward her. There was no fire at this end of the stable, but that didn't mean the whole building couldn't explode in flames in a matter of moments.

She pushed against the door leading to the corrals behind the building, but it didn't budge. "Eamon! The door won't open!" Panicked, the horses reared and screamed. Those that could, turned around and ran toward the fire at the other entrance.

He brought the mares to her, then pushed against the door as well. "Damn! I don't remember bolting this door." He glanced back toward the opposite entrance. Engulfed in fire, the doorframe was a beacon in the darkness, but a potentially deadly one. They didn't have much choice though. "There's no time."

He grabbed the halters of the closest mares, one in each hand, gave a sharp whistle, and ran toward the open doorway with the mares in tow. The other horses, those milling around Theo, followed him out into the barnyard where Quincy, Lou, and Wynn were already filling buckets from the water pump at the edge of Granny's garden. He didn't stop his progress and rounded the side of the building, looking back for a glimpse of Theo. She should be right behind him.

She rode past him on Pumpkin's bare back, her hands gripping his mane, whistling and calling to the mares. His heart jolted at the sight. He let go of the halters, confident she'd lead them to safety, then broke stride and backtracked.

He skidded to a halt in front of the stable. The flames were higher, the old wood snapping and crackling as the blaze grew. Hart and the rest of the guests, summoned by the bell Theo had rung earlier, formed a line and passed buckets of water from hand to hand. Lou and Wynn manned the water pump in front of the garden and kept the supply coming. The younger children were gathered around Granny on the back porch, but the expressions on their faces, particularly Gabby's, wrenched his heart. He could imagine her terror at reliving the nightmare that had left scars on her little body. He wanted to comfort her and let her know everything would be all right, but he couldn't. Not yet. Not until every last spark, every last flame, was extinguished.

Eamon took his place at the head of the line, grabbed the pail handed to him, and tossed water at the blaze.

Wood sizzled and crackled, popped, and hissed. Smoke billowed.

How many buckets of water he threw at the fire, he didn't know. He'd lost count by the fifteenth one. His shoulders screamed from the repeated actions. Smoke made his eyes water and his throat burn until finally, exhausted and overwhelmed with emotion, he dropped the last empty bucket on the ground. The fire was out, leaving charred wooden planks and a scorched smell that stuck in his nose and filled his lungs. All of them working together had saved the stable. Only the front, the awning above, and a small portion of the left side had been burned, but that could be repaired. The horses were safe as were the children, which was all that mattered.

"Is everyone all right?" he asked as his gaze swept over Theo's guests, the children, Quincy, and the older boys.

There was a chorus in the affirmative as they turned, almost as one, and headed for Marianne and the coffeepot she held in her hand. Eamon breathed a sigh of relief, grateful no one had been hurt, though he was certain they were all exhausted. They had done well. All of them. Quincy. Lou and Wynn. Hart and the other breeders. He lifted his gaze to the heavens and said a silent prayer of thanksgiving, then lowered his eyes and searched for Theo. He'd been so busy throwing water on the fire, he hadn't seen her come back from the paddock.

He spotted her in front of the stable. She stood next to Granny now, facing the building that had once been her pride, head down, shoulders slumped. The children were gathered around her, Gabby's head buried against her skirts. There were small black spots on her white blouse, probably burns from the embers produced by the fire. She nodded at something Granny said, then lifted her head, and stood up straight, her back moving as she took a deep breath.

He headed toward her. "Theo? Are you all right?"

She turned and swiped at her dirty, tear-stained face, smearing the soot and sweat over her features instead of wiping it clean, then winced and hid her hands behind her back. "I'm fine." Her husky voice seemed much hoarser than usual.

He drew closer, and she retreated, right into Granny's arms. He reached for her, gathering her close, but she stiffened in his arms. "Don't."

He understood, probably better than she might imagine. For a strong woman, this bit of kindness might be her undoing, and by the looks of her, she had already cried and didn't want to continue in front of the children. They'd never seen her anything but brave and undaunted, if what Quincy had told him had been true.

Releasing her from his embrace, he reached for her hands. She winced again and his stomach turned. More gently now, he turned her hands over and looked at her palms. They were red and raw, burned, he suspected, when she tried to lift the heavy beam that had bolted the door closed. The blisters were broken now and oozed blood. "Your hands!"

"I'll be fine." She tried to pull away but gave a small cry instead. Again, Eamon released her, but she moved quickly, flipping his hands over to inspect them as he had inspected hers. "And look who's talking? Your hands are just as bad as mine."

Gabby stepped between them and examined both their hands, her touch gentle. "Now you'll have scars just like mine."

"Yes, Gabby, just like yours," Theo said as she drew girl closer.

"Granny can fix it." She smiled then, the front tooth she'd recently lost making her more adorable than before. "She can fix anything."

Eamon had to resist the urge to hug her. "Yes, she can."

• • •

Aldrich paced, pausing now and then to stare at Tell. His stomach clenched as did his hands, and the notion to throttle the man in front of him flitted into his brain. "You tried to burn down her stable? With all that valuable horseflesh inside?" He scoffed, then slammed his hand on the desktop. "Damn it! I want those horses. Hell, I want the whole farm!"

"Don't forget, you want the woman, too." Tell's words came out a little slurred, and his bloodshot eyes blinked repeatedly, as if the man had trouble focusing. He probably did after pouring rotgut whiskey down his gullet for the past two days. He claimed it was the only way to ease the pain of the dog bites. He had two of them—one on his left foreman, now wrapped in a bandage. Red splotches of blood seeped through the white cotton, signifying the bite was deep. It would leave a scar. The other bite would leave a bigger scar, and Logan would be reminded of it every time he sat down.

In Aldrich's opinion, it served him right, and if he wasn't so angry and frustrated, he would have found Logan's predicament amusing. He could imagine the scenario as Logan described it— the duck distracting him while the dog snuck up behind him without a sound to sink his teeth into his arm as he lit the whiskey-soaked bales of straw piled up against the front of the stable. He could imagine Logan's surprise and pictured him trying to shake the dog loose, all the while keeping his mouth shut so he wouldn't wake anyone in the house. Better still, Aldrich could see Logan running away, the dog hot on his trail, catching up to him at least once to bite him on the ass and rip his trousers in the process.

Yes, he could see it all, but it didn't lessen his anger, nor did it get him what he wanted. Theo's farm. Her mutt had succeeded in his mission, whereas Logan had failed, and the damage to Theo's stable wasn't nearly half as bad as it could have been, or so he'd heard. None of the horses had been hurt, and the structure could be repaired.

He slowly counted to ten, trying to keep his temper. It wasn't easy, not with a barely sober gunman slumping in the chair before him.

Logan pulled a cigarette from his shirt pocket, tapped it a couple times on the arm of the chair, and popped the end into his mouth as if he hadn't a care in the world. He stood and dug the silver match safe from his trouser pocket, wincing as he did so, then lit the cigarette. Smoke curled to the ceiling as he limped over to the liquor cabinet.

"What the hell were you thinking?"

The man shrugged and took a long, slow drag on his cigarette. The tip burned bright red, and ashes dropped to the fine Persian carpet on the floor. As the smoke left his mouth, he said, "I didn't intend to start a fire. It just kinda happened."

"Just kinda happened." Aldrich repeated, letting heavy sarcasm creep into his voice. Logan didn't seem to notice it and kept talking.

"I snuck onto the farm a couple times, just to watch 'em, ya know? She's got a sweet setup. Nice place, even with all them brats runnin' around. You were right, she's fuckin' him. Can't say I blame the man for takin' what she's offerin'. Wouldn't mind takin' some of that m'self." He chuckled, then grew serious. "I don't know why you're so hot under the collar, Pearce. I saw an opportunity, and I couldn't pass it up. All those bales of straw piled up against the front of the stable. It was just too good to be true."

Logan shrugged again, stuck the cigarette in his mouth, and reached for one of the bottles of whiskey cluttering the surface of the cabinet. "Didn't take much to set those bales on fire, just my sippin' whiskey. I thought it was a good idea. Woulda done more except for that damned dog! Never heard him sneaking up behind me. He never even barked. Not once. Followed me for a while, too, and tried to bite me again, but I hit him over the head with my gun. Wanted to shoot him, but didn't want anyone to hear the gunfire."

Aldrich grabbed the bottle from his hand. "I don't pay you to think, Logan! I pay you to do as you're told!"

He took the cigarette from his mouth and squinted. "I wouldn't do that again, if I were you."

Aldrich lifted a brow and stared the man down, not the least bit afraid. As Logan had shown, he did best when he followed orders and didn't think for himself. And though he might be intimidating to nearly everyone else, he wasn't to those who knew him well. In truth, the man was a coward.

After a moment, Logan turned away and chose a different bottle. Aldrich took that bottle, too. "I suggest you sober up and figure out a way to get rid of MacDermott without damaging my property. And I suggest you do it now." He put both bottles back on the cabinet but continued to glare at the gunman. "Call him out."

"Call him out?" Logan repeated, rather stupidly.

Aldrich nodded, liking the idea more and more as it settled in his mind. Who knew? If Logan and MacDermott killed each other, two of his problems would be solved. "You heard me. Challenge him. The sooner, the better."

"Are you out of your fuckin' mind, Pearce? I ain't gonna call him out." Logan backed up a few steps and bumped into the chair, hitting himself where the dog had taken a chunk out of his behind. "Shit!" He sidestepped.

"Why not? Are you afraid?"

"Hell no, I ain't afraid."

He lied. Aldrich could smell his fear, see it in the weariness of the man's eyes and the paleness of his face.

Logan scowled but eventually gave a quick nod and limped out of the study. Aldrich watched him go and smiled. He liked nothing more than getting the better of someone who thought he was meaner and tougher than himself.

Chapter 14

"I'm so sorry."

"This wasn't your fault, Theo. There's no reason to apologize." Hart leaned over and kissed her on the cheek. He had been the first to arrive for the breeding season and the last to leave. Her other guests had made arrangements to go home while the stable still smoldered, since the season was over due to the circumstances. Hart had stayed another day.

He climbed into the seat of the wagon he'd rented from the livery in town, his luggage piled into the back, tickets in his pocket for the late morning train. Their lead lines tied around one of the vehicle's wooden slats, Gloriana and Phoebe waited patiently for their trip to Hart's farm. "I can stay, Theo. I can help you rebuild. I ..." He gazed into her eyes. "I would be honored if you'd marry me."

"Thank you, Hart, but I can't." She laid her bandaged hand on his hand. "I love you dearly, but you deserve passion and ... and so much more. Thank you for asking though."

"Very well," he said, his voice filled with disappointment before he found his usual joie de vivre. "I'll be back next year. If you need me in the meantime, you know where I'll be."

Theo nodded, unable to speak over the lump in her throat as he flicked the reins. Moving the wagon forward, then around the corner of the house, he disappeared from view. She wiped the tears from her eyes, the wetness absorbed by the bandages, and took a deep breath, then turned to see Eamon come out of the stable. He didn't see her, intent on cleaning up the mess left by both the fire and the water used to put it out. He was nearly finished repairing what he could with the help of Lou, Wynn, and Quincy. They'd knocked down the worst of the charred boards and covered the gaping holes with pieces of canvas.

He'd only taken a few swipes at the straw when he stopped and leaned the rake against the fire-scorched wall. Bandaged hands on his hips, gaze focused on the ground, he didn't move, just studied the nearly bare patch of earth at his feet. After a moment, he unwrapped the bandage from his right hand and stuffed the strips of white cotton into his trouser pocket, then squatted on his haunches. He moved some straw out of his way with his finger and picked something up. He twisted and turned the object, even bringing it up to his nose to sniff at it.

Curious, Theo headed in his direction. The smell of smoke still hung in the air even though the fire had been out for two days now. Indeed, the acrid odor seemed to be everywhere ... on her clothes, in her hair ... in her very soul, but life on the farm went on, as it must. "What are you looking for?"

Eamon glanced up at her and squinted against the early morning sun, despite the brim of his hat shadowing his face. "How and why the fire started." He held out his hand. In the middle of his palm, saturated and falling apart, but still recognizable, was a half-smoked cigarette. "I think this was the cause or, at the very least, part of it, but it doesn't belong to any one of us. Quincy and I smoke pipes, and one of your guests smoked a cigar. No one here smokes cigarettes."

Her heartbeat picked up its pace, and her stomach clenched as the unthinkable came to her. "Did someone set fire to my stable on purpose?"

He stuffed what was left of the half-smoked cigarette in his shirt pocket and straightened. "I believe so."

"But why? I don't understand."

"I don't know, Theo." He reached for her bandaged hand, and she gladly gave it to him, accepting this small gesture of comfort. "Do you have any enemies? Someone who wants to hurt you?"

She shook her head. As far as she knew, no one would want to hurt her. She was a good neighbor, caring for those around her, and she always tried to be kind, no matter the circumstances. The only ones who might wish her bad luck were Pearce and his son. She had feared Aldrich's reprisal after she rebuffed his offer of marriage, but there had been none. The fancy lawyers he sent to convince her to sell the farm to him had been nothing more than a nuisance. And AJ? Another bother, but completely harmless.

No, Aldrich would never set fire to her stable. He knew the value of the horses. He wanted the farm, but he would never do something like this to get it. That wasn't like him—fire was too obvious. His methods to get what he wanted were more subtle, for the most part, though he wasn't above using fear and intimidation as his weapons, not to mention his fancy, back east attorneys who could twist words like Marianne twisted dough to make pretzels.

"I can think of no one who would want to hurt me this way, Eamon. Not one single person." Tears filled her eyes. They seemed to be coming more easily now, leaving her throat raw and her heart bruised. She had cried not only in Eamon's arms but Granny's and Marianne's, too, but never in front of the children. For them, she maintained a positive attitude, no matter how much her heart was breaking.

"Maybe we should have the sheriff come out and take a look. At least report what happened." He shrugged his broad shoulders. "Perhaps there have been other fires."

"Other fires? Wouldn't we have heard something about that? Quincy, I'm sure, would have said something if there had been mention in the newspaper."

Again, he shrugged, then pushed the brim of his hat higher on his forehead. "Maybe they haven't been reported. Maybe no one suspects arson." He shifted his weight from one leg to the other as he removed the bandage from his left hand and stuffed the material in his pocket. "There could be someone out there setting fires because he likes to do it. I've heard about people like that. And it could have nothing to do with you or your farm. It could be just a random act."

"A random act?" Theo repeated as anger flooded her. She'd been upset, but she hadn't been angry ... not until this very moment. "Why? Why should someone have the right to ... to ruin everything I've worked for because he likes to see fire? Why pick my farm? I have valuable animals here. More importantly, I have *children* here, one who has already been through a fire that nearly cost her her life, and an old woman who doesn't move as fast as she used to. People I love, Eamon!" Panic rose with the anger even though she was not usually a woman who gave in to hysterics. She'd always been calm and in control, but thinking about who she could have lost was too much.

She swiped the wetness from her eyes, frustrated that she should cry when what she really wanted to do was hit something. Or someone. Hard. "What if it hadn't been the stable, but the house that had been set on fire? What if we'd been too late? What if—"

"Theo!" He reached for her, his hands coming up to rest against both cheeks, his skin hot and rough from the burns he'd suffered putting out the fire. His silvery-gray eyes bored into hers. "Stop and take a breath."

Startled, she did as she was told.

"Again."

The panic began to pass, but not the fury, as she drew more air into her lungs.

He released her, but didn't move away. Instead, his gaze remained steady, and his voice lowered in pitch. "Listen to me. Everyone is fine. The children. The horses. Granny. No one was hurt. The stable can be repaired, and Happy will be his old self again in no time at all."

She shook her head, knowing he lied to her. Happy had finally come home after the older boys, Lou and Wynn, had scoured the surrounding woods calling his name. He hadn't been the same dog since—he stayed in his box on the porch more often than not, his eyes alert but so sad, as if he'd lost his joy. Mallory and the cats sensed the difference in him, too.

"He'll come around," he repeated, as if he could feel the doubt in her heart. He moved closer to her, then reached out to caress the side of her face, wiping a tear from her cheek with his thumb.

Theo leaned into his soft touch and gathered strength from his strength, letting it soothe her troubled soul.

"Let's go into town."

"Town?" The suggestion caught her by surprise. Eamon never went to town, though Quincy had offered several times. Indeed, this would be the first time—he hadn't left the farm since the moment he arrived. If he needed something, he had Quincy pick it up on one of his daily trips. He was trying to distract her, and despite everything, her spirits lifted, the sweet gesture nearly bringing her to tears—again.

He nodded, his warm gaze roaming over her face, his hand still resting against her cheek. "Why not? I know Quincy was going to pick up wood at the lumber yard to start repairing the stable, but there's no reason why we can't do that. And we can bring the children." He glanced around like he was about to impart a deep, dark secret, then grinned. For a moment, Theo caught a glimpse of him as a little boy up to mischief. "Quincy told me there's a new ice cream shop on Main Street. Marianne is a fantastic cook, but she doesn't make ice cream and I've got a powerful hankering."

"A powerful hankering, huh?"

"Yes, ma'am. Right powerful." He grinned, and once again, she saw a bit of the little boy he'd been. She had no doubts he'd been a good son, but her woman's intuition told her he had added many gray hairs to his mother's head.

"All right." She pulled away from him and swiped at her face once more, removing the last of her tears. "We'll go into town.

Thomas needs a new pair of shoes anyway, and we can always use more hair ribbons." She rose up on her toes and touched her lips to his, despite who may be looking. "Thank you."

"For what?"

"For just ..." She had no words so she simply shrugged. "Thank you."

Eamon touched the brim of his hat with the side of his finger and gave her a lopsided smile. "My pleasure, ma'am." He lowered his voice to that deep rich timbre that always sent a shiver down her spine. "Why don't you get yourself and the children ready while I talk to Quincy and hitch up the buckboard?"

"Meet you here in fifteen minutes?"

"Better make it twenty."

• • •

She turned away, the hem of her split skirt swirling around her boots, and started walking toward the house. He admired the sway of her hips and couldn't resist the temptation of her perfect backside. With a chuckle, he took a few steps after her, then gave her a love pat on the behind.

"Eamon!" Theo shouted, then dissolved into giggles, as he hoped she would.

He laughed as she picked up her pace and disappeared into the house, then turned toward the stable to grab the rake he'd left leaning against the wall.

"I saw that."

Eamon jumped, startled, as Quincy came around from the side of the building, took the unlit pipe from his mouth, and grinned.

"Nice to know people still take my advice. Except for this"—he moved his hand to encompass the burned façade of the stable— "she seems happy. Happier than I've seen her in a long time. It's good to see."

"I ... It's ..." His face heated as he tried to stammer out a comment, but Quincy wasn't done and held up his hand.

"You're happy, too. I'm glad you finally realized what we all already knew."

"And what was that?"

"That you're worthy of friendship ... and love." He stuck the stem of the pipe between his teeth and clamped down on it as he moved closer. Again, he gestured to the burned wall of the building, effectively closing the subject of Theo's happiness, and much to Eamon's relief, he didn't ask if Theo knew of his past. "Didn't mean to eavesdrop either, but I heard you talking about someone setting this fire deliberately. I agree with you."

Quincy reached into his trouser pocket and pulled out a wadded handkerchief. "Found these." As he unwrapped it, the smell of tobacco rose, different from the fragrant blend both he and Quincy used in their pipes. More half-smoked cigarettes littered the square of white, all were flattened, as if crushed by the sole of a shoe when the smoker was done. "Someone has been here, watching us. Not sure how long or why—or who for that matter—"

"Where did you find these?"

"Found a couple behind the playhouse." He gestured toward the former gypsy wagon. "Found a few more outside your window."

Eamon stiffened as the implication became clear. Sweat began to gather on his forehead beneath the band of his hat. "You mean someone was standing on my front porch, smoking cigarettes, and looking in my window?"

The man shook his head. "Not your porch window, Eamon, the other one. Whoever it is, he isn't stupid. He's staying to the shadows, and I'm thinkin' he's only been here after dark."

More perspiration dampened his back despite the cold chill that moved down his spine. What had the intruder seen? With a sinking feeling deep in his stomach, the answer came to him immediately—the trespasser had witnessed him making love to Theo. That alone made his gut twist. "Why didn't the dog let us know someone was here, watching?"

Quincy shrugged. "Don't rightly know. Happy *is* getting older. You may not realize it, and he certainly doesn't act like it, but he's almost fourteen and probably doesn't hear as well as he used to. And maybe he just got used to people being here. We did have a house full of Theo's guests. Plus, if whoever it was came through the woods and around the back of the playhouse and the barn, he wouldn't be seen from Happy's bed on the porch. Morning Mist is pretty big. A person could sneak on the property and not be seen at all." He tilted his head, then handed over the handkerchief with the cigarettes. "It's probably a good idea to see the sheriff, like you said. If nothing else than to warn him there may be an arsonist in Pearce."

Eamon gently folded the handkerchief and put it in his pocket.

"Come on, I'll help you get the buckboard ready." The older man led the way into the barn. They worked in silence as they hitched up the draft horses. Once all the leather straps were tightened and checked, Eamon headed for his room while the older man drew the buckboard into the barnyard.

"You be careful in Pearce." Quincy spoke around the pipe stem in his mouth when Eamon returned a few minutes later. "I'm sure it's changed a lot since you were there last. And you keep an eye on our girl."

As soon as he said the words, the back door slammed and Gabby, followed by Thomas and Charlotte, raced across the porch. "I call shotgun." For such a little girl, she could certainly move fast, outpacing her companions.

"Here you go, poppet." Quincy lifted Gabby into the back of the buckboard. "No shotgun for you. Now you sit still and hold on tight."

"Okay, Quinthy," she lisped, her speech impaired by the recent loss of the other front tooth. Charlotte and Thomas joined her in the back of the wagon.

The door slammed one more time, and Theo crossed the porch, a small drawstring purse swinging from her wrist. Eamon's pulse picked up, and his heart hammered in his chest. She had changed from her usual uniform of split skirt and white blouse to a dress in soft green with slightly darker green stripes that shimmered as she walked. She'd even done her hair, taking the whiskey-colored tresses down from her customary ponytail and letting the curls cascade over her shoulders instead.

He drank in the sight of her, then shook his head as his gaze drifted down to her feet. She had changed her dress and her hair for their trip to town, but she hadn't changed her old, well-worn boots, which peeked out from the hem of her skirt as she walked.

He leaned against the side of the wagon, just admiring her, his lips stretching into a grin when Granny stuck her head out the door and called after her, "I could use some peppermint sticks."

Theo turned around and walked backward, giving the woman her attention and Eamon an eyeful of that perfect backside. "How many?"

"Whatever Mr. Gentry has in stock."

"Yes, ma'am." She turned again and strode up to the buckboard in the barnyard. Without a word, Eamon took her hand in his and helped her into her seat. He climbed up beside her and gathered the reins in his hands.

"Everyone ready?"

After a chorus of yeses met his ears, he flicked his wrists and clicked his tongue. The horses responded instantly, moving the wagon down the drive like they'd done a thousand times before.

A mix of emotions tumbled through him, like water rushing over boulders in a stream, as he guided the buckboard between the two towering evergreen trees at the end of the drive and turned onto the road that would lead him to Pearce. The prospect of meeting someone he'd known when he'd been a Marshal made him a bit nervous, but not so much that he wanted to turn back. Besides, Theo needed this outing. He was doing it for her more than himself, and that made the difference.

Despite the fire and the decision for Theo's guests to leave earlier than expected, the half-smoked cigarettes, and the fact that someone had been watching them, he still counted his blessings. He had so much to be grateful for. He turned his head and glanced at the children in the bed of the wagon. Their bright smiles, even from Charlotte, warmed him just as much as the sun did. He loved them dearly, and he thought they loved him as well, but the biggest blessing on his list? Theo.

Emotions so strong they couldn't be contained swelled within him, and he had no choice but to release them. He began to sing, his voice as strong as his emotions. Strange, he wasn't embarrassed, not even when Charlotte declared in what he thought was mock horror, "He's doing it again," and Theo turned to study him, her eyes dancing with both curiosity and pleasure.

"Come on, you know the words. I know you do," he encouraged her.

She gave a slight nod, and then her voice, sweet and pure, the perfect counterpart to his baritone, joined with his. The children sang as well, and one song led to another. Before he knew it, they were entering the bustling town of Pearce, Colorado.

The town had changed—nearly doubling in size—since the last time he was here. There were more businesses ... and more people. Eamon maneuvered the buckboard down the main thoroughfare and stopped at the entrance to the lumberyard. He set the brake, then climbed down before running around the wagon to help Theo, though she didn't seem to need it. She was already on the ground, her arms stretched up to help Gabby.

"Why don't you take the children and buy Thomas's shoes while I get the lumber we need. I'll meet you—" He grinned and shrugged. "I have no idea where to meet you." He lowered his voice so the children wouldn't hear. "And I have no idea where the ice cream shop is, either. Quincy said it's at the corner of Elm and Main." He knew Main Street, but there hadn't been an Elm Street when he was here last. At least, he didn't remember it, but then, when he visited here, it was to pick up a prisoner to transport him elsewhere.

"Elm and Main? That isn't far from here at all. In fact, it's just past the town square and the hotel where Quincy delivers our milk and butter." She pointed to the clock tower of a three-story building visible over the rooftops of several businesses that lined Main Street. He did remember the hotel—and the town square— from previous visits, but he'd never stayed there. He had always wanted to. Perhaps he and Theo should honeymoon there.

Startled by the thought, but finding it wholly agreeable, he grinned, amazed by the change in his life. When he rode onto Morning Mist Farms that fateful day, he hadn't planned on Theo Danforth filling the ache in his empty belly or on anything more than working for her for a couple weeks before he took to the lonely road again, and now, not only had he fallen in love with her—and her family—he wanted to marry her. He could imagine them in forty years, surrounded by grandchildren, still breeding and training champion racehorses, still in love, still ...

Nice dream, MacDermott, but does she love you? Would she even consider marrying you? Hell, man, you haven't even told her that you love her. Nor have you said a word about your past. How will she feel when she finds out who and what you were? When she learns about Kieran, Mary—

"Eamon?" Theo touched his arm, drawing his attention, then gestured to a storefront not thirty yards from where they stood. A sign swayed in the breeze, proclaiming the name "Charles Wright,

Fine Shoes" in fancy black letters on a white background. "Mr. Wright's shop is right there. You can meet us at the shop when you're done with the lumber. If we're done before you, we'll come to the lumberyard." She took Gabby's hand in hers. "Have them put the lumber on my account." She started walking down the street toward the shoemaker's shop, Thomas and Charlotte right behind her.

"I'll take care of it, Theo," he called after her, then climbed back into his seat, but he didn't pull the buckboard into the lumberyard. Instead, still reeling from the idea of marriage that had popped into his head and the devil on his shoulder trying to talk him out of it, he kept his focus on her until she let herself and the children into the shoemaker's shop, then flicked the reins and guided the horses into the lumberyard.

He had no intention of putting the lumber on her account as she asked. He hadn't spent any of the salary he'd earned except for a few pouches of tobacco. If he could do this for her after all she'd done for him, he'd be more than glad, though it didn't seem enough. What was a few dollars compared to being able to forgive himself? To look in the mirror and not be ashamed of what he saw? Those things were priceless ... and they were just the beginning. He had a family again, and that was worth more than all the gold and silver mined from the Colorado mountains.

After he conducted his business with the owner of the lumberyard, a very obliging man who was more than happy to accommodate him, Eamon left the buckboard with one of the employees as instructed. By the time he, Theo, and the children finished their ice cream, his order should fill the wagon, and they could be on their way home.

He strode up the street, peering into the windows of the shops he passed. At the cobbler's shop, he watched Theo hand money to the shoemaker. He couldn't hear the words he and Theo exchanged, but he could certainly discern the conversation. Thomas was growing like a weed, almost three inches seemingly overnight, hence the need for new shoes sooner than Theo had expected. His gaze dropped to Thomas's feet, then Charlotte's, and finally, Gabby's. All three sported new footwear. He couldn't see Theo's shoes but assumed she hadn't gotten a new pair for herself. As frugal as she was, she wouldn't spend the money unless it was absolutely necessary.

He leaned against a post that held up the awning in front of the building to wait and watch the passersby. He nodded a few times in response to a greeting thrown his way, touched the brim of his hat in deference to the ladies. No one, not one person, recognized him. What had he thought? That people would look at him and point, proclaiming him a coward for hanging up his guns?

He turned around and focused his gaze on the shops on the other side of the street. A man stood at the big, plate glass window of the building directly across from him, hands on his hips, shirt sleeves rolled up past his elbows, the top of his bald head coming just beneath the words "Edwin Dancy, Editor" painted on the window in black and gold. Above that, also painted in black and gold, the letters bigger and bolder, was The Pearce Intelligencer. He recognized the name, though he hadn't read a newspaper in years. Quincy, however, read every word of the *Intelligencer* and often shared what he read aloud, believing that everyone needed to know what happened in the world beyond Morning Mist.

The bald man he assumed was Edwin Dancy stared at him, then, as if embarrassed to be caught being so rude, he gave a quick nod and moved away from the window. Eamon didn't give it another thought. He turned his attention back to the shoemaker's shop as the bell over the door jingled. Gabby rushed toward him, her grin angelic, even with her two missing front teeth. "Look, Mr. MacDermott, I got new shoes!"

"Very nice, Gabby." He moved away from the post and turned his attention to Charlotte, who hung back just a little. "What about you, Charlie?"

The girl beamed, as he hoped she would. She was still shy around him, but she was getting better, especially when he called her "Charlie." She showed him her shoes, then hid behind her brother.

Theo approached him, and for a moment, there was no one else in the world ... just her. She handed him a burlap sack with the children's old shoes and glanced past him. "You finished sooner than I expected. Where's the wagon?"

"I left it at the lumberyard. Our order should be completed by the time we finish our ice cream." At the mention of ice cream, the children's faces broke into grins of surprise. He moved away from the post and held out his arm. "I thought we could walk." He grinned as his gaze passed over the children's footwear. "Give those new shoes a chance to break in."

Theo slipped her hand into the crook of his elbow. She gestured to the sack in his other hand. "I thought we'd drop those off at the church. They're still in good shape, and I'm sure Pastor Engvall knows someone who could use them."

"Of course."

Chest puffed out with pride, Eamon strode down the raised sidewalk. He had Theo beside him and the children he thought of as his own in front of him. Nothing could dim the happiness coursing through him.

"Get the hell outa my way!" The belligerent tone accompanied a man pushing his way through the batwing doors of the Cattleman's Saloon, stopping Eamon in his tracks.

In an instant, the world disappeared—the people on the sidewalk and in the street, Theo beside him, her hand tucked into the crook of his elbow, the children walking in front of him. Eamon's breath wheezed in his throat, his lungs demanding life-saving air that seemed just out of reach. The bright sunlight of only a moment before faded to the sepia tone of photographs as his eyes took in the hellish visage of Tell Logan. His heart raced even as his blood froze.

He'd never forget that face. Or that voice. How could he? He saw it every day ... in his nightmares and even when his eyes were wide open. That face had emblazoned itself in his memory, along with those of Kieran, Mary, and Matthew. That face belonged to the man who'd shot him and left him for dead on the front porch of Whispering Pines, his brother's ranch, so long ago.

His stomach clenched, and bile rose to the back of his throat as the man sauntered down the raised wooden sidewalk as if he hadn't a care in the world. Without conscious thought, Eamon dropped the burlap sack in his hand and reached for his guns, but they weren't there.

They hadn't been for a long time. Even if they were, there wasn't much he could do, not with all the townspeople crowding the sidewalk, and most definitely not with Theo and the children nearby. He would never put someone in harm's way. Never. Least of all those who had become more important to him than breathing.

"Eamon? Are you all right?" He heard her voice as if through a dense mist. "You look like you've seen a ghost."

He took a gulp of air. "I think I have. We should go."

"But we promised the children ice cream, and we have to drop off the shoes."

Eamon studied her face, then glanced at the children. Anticipation had put smiles on their features. He couldn't deny them this small pleasure, despite the anxiety churning in his gut.

"I'll meet you at the ice cream parlor." He reached down and picked up the sack he'd dropped, then handed it to her. "There's something I need to do."

"But Eamon—"

He didn't let her finish. He brought her hand up to his lips and kissed her knuckles, then repeated, "I'll meet you there."

She gazed into his eyes for what seemed like forever, but in reality, was only a moment or two before she gave a slight nod. "All right, Eamon." She squeezed his hand, then ushered the children across the street. She turned once, her gaze intent, gave another slight nod, and headed toward the town square, Gabby's hand in hers.

Eamon forced himself to breathe as he watched her, his mind in turmoil, every muscle in his body tense and poised to go after the man who had so drastically changed his life. Without his pistols though, he'd be asking for certain death ... and he had too much to live for now to let that happen, but that didn't stop him from following the man.

Chapter 15

With the children finally settled in bed, Theo wandered downstairs, intent on brewing a cup of Granny's special tea. It might just take the hurt away from her head. She didn't hold out much hope that it would do anything for her heart.

Something happened today—something bad—but she couldn't exactly say what it was, except that Eamon had changed. And she didn't know why, nor could she explain it to the children, though they'd peppered her with questions. He'd gone from smiling and laughing to shutting her out—shutting them all out—in a split second, all the excitement from their excursion gone in the blink of an eye.

He arrived at the ice cream parlor long after they'd finished their treat, his features taut, his dark mustache standing out in stark relief against the paleness of his perspiring face, but it was what she'd seen in his eyes that frightened her the most, and the ride back to the farm was made in eerie silence. Eamon wouldn't look at her or the children, and the expression on his face did not invite questions. Nothing had changed by the time they'd arrived home, and as soon as he took care of the horses and the lumber, he shut himself in his room. The summons to dinner had come and gone, the nightly chores completed without his help.

Quincy was waiting for her when she entered the kitchen, a bottle of brandy and two glasses on the table. She didn't want to talk, but it didn't look like she had much choice. At least, it was just Quincy and not Marianne. Or Granny. She didn't know if she could handle the expressions on their faces, though she had suffered through their kindness and concern all through dinner as they had seen the change in Eamon immediately. He hadn't been rude, he'd just ... closed in on himself, becoming sullen and so utterly sad.

"You know I love you like my daughter, right?" Quincy asked as he pulled out a chair for her, his voice so gentle and concerned, it brought a lump to her throat. She nodded as she took her seat.

"And you know I've grown quite fond of the big guy outside, right?" Again, she nodded, unable to speak. He poured a glass of the brandy and handed it to her, then asked, rather bluntly, "What happened in town today?"

Theo took a sip, letting the warmth of the liquor ease some of the tightness in her throat. "I don't know. Everything was fine one minute, and the next, it was ... different."

"What were you doing when it became 'different'?" Quincy pulled out the chair beside her, then poured his own glass of brandy.

She shrugged and tried to put the pieces together so she could explain, but how could she when there was no explanation? "We were walking to that new ice cream shop you told him about. He was happy, laughing at something Charlotte said, when someone came out of the Cattleman's Saloon—a man—and almost slammed into him. When I looked at Eamon, he'd gone completely white, like he had no blood left in his body. If I didn't know any better, I would swear he saw a ghost. I even made that comment, but he didn't laugh. He didn't even smile."

She took a deep breath and studied the brandy in her glass, the amber brew reflecting the light from the candle on the table. "I saw something in his eyes, Quincy, something I never want to see again."

"What did you see?" Still the same gentle voice, but this time, edged with apprehension.

Tears pricked her eyes, and she blinked as she looked into her trusted friend's concerned face. "Fear. I saw fear ... and hopelessness. Despair. It ... I ..." She couldn't finish as her throat closed over the words.

He gave a slight nod, then grasped his glass and swallowed the contents in one gulp. He opened his mouth, then closed it again and poured himself another, downing that one as well before he said, "You should talk to him."

"I know. I just ... don't know what to say. What if he continues to shut me out? What if he won't talk to me?"

The older man studied her, his gaze intent on her face. "Just be patient with him. He has something to tell you—something hard—but something you should know considering how you feel about him. And how he feels about you."

His words were cryptic, and she stared at him, her mind working furiously. The expression in his eyes, which weren't twinkling as they usually did, told her he may know what happened earlier today, even though he hadn't been there, but whatever it was, he didn't feel he could share it with her. "You're scaring me."

"I don't mean to."

"Can't you tell me?"

He sighed deeply, then reached for the brandy bottle one more time. He poured the liquor into the glass and took a sip this time. "It's not my place. It has to come from him."

Despite her fear, Theo reached deep inside herself and took hold of her courage. She stood, though her knees were quaking. "You're a good man, Quincy Burke, and a good friend. To both of us." She squeezed his shoulder gently, grabbed the bottle of brandy and her glass, and then let herself out of the house, closing the door softly behind her.

The stars were out, the moon full and casting a bright light as she made her way across the barnyard to Eamon's room, her heart pounding, her body trembling, as afraid and unsure as the first time she'd gone to his room.

•••

Eamon paced, going from one end of his small room to the other, his boot heels loud on the wood floor, then muffled when he trod over the small throw rug between the bed and the chair. Night had descended long ago, though it couldn't match the darkness in his heart. The small lantern he'd lit earlier couldn't chase away the gloom either or the thoughts in his mind.

He'd followed Logan as far as the edge of town, his scar throbbing with each fall of his foot, only to lose him when he mounted his horse and rode north. To where? A hideout in the hills, a place where he laid low? Eamon had racked his brain, trying to remember what lay north of Pearce, and could only recall several homesteads and a few small ranches, none of which would willingly hire an outlaw.

Another thought clamored into his head, one that made his stomach twist with guilt and rage. Was it Logan who had been watching them and set fire to the stable? He shook his head, disregarding the idea as quickly as it came to him. Arson had never been Logan's way of killing—he'd rather just shoot someone and be done with it—but it did raise more questions, adding to the turmoil already in his mind. Did Logan even know he was here? He hadn't been off the farm until today. He supposed it was possible Quincy or one of the children might have mentioned him to someone in town, but who would talk to Logan? And why would Logan be after him? The outlaw thought he was dead. Unless ...

Could Logan have been hired to chase Theo away from Morning Mist? Both Theo and Quincy said Pearce had made several offers, even sending his fancy New York lawyers—as well as his son, AJ—to try to convince Theo to sell, but would he sink so low as to join forces with a known criminal to ... what? Intimidate her into giving Pearce what he wanted? Kill her? Quincy said one never knew what Aldrich Pearce would want nor to what lengths he would go in order to get it. Was he capable of murder? Perhaps not, but he wasn't above hiring someone else to do his dirty work.

Eamon had no answers to the barrage of questions in his brain, which only served to make him more agitated. He forced air into his lungs and sat on the edge of the bed, but shot to his feet and started pacing again in moments, unable to sit still. If he kept on like this, he'd wear a path in the hardwood floor ... or make his heart stop. It already hurt, pounding against his ribcage like it longed to be free of his body. He laid his hand over the place where Logan's bullet nearly took his life and pressed—hard—hoping to stop the familiar ache from spreading and stealing his breath, hoping to find the courage to do what he needed to do, but afraid that taking Logan's life would irreparably change his own.

Theo.

How could he tell her of his intentions? How could he tell her he'd be gone by the time the sun rose in the morning to search for the man who nearly killed him? Perhaps Logan would finish what he started this time, and when the bullet hit him, he'd draw his last breath.

He forced the thought from his mind. He'd have to make sure that wouldn't happen. He had too much to live for now.

But even as the knowledge and fear ripped through his mind, he stopped in front of the armoire and reached into the bottom to pull out the burlap wrapped package. He held the parcel reverently in his hand, then sat in the chair next to the small Ben Franklin stove. Slipping the knot in the leather tie holding the package closed, he unveiled the tools of the trade he'd given up—his guns.

A sigh escaped him as he removed one of the pistols from its holster and tested the weight in his hand. Strange, the gun didn't feel odd or heavy. It felt right. Comfortable. The pearl handle gleamed in the light of the lantern.

A knock sounded on his door, followed by Theo's husky voice. "Eamon?"

He rose from his chair, slipped the pistol back in the holster, and slid everything beneath the pillow on his bed before striding across the room. He took a couple deep breaths, then, struggling to keep anger and fear from showing on his face, opened the door, but not enough so she could come in.

Theo didn't push her way into his sanctuary. She stood on the little porch and stared at him. She said not a word, but she made it clear with her expression that she was coming inside whether he wanted her to or not.

After a moment, Eamon opened the door wider. She stepped past him, shoved the brandy bottle into his hand, and sat on the bed where they'd made love the night before, her hand coming perilously close to the guns beneath the pillow. She studied him, her gaze roaming over his face. He saw no anger, only her concern for him ... and her curiosity. He'd been so careful about not revealing his past ... or why he ran from it, but he couldn't do that anymore.

"What happened today, Eamon?"

Eamon opened his mouth, but no words would come forth. Perhaps they'd been locked in his chest for so long, he couldn't speak of it.

"Please tell me."

"Tell Logan," he finally uttered, his throat so tight he could barely get the name out.

"Who's Logan? Tell him what?" She shook her head. "I'm sorry. I don't know what you're talking about." She patted the bed, inviting him to sit. "Start at the beginning. Help me to understand what happened that made you change from happy to ... to afraid in seconds."

The request tumbled from her lips, the expression on her face almost his undoing. He should never have stayed here. Hell, he should never have fallen in love with her. He placed the brandy on the little table near the stove and started pacing again, unable to remain still, hardly knowing how to begin ... or even where to begin.

He studied her and saw the wariness in her eyes, the tightening of the skin around her mouth. Hurting her had never been his intention, but he was doing that now with his silence. Quincy was right. She deserved to know, no matter how afraid he was to tell her. "I ..." He cleared his throat and tried again. "I was a U.S. Marshal. I was good at it, but then, I'd been taught from an early age about the law and enforcing it. My father was a lawman. So were two of my brothers."

"What happened, Eamon? You aren't a Marshal now. I don't think you have been for a while."

He shook his head. "I walked away from that life. Gave it up."

"Why?"

"Because I killed them." If his statement upset her, she tried not to show it, but he knew her too well now. He could see the slight change in the color of her eyes, hear the subtle indrawn breath.

"Killed who?"

"My brother." He swallowed over the constriction in his throat and continued, "His wife. Their son, Matthew."

"I don't believe that, Eamon," she cut him off. "I don't believe you killed anyone, least of all your family. You're a good man. I see it in how you treat the children and the animals. I see it in how solicitous you are of Granny. What's more, I know this here." She laid her hand over her heart.

"I may not have pulled the trigger," he shook his head, and for a moment, her image blurred as his eyes misted with tears, "but it's my fault they're dead just the same."

She didn't say a word, didn't refute his statement, but simply looked at him. There was no condemnation on her face, only kindness and love, but it was the soft glow in her eyes that finally convinced him he could reveal everything. He grabbed the brandy and filled her glass, then poured one for himself. He took a swallow and allowed the warmth of the liquid to help loosen his tongue. Then, glass in hand, he resumed pacing.

"We had a good life growing up, even though we moved around a lot. Da was a lawman, but never liked to stay in one place for very long. Mam and us kids followed him from place to place, town to town, until we settled for good in Colorado. Da loved it here. So did Mam."

He glanced at her. She sat in the same position, but her body wasn't nearly as stiff. She sipped at the amber liquid, raising the glass to her lips, but she never took her eyes off him. Encouraged, he continued, "My oldest brother hated moving around so much. He swore he'd never move again once he 'growed' up, and he didn't. He married Mary Campbell, a lovely young widow with a son and a ranch on the verge of bankruptcy. He put down roots, and he was happy—loved Mary, loved her son and their daughter, loved working the ranch together. It was a hard life, but a good one. They were beginning to make a profit, breeding racehorses, like you do. I was so proud of them and happy they'd found each other."

He stopped pacing, slumped into the chair opposite her, and picked up the pipe resting in a glass dish on the table. He gestured with it. "My father's pipe. Mam gave one to each of us boys after Da passed away." He studied the fine wood grain of the pipe's bowl, assailed with memories of life before the Logans changed everything. The scar on his chest throbbed, and he put the pipe back in the dish. "Teague became deputy, then took over as sheriff after Da died. Brock was already keeping the peace in Colorado Springs by that time, and I was a U.S. Marshal, traveling from place to place. We managed to see each other as often as possible, even more so after Mam passed away a few months after Da."

He scrubbed his hand over his face, weary deep down in his bones, still afraid to tell her everything, but knowing he must, whether he wanted to or not. Knowing and doing were two different things, but if he wanted any kind of future with Theo—and he did—he had to try, no matter how much it hurt. "It all changed so fast, I ..." He swallowed the rest of his words along with his brandy, then poured them both more, leaning across the space between the bed and his chair.

"What happened?"

"The Logan Gang."

She gasped but, otherwise, did not interrupt.

"They tried to steal Kieran's horses. The older members of the gang had gotten away—along with several valuable horses—but the youngest member, Jefferson, hadn't been so lucky. Kieran caught him and dragged him to town. Teague locked him up." He took another drink, then placed his glass on the table.

"I wasn't there at that point—I was in Canon City with a prisoner, but my understanding from Teague was that the moment Jefferson was put in the jail cell, he started promising—threatening really—that his brothers would spring him, no matter what it took. We all knew about the Logan Gang, knew what they were capable of, had seen the destruction and devastation they could leave in their wake, so Teague took the threat seriously. How could he not? He telegraphed Brock and me."

He stood and strode to the window, resting his hands on the sill as his gaze took in the stable and Granny's garden in the moon's glow. "Traveler and I left Canon City immediately, and I admit, I nearly killed my horse, forcing him to run too hard for too long—"

His words ran dry, but the pain in his heart remained. He'd always heard that confession was good for the soul, but it certainly wasn't helping him. His heart hurt just as much as it always did. The scar left from Logan's bullet throbbed with each beat as he confessed to the event that started his lonely journey, until he found Morning Mist Farms—and her. "I was late anyway, Theo. I was supposed to help Brock move Kieran and his family to a safe place, but Traveler picked up a rock in his shoe and I lost valuable time removing it. When I finally arrived at Whispering Pines, I thought everything was all right ... but I was wrong."

He licked his dry lips. "I heard the back door banging against the house—at least, that's what I thought it was at the time—but it wasn't. The sound I'd heard was the shots that killed Kieran, Mary, and Matthew. The only ones who had survived the shooting were Brock and Desi Lyn, Kieran's young daughter, and Brock almost didn't make it. I couldn't save them." He drew a deep breath, unable to help the shiver that raced up his spine. "Hell, I couldn't even save myself. Tell Logan shot me on the front porch. Stood not twenty feet away and pulled the trigger. And he smiled as he did it. Teague found us later."

There was more, so much more to tell her. He swallowed, and forged on despite his pain ... and hers, for surely that would come. "He'd come to the ranch after the Logans shot up the town in their attempt to free Jefferson. So many dead, including most of the Logans. So many wounded. Too much heartbreak." He took a breath and finally admitted his deepest secret. "I ... I could have stopped it before it even happened, Theo. I could have chased down and caught the Logans when I had the chance several weeks before ... before they rode into town, before they shot up everything and everyone, but it wasn't possible at the time. I already had three prisoners I was bringing to Canon City ..."

He stopped, unable to continue without looking into her beautiful eyes, even though he was afraid of what he might see. Fear. Revulsion.

He didn't see any of those things when he turned around. Instead, her eyes were wide in her pale face, bright with the tears that filled them, her lashes spiky from those that had already fallen down her cheeks. Her body trembled so violently, he thought she would break apart. The brandy glass slipped from her hand but didn't break as it dropped to the thick rug on the floor. He rushed to her side and pressed the palm of his hand to her cheek.

She moved, purposefully dislodging his hand from her face, but her gaze continued to bore into him.

"Theo? Are you—?"

"Kieran MacDermott was your brother?" She interrupted him before he had a chance to finish asking his question, her voice so tight and filled with anguish, he winced, feeling her pain as keenly as he felt his own. He wanted to touch her, hold her, give comfort as all the truths settled in her mind, but she wouldn't have allowed that ... and he knew it.

"Yes."

"The little town where all this happened was Paradise Falls, wasn't it?"

"Yes. Almost three years ago now."

She drew in her breath sharply, a gasp of horror that changed to a cry of utter pain as she jumped to her feet and ran from his room. From him. As he had feared, but he couldn't let her go.

Theo made it past the water pump and nearly to the gypsy wagon turned playhouse before she stopped and dropped to the ground. She held herself, arms folded across her stomach, as if in physical pain and rocked. She didn't cry, didn't wail to the heavens over her loss, although he wouldn't have blamed her if she had. He came up behind her, sank to his knees, and wrapped his arms around her. Or tried to. She pushed him away and held herself tighter.

His heart thundered in his chest at her rejection. "Theo? Talk to me."

She gulped air, then wiped her face with the back of her hand, and turned to face him. "I was there. We were there. In Paradise Falls. That's where ..." She inhaled deeply and swallowed, her throat moving. The pain in her eyes and on her face was almost his undoing. His heart hurt, the pain worse than anything he'd ever experienced. Even getting shot didn't compare to what he felt now.

He tried once more to wrap his arms around her, afraid she'd run from him again, but she didn't want him. He let her push him away. Defeated and utterly ashamed, he rose to his feet and just stood there, waiting for what she would do next, not knowing what to say or do to ease her pain.

"That's where I lost Henry. A shootout in the streets of that quiet little town. Henry and I were leaving the hotel when the shooting started. We had just bought Daphne from Whispering Pines, from Kieran, and were making arrangements to come home." Her eyes wide and shiny with tears, her voice barely above a whisper, her gaze searched his face. "But you knew that, didn't you?" Her breath hitched as she swiped the tears from her eyes, her cheeks. "You've known all along who I was and what happened to Henry."

Eamon shook his head. "I swear to you, I didn't know who you were when I first came here. How could I?" He hung his head. He'd known telling her would be hard, would probably break his heart, but he hadn't expected the pain would be this devastating. "I ... I realized later. Something Quincy said struck a memory for me, but I ... I couldn't tell you. I was a coward. I thought about leaving so many times. I could have been gone and you'd never know, but I ... I fell in love with you, Theo." Her eyes widened at that, but she didn't interrupt. "And this place. The children ..." He swallowed over the lump in his throat and blinked back the tears blurring his vision.

"I couldn't leave, couldn't force myself to walk away like I'd done so many times before. You helped me—you all did—made me see that despite what happened, I was still a good man, I still had value. I was worthy." He took a breath and searched her face, looking for forgiveness and for what he saw in her eyes when they made love. "Don't hate me. Please." His voice cracked, the constriction in his throat so tight, he could hardly speak. "I don't think I could bear it."

She studied him, her gaze intent, the moon's glow clearly showing her indecision—and pain—as those emotions played over her features. She was hurt—so very hurt. He'd known she would be, which was why he couldn't tell her of his past and the part that he had played in hers, however inadvertently. "Am I still worthy, Theo? Can you forgive me?" He held out his hand, palm up, his breath stuck in his lungs, his heart pounding much too fast.

If she didn't take his hand, he'd know.

It only took a moment before she placed her hand in his, but in his heart and mind, that moment seemed to take forever.

"There is nothing to forgive, Eamon. I understand why you didn't tell me. It hurt too much for both of us. I don't blame you for what happened."

Her voice, normally hoarse and throaty, was crystal clear, and the relief washing through him nearly brought him to his knees. How he remained standing became a mystery.

"And I could never hate you. I love you too much to hate you."

She loves me. She forgives me. He helped her stand so he could pull her into his arms. She came willingly and wrapped her arms around him, squeezing tight. The scent of roses wafted from her hair, filling him with a sense of peace, despite the knowledge that come morning, he'd be gone. Despite the fact he loved her and she returned the feeling—perhaps because of it—he would never be able to live his life in peace while Tell Logan still breathed. And he would never be able to hunt for the man who'd almost killed him if Theo hadn't forgiven him.

Theo pulled away from him but remained in his embrace. She studied his face, then tilted her head. "There's more, isn't there? More you want to tell me. I'm not sure I'm strong enough to hear it." She gave a shaky, nervous laugh just before her knees buckled.

He lifted her in his arms and carried her back to his room where he laid her on his bed, then picked up the glass from the floor. He turned away, grabbed the bottle of brandy from the small table, and poured the amber liquid, filling just the very bottom of her glass, then thought better of it and added another dollop. She'd need it for what he needed to tell her now.

"What is this?"

The strident tone in her voice startled him, and he ended up pouring more of the liquor into the glass than he intended. He took a deep breath, put the bottle down, and turned to see Theo sitting up, the pillow on her lap, his gun belt in her hand, and her face—dear Lord!—her face was so pale, even her lips. He struggled to ignore the sinking feeling in his stomach. He had wanted to explain to her why he needed to go after Logan in his own way, in his own time, but his time had run out. "You're going after him, aren't you?"

Eamon tried to give her the liquor, but she wouldn't take it. He set it down on the little table, let out his breath in a long sigh, and took his gun belt from her hands. "Yes. I'm going after him."

"Why you, Eamon?" She shot up from the bed, her movements quick and agitated. "Let the law handle it. Report what you've seen and what you've heard to the sheriff, and let him arrest this Logan person."

"I've already been to the sheriff, Theo, while you and the children had ice cream. He's not going to do a thing about it. He told me as much."

"Eamon, you can't ..."

He studied her, his gaze roaming over her face. Anxiety and fear made her eyes darker. Her voice trembled, as did her entire being. Despite what he saw and how it broke his heart, he simply shook his head. "I have to do this. That man ... that man left me for dead. That man is responsible for killing innocent people. That man, I believe, is the one who set your stable on fire." He grabbed her, then drew her close even though she stiffened in his arms. "I'm doing this for you. For us."

She pulled away from him as fresh tears filled her eyes. "You're not doing this for me. It's for you. So you can have your revenge."

"It's not revenge, Theo. It's justice."

"The hell it is!" She yanked herself out of his arms and stumbled across the room, once again running from him. This time, he had to let her go. She gulped air as she opened the door and stood on the threshold. "He'll kill you, Eamon. His brothers took my Henry from me, and he'll take you, too."

"I'm sorry, Theo."

"I love you, damn it, and I want to build a life with you, but if you do this—if you leave to search for him—don't come back." She closed the door softly behind her. It took every ounce of willpower he possessed to not chase after her again. He closed his eyes and silently counted to ten, then ten again. Finally, he strapped his gun belt around his hips, the weight familiar, like an old friend. He fitted his hat to his head, grabbed his bedroll and the saddlebags he'd packed earlier, and took one last look around. Spotting his pipe, he swiped it from the tabletop and slipped it into his shirt pocket. His gaze drifted to the bed. Memories assailed him, and he forced himself to turn away. He blew out the lantern, leaving the room in darkness—like his heart.

Theo was nowhere in sight as he made his way into the barn and lit a lantern. Traveler nickered at him as he pulled his worn leather saddle from the shelf where it had been since he rode onto the farm. "Are you ready to ride, my friend?" The horse tossed his head and shuffled around his stall, seemingly anxious to run as Eamon placed a blanket, then a saddle on his back and tightened the cinches.

He led Traveler past the barn's big, open entrance, went back inside to blow out the lantern and close the door, and then climbed into the saddle and gently nudged the horse into a walk. He did not look back—his resolve would have faltered if he did—as he guided Traveler down the drive and turned onto the road that would bring him to Pearce ... and the possibility he would meet his Maker sooner rather than later.

Chapter 16

He was gone.

Theo had stood by the window in her bedroom last night and watched Eamon ride away. He never turned around, never looked back. And she hadn't moved since, standing like a statue in this one spot, her gaze focused on the drive where it turned onto the road to Pearce. The last image she had of him was his broad back and the moonlight reflecting off the silver band on his hat.

Regret filled her while a litany of recriminations abounded in her mind. She shouldn't have walked out on him. She shouldn't have let him go. She certainly shouldn't have told him not to come back, but she had hoped by doing so, she'd make him realize what he would lose if he left. It hadn't—which hurt her even more. And made her angry. It was one thing to keep his past a secret, especially when it involved her, no matter how indirectly. She could forgive him for that—and had—but it was another thing entirely to purposefully put himself in harm's way. Seeking out Tell Logan bordered on insanity.

He'd get himself killed ... leaving her once again to mourn a man she loved.

It had taken every ounce of willpower she possessed not to ride out after him and make him stop this madness. It wouldn't have done her any good if she had. He was determined to see this through, and nothing she said or did would change his mind. After all this time, she knew him well enough to know that.

Theo wiped her eyes for the hundredth time and forced herself to breathe. She'd cried all night. From the moment she closed the door to Eamon's room and moved across the barnyard like a ghost, she hadn't stopped crying, her heart broken in so many pieces. She hadn't slept either, and her eyes were gritty and swollen. Her chest and throat hurt from sobbing, and her head pounded in unison with her heart.

She had to pull herself together. Gabby and Charlotte would be here any minute so she could brush their hair. They'd know instantly she'd been crying. And they'd want to know why. There would be the inevitable questions—questions she didn't want to answer. This wouldn't be the first time she'd have to tell the children one of the farm hands had left, but this was different.

This was Eamon. He hadn't been just a farm hand. He'd been a friend, someone they cared about.

The girls had grown close to him, as had everyone else. She drew in her breath. At least, she wouldn't have to tell *everyone* he was gone. Quincy, Lou, and Wynn would already know as he wouldn't be there to help with the morning milking. They, most likely, would tell Marianne and Granny, but she'd still have to tell Thomas. The knowledge sat in her stomach like a rock. The boy would be just as devastated as the girls, which made her heart hurt more.

She turned to her bed, the idea forming in her head that she could take refuge on the soft mattress and never move from it again, but she couldn't crawl under the blankets and hide ... as much as she wanted to. She had responsibilities—a farm to run, horses to take care of, children to raise. She hadn't curled up on the bed and let the world pass by when Henry died—for the same reasons—and she had mourned his passing as she worked.

This was a different kind of mourning though. Eamon wasn't dead ... but he might end up that way.

Taking another deep breath, she forced herself away from the window and moved across the room toward her bureau and the washbasin. She splashed the cold liquid on her face, then dipped the washcloth into the water, and pressed it against her eyes. The coolness felt good on her hot skin, but only lasted as long as she held the washcloth in place. She dipped the cloth in the water again, then pulled the chair away from the vanity and sat. The reflection in the mirror stared back at her. The cold water hadn't helped. Her eyes were still swollen.

She heard the thump, thump, thump of stocking-clad feet racing down the hall, accompanied by little girl giggles and quickly pinched her cheeks to add some color. She turned away from her image as Charlotte and Gabby skidded to a halt at her doorway. In an instant, giggles stopped and smiles faded, and Theo found herself on the receiving end of the most unflinching scrutiny.

"What's wrong, Mama Theo?" Gabby asked immediately ... as Theo had known she would. Out of the three children, Gabby was the most perceptive ... and the most inquisitive. Charlotte tended to let others take the lead, hiding behind her innate shyness, and Thomas, embarrassed by his stutter, which sometimes made speaking a difficult experience for him, was inclined to remain quiet, but Gabby? If she had a question, she asked it. If she was happy, everyone in the world knew it, just as they all knew when she was sad. The girl didn't hide her emotions or her curiosity. They were there on her face and in her eyes ... as they were right now.

"Will you go get your brother, Charlotte? I'd like to talk to all of you."

Charlotte gave a quick nod, then raced off. Gabby remained in the doorway and didn't move except for twisting her fingers together, but her gaze remained intent, so much so that Theo had to close her eyes for a moment to gather her strength. It didn't help. Even with her eyes closed, she still felt the intensity of Gabby's stare. She opened her eyes and tried to smile.

"Come in, Gabby. Please."

The little girl hesitated, then slowly moved from the doorway. She said nothing as she crossed the room, climbed on the bed, and sat with her legs dangling over the side, her head tilted slightly. She didn't even blink.

Thomas and Charlotte arrived a moment later. They hovered in the doorway for a moment or two, then shuffled to the bed like men walking to the hangman's noose and climbed onto the mattress beside Gabby, their faces reflecting their confusion. They might not have been as perceptive as Gabby, but they certainly knew when something wasn't right. Their morning routine had been broken, which only happened on very rare occasions, usually when someone was ill or Granny's arthritis hurt more than usual.

Theo sat in the vanity chair and faced the children lined up on her bed. The expressions on their faces made her draw in her breath. There really was no easy way to tell them, no magic words that wouldn't make the news hurt less. Keeping her tone as neutral as possible, she said, "Mr. MacDermott has gone away."

"Like Mama and Papa went away? And Papa Henry?" Charlotte's eyes filled with tears instantly, and she reached for Thomas. He put his arm around her shoulder.

"No, Charlotte, not like that at all." She inhaled, struggling to keep her emotions in check, but it was so damned hard. She had had to tell both Charlotte and Thomas when their parents had died from diphtheria. The children had been here when she'd come home from Paradise Falls without Henry, and she'd had to tell them that Henry had died and gone to heaven like their parents. It had been difficult then, but somehow, this seemed more so. Angela and Thomas White Senior hadn't wanted to die of a dreadful illness, and Henry hadn't wanted to be killed by a bullet from an outlaw's gun. Dying hadn't been their choice, but Eamon? He had a choice, whether he chose to believe it or not. "Mr. MacDermott just couldn't stay here anymore."

"But why? Doesn't he like us?"

"Of course he likes us, rosebud." She couldn't tell these sweet children the truth or make him any less in their eyes. She also didn't want to worry them. Telling them their friend was searching for an outlaw to kill him—and might end up dead himself—was not something one did to a child. No, it was best to keep the explanation as simple as possible. "How could he not? He just had to go. Sometimes that happens."

"Will he c-c-come back?"

Theo shook her head and swallowed hard against the constriction her throat. "No, Thomas, I'm afraid not."

The boy gave a solemn nod, accepting the circumstances and her explanation, though he certainly didn't like it. Unshed tears made his eyes shiny, but he didn't cry. He slid off the bed. "I'm gonna help Quincy with the m-m-milking. Come on, Charlotte." He held out his hand, and Charlotte climbed down from the bed and took it.

Gabby remained behind after they left the room, then jumped off the bed, her sock-clad feet making a soft thump on the floor. She reached up, and Theo thought she'd be getting a hug from the little girl, but instead, Gabby put her hands on each side of her face and looked deeply into her eyes. After a moment, she touched her forehead to Theo's, then pulled back, never taking her hands from their position. "Don't worry, Mama Theo. Mr. MacDermott will be okay." She dropped her hands to her sides, then shoved them into the pockets of her trousers and rocked back on her heels. "And he'll come back as soon as he takes care of business."

Theo drew back, a little surprised by Gabby's choice of words, and the fact that she seemed to know something she hadn't been told.

"How do you know?"

The girl grinned like she had a secret, one that she couldn't wait to share. Her eyes fairly glowed, and her chest puffed out. "His guardian angel told me."

"Eamon has a guardian angel?"

The girl nodded with enthusiasm. "Yes, ma'am. I've seen him, but I don't think Charlotte or Tommy have. I don't think Mr.

MacDermott sees him, either. He was leaning against the corral fence one time when Mr. MacDermott was brushing Daphne. He smiled at me."

"What does this guardian angel look like?"

"He's tall, like Mr. MacDermott, but he isn't dark like him. His hair is light, like Charlotte's, and he brushes it back from his forehead." She demonstrated, pushing her hair off her forehead and smoothing it back against her head. "I think he had stuff in it to make it stay there 'cause his hair didn't move when he took off his hat. Oh, and he had nice eyes. They were all crinkly when he smiled."

Theo's jaw dropped open as Gabby described Henry Danforth to a T, though she'd never met him. She had seen the photograph of him in the office though, many times. Yes, that was it. She saw the photograph, and somehow, in her imagination, the man in the photograph became Eamon's guardian angel.

"I don't think his angel will let anything happen to him," she said and skipped from the room, not the least bit worried or upset that Eamon had gone. Theo wished she could say the same for herself, and though she didn't believe in guardian angels like Gabby did, she still bowed her head and prayed for Eamon's safety.

* * *

Eamon dismounted in front of the Cattleman's Saloon and flipped Traveler's reins around the post, then took the stairs to the raised porch two at a time. He sauntered through the batwing doors and took a look around. The room was empty except for a man who made busy work of wiping tables and straightening chairs—such a different sight than when he'd been here last night. The place had been bustling then, the bartender sliding mugs of beer and whiskey down the long mahogany bar to his waiting patrons. The tables had been filled with men intent on poker or faro or other games of chance, but Logan hadn't been there. He hadn't been in the next saloon Eamon walked into or the next, but he would find him. Or better yet, make Logan find *him*.

That was the idea he'd come up with after his fruitless search the night before. Exhausted and heartsore, he hadn't gotten a hotel room. Instead, he'd made a small camp outside of town and slept under the stars. Or tried to sleep, but every time he closed his eyes, he saw Theo's face. Even with his eyes open, he saw her face and the hurt he had put there. She hadn't understood his need to find Logan ... and kill him. She probably never would. Theo Danforth was all about love and kindness ... there was no room in her heart for revenge, even after what had happened to Henry.

He shook himself, firmly placing himself in the here and now. He'd have plenty of time later to regret walking out on Theo and giving up the best thing that had ever happened to him ... if he lived.

"We ain't open," the man said as he glanced in Eamon's direction, then went back to his task. He wasn't the bartender from last night. Perhaps he was the owner or maybe just the person who cleaned up after everyone else.

"I'm looking for Tell Logan."

The man stopped wiping the table and straightened. He let his gaze wander around the empty room, then looked at Eamon like he was the stupidest man on earth. "Well, he ain't here, an' I got work to do." He pointed to the batwing doors with the rag in his hand. "That door swings both ways. Why doncha look somewhere else?"

Eamon didn't let the expression on the man's face or his rudeness bother him. He'd been on the receiving end of that particular look more than once, and he wasn't about to leave just yet either. "I have a message for him the next time you see him."

"I ain't no messenger service, mister." He went back to wiping the table. After a moment, he stopped, both hands as well as the rag on the table, sighed deeply, and gave his full attention to Eamon. "You ain't goin' away, are ya?"

Eamon shook his head.

The man sighed again, then straightened and put his hands on his hips. "Ah, hell, what is it? If I see 'im, I'll tell 'im."

"Let Tell Logan know that Eamon MacDermott is looking for him."

...

Aldrich Pearce sat back in his chair, put his feet up on his desk, and blew smoke rings at the ceiling. He grinned as those smoke rings dissipated. In fact, he'd been smiling all day and just barely resisted the urge to rub his hands together with glee. From the moment he'd heard Eamon MacDermott walked into the Cattleman and left a message for Tell Logan, then proceeded to visit every saloon and brothel after that, his day had brightened. He couldn't have manipulated a better plan.

What better way to get rid of a lazy, too big for his britches outlaw he was tired of paying and the former Marshal who stood in the way of what he wanted? Pit them against each other in a shootout that pretty much assured him neither would remain standing. Now all he had to do was push Logan to meet the man and accomplish the deed. So far, he'd been stubborn about it and Aldrich was getting tired of waiting.

"What are you so happy about?" AJ sauntered into the study and strode directly to the bar to pour himself a whiskey. He glanced at the nearly empty glass on the desk, then brought the bottle and poured more of the dark liquid into it, left the bottle on the desk, and lowered himself into a deeply cushioned chair. He crossed his legs, adjusted the sharp crease in his trousers, and then took a sip of the fine whiskey.

Aldrich studied his son and noticed immediately that he hadn't slurred his words. The second, third, and fourth things he noticed in quick succession were that AJ's hands weren't shaking, he was freshly groomed, and he was immaculately dressed in the new suit that had just arrived from New York. In fact, he appeared downright sober, a sharp contrast to how he'd been ever since Theo had made it clear she wasn't interested in him ... and never would be. Even so, AJ had held out hope she would come around, but that hadn't happened either, much to AJ's chagrin and Aldrich's delight. Indeed, he had taken great pleasure in letting his son know Theo and her hired hand were lovers, dashing any dreams the young man may have had, but none of his own.

The information hadn't bothered Aldrich at all, neither the hearing of it nor the telling. Actually, knowing that Theo had taken MacDermott as her lover fell right into his plans, especially since MacDermott was the former U.S. Marshal who just happened to have a personal history with the outlaw in his employ. Manipulation worked best when emotions came into play.

"Have you heard?"

"Heard what?"

Aldrich smiled and sat up straight, his stomach full of butterflies caused by his excitement over the turn of events. "MacDermott has been leaving messages all over town. He's looking for Logan. I think he's determined to finish what Logan started years ago."

"And that makes you happy?"

"Of course. I have no doubt they'll kill each other, which takes care of two of my problems with one fell swoop."

AJ stiffened in his chair, but didn't say a word, not quite the response Aldrich had hoped. He decided to let it go. "Do you know where he is?"

"Who?"

"Logan, of course."

AJ shook his head. "Haven't seen him. And I don't want to see him. Nor will I go looking for him. I have plans for this evening." He took a sip of whiskey, then licked his lips. "I actually have plans for the rest of my life, Father. In fact, this will be the last drink we ever share."

"Last drink? Plans? What the hell are you talking about?"

"You see, I've learned a few things over the past couple months. I've watched you and how you treat people, and I've come to the conclusion that you're simply a bully. Oh, not in the truest definition of the word, Father, because you don't actually badger and intimidate people yourself, except for me and maybe one or two others. You let others do that for you. Outlaws and hired guns and lawyers who are as ruthless and manipulative as you are. They all carry out your orders while you stay behind the scenes and direct them like we're in some kind of play." He very carefully put his drink on the table beside him and pushed it farther away. "This isn't a play and the people ... never mind. Let's just say I can no longer stomach the sight of you. I'm leaving and I'm not coming back."

Aldrich let the insult flow over him. Besides, he couldn't argue with the truth. He *was* a bully. Actually, he was rather proud of that, considering where he came from. "Where will you go? What will you do?"

"Does it matter? Do you really care?" AJ stood but his gaze never faltered. "I heard about the fire out at Morning Mist. You went too far."

"I didn't start that fire, son. It was Logan."

AJ shook his head. "Doesn't matter who started it. People could have been hurt. Or killed." He picked up his glass and turned it in his hand, but he didn't take a drink. "I've had enough of your manipulations and interfering in people's lives because you want something you can't have. Like Theo. She's a good woman, kind to a fault, but because she doesn't want you—or me, for that matter—you want to take her farm, want her to lose everything she's worked for. It isn't right. Theo doesn't deserve it. And neither do I." He put his drink down with a final thunk, then walked toward the door, a slight bounce in his step.

"If you walk out that door, we're done. You won't get a penny from me."

AJ stopped in the doorway. "I don't want your blood money, Father." His shoulders tensed, then relaxed before he turned around. "I never wanted it. Oh, there were advantages to being the son of the richest man in Colorado, but the price you demanded was too high." He took a deep breath. "There was only one thing I really wanted from you, but it just so happens that the one thing I wanted was the one thing you couldn't give me. I've been educated, I've traveled the world, I have everything that money can buy, but I was never loved, not after Mother died. I don't think you're capable of that emotion."

And with that, AJ turned once more and walked out the door. Aldrich stood behind his desk and watched his son give instructions to Wilson, shake his hand, then say good-bye. A moment later, the door closed softly behind him.

Aldrich moved into his chair and pursed his lips. A minor setback. Nothing more. He had intended to have AJ head over to Mimi's bordello to fetch Logan and bring him back to the house. He'd have to find some other way, as he couldn't be seen entering or leaving a brothel. He had a reputation to uphold. After a moment, he scribbled a note and yelled, "Wilson!"

"Yes, sir?" The man moved from the foyer and into the study on silent feet, as was his custom.

"Take this to Tell Logan." He held out the folded note. "This time of night, he'll be at Mimi's."

"Mimi's, sir? I don't believe I've ever ..." His voice trailed off, evidence of his discomfort.

Aldrich stared at the man and noticed the peculiar green cast to his features. A proper English butler, trained in London many,

many years ago, visiting a brothel would be odd to him. He'd never permit himself that particular pleasure. Aldrich chuckled. The man didn't know what he'd been missing. "Never been to Mimi's, have you, Wilson?"

"No, sir, I have not." The man gave a slight bow as he accepted the note and started backing out of the room, then stopped in the doorway. "Sir?"

"What is it, Wilson?"

"It has been …" He took a deep breath and began again. "It has been quite an experience to serve you, sir. However, delivering this note as well as bringing Mr. Logan back here will be my last official act. I will be leaving posthaste, as young Master Pearce has done." He bowed again and backed into the foyer.

Aldrich sat back in his chair and let out a long sigh. How could such a wonderful day go to shit so damned quickly? He shook his head. AJ could leave. Wilson could leave, too, and it didn't matter. None of it mattered … as long as he got what he wanted in the end.

Chapter 17

"Did you see him? Talk to him? Is he all right?"

Theo didn't wait until Quincy brought the buckboard to a halt in the barnyard before she badgered him with questions. It had been three days since Eamon had left. Three days of not knowing if he'd found and killed Logan, or if Logan had killed him, and the not knowing tore her up inside. The recriminations she'd suffered after he first left had multiplied to the point where she couldn't sleep, couldn't eat, couldn't even hold a coherent thought in her head except for him.

"Hold on there, Theo." Quincy sawed on the reins and slowed the wagon down. "Let me stop first."

Theo backed up a couple steps and waited, although that wasn't what she wanted. What she wanted was to climb up in the seat, grab the reins from his hands, turn the buckboard around, and head back into Pearce. What she wanted ... was Eamon.

"I saw him." Quincy jumped from his seat and started to lead the horses into the barn. "He's ... determined. Frustrated at the moment, but still very resigned to finishing what someone else started. We shared a cup of coffee at the White Palace Hotel—he's staying there, by the way."

"I should go to him." She followed him, catching every word he said over his shoulder. It wasn't easy with the horse's harnesses jingling and the creaking of the old wooden buckboard. "I should bring him back here with me. I should persuade him that killing Logan isn't what he wants or needs to do."

Quincy stopped and turned around. Theo stopped as well and backed up a step. There was something on his face she'd never seen before—judgment. That pulled her up short. She'd never seen that look before. "You think it's my fault he's gone and not coming back."

"No, not that he's gone, Theo. I know … I know how hard leaving must have been for him." He took a deep breath, then unhitched the horses from the wagon. "But I also know that this is something he has to do. He's not going to stop looking for Logan or stop calling him out. It's a matter of honor now."

"Honor? How can it be honor to stand in the middle of the street and get yourself killed?" Theo threw up her hands in disgust and fear. "It's foolishness and …"

"His choice, Theo," Quincy said as he began removing the harnesses. He glanced at her as his fingers manipulated leather straps and metal buckles. "He could have stayed here on the farm and let matters rest, but what would that have done to him?" He hung up the harnesses, then grabbed a currycomb. He spoke while he worked. "Do you remember what he was like when he first came here? He rarely smiled, and when he did, it never reached his eyes. He didn't speak very much either and he was so … unhappy. So filled with guilt, but over the weeks and months, he changed. He smiled more. He laughed. He even started singing!"

Finished with one of the horses, Quincy led the gelding outside to the pasture behind the barn, but he never stopped speaking and his voice faded and swelled as he moved from one place to another. "You did that for him. You and Granny. The children. Marianne. I like to think even I had something to do with the change in him." He began to groom the other horse, and once again, she lost sight of him except for his hat and feet. "I would hate to see him go back to being so unhappy, and that's what would happen if he didn't go after Logan. A man can't live constantly looking over his shoulder, Theo, waiting for a bullet to end his life … or that of someone else he loves."

"But—"

"Don't go to Pearce, Theo," he cut her off and she stiffened. He'd never spoken to her like this before either, his voice stern and commanding—the voice he used with the children sometimes. "Leave him be. I'm saying this as your friend. If you are there when he meets Logan, it'll ruin his concentration and he'll need every bit of it if he's to be successful." He paused in his actions and raised his head, his intent gaze connecting with hers. "As for him not coming back, as I recall, you told him not to."

Theo sat heavily on a bale of hay and plucked at her split skirt with numb fingers, her vision blurring as tears made focusing difficult. "I only said it because I didn't want him to leave." She wiped at her eyes, removing the wetness that never seemed to be far away, though how she had any tears left was beyond her comprehension. "I thought if he loved me like he said he did, he would stay."

"He does love you." He laid the currycomb on the shelf, then sat beside her, putting his arm around her shoulders. She felt the comfort one friend had for another, but it wasn't enough. It wasn't Eamon holding her. "He has for a long time, honey, but sometimes ..." He heaved a sigh. "I know you don't understand."

"No, I don't. If he loved me, how could he leave?" And with that, she buried her face against his chest and burst into the sobs she'd been holding at bay.

• • •

Eamon left the shot of whiskey on the table untouched, and exited the Cattleman's Saloon through the back door. Frustration and anger made the muscles in his back and shoulders tense. Three days and he still hadn't found Logan.

The outlaw hadn't sought him out either, despite the messages Eamon had left all over Pearce. Word had spread among the townspeople though, creating an almost carnival feel. Curious gazes followed him now wherever he went.

Was that why Logan hadn't approached him? Afraid that a confrontation would be witnessed? Was someone hiding him? Or had he left town? If anyone knew of his whereabouts, they weren't sharing the information with him, though he supposed he understood why. No one really knew Eamon MacDermott or why he was looking for Logan.

He untied Traveler's reins from the post, but didn't mount up. Instead, he led the horse down the alley between the saloon and the building next door. He'd return to the spot outside of town where he'd camped his first night, get in more practice shooting at the tin cans he'd found and set up there. He could use it. His hands were still sore and stiff from his burns, despite the healing cream Granny had repeatedly massaged into the damaged skin. Later, when the sun went down, he'd try his luck again, visiting the same brothels and saloons he'd already been to three times.

He felt it then. The hair on the back of his neck stood straight up, and his stomach churned. He drew air into his lungs, certain beyond doubt that Logan stood behind him. Logan was quite capable of shooting someone when his back was turned. The man had no scruples.

Eamon took another deep breath, dropped Traveler's reins, and turned slowly, his hands relaxed at his sides.

"Heard you was lookin' for me, MacDermott." Logan leaned against the wall of the saloon as if he didn't have a care in the world, but looks were deceiving. He was nervous. Eamon could hear it in his voice, see it in the tenseness of his body. Any closer and he might have smelled it, too.

For the first time in three days, he smiled as he gave Traveler a slap on the rump, making the horse race from the alley. Once Traveler cleared the passageway, he stopped and waited, as he'd been trained to do, and Eamon focused his attention on Logan.

"Just giving you the opportunity to finish what you started. A chance to try to kill me again ... if I don't kill you first."

"Think you're that good, do ya? I seem to recall the last time we met, you froze. Your pistol never even cleared leather."

Eamon let the reminder pass, refusing to allow Logan to rattle him, his gaze intent on that damned face, the one that haunted his dreams for far too long. He forced himself to relax his shoulders. His hand twitched though, aching to feel the solid grip of his pistol, and his heart pounded much too fast, but he was ready ... to either kill Logan or meet his Maker. One way or the other, this would end. "Try me."

"You sure you want to die today, MacDermott? What about that sweet woman you been fuckin'?" He grinned, revealing tobacco-stained teeth. "Sure wouldn't mind gettin' a taste o' her m'self."

Anger rushed though him, and Eamon tensed as Logan's grin widened. For that statement alone, he deserved to die, but he recognized what the outlaw was trying to do—make him lose control to the rage sweeping through him. He took a deep breath and refused to rise to the bait. He needed to remain calm and keep all his attention on his enemy. To lose focus would mean his death. "You started the fire."

Logan laughed but admitted nothing as he moved away from the wall and took his stance, his legs spread, his hands down at his sides, close to the holsters tied to his thighs.

They stood not more than fifteen yards away from each other, absolutely still. A gust of wind whistled through the alley as the sun ducked behind a cloud, shrouding the passageway in gray shadows for what seemed an eternity but was truly only a moment or two. The sounds from the crowd gathering in the street dimmed to a low hum that buzzed in the background.

Logan blinked. Eamon remembered that from the first confrontation he'd had with him. The moment before he drew his pistol on that long-ago day, he had blinked. Twice.

He waited, his breath stuck in his lungs, muscles tense, every beat of his heart thumping in his ears. His focus narrowed until all he could see was Tell Logan. Outlaw. Murderer. Soon to be dead man.

Logan blinked again.

Eamon pulled his pistol from its holster and fired, but Logan was fast. The outlaw pulled his pistol from its holster and fired a split second before he did, but his speed did not equal accuracy. There was no pain—at least, not yet—although he'd been shot, the bullet piercing the muscle of his left arm.

Logan's eyes opened wide before he looked down at the blood blossoming from the wound in his chest. He crumpled to the ground, almost in slow motion, the surprise registering on his face becoming permanent in death.

Eamon clamped a hand over his wound and walked toward the man lying in the dirt. He kicked the gun from his lifeless hand, and just to be certain, bent down and touched his bloody fingers to the man's neck. No pulse. No sign of a heartbeat at all. Tell Logan was truly dead.

He felt no elation, but a deep sense of justice filled him and the guilt he'd carried around with him for so long finally lifted. Still, his stomach churned, threatening to rid itself of the breakfast he'd had earlier. He'd never killed another man like this before. A wave of dizziness made him pitch forward a little, and he sat heavily on the ground, his arm now throbbing where Logan's bullet had found its mark, the pain blooming as blood stained the sleeve of his shirt.

At least he hadn't been shot in the chest again. His heart still beat.

With shaking hands, he took the neckerchief from his neck and tied it around his arm, using his teeth to hold one end while he tightened the knot, then rose, a little unsteadily, to his feet. He looked toward the street and the crowd of people gathered there.

Sheriff Call moved away from the crowd and approached him. He looked at the dead man on the ground, then at Eamon as he lifted the brim of his hat with his fingertip. "Mighty fancy shootin', MacDermott. Glad to see you're still standin'."

Eamon acknowledged the statement with a nod, then said, "Make sure the bounty goes to Theodosia Danforth out at Morning Mist Farms."

"Sure thing. I'll take care of it."

Eamon walked away, his legs a little wobbly. He edged through the crowd, turning this way and that, every bump against his arm a new experience in pain.

Despite his suddenly dry mouth, he whistled and Traveler trotted toward him.

"Mister, you know you're bleeding?" A young man, perched at the top of the column that supported the second-floor balcony of the saloon, stated the obvious as Eamon grabbed Traveler's reins. No more than twelve or thirteen, his eyes were alight with wonder at the spectacle he just witnessed—and from a great vantage point at that. "I can take you to Doc Foster's. It isn't far from here." He shimmied from his post and landed on his feet. Dust plumes rose up to coat his shoes. "Might wanna do that before you fall down."

Eamon glanced at his arm. Despite the neckerchief, blood still oozed from the wound, soaking the cloth. Bright red droplets plinked to the dirt from his fingertips. No wonder his mouth was dry and little spots floated before his eyes. He'd lost some blood. Maybe a lot of it.

"Lead the way, son."

• • •

Hell and damnation!

Aldrich spit in the dirt and cursed his luck, which had been with him just a little while ago when word had spread through the town that Logan and MacDermott were finally meeting, not in the middle of Main Street as he had hoped, but in an alley beside the Cattleman's Saloon. He'd been at the sheriff's office just down the street when an older gentleman reported what he thought was a gunfight. He and the sheriff had jostled their way through the crowd, arriving just in time to see both men draw. Logan had been a little faster, and for a moment, elation had zinged through Aldrich, but that triumph hadn't lasted.

Although the outlaw had fired first, he hadn't killed MacDermott. Instead, his face still contorted in an expression of surprise, blood soaking the front of his shirt, Tell Logan lay at the sheriff's feet, dead.

Aldrich backed away from the crowd at the end of the alley and watched a young man lead Eamon MacDermott up the street, toward Dr. Foster's home office. Frustration rippled through him. MacDermott, though wounded, would live to see another day.

He swallowed his disappointment and forced himself to think of another solution. He could hire another man willing to do his dirty work and kill MacDermott, but that would take time and it was time he couldn't afford. The need to have Theo and her farm had become all encompassing. Hell, he hardly thought of anything else now. He could lay in wait on the road to Morning Mist Farms and shoot MacDermott from the shadows. That would solve his most immediate problem, but in truth, he found pulling the trigger and shooting someone distasteful. That's why he had kept Logan on his payroll for so long. The outlaw wasn't squeamish at all about killing anyone, which had been one of the few things he'd liked about the man.

A sigh escaped him as he found himself alone in the street, in the same position as before, his gaze intent on the former Marshal's back. He hadn't even noticed when the crowd dispersed or when Logan's body was taken away, so lost was he in his own thoughts.

Still, there might be a chance, a slight one, but one he had to try, while MacDermott was otherwise occupied. If he could get to Theo first, before MacDermott—

He hurried up the street to collect his buggy ... and the justice of the peace, who just happened to be on his payroll.

• • •

Less than an hour after the young man brought him to Doctor Foster's home office, Eamon sported a clean, white bandage around the upper part of his arm to hide the multitude of thick, black stitches that had closed the wound and finally stopped the bleeding. The bullet had gone clean through, which, in Doctor Foster's opinion, was better than being lodged in the muscle or bone. Eamon replaced his ruined shirt with a clean one he'd pulled from his saddlebag while Doctor Foster gave him instructions on how to care for his injury. "Thanks, Doc. I appreciate it."

"Nice to finally meet you, MacDermott." The doctor extended his hand after he opened the front door. "Wish it were under better circumstances." Eamon clasped the hand he offered and shook. "Give my regards to Theo." Doc Foster grinned, showing pearl-white teeth beneath an impressive handlebar mustache. "And the rest of her clan."

Eamon simply nodded as he stepped down the porch stairs, untied Traveler's reins from the hitching post in front of the doctor's house, and climbed into the saddle, already feeling a pull on the stitches. If he wasn't careful, he'd rip them out. Theo could fix it, though. Or Granny. And maybe even Gabby could learn something.

A sigh escaped him at how easily Theo's name came to mind, but she hadn't been far from his thoughts at all—no matter how hard he tried. He missed her—missed all of them—but her most especially. The way sunlight played on her whiskey-colored hair, bringing out the burnished reds and golds, the way her smile lit up her entire face and made the corners of her eyes crinkle. The way she loved him.

He nudged Traveler forward and rode west, toward the Rockies and Paradise Falls on the other side of the mountain range. He hadn't progressed very far when he came upon a river. He dismounted and led the horse closer to the water's edge.

As Traveler drank, he hunkered down and picked up a small, flat rock, one of a thousand littering the bank. He threw it, making it skim across the surface of the water, but his thoughts weren't on the rings left in the rock's wake—they were on Theo, as they always seemed to be. What was she doing right now? Training the horses? Comforting the children, her soft touch taking away whatever ailed them? Laughing with Granny or Marianne or Quincy? Forgiving people and teaching them that their lives were worthwhile?

"What do you think, Traveler? Did she mean it when she said don't come back?" The horse finished drinking, then shook his head, flinging droplets of water at him. "Well, that's no help."

With a sigh, he hefted himself into the saddle, careful of his wounded arm and lightly nudged the horse's sides. Traveler didn't move. He tugged on the reins, again lightly, and once again, Traveler remained still except for shaking his head and nickering. "What is wrong with you?"

In answer to his question, the horse turned his head and just looked at him, his expression very much like the one Nessie wore the first time he tried to milk her so long ago, a combination of exasperation and humor.

Eamon let out a chuckle as he finally understood. "All right, Traveler, let's go home."

Chapter 18

It was quiet. Too quiet. And Theo found the silence deafening. The usual noises—the neighing of the horses, the lowing of the cows in the pasture, and the chickens clucking from their pen—were missing. Mallory and the cats were out in the paddocks. Happy rested on his bed, still not himself. Even the children, normally rambunctious and full of mischief, seemed unusually subdued as they left the playhouse in answer to the dinner bell.

They missed Eamon, as did she, and asked constantly when he was coming back, especially Gabby, who didn't believe for one minute he wouldn't.

Theo closed her eyes as she brushed Daphne, Eamon's favorite out of all the Morning Mist horses. She understood the connection now, the emotional bond between them. After all, Daphne had been bred and raised at Kieran's farm, Whispering Pines, before tragedy had struck ... for all of them. "What should I do, Daphne?"

The horse tossed her head and whinnied, but provided no answers.

"Still talking to the animals, I see." Amusement made his tone light and charming.

Startled, Theo spun around and couldn't help the gasp that escaped her. "Aldrich!"

"Hello, Theo."

"What are you doing here? Are you interested in purchasing one of my horses?"

"No, not today." His eyes darted from side to side, then came to rest on her as he took a step closer.

There was something odd about him. Very odd. Normally fastidious about his appearance, he seemed to not care at the moment. His clothes were wrinkled as if he'd slept in them, and his hair stood up on end, like he'd run his fingers through it repeatedly. Or just hadn't brushed it that morning.

She backed away a step and bumped into Daphne. She could retreat no farther. "Then why are you here?"

"Smile, my dear." He advanced on her, and even though he encouraged her to smile, he did not. "Today is our wedding day."

"Are you insane? I'm not going to marry you. I've told you that before. I have not changed my mind."

Theo gasped as Aldrich grabbed her, his fingers digging painfully into her arm. He forced her closer to him, his gaze boring into hers. She noticed a small twitch at the corner of his left eye. Aside from that, his whole demeanor said he was a man with a mission. Confident. Arrogant. Unwilling to take no for an answer.

"Not insane, my dear." He lowered his voice, his lips close to her ear. "Determined to get what I want." He licked her throat, and a shudder of revulsion wracked her. "Now, where is the rest of the family? You wouldn't want them to miss the nuptials, would you?"

"You've lost your mind." She tried to pull out of his grasp, but he was too strong and his fingers bit deeper into her flesh with cruel intention.

"No, I don't think so. I'm finally thinking right. I've waited for you a long time, Theo. A very long time. I'm done waiting. I mean to have you." He chuckled then, but it wasn't with amusement. It was madness, pure and simple. "You gave it to MacDermott, so you can give it to me, too, but you don't have to be willing. I don't care either way. I will have you." His hot breath in her face made her stomach turn almost as much as his words. She'd heard things about Aldrich Pearce, things she hadn't wanted to know about how he treated his late wife and his succession of mistresses, things that had repulsed her. And now, he was here, showing her by his actions the rumors were true.

"Let's go share the happy news." His lips formed a smile that didn't reach his crazed eyes—as if she were in full agreement with his plans.

Theo didn't move.

"Playing hard to get, are we? You're too old to be considered a coquette, my dear." His words were deceptively smooth and cajoling, not at all in keeping with the jerk he gave her.

Theo stumbled with the force of his strength, nearly falling to her knees. She had no doubts he would drag her if necessary. Gaining her footing as well as her dignity, she drew herself up and took a step, but that wasn't good enough for Aldrich. He yanked her again, and this time, she did fall. He let her go for a moment, but that was only to grab her more forcefully, his hands now gripping both arms as he pulled her to her feet and against him, so tightly, she could feel his full erection against her belly. The churning in her stomach worsened. "Don't force me to be unkind, Theo," he warned as he released her, then caught her arm in his steel-like grip and forced her to walk across the barnyard toward the house.

An older man in an ill-fitting black suit stood on the back porch, his hat in one hand, a book in the other. She knew him— Mr. Parish, the justice of the peace—and it was clear he wasn't there to help her. Just the opposite.

She had no choice. She'd have to help herself. There was no way she would allow this man into her home or anywhere near the children. She stomped on Aldrich's foot as hard as she could. As expected, he yelped and let her go. She'd only managed to take a step when he grabbed her ponytail and dragged her back to him. The pain made her eyes water.

"Keep it up, Theo. I enjoy some spunk in my women. It'll make the wedding night that much more exciting."

Theo's stomach twisted at the thought, and bile flooded her throat, threatening to choke her as he half dragged, half pulled her through the porch. Happy rose from his bed, teeth bared, and lunged toward Pearce, but the man was quick and kicked him. The dog cried out the same time Theo did and shook his head, perhaps dazed by the action, as Pearce neatly sidestepped him and dragged her into the house.

Conversation ceased in an instant, the happy chatter dying as everyone around the dinner table turned.

"Aldrich!" Granny exclaimed as she rose stiffly from her seat at the same time Quincy stood. "What is the meaning of this?"

"There's going to be a wedding," Aldrich announced, then immediately turned his attention to Quincy. "You." He motioned toward the cellar door with his head. "Get in there. Take those two with you." He gestured toward Lou and Wynn. "You." He pointed at Marianne, who stood perfectly still, a plate of fried chicken in her hands, her face pale. "Lock them in."

Her cheeks flushed, the redness standing out on her white face. "I will not!"

"You will and you'll do it now."

Theo bit back the scream of pain as his fingers dug deeper into her arm. Her hand began to tingle; his grip was so tight. "It's all right, Marianne. Do what he says. Then take Granny and the children and go outside."

"No, the children stay. So will the old woman."

"Aldrich, please, I'll do whatever you say. Let them go." She hated the weakness in her voice, but any ploy was better than the rage that might push him to do more harm.

He loosened his grip on her, but not enough. "I don't think so, Theo. You see, they are my leverage," he held up the revolver he pulled from his pocket and pointed it at each member of her family one at a time, "more so than this. You'll do what I say because you won't want anyone to get hurt." He lowered his voice and moved his mouth closer to her ear. "And you know I won't hesitate to pull the trigger."

He wouldn't. She knew that. "Marianne, Quincy. Please." She heard the fear in her own shaking voice, but it wasn't fear for herself. It was for her family. Pearce had guessed that much right, gambling on the fact she loved them more than she loved herself. "Do what he says."

"The boys, too," he reminded her.

Marianne put the platter of chicken on the table as Lou and Wynn stiffly rose from their seats and started slowly walking toward the cellar. "I wouldn't try anything," Pearce warned and raised the pistol once more. He made a show of pointing the revolver first on Thomas, then on Charlotte, then lastly, on Gabby. Wide, blue eyes watered as the little girl's chin trembled.

Theo's heart thundered in her chest. Mr. Parish entered the kitchen, dropped his hat on the chair beside the door, and swept the cellar door open with a flourish. He gave a slight bow as Quincy, Wynn, and Lou stepped onto the stairs that would lead them down to the basement, then slammed the door closed after them. He moved aside only so Marianne could lock it, then took the key from her hand.

"Very good." Pearce waved the revolver at Marianne and pointed to the sink with it. "Now get over there and keep your mouth shut."

Marianne nodded and moved slowly toward the table, her intention clear—comfort the children, who sat staring at Theo and Pearce with tears in their fear-filled eyes.

"Mrs. Burke, it wouldn't bother me at all to shoot you right now."

Once again, Marianne nodded, bypassed the table, and moved to the sink. She leaned against the counter and folded her arms across her chest, her expression filled with the desire to do him bodily harm.

"Stop this right now, Aldrich!" Granny demanded as she slammed her open hand against the table, drawing his attention.

"Shut up, old woman!" The revolver leveled in her direction. Granny's mouth shut with an audible click of her teeth, her face white except for the twin spots of red on her cheeks. He chuckled, obviously pleased, and turned toward Mr. Parish. "Now then, let's get on with the ceremony. Mr. Parish, if you will?"

The man began to read, but Theo heard nothing. Her mind scrambled for a way to get out of this ... this nightmare ... without anyone getting hurt, but came up blank. He was too strong, his grip too tight on her arm, the tingling in her fingers gone now— she felt only coldness in her hand ... and in her heart.

Eamon! her brain screamed, though he couldn't hear her. He'd gone, and she was the reason. She'd told him not to come back if he went after Logan. And yet, she still looked toward the kitchen door, hoping he'd walk through it any minute and save her. Save them all.

"You keep looking at the door, my dear. Why is that?" He lowered his voice and leaned a little closer. As if reading her mind, he asked, "Could it be you're thinking MacDermott will burst through that door and save you?" He laughed then, the sound rising up from his chest to instill terror in her heart. "He's not coming. He's dead."

The tears were instantaneous and, with it, rage beyond comprehension. Despite the grip he had on her arm and the fact her hand was numb, Theo yanked herself free of his grasp and whirled on him, her open hand aiming straight for his face, but it was a mistake because desperate men did desperate things.

And Aldrich Pearce was becoming a desperate man.

He smacked her hard across the face with such force, pain exploded in her cheek and she staggered across the room, landing in a heap at Marianne's feet. He turned quickly and grabbed Charlotte, plucking her from her seat as if she weighed nothing. He held her against him while she cried, the bore of the pistol resting against her temple.

"If we are done with the theatrics?" He pressed the gun a little harder against the child's head. "Mr. Parish? Please continue."

. . .

Eamon slowed Traveler to a walk as he turned into the drive, unsure of the reception he'd receive, but determined to see Theo, no matter the outcome. She could still be of a mind to see him gone, but he'd never know if he didn't try.

He came around the side of the house to the barnyard, and it hit him in an instant. Something wasn't right. It was much too quiet. He didn't hear the children laughing, didn't see Quincy and the boys bringing the cows in from the field, didn't see Theo.

Sunlight filtered through the trees as it lowered into the horizon.

Of course. Dinnertime. The family would be gathered in the warm kitchen, having one of Marianne's wonderful meals. What was it tonight? Fried chicken? Her famous meatloaf with peach cobbler for dessert?

His stomach growled as he pictured the table laden with her excellent cooking.

A buggy was parked near the stable. He recognized it instantly as the fancy rig AJ Pearce had driven when he'd come to the farm. Eamon drew Traveler up beside it and dismounted.

"Psst. MacDermott!" A loud stage whisper came from the shadows of the stable to his right and the piece of canvas where the door should have been moved. Eamon walked toward it, his hands at his sides but ready to pull his pistol if need be. A moment later, AJ peeked out from the side of the canvas.

"AJ? What are you doing here? Why are you hiding?"

"Keep it down," he hissed, still in the stage whisper, and motioned toward the house. "My ... my father is in there. He has Theo, and he's trying to force her to marry him."

"What?" His heart pounded as fear for Theo twisted through him. From what he'd learned about Pearce, there was no telling what the man was capable of doing. "Why?"

The man had the good graces to look not only afraid, but embarrassed. "He … he wants her."

"I thought he wanted the farm." Anger surged through him now, competing with the fear already in residence, and his hands balled into fists.

AJ's eyes darted to the left, then the right, then down, everywhere but on Eamon's face. "He does, but he wants her, too. He's always wanted her."

"And that's why you're hiding in the stable?" He could barely keep the disdain from his voice. He had no tolerance for cowards. Or stupidity.

"I was going to try to stop him, but I … I can't."

Eamon gave a short nod. He didn't begin to understand how a grown man could be so afraid of his father. He understood respect. And love. He'd had both for his father, but this fear … it wasn't right. "Then stay here and stay out of the way." He left AJ hiding behind the canvas. Keeping to the shadows of the fading sun, he skirted the stable and the barn to come up behind the playhouse, then slowed his steps and gained the back porch. He tiptoed across the porch so the sound of his boots on the hardwood wouldn't be heard within the house.

Happy rose from his bed, his tail in full wag, and staggered toward him. As thrilled as he was to see the dog, now wasn't the best time. "Go lay down," he ordered in the same stage whisper AJ had used. Obedient as always, the dog whimpered and climbed back into his bed, and Eamon turned his attention back to the task at hand.

The kitchen windows were open to catch the evening breeze. Eamon peeked through the lacy curtains, which made everything seem fuzzy. Fear clutched at his heart. The scene before him was something out of a nightmare. Theo stood near the sink, shielding Gabby as best she could. Marianne and Granny were beside her, faces pale with fear. Thomas stood next to them, his hands balled into fists, a scowl affixed to his young face, and a strange man in a black suit rested against the icebox, a well-worn book in his hands, seemingly out of place, unconcerned and unaffected by the events taking place in front of him. He mumbled words that sounded very much like marriage vows to Eamon's ears.

And Pearce? He stood by the table, his back at an angle to the kitchen door and he held Charlotte. Sweet, shy little Charlotte. Eamon heard her crying and his anger knew no bounds, but he had to be careful. He could simply shoot the man right now, but even if he only winged Pearce, he didn't want the children to witness such an act—not from himself. They'd seen enough ... shooting Pearce would only add to their nightmares. And what if he missed? What if the bullet ricocheted and hit one of the children? He couldn't risk it.

"L-l-let her g-go!" Thomas demanded and took a step forward. His fists raised in the boxing stance Eamon had taught him just a few short weeks ago.

Pearce laughed, then mocked his stutter. "G-g-get back over there with the wo-wo-women, mama's boy!" He pulled Charlotte closer with one arm and waved the revolver at Thomas before placing the bore of the pistol against Charlotte's head. The girl cried harder.

With reluctance, Thomas lowered his hands and took a step back, but there was murder in his eyes. If he could, he'd physically harm the man holding his sister hostage. The same could be said for Marianne and Granny. Both women wore their feelings on their faces, but it was Theo he feared for most. There was no kindness in her eyes, Eamon noticed as his gaze settled on her. Not now. Rage flowed from her, and her eyes sparkled with warning.

Don't do anything stupid, he silently prayed.

The prayer did little good. She hadn't heard it and if she had, it wouldn't have mattered. She pushed Gabby at Granny, then reached for Thomas, and shoved him toward Marianne so quickly, the women only had time to gasp. Once the children were safe, she advanced on Pearce. "You will not hurt my children!" She hauled back and slapped him hard across the face, the sound echoing in the room. She grabbed Charlotte and pushed her toward Marianne's waiting arms.

Seeing an opportunity, the only one at hand, Eamon pushed through the kitchen door at the same time the door to the cellar crashed to the floor with a horrendous bang. Startled, Pearce was momentarily without a hostage ... and without his wits about him.

Quincy glanced his way as he exited the cellar, but only for a second. "Glad you're back, MacDermott." He grinned as, without another word between them, they tackled Pearce to the floor and Lou and Wynn stood in front of the startled man in the black suit.

Subdued, breathing heavily beneath the weight of both Eamon and Quincy, Pearce snarled, "You'll regret this, MacDermott! You, too, Burke! Unhand me! Now!"

"You got this, Quince?"

Straddling Pearce's hips, Quincy grinned. "You bet."

Eamon rose to his feet and glanced at Marianne. "Tie his hands."

"Gladly." Marianne grabbed rope from one of the drawers and made quick work of securing Pearce's hands behind his back. When Quincy rolled him over, she stuffed a handkerchief in his mouth to stop the vile words issuing forth, then wiped her hands against her apron as if touching him made her dirty.

"Is everyone all right?" Eamon asked, but his gaze wasn't on anyone other than Theo. Aside from the red handprint on her face, she appeared shaken but unharmed. Still angry, if her expression was any indication, but not so angry that she didn't walk straight into his arms.

"You're not dead," she whispered and held him tight.

"No, sweetheart, I'm not dead."

"I'm so sorry. I should never have told you not to come back. I was wrong."

"Aren't you glad I didn't listen?" Eamon kissed her then, his lips taking possession of hers regardless of who saw. No more hiding. He loved this woman, and he wanted everyone to know. No one said a word, as if his actions were expected ... and accepted as a matter of course. When he broke the kiss, he gazed into her eyes.

She lightly caressed his cheek, her eyes shiny with unshed tears. "I love you, Eamon MacDermott."

Before he could respond with the same, Gabby wrapped her little arms around both of them. "I knew you'd come back!" She was quickly joined by Thomas, Charlotte, and Granny. Love filled his heart, and Eamon's throat constricted. He cleared it, then studied each of the children one by one. Aside from tear stains on their faces, they all seemed to be unharmed. "Granny, why don't you take them in the other room? They don't need to see all this."

"Good thinking, Eamon." She ushered the children into the parlor but stopped before entering herself. She took a deep breath, then turned to face him, her eyes glowing softly beneath the sudden onslaught of tears. "I'm glad you came back."

"As am I." A slow grin curled his lips.

She nodded, then disappeared into the parlor. Eamon watched her go, then turned toward Quincy, who stood with his foot on Pearce's chest. "How'd you get out of the cellar?"

Quincy grinned. "Show 'em, Lou."

The young man opened his hand and showed them the hinges he had removed from the door. "I've been meaning to fix them. They've been loose for a while now."

"What about Pearce?" Theo asked as she stared at the man, her expression not at all forgiving, despite the fact the children had not been hurt.

"I'll take him to the sheriff."

"I wouldn't bring him to Sheriff Call," AJ said as he entered the kitchen, his hat in his hand. He nodded to everyone, then moved closer to Theo, his gaze on his father before rising up to meet hers. "I'm so sorry about all this, Theo. And for the part I played in it. I never thought he'd come after you like this."

"It's all right, AJ. I think I understand. For the first time in his life, he couldn't have what he wanted, and it made him angry and unreasonable."

AJ gave a nod. "You're very kind. You always were."

"Why can't we bring him to Sheriff Call?" Quincy asked as he moved his foot a little and pressed harder on Pearce's chest to keep the man still.

AJ turned his attention to Quincy. "He's on father's payroll, along with a host of others. Including him." He pointed at the small man still standing in front of the icebox, now slack-jawed and clutching his Bible. "I'll take him back to town with me, if you don't mind. I have my horse."

"That's fine." Eamon shrugged. "As far as your father is concerned, I can still lock him in the jail. I'll take the key so Call doesn't let him out, and we can all wait for the U.S. Marshal together."

"Again, I'm sorry." AJ held out his hand to both Theo and Eamon, then put his hat on his head, nodded toward Marianne and Quincy, and escorted the older gentleman outside. A few moments later, the sound of his horse's hooves meeting hard-packed dirt reached them.

"You'll come back, won't you?" Theo melted into his arms again.

"You're not getting rid of me that easily." He kissed her again—he'd never get enough of the taste of her lips. "I love you, Theodosia Danforth. I have for a long time." He lowered his voice and pressed his forehead to hers. "I'll be back before you know it."

"What about Logan?"

Eamon shook his head. "No need to worry about him anymore. He'll never hurt anyone again."

She breathed a sigh and finally let him go. Eamon kissed the tip of her nose, then helped Quincy lift Pearce to his feet. The man tried to fight, but there wasn't much he could do with his hands tied behind him.

Half carrying, half dragging him, they made it to the buggy and shoved Pearce none too gently into the deeply cushioned seat. Quincy climbed into the driver's seat, took the reins, and started the carriage moving while Eamon stuck his foot in Traveler's stirrup and lifted himself into the saddle.

He waved one last time to the family standing on the back porch, then faced forward, Traveler's reins held loosely in his hands as he nudged the horse to break into a trot and caught up to Quincy and Pearce's fancy rig.

"You gonna marry that girl?" Quincy asked as they turned out of the drive and onto the road to town.

"If she'll have me." He grinned.

"Oh, she'll have you." Quincy chuckled, then faced forward and concentrated on what was ahead of him. Eamon did the same. Despite the ache in his arm—he didn't think he'd pulled out any stitches when he tackled Pearce, but he couldn't be sure—and in the face of everything he'd been through in the past few hours, he was happy. Actually, happier than he'd ever been. He hadn't been late this time. Hadn't lost anyone he loved like he had in the past. The events could have turned out badly, but they hadn't, and for that, he was grateful.

A smile curved his mouth just as the buggy swerved, making Traveler rear up on his hind legs.

Eamon brought his mount under control and looked to his left. Fear struck his heart, almost as much as earlier when he saw Charlotte in Pearce's bruising hold. Somehow, Pearce had wriggled his hands free from the rope that bound him. He and Quincy struggled over a revolver while Quincy tried to avoid being shot and stop the buggy at the same time.

Where the revolver had come from, Eamon had no clue. Maybe Aldrich had hidden it under the buggy's seat but it didn't matter. What mattered was that Aldrich would never stop, never accept defeat. He had been waiting, biding his time until he could make his move, and he didn't seem to care who was killed in the process.

"Pearce! Stop!"

Enraged, Pearce succeeded in gaining possession of the revolver with a strength born of fear and perhaps insanity. In one smooth motion, he smacked Quincy on the side of the head with the revolver then turned it on Eamon.

"Rot in hell, MacDermott." Spittle sprayed from his mouth as he aimed the weapon.

Eamon drew his pistol and fired at the same time Pearce did.

Epilogue

"I remember the first time I saw you." Eamon grabbed a lock of Theo's whiskey-colored hair and twirled it around his finger. Sunlight played on the silken strands, bringing out the deep reds and golden browns. He smoothed the curl back into place and lowered his hand to caress her bare shoulder. Her skin, satin to the touch, had been warmed by the sun shining down on them as they lay on a blanket on the soft grass not far from the swimming hole.

Theo rested her head on his chest, exactly where he wanted her to be—close to his heart. Always. Her body vibrated as she chuckled, then lifted her head to gaze into his eyes. He loved it when she looked at him like that, her green eyes shimmering with the love they shared, her face still aglow from spent passion. "I held a shotgun on you."

He laughed, the sound bubbling up from his chest. For a man who hadn't laughed much before they met, he laughed a lot now. And he liked it. So many changes had happened for him since the moment he saw her. Family, always important to him, had become more so. He'd gone to see his brother, Teague, in Paradise Falls after Tell Logan died so he could impart the news in person. They kept in touch with letters now. He'd yet to see his brother, Brock, though they reconnected in correspondence as well.

And he'd learned how to forgive himself and love like she did, with her whole heart. He chuckled again, then drew in his breath as memories assailed him—precious ones, so different from the ones he'd carried with him for so long. "I think I fell in love with you in that moment. You were unapologetic and angry and so beautiful. For a minute there, I thought you were going to shoot me, but you didn't. Instead, you offered me a job but so much more than that. You gave me kindness when I didn't think I deserved it." He rolled on to his side and faced her, the back of his hand lightly caressing her face. "I'm glad you did." He dipped his head to capture her sweet lips beneath his own. "If you hadn't, I don't know what I would have done. I was ... lost, Theo, until I found you."

"I'm sure you would have found another woman, Eamon. You're a good man." She pulled him closer, wrapping her arms around him, her warm fingers entangled in his hair.

Could anyone be luckier? Or happier than he?

"No, there isn't any other woman for me. Just you. Always you." He laughed again, then nuzzled the sweet spot between her ear and collarbone. Theo trembled in his embrace, as he knew she would. He loved that as well. "Do you know what tomorrow is?"

"Saturday?" she whispered against his skin, and it was his turn to shiver.

"I'm serious."

"Could it be our anniversary?"

"Why, yes, I do believe it is! Two years, Theo, since I put my ring on your finger." He sighed, remembering the day. The pastor had come out to the farm and married them in front of a few witnesses—the most important ones—the children, Marianne, Quincy, and Granny, who beamed as if she had planned it all from the beginning. And perhaps she had. "Two years since you made me the happiest man alive."

"That's not such a long time. I can see us still sneaking out to our spot right here and making love for the next forty years."

"Forty?" he groaned, teasing her. If forty years with her was all he could have, then he'd take it though it wasn't nearly enough. "That's only if you don't wear me out."

She pulled out of his arms and sat up, hugging her knees to her bare chest. Sunlight dappled her skin as the trees around them swayed with the breeze. Eamon couldn't resist. He sat up behind her and once again, wrapped his arms around her. She turned her head and laughed. "If there is anyone who will wear you out, it's our son. I thought Gabby, Charlotte, and Thomas were a handful when they were younger, but they don't hold a candle to EJ." She laughed again and the sound filled him. "Do you know what I found your son doing yesterday?"

"No, what?"

Theo leaned against him and stretched out her legs, crossing them at the ankle. "Babbling to Daphne, trying to persuade her to let him ride her, I would assume. She was so gentle with him. Actually laid down in the field and let him climb on her back. I've never seen a horse do that before." She reached up and rested her hand on his cheek. Eamon nuzzled her wrist, knowing how sensitive she was there. "How he got all the way out to the pasture is another matter. I only turned my back for one minute."

"Little scamp. He must have some of your magic with animals." Pride made his chest puff out. He adored his eighteen-month-old son, seeing a lot of himself as well as his brothers in the MacDermott gray eyes he'd inherited and the constant mischief he sought. And he did have Theo's touch with the horses, especially the young colts and fillies Pumpkin had sired. This past year had seen five born on the farm and six born to the mares the breeders brought to Morning Mist. The previous year, there had been four births on the farm, and the breeders who had come the year of the fire were thrilled that all their mares had birthed healthy, spirited offspring. Hart Jameson was especially pleased when Gloriana foaled twins and came back the following year to try his luck with three more mares. All of them showed great racing promise. "Speaking of children, don't you think it's time to tell me your secret?"

"What secret?" She threw him a glance, her eyes wide and guileless.

"EJ is going to have a brother or sister."

She grinned. "How did you know?"

He shrugged. "I just do." His hand drifted down to rest first over her fuller breasts, then her rounded belly. "Am I right?"

A blush spread up her cheeks and her eyes glowed as she nodded.

Love filled his heart, and tears blurred his vision. To think, a few short years ago, he stumbled upon a place of magic, a desperate man who didn't think he deserved to be loved or accepted or forgiven and a woman, who despite her own heartbreak, had shown him that he was deserving. The changes hadn't come overnight, but they had come, and it all started with a kiss in the morning mist.

About the Author

Marie Patrick has always had a love affair with words and books, but it wasn't until a trip to Arizona, where she now makes her home with her husband and her furry, four-legged "girl," that she became inspired to write about the sometimes desolate, yet beautiful landscape. Her inspiration doesn't just come from the Wild West, though. It comes from history itself. She is fascinated with pirates and men in uniform and lawmen with shiny badges. When not writing or researching her favorite topics, she can usually be found curled up with a good book. Marie loves to hear from her readers. Drop her a note at Akamariep@aol.com, or visit her website at www.mariepatrick.com.

www.ingramcontent.com/pod-product-compliance
Lightning Source LLC
Chambersburg PA
CBHW010442100726
47904CB00008B/2453